Broken in Two

"Don't miss this exceptional book if you are into Native American lore: unbeatable suspense in a world where miracles do happen." —*Rocky Mountain News*

"Ms. Baker has once again given us a mythical, magical page-turner that will keep you glued to its pages. A Native American romantic gem!" —*Rendezvous*

Legend

"Laura Baker's LEGEND is a page-turner from beginning to end. A skillfully crafted mystery, laced with Native American mysticism and romance is a sure-to-please read." —Dinah McCall

"Laura Baker is a truly dazzling new find. Her second novel, LEGEND, is a marvelous example of romantic suspense deftly blended with Native American beliefs." —*Romantic Times*

Stargazer

"A fast-paced, well-plotted story. A larger-than-life hero and a heroine who is his match. Here's one you'll enjoy!" —Kat Martin

"STARGAZER is absolutely magical. Laura Baker has created a wonderful hero, and a tale to savor. Don't miss it!" —Megan Chance

"Promising new author Laura Baker makes a winning debut with this uniquely spellbinding tale. STARGAZER focuses on the internal and external conflict of those torn between the ways of the past and the reality of the present." —*Romantic Times*

Raven

Laura Baker

St. Martin's Paperbacks

RAVEN

Copyright © 2001 by Laura Baker.

ISBN: 0-312-97709-3

Printed in the United States of America

St. Martin's Paperbacks edition / February 2001

St. Martin's Paperbacks are published by St. Martin's Press, 175 Fifth Avenue, New York, N.Y. 10010.

10 9 8 7 6 5 4 3 2 1

This book is dedicated to my son, Nick.
Wherever you go, whatever you do
you are always in my heart

WITH WARMEST THANKS

to Steve Fleming, District Staff Ranger of the Bureau of Land Management in Albuquerque for taking the time to answer my questions. Any mistakes in this story with regard to the investigation of archaeological crimes are entirely my own.

to Al Castanza, man extraordinaire, for helping me to understand surveillance systems. Great conversations, amazing e-mails . . . you are full of surprises.

to my editor, Glenda Howard, for her enthusiasm and patience; and most of all for truly caring about delivering a great story.

to Karen Solem, who has blurred all the lines as editor, friend, and agent.

to Sandy and Robin. God knew I was going to have a tough year and he gave me you.

and, as always, to my valued readers. I am grateful to you all and treasure your heartfelt letters.

Raven

Chapter 1

THE raven soared above the canyon floor, his short, loud calls echoing off the cliff walls. On powerful wings, the great black bird glided to rest on the base of an upturned Anasazi vessel. The two girls scrambled easily over the treacherous ground in pursuit. The ten-year-old reached the pot first, her squeals of delight filling the canyon.

"Oh, Blackjack, what have you found?" She descended on the pot, her fingers digging at the surrounding dirt. The raven let out a loud protest.

"Tilly! Wait!" Rheada pleaded against her younger sister's determination. "Blackjack is warning you!"

"Then why did he land here?" Tilly protested, still digging.

Blackjack pecked at the air close to Tilly's fingers. She swatted a hand at him. "Stop it, you crazy bird."

Rheada grabbed one of Tilly's arms. "No, Tilly, you can't dig for this one. Blackjack was just testing you."

Tilly paused and glared at the bird. "You think that bird knows everything."

Blackjack raised his head and crowed. The sound echoed between the cliffs and reverberated through Rheada. She gazed warmly at her bird. "He does," she said quietly. She believed that with all her heart.

"Well, he doesn't know more than Daddy." Tilly stood abruptly and walked away, her anger stirring the surrounding air.

"Tilly, don't be mad," Rheada called after her.

But her sister didn't stop. She only slowed long enough to yell over her shoulder, "Daddy told us to find more pots."

Tilly knew as well as Rheada that what their father wanted wasn't just pots. He wanted the mask. He had hunted for the mask for as long as Rheada could remember. Now he was sure he was close. He could *feel* it, he said.

Rheada felt something, too: a scary eeriness that hung in

the air as if the canyons were imprinted with a great terror. She thought of her father's stories about the mask and shuddered. If anything were to have the curse of the Anasazi, Rheada was sure that would be the mask.

Blackjack flapped his wings and rose easily above their heads, then landed on another pot. He gave two excited calls.

Tilly walked to Blackjack's choice, knelt and began to dig. The raven stepped gingerly, holding his perch.

Rheada sat down beside her sister. They worked side by side, quietly. Rheada dug at the dirt several inches from the pot. "Loosen this dirt first, Tilly, or you'll break the pot."

Blackjack, with two efficient flaps of his wings, settled on her shoulders, his huge body a hefty but welcome weight. Rheada rubbed her nose in his breast feathers and she could feel the swift beating of his heart. Her own excitement rose, anticipating the find.

"It's already broken," Tilly pronounced and stood, her eager gaze taking in the rest of the canyon for more promising treasures.

"It's still beautiful," Rheada murmured. She trailed her finger with care along the crack, then closed her eyes and laid her palm against the warm roundness of the pot. Just because it was flawed didn't mean it wasn't good.

Blackjack shifted on her shoulder, then tugged on some strands of her hair, but Rheada ignored him.

Blackjack screeched right into her ear.

"Ow, Blackjack!" Rheada clapped a hand over her ringing ear. She glared at the huge bird, but his gaze was fixed high on the cliff face. His talons gripped her shoulder, piercing the light cotton shirt. "Blackjack, you're hurting me!"

The black bird pushed off and flew straight up the cliff. Rheada looked past him and saw the reason for his concern. Tilly had discovered a ruin perched high on the canyon wall. Her small frame clung to the rock face at a dangerous angle.

Rheada clambered up the talus slope, her breath tight, praying Tilly wouldn't fall. She had to pause at the top of the conical slide of debris to figure the best way to reach her sister. She saw Blackjack perched above Tilly, his harsh caws aimed at her. Rheada had to agree with his angry rebukes, but now was not the time to scold Tilly—later, after she had Tilly safe, then she would lecture her. Not that her sister would listen—

words of caution seemed to bounce right off her, as if she were protected by an impenetrable shield.

As Rheada stretched for jagged handholds, dragging herself higher, the grating sandstone only inches from her face, the thought flashed through her that she was forever chasing after her sister. Tilly plunged headlong through every moment. With fearless curiosity and barely a thought, she swept Rheada along on breathless adventures; and more times than Rheada could count, she had had to come to Tilly's rescue. A prick of anger stabbed Rheada's heart.

A shower of pebbles and sand cascaded over Rheada, pelting her arms. She squinted through the hazy curtain of dust to where Tilly should be, but her sister wasn't there. Rheada stole a frantic look below. No Tilly.

A lump of tension lodged in Rheada's throat. What if this time Rheada failed to get to her sister in time?

"Hang on, Tilly!" Rheada cried, hoping her sister was just beyond her sight. "I'm coming." Her call sounded weak and desperate.

Rheada struggled onto a narrow ledge and stood, hugging her body against the rock wall. She shimmied along the edge, inches at a time. The ledge gradually widened and Rheada rounded a curve to find herself on the entrance path of the ruin. Tilly's head popped up from inside a crumbling adobe room, a huge smile on her dirt-smudged face.

"Hey, slowpoke! Wait till you see what I found!"

Fierce relief flooded Rheada. She stared in disbelief at her nonplussed sister chattering gaily about her discovery. Rheada's heart beat in her throat, her legs shook from exertion, and the fear that had driven her up a hundred feet of canyon wall now held a jagged edge of anger.

Blackjack wasn't any happier. His nagging caws had heightened to shrieks. Rheada recognized her bird's frantic squawks as a warning that whatever Tilly had found was best left buried.

"It's not safe here, Tilly." Rheada immediately wished she had picked other words—ones that wouldn't feed Tilly's need for challenge.

Tilly scowled back. "You're just jealous I found this place first."

"Jealous? I was scared. You ran off, without a word."

"Just because you're two years older than me, you don't boss me, Rheada. You're not my mother."

The fear Rheada had felt, the anger of having to chase after Tilly again, now lodged in her throat. If she didn't watch after Tilly, who would?

"Come on, Rheada," Tilly begged. "Come see what I found." She slanted an excited look to the room behind her.

Rheada smiled inwardly at her sister's bright-eyed enthusiasm, undampened even by Rheada's scolding. She gazed at her sister—a smaller version of herself, she knew, because Daddy always said so. The only difference was how they wore their hair: Rheada pulled hers back in a thick braid. Tilly, of course, let her long, black hair hang free. It fell in a thick mane around her small face, giving her the appearance of peeking out from under a black hood, large light brown eyes taking in everything.

Rheada loved her sister—even when Tilly's unbridled enthusiasm took them places they shouldn't go. Tilly owned Rheada's heart.

Rheada approached the remnants of the outer pueblo wall. "Okay, show me what you found, Tilly, then we have to leave."

Blackjack paced along the top of an enclosed room, protesting. Rheada trusted the black bird's instincts and her own wariness grew with each additional minute they lingered.

Before she slipped beneath the doorway to join Tilly, Rheada ran a reassuring hand down the raven's back. "It's okay, Blackjack, we'll leave soon."

Rheada found Tilly in the corner, crouched over a dark mound. "What is it?" she murmured.

"You don't have to whisper, silly." Though Tilly's own voice was lowered.

Rheada couldn't resist a shimmer of excitement at the thought of what wonderful, precious thing the ancients had left.

She crept closer. Tilly reached a hand for the shadowed mound. Suddenly, Rheada recognized the dark shape of a basket, painstakingly woven of yucca fibers, in the exact size to fit over a human head. She knew instantly what lay beneath and cried out to stop Tilly. But she was too late. Tilly lifted aside the perfectly preserved basket and revealed a cache of plain shell necklaces.

"See? I found jewelry. Daddy won't believe it."

Rheada breathed out. "They're beautiful," she agreed. "Put the basket back, Tilly. It's a grave."

"I know that. I knew it was a burial when I saw the basket."

The fact that her sister had gone ahead and lifted the basket both appalled. Rheada and left her in awe of Tilly's fearlessness.

"Rheada, look!" Tilly pointed to petroglyphs carved into the cave wall high above.

Rheada could make out a dozen birds, their wings outstretched. Beneath them was a spiral, circling ever wider as if rising and sending the birds in a flurry of flight.

She knew this carving. She had seen it 'once before, long ago, when Daddy had taken her to the special cave, deep in the forested canyon country of southern Colorado. There, an Anasazi woman lay buried surrounded by riches of turquoise: necklaces, inlaid shells, carved animal fetishes. Daddy said he had never seen such wealth buried with one of the ancients. She must have been important, yet she was buried alone, far from any of the Anasazi villages.

It was that very place where Blackjack had come to her, from out of the shadows, as if he were the guardian of the burial. In his mouth was a strand of turquoise beads. Rheada's hand rose to her neck, to the necklace she had worn ever since.

"What does it mean, Rheada?"

Rheada looked down at *this* burial that Tilly had uncovered. "This person was special, Tilly. It means we need to leave the burial alone."

Blackjack squawked, a low sound that she immediately understood and that sent shivers over her arms.

"Come on." Rheada jumped up. "It's time to go." She took Tilly's arm, partly lifting her.

Tilly shook loose. "You never want to do what I want to do, Rheada."

"That's because you choose dangerous things, Tilly. If you don't believe me, believe Blackjack."

He stared at Tilly, his keen eyes flints of black.

Rheada walked out of the cold gloom of the ruin to the edge of the cliff and stood in the sunlight. She heard sharp squawks and Tilly's raised voice, the sounds of her sister arguing in vain with a bird. Blackjack obviously had more stamina, or more determination than Rheada, for soon Tilly emerged.

As they made their way down the cliff, Blackjack persisted in his protests, hovering over Tilly like an angry black cloud, until Rheada almost sympathized with her sister. Tilly had only wanted to play. She had wanted to put on the beautiful necklaces and pretend. Rheada couldn't blame her for that. Even Rheada had felt the urge.

But Rheada knew better than to mess with sacred objects. The curse of the Anasazi was a real, deadly power. Tilly should know that by now, too. A part of Rheada worried that Tilly just didn't believe in the power of the Anasazi.

They reached the bottom of the talus slope and Rheada knelt beside the overturned pot. Carefully, she dug a trench in the sand surrounding the vessel.

"Why are you bothering with that broken pot?"

Rheada looked up at Tilly, who stood off to the side, a stubborn set to her jaw.

"Just because something isn't perfect doesn't mean it's not worth saving," Rheada replied. She smiled inwardly at the relentless will of her sister. "How do you think it ended up here?" she asked, hoping to soften Tilly with a guessing game.

"They probably tossed it out with the garbage," Tilly said gruffly with a nod to the ruin, but her lips contorted to a sly smirk. Soon, she was kneeling alongside Rheada, her fingers brushing her sister's as they both dug at the dirt. Blackjack strutted around the girls, occasionally scratching at the ground as if to help.

Suddenly, Tilly asked, "Who do you think was buried up there?"

Rheada followed Tilly's gaze to the ruin. "I wish I knew."

"But it was someone important."

"Yes, someone important," Rheada said, working her fingers around the pot.

"Well, if it was someone important, why weren't the necklaces buried?"

Rheada glanced up at Tilly. Her sister's forehead was furrowed in thought. "I don't know, Tilly. Maybe Daddy knows."

"Well, maybe," Tilly said, "someone *else* hid the necklaces there. You know, years later, stuck them under the basket." Tilly's words came out in a rush, as if this were all she'd been thinking about.

Rheada looked at her sister in disbelief. "Would *you* hide something in a grave?"

"Maybe," Tilly said, a bit defensively.

Rheada shook her head in amazement at Tilly's fearlessness. She had no doubt her sister *could* consider using a burial as a hiding place.

They worked together on the buried pot, Rheada taking the weight of the pot, carefully jiggling it loose as Tilly cleared away handfuls of dirt. Finally, Rheada lifted it free, and fell back on her rump with a long, tubular vessel in her lap.

"Oh, my gosh," Tilly breathed. "Another one."

Rheada stared at the rare cylinder pot resting across her legs, the second one they had found in two days.

"Is it as old as the other one?"

Rheada ran her hand over the carefully shaped clay. "I don't know, Tilly . . ." Her words trailed off in wonder. "Maybe eight hundred years?" Rheada looked up at her sister and their eyes met in mutual excitement.

Rheada laid the clay cylinder on the ground, and she and Tilly gently brushed off the dark, cold remnants of the deep earth that had held the pot so close, for so many hundreds of years.

Rheada was the first to see the thick, black lines of paint. "Look at this, Tilly!" Her fingers whisked more dirt from the pot.

A design emerged. Both girls sat back in utter silence. A crude painted face stared back at them. Black squares were the eyes; a downward stroke of black was a nose; and for the mouth there was a small circle of black. Above the eyes, spanning the width of the face, was a black triangle with stepped sides. Rheada traced the perfectly drawn round mouth. It could be singing, or telling stories . . . or warning.

A realization dawned on her. A chill skittered up her arms.

"Poseyemu." Tilly uttered the name first.

"Maybe," Rheada said, trying to forestall the fear that was creeping through her. She thought of the story her father told about the daughter of a Chaco priest forced to marry an Aztec warlord. Their child was meant to be the leader of the empire.

The mask made for him symbolized the two powers as one. But he was killed. And the reign of terror tore Chaco apart.

"There should be two sides, *two* masks," Tilly said with authority.

"You're right." As soon as she uttered the words, Rheada's heart jumped in her chest. And before Rheada could stop her sister, Tilly's hands were rolling the pot over in the sand.

Right away, Rheada could see the distinct black beneath the caked-on earth. Her hands trembling, she helped Tilly sweep away dirt. Swaths of black paint emerged—harsh, bold lines that made Rheada's hands tremble even more.

When they finally uncovered the painting, Rheada's breath stuck in her throat.

"Oh, my gosh," gasped Tilly.

Rheada couldn't speak. She could only stare at the terrifying face she had unearthed. Tiny white eyes glared back at her. The mouth was a slash of angry white. The entire face was fierce and menacing—a frightening opposite to the other side.

"The two sides. Just like Daddy said," Tilly whispered.

Rheada stared at the pot, fixated by the intense face on this side, and the notion of the good, almost *merciful,* face on the other. In her mind, she saw them together, one on top of the other, becoming one powerful man . . . the ancient hero who saved the Anasazi.

Her heart pounded, each beat sharper than the last—as if she were running hard. But toward something or away? Her head was light, as if with excitement . . . or fear.

"Rheada, are you okay?"

Rheada nodded, though the gesture took effort. She was not okay. And she knew right then that the real mask, wherever it was hidden, should *stay* hidden.

"Wait till Daddy sees this!" Tilly exclaimed.

For the first time in her young life, Rheada wasn't eager to show their father the find. She looked at the hole in the ground and even had the fleeting thought of sticking the pot back in and covering it with dirt. Then it would be safe. *She* would be safe.

The notion was ridiculous. Daddy protected them and everything they found.

It took the two of them to carry the pot, laid across their

outstretched arms like a baby. For the first hour, the girls walked in silence, Blackjack sitting balanced on Rheada's shoulder, though at times he flapped around Tilly, pecking at the tail of her shirt. Rheada's own thoughts spun around the pot and their amazing find. And gradually, with each step toward home, her worry changed to excitement, spiraling through her in anticipation of what their father would say. He would be so proud.

By the time they reached the confluence of sandy washes—their landmark to the side canyon protecting the family camp—the sun had already relinquished its hold on the deep canyons. The cliff walls again claimed their domain, stretching long shadowy fingers across the canyon floor to the opposite side.

Blackjack usually took the lead, his short calls guiding the girls. But tonight, he hovered in front of them, squawking, blocking their steps.

"Blackjack! Move!" Rheada tried to angle around the pesky bird.

Brack!

He screeched so close to her, Rheada's ears rang. She couldn't cover them without dropping the pot.

Brack!

"Blackjack! Stop it!"

He flapped his wings frantically and forced them off the path. Rheada and Tilly set the pot on the ground. Rheada rose, intending to scold her bird. She could see the glow of their father's campfire in the distance.

"Blackjack," she hissed. "What's wrong with you? We want to go home—"

Just then, she saw that more than her father's tall silhouette stood by the fire. Another man faced him.

Rheada's eyes narrowed on the stranger. Daddy had always warned the girls never to talk to others about the wonderful things they found in the canyons.

"What do we do?" Tilly whispered.

Caw! Blackjack issued the order as he lifted from beside them and flew straight down the canyon to the campfire.

Rheada looked at her sister and saw the silent agreement. They both crouched beside the pot and watched. Blackjack landed on the ground at their father's feet.

Brack! His call echoed off the cliffs.

"Go away!" their father yelled. He took a step toward Blackjack, but his gaze was down the canyon, and his voice held a warning. Suddenly, Rheada knew his message was for her and Tilly: He wanted them to leave. A part of Rheada had the same urge—to run back in the direction from where she and Tilly had come. But what if their father was in danger?

"Stay here," she said to Tilly. "I'll be right back." She crept along the dry wash, until she was as close as she dared. Rheada saw her father glance quickly down the canyon, then he faced the stranger.

"How did you find me?"

"It wasn't easy." The man looked up from where he was crouched by the fire. "You've got yourself holed up pretty good back here." The man barked out a laugh that sent shivers up Rheada's arms.

"So, why are you here?" her father asked.

"I want to see what you have for me." The glow of light from the fire made harsh lines on the stranger's face.

"We're supposed to meet in five days. That was the arrangement."

"And I made a new arrangement." He rose and faced her father. "Now what have you got?"

Rheada didn't like the tone of his voice, or the way he stared at her father. She wished her father would just tell him to leave.

Her father took a step toward the stranger. "You think I keep the stuff with me? I'm not an idiot."

What stuff? Rheada thought. She wished she could understand what her father was talking about.

"I didn't go to all this trouble for nothing, Samuels. You must have something around."

"Just what the hell is the emergency?"

The man paused, then, "I've got my hooks in a big buyer. But he's new and I need to reel him in now, before he leaves for Germany. We can do the rest of the business by shipments."

"How big?" her father asked.

The stranger smiled. The fire's flames lit his eyes. "Big."

Her father's gaze shifted down the canyon. He ran a hand over his jaw. Rheada recognized the gesture from when he was thinking something through. The next moment, he walked out of the firelight. He was back a few minutes later, carrying the cylinder pot that she and Tilly had found just yesterday. Why would her father show one of their rarest finds to this rude man? She felt a sickening flutter in her stomach.

"This ought to impress your buyer. I'd guess it to be eleven hundred A.D."

"Doesn't make any sense finding this so far north of Chaco." The stranger's eyes narrowed. "Just where did you say you found it?"

"Nice try. But you can forget an answer."

Rheada had never heard her father sound so threatening. The man didn't seem to care, though. He just shrugged.

"It makes perfect sense finding it up here," her father continued. "Everyone knows the Anasazi fled north from Chaco Canyon and built the cliff dwellings. There has just never been any direct, tangible proof. Until now."

There was a reverence in her father's voice. Rheada leaned closer. She loved her father's stories.

The stranger was kneeling by the pot. He looked up at her father. "It's nice. But you *know* what I really want."

"I haven't found it."

"Not yet, you mean."

Her father looked down the canyon, and though Rheada couldn't see his eyes, she could almost *feel* the intense stare. Suddenly, she knew exactly what they were talking about: the mask. "That's right. Not yet."

But there was a sliver of doubt in his voice. Rheada wanted to jump up and tell her father that they were close, that his story was true. Her fear about the mask was buried in an avalanche of love for her father.

"You wouldn't lie to me, would you?"

"It's out there." Her father's voice was harsh. "Sometimes I wonder if it should *stay* out there."

That her father's words echoed Rheada's own thoughts plumbed right to her core. She nearly ran to him to hug him close. God, how she loved her father.

"Don't even think of crossing me, Samuels."

The stranger's threat hung in the air. Her father stared down at the man. "You're an idiot if you think your threat concerns me. You're *nothing* compared to the power that's in the mask." Her father advanced on the man. "The combined forces of the Anasazi and Aztec Indians are in that mask. You think you worry me?"

The stranger gave a snort. "Save the drama for the buyers, Samuels. They love that shit." He turned back to the pot. "As for this pot—"

"What my grandfather would have given to see this . . ." Her father's words trailed off.

"Yeah, well, if he'd found it, the museum that paid him to loot would have gotten the pot for pennies compared to what I'm prepared to offer. I'll give you one thousand."

Rheada couldn't believe what she was hearing. This man must be crazy if he thought her father would take money for the pot. He loved them even more than she did.

Her father laughed. "As a down payment, you mean?"

Rheada had the desperate sense the conversation had taken a wrong turn—one she couldn't understand, yet somehow knew she didn't like.

"Fifteen hundred," the stranger said.

"Your buyer will pay eight times that because you have the only Chaco cylinder pot found outside Chaco Canyon."

Rheada couldn't believe her ears: that her father was actually selling their pot! Her desperation rose to full-blown anxiety.

"No!"

Suddenly, Blackjack was in her face.

Brack! Brack! Brack! he screeched at her. His wings flapped furiously, blocking her.

Rheada saw her father's head jerk toward her, alarm on his face. She heard him say, "I'll take three thousand. Now get out of here."

Rheada tried to fight past Blackjack to get to her father, but Blackjack drove her back down. He flew at her, forcing her to retreat farther and farther. She stumbled over a rut and fell backward. She could hear the sound of a Jeep rumble past the arroyo.

Her father appeared over the ridge of the wash. His face was lined with concern, then relief when he saw her. "Rheada, are you okay?"

"Daddy, you can't sell the pot!"

He stared down at Rheada, the relief on his face gone,

replaced with a sadness. For a moment, Rheada hoped he
would explain that she had misunderstood. He treasured the
pots. He would never sell them.

"Rheada, this is what we do," he said. "We find pots and
we sell them. That's how I make a living. That's how it's
always been."

"But you said you kept the pots. You said you protected
them."

Her father let out a long sigh. "When the pots find a place
in someone's home, then they are safe. Out here they aren't
safe. You can understand that."

Rheada couldn't understand that. The swirl of confusion
had swept to her stomach, churning her insides, threatening to
make her sick.

"But they don't belong to you," she said, looking up at her
father, hoping he would change back, any minute, to the man
she knew.

"The people they belong to are dead, Rheada. Now that's
enough." He straightened and walked away.

The pain of his betrayal squeezed Rheada's heart and
flooded her with an ache that pressed behind her eyes, forcing
them to cloud. She staggered to her feet and crept back toward
Tilly. Her sister's eyes were wide.

"What happened?"

The truth Rheada didn't want to face fell from her lips. "He
lied to us." She bent to lift the pot. Tilly helped and walked
alongside.

As if guided by her heart, Rheada's legs took her to the
one place where she could find solace. Blinded by the dark
grip on her heart, blacker than the night, Rheada found her
cave. From a small niche, she took a box of matches and lit
the candle. The black cavern transformed, with the instant
flicker of light, to a treasure haven.

Rows of pots hugged the walls. Remnants of yucca-frond
sandals poked above the rim of a woven basket. Rheada had
collected the relics from ancient refuse dumps or found them
on obscure trails. None were sacred and many were chipped
or even broken, but they filled her with a joy she couldn't
explain. She only had to gaze on the pieces to be swept away
for hours on daydreams about the ancient ones. Rheada placed
the vessel they had found on the ground.

She stared at the two-faced pot and felt a fear grow inside her. Everything was wrong, so wrong, and she didn't know how to make it right. Maybe if she put the pot back, she thought desperately. Maybe it had the curse of the Anasazi and they were all doomed.

Except Blackjack would never have let them dig up the pot if it were dangerous. So that didn't make sense. But nothing made sense right now.

Tilly sat down beside her and broke the long silence. "What's the matter, Rheada?" She slipped her hand within Rheada's. Rheada squeezed the small hand and the tears she had contained started to flow over her cheeks.

Rheada looked away, and lifted her chin, until the tears subsided. How could she tell Tilly that their father stole pots? That he sold them?

"Rheada, I have something for you."

Rheada glanced aside and saw Tilly pull a necklace from her pocket—one of the necklaces she had uncovered in the burial. Tilly had disobeyed, but now she offered the precious strand of shell-beads to her sister.

"You have to promise not to be mad."

Rheada swallowed over choking emotions. "I'm not mad, Tilly," she managed. "But you know we'll have to put them back tomorrow."

"I know," Tilly admitted. "But they make you happy now."

Rheada let the hand-cut shells run across her fingers and she couldn't help a small, wondrous smile. She pictured a man placing the necklace around a girl's neck, his eyes full of love, and she realized she was seeing her father and herself. Her throat constricted with new pain.

"When I grow up, I'll protect the old things. I won't be a thief." She looked at her sister, the only person she could trust.

Chapter 2

ANOTHER tourist had taken a potshard and risked the wrath of the Anasazi. Over the past six months, Rheada had received over a dozen of these packages—different sizes and shapes of envelopes, but all bulging about the middle; all addressed seemingly in haste, with the same element of desperation.

Sometimes a letter would accompany the shard, the writer begging forgiveness, pleading with Rheada to return the shard—please, right away, before more bad luck befell the pilferer.

This envelope had been stapled, then taped, then stapled again. Rheada cut and ripped, finally breaking through all the layers. She tilted the package. A bundle of tissue slid onto the desk and with it floated a slip of paper. Scrawled print said only, "taken from Ayah'i. The Place Below." It was the ruin she had stumbled upon just three weeks ago.

Rheada eyed the tissue bundle, but didn't reach for it. She had hoped to put that day behind her . . . and that ruin.

She had only meant to find a different route home to Aztec. Some in the tour group had complained about taking yet another unplanned side trip. Others had joined in what they perceived as her spirit of adventure. In truth, Rheada had simply been anxious to get off the highway. She hated the hard, black two-lane roads; she hated the sound of tires on the road; and she couldn't get used to the speed at which people traveled.

South of Aztec, she had spotted a dirt road angling east across the plateau and told Henry to take it. The road had serpentined down the side of a mesa into a valley. She might never have noticed the lone mound on the horizon, but in the perfectly blue sky, clouds had gathered only there, hovering, a halo of swirling gray above this one bluff, a solitary cone of dark earth. She knew instinctively she was gazing on the site of a ruin, a shadowy monument rising from the past.

The group clambered one hundred feet to the top, their

enthusiasm dissolving when all they found was a meager pile of stones.

Rheada, however, saw much more: masonry techniques that weren't Chacoan, or that of any other indigenous Indians of the Southwest for that matter. She had stared, at first disbelieving. But nothing could change the obvious: The ruin was built by Aztecs.

Rheada had stood on that windblown bluff, and stared north in the direction of where thousands of Anasazi had fled into the cliffs. No one knew who the enemy was that had chased them. But here, standing between them and the great city of Chaco they had abandoned, was an Aztec outpost.

It was a discovery that would make even Tilly proud . . . but had made Rheada nervous. A familiar disquiet had fled over her skin . . . along with a clear image of the mask. And Rheada *knew* the place harbored secrets meant to remain hidden.

How she wished that Tilly and Blackjack were with her.

By habit, Rheada touched her hand to her neck, reaching for the turquoise necklace Blackjack had given her but which Rheada no longer wore. It was back in the canyons, along with Blackjack and Tilly and all the things that had been precious in her life.

Rheada raised her head to her office and the clean white walls. She let her gaze linger on her pencil drawings, framed now—her only keepsakes from the canyons. Beyond, through the window, was the porch and original living room of the old adobe house, now all enclosed for the business entrance.

She could see Tilly here, enjoying the novelty of high, straight walls instead of the sloping tent roofs; she could hear Tilly giggling as she tested water faucets and switched on and off the lights.

She should be here. This had been their plan, their dream: They would escape the canyons and build a legitimate life, together.

Rheada's eyes stung from a sudden emptiness and yearning. How could she ever redeem the past without her sister?

Rheada stared at the bundle of tissue on her desk. It was wrapped with more tape, more wrapping, layer upon layer; an excessive amount . . . a fearful amount.

Sudden dread skittered through Rheada. Her hands stilled.

She could almost hear Blackjack's sharp caws of warning. Instinct told her to set this piece aside; if she were still living in the canyon, she would give it wide berth.

But she wasn't in the canyon anymore and she couldn't simply walk away.

Tentatively, she pulled back a piece of tape, then another, her anxiety mounting beyond any she had suffered with previous returned shards. Whatever lay within her hands commanded her respect.

The last bit of tissue fell away and a pottery shard fell onto her palm. She had never before seen such a beautiful piece. The white background was painted with not only black, but also red. She turned the circle of pottery between her fingers, her eyes following the lines of paint. Suddenly, the pattern was clear, unmistakable. Rheada's breath caught in her throat. The drawing was a figure of a bird—a raven, like her namesake . . . like the name she had carried for the nine years since her father's death.

The shard dropped from her hands onto the tissue and Rheada pushed back from the desk, her thoughts racing. Did someone know her identity? She grabbed the envelope and flipped it over, but there wasn't a return address. She peered inside the envelope, but there was no other note—not a mention of threats, or blackmail.

Rheada took several breaths, trying to calm herself—except she couldn't dispel the scary eeriness flooding her.

Rheada heard Tilly's voice mocking her, *You can't escape the past, Rheada.*

Rheada's throat clenched at a rush of emotion. God, how she wished her sister were here. With Tilly beside her, Rheada could face anything. Sometimes she lay awake at night wondering how she could ever do this. What right did she have to want an honest life? But then she would see her sister's face as it was that one terrible day when Tilly had found their father in a heap at the bottom of a cliff. Her cheeks were stained with tears, her voice was raw from screaming, but her eyes . . . her eyes were so intense that Rheada felt a strength surge from Tilly straight through her. It was Tilly who had said, *We can do this, Rheada, we can make it on our own.*

Except Rheada had never meant to make it without Tilly.

Now she had to find the strength to continue on her own.

She had to make this life work, make the dream come true . . . and maybe then she could convince Tilly to join her.

Rheada pulled her gaze back to the shard. It was just a piece of pottery and she had a duty. She had made a vow to the Anasazi. Today, after the tour, she would return this artifact to its home and let it again rest in peace.

She gathered her courage and picked up the shard with her thumb and forefinger. It was only a piece of pottery, she told herself again, picked up by a tourist and now returned. It was not an omen of bad luck.

Rheada wished that she believed in coincidences. But she didn't. Things happened for a reason.

Here, my name is Kee.

He repeated the name silently, invoking the identity, his mind seeking the remnants of that man—the one he had been, the one who was not a criminal . . . the one who was not a murderer.

His thoughts stumbled, catching on the nightmare.

He leaned into the brick building and pressed his forehead to the jagged masonry, bearing down on the edgy roughness, but nothing could stop the horrible visions from rising.

Once again, he heard the man's screams. He heard Crow yell at the others to throw on more dirt . . .

. . . and he had stood by and watched.

That could have been him. Since Crow had meant to bury alive the undercover agent, that *should* have been him.

Instead, he had managed to set up one of their own and saved his own skin.

I did what I had to do. For her.

Sarah's face floated to him, just as he remembered her— young, innocent, her life ahead of her. Pain spiked through him, forcing his lips back in silent agony. The ache charged through him, drawing his hands into fists.

"Son, are you all right?"

A gentle hand closed around his arm. He looked down at an old woman in a flowered hat, her eyes full of concern.

"I'm fine. Just getting my bearings," he said, harsher than he intended.

She stepped back, startled, then hurried past him and down the sidewalk. He stared after her and the damn cheery flowers bouncing on her head. She was right to be scared of him.

To hell with her. To hell with my own pitiful conscience.

He had let a man die, but he was also one step closer in his hunt to finding the murderer of his sister.

When the crew regrouped in about a month, Crow expected Kee and he would be there. Not that Kee gave a damn about whatever illegal activities Crow was up to. But that murdering son of a bitch actually trusted Kee: He had no idea Kee was undercover for the Bureau of Land Management. Through Crow, Kee would somehow find his way to Raven, the most elusive of all pot thieves. Then, he would have his revenge for his sister.

But for now, his name was Kee. It was the only truth left him in the fortress of lies he had built.

He drew a ragged breath, pushed away from the wall, and opened the door to the bar. He strode to the back, the old plank floor creaking beneath his footsteps. His passing gaze took in the familiar faces of the patrons. He recognized the smells: the polished wood; clay from the shoes of the ranchers; soapy dishwater in the sink behind the bar; and cigarette smoke, caught by the morning light in a ghostly haze. Though he had been to the edge of hell and back, nothing here had changed.

Kee angled a chair and slid into the shadows, his back to the corner, his eyes on the door. The vantage was instantly familiar, the habit as natural as any survival instinct.

He was damn good at surviving.

He shifted his weight on the chair, trying for the ease any normal man could find in a simple damn chair in a bar— except he hadn't seen a chair, or any other piece of furniture, in eight months. The chair's rounded back hit him just below the shoulder blades; the hard, flat seat gave no more comfort than a cold boulder. He cursed his own body—now more accustomed to crouching in the clandestine darkness of a cave or hunched at the edge of an open-pit grave.

"Welcome back, Blackburn. You get the job done?" A long-neck bottle of beer appeared in front of Kee.

He shoved the memories deep and donned the mask he presented to the bartender—and everyone else in Aztec. "For now," Kee said with a glance up to Max.

The big man's expression sobered. His brow furrowed and

he looked at Kee a little too long. "A lot of wild country out there to map," Max said finally.

"Yeah." Kee pulled his gaze back to the beer.

After a moment, Kee could hear Max walk back to the bar. He heard the rustle of the newspaper Max kept at the counter and perused all day. Over all that, he could still hear the concern in Max's voice. Maybe it had been a mistake to come straight back here. Max was too perceptive, too observant. Of course, those same qualities were the reason why Kee had cultivated him. The bartender seemed to know everyone and what they were up to. After his long absence, Kee had a yearning to know that at least nothing here, in his sanctuary, had changed.

He grabbed the bottle from the table and lifted it to his lips. His first taste of cold beer in eight months sent a rush through his body: biting his tongue, swirling down his gullet. He had to struggle not to release a groan of consummate pleasure.

Kee gripped the bottle, let the cold sweat seep into his fingers, through his palm. For just a moment, his fingers wrapped around the chilled bottle in the same way as other men, Kee could even imagine himself a part of humanity.

Except he knew better.

A burst of sunshine filled the entrance. Kee squinted his eyes at the person in the doorway—a shadow, really, against the bright morning light—but he could distinguish slender curves, wisps of hair around her face. She looked like an angel.

For a hazy, off-balance second, his heart jerked at the possibility: Was it Sarah?

As if an apparition, her shimmering form drifted across the threshold. The bottle slipped down his fingers, clunked on the table, forgotten, as he stared.

Someone closed the door. Familiar darkness returned. The vision dissolved and reality gripped his heart. It couldn't be Sarah. She was dead. Seduced into the night by the legend of Raven.

Kee gasped at the sudden ache in his chest. His hand found the beer and he brought it to his mouth, his movement awkward, stiff.

He closed his eyes and took a long drink, letting the liquid fill the hole within, weight him with reality. He opened his eyes, expecting her to be gone, yet there she stood, two tables over, where a man lay slumped, facedown on the table, his hand still clutching a glass.

"Henry?" She placed both hands on the table and gave it a shake. The table wobbled and the man's head lolled from side to side. Beyond that, though, he didn't move.

"Henry!" She thumped the table with the flat of her hand.

"He can't hear you, Rheada," Max offered. "He's been out for a couple hours."

She straightened, still staring at the disheveled lump. "I don't believe this. I have a tour."

Kee couldn't pull his gaze away from her. He saw now that her hair was pulled back into a long braid. High cheekbones accentuated her slender face. She was part Indian; maybe full Indian. Kee leaned closer, curious.

She thumped the table again. "Henry, please. Wake up."

Max walked over to her and laid a hand on her shoulder. "Even if you wake him, Rheada, he won't be any use. I'd be surprised if he could walk. He sure as hell can't drive. When does your tour start?"

"Twenty minutes ago," she said with an edge, staring at Henry. Then she looked at Max. "It was scheduled for nine. I've got people waiting at the office."

"Guess you'll have to cancel."

"I'm not canceling," she stated. She paced a few steps out and back.

"Just give them a rain check for tomorrow, Rheada. You don't have to offer any refund."

"It's not the money, Max."

She gave a hard sigh. Determination centered in the tilt of her chin.

"How about one of you fellas helping out?" Max didn't have to raise his voice much to carry to the few patrons. They were already watching the scene with mild interest; though, as soon as Max made the request, every man turned back to his drink.

"You just have to drive the bus," she announced. "Five hours total. I pay forty dollars."

A couple of men perked up at that.

"You also get lunch," she added, as if that would clinch the deal.

Kee couldn't help a small chuckle. She jerked her head to him, opened her mouth as if to say something, but then just looked at him. Her gaze held his; light-brown eyes, wide oval, like a cabochon of agate. She studied him, her eyes intent, and Kee stared back, unable to tear his gaze away. Something about her was familiar—not that he knew her or had ever met her; but he recognized an inexplicable trait, an element he couldn't name.

A chair hit the floor. Rheada broke the gaze and turned calmly to the noise. Kee glanced beyond her to see a man bracing himself on the table. "I'll drive," he said, staggering over to her. "Where you wanna go?"

She didn't answer him. Instead, she faced Kee. "What about you?"

Her directness intrigued Kee, but he shook his head. "Don't drive tours. Sorry."

Max raised a brow. Kee had the sense he had just disappointed the big man.

"They're more than tours," she said. She walked to Kee's table and stopped, her slim waist directly in Kee's line of vision.

He lowered his gaze to his beer. "Not interested."

She slid the brochure to the edge of the table, right beneath Kee's face. The words "Legendary Tours" filled the top in a Gothic print. "Takes you to mythic places in the heart of Indian country," Kee read. "Travel the back roads to hidden meadows, soothing hot springs, and secret caves."

"Sounds great." He pushed the brochure away. "Max, why don't you take the day off?"

Max smirked. "Seems to me the two of you got a lot in common."

Kee slid a glance to Max—one he hoped would silence the meddling bartender.

The big man smiled, undaunted. "You map the wilderness. She gives tours. Sometimes to places *off* the map. You just might learn something." Max turned to Rheada. "Right?"

Kee swore he could *feel* her gaze on him.

"Never mind, Max," she said.

Kee heard her walk away. Unable to resist, he glanced up just as she reached the door. There was a blast of sunshine, then blessed darkness, as she left the bar.

Kee tilted the chair back until it rested against the wall and stared at the door.

Who the hell is Rheada? What else had changed in his sanctuary while he was gone?

From the corner of his eye, Kee could see Max still standing by his table.

"So you two know each other?" Max asked.

"What are you talking about?"

Max shrugged. "Because of the way you looked at her."

Kee took a swig from the bottle, feigning disinterest. "No. Don't know her." But in his mind he saw her eyes, staring at him.

Max made a move to walk away.

"You want to bring me another beer?" Kee asked the back of the bartender.

Max turned and faced Kee. The big man's eyes flared. "You don't need another beer. You already look like hell, Kee." He shook his head. "What happened to you?"

Kee set his jaw. *Nothing. Nothing has happened to me.*

The ache returned. He downed the rest of the beer, but the hollowness didn't go away. "What's the deal, Max? You trying to make points with this woman?"

Max paused, his lips flattened. "You really got ornery out there." He turned away. "I like her, is all," he said over his shoulder. Back at the bar, he picked up his newspaper. "And the tourists like her," he added.

Kee let out a sigh. "The last place I want to go is back into the damn wilderness. Especially with a carload of tourists."

"I've heard she gives pretty unique tours," Max continued. "She took the group to some Indian ruins. Ones I didn't even know about."

Kee slid his gaze to Max. "What ruins?"

Max glanced over the top of his newspaper. "Turns out there's a site east of here."

Kee let the chair down slowly. "There's no site east of here."

"Yeah, big surprise. Especially since it turns out to be Aztec." Max lowered the newspaper.

"As in Aztec Indians from Mexico?"

"Yeah, it's been in the news. The ruin has even been mentioned in an election going on in Mexico. Some new international Indian group is electing their president. One of the candidates is using this discovery to bolster his campaign—"

"What is she, some student of archaeology?" Kee interrupted Max, or the man would go on forever.

Max chuckled. "She can't be a student, not with the money she's been spending, unless she has some backing."

"What do you mean?"

"She paid for that whole business in cash."

"All cash?"

"That's what I hear. Even the customized van."

Kee stared at the door, but what he saw was the look in her eyes, a look he hadn't been able to place, until now. It was the look of someone with secrets.

His blood pumped fast, fired by instincts he knew better than to ignore.

Kee pushed away from the table and stood, grabbing the brochure. He caught Max's curious glance.

"You changed your mind?"

"Guess so." Kee started for the door.

"This can be your good deed for the day," Max called out.

"I don't need a good deed." Kee pulled open the heavy oak door and stepped into the sunshine.

"Right." Max choked out a laugh.

Chapter 3

RHEADA had seen worse in the eyes of men. In the years after their father died, when she and Tilly had had to make a living on their own, she had seen much worse. The look in the eyes of *those* men could make sand crawl into the shadows.

He didn't have *that* in his eyes.

Still, she had recognized a quality in his gaze—the one that sized her up, judged her as friend or foe, as someone to be trusted or avoided. She had seen that same scrutiny in the eyes of other men—outlaws, thieves, and loners. It was a gaze that harbored secrets and issued warnings at the same time.

It was the gaze by which they recognized each other and knew their own kind.

Which must have been the reason why she had asked him to drive.

Rheada scolded herself. She had to be more careful, not so impulsive. That was a Tilly maneuver . . . and one that had always led to trouble for both of them. Rheada knew better.

She reached the end of the sidewalk and gazed across the street to her home, her business. Tall cottonwoods framed the small adobe. Window planters overflowed with flowers. A neat brick walk led from the parking area to the front door.

She had a house, an address; and yet as hard as she stared she feared it was as fleeting as a mirage of water on deathly hot ground. Her heart pinched with a dread that this too would be impermanent and no more real than the imaginary stories of the Anasazi she used to create.

Melancholy, stealthy and cloaked in memories, stole through Rheada, casting shadows of doubt. Could she make this life work?

Rheada's hand went to her pocket where she felt the shard, like a remnant of her past haunting her. With new determination, she stepped from the curb, her place of business straight ahead. She heard the high whir of tires on the street and looked up just as a Jeep ground to a halt at her side. It was the man from the bar.

She now noticed the Indian blood in his heritage—Apache or Navajo, she guessed from the lean length of him folded into the seat. Sunlight seemed to hold him in low regard, cutting his face with dark lines and harsh angles. But when he raised his hooded gaze to hers, power beyond the sun leaped straight from him to her.

"I changed my mind," he stated.

Rheada's heart bumped as if she had stumbled and barely caught herself. "I have, too," she finally answered, and kept walking.

The Jeep angled, blocking her. "You changed your mind about what?"

"About a driver."

"You're canceling the tour?"

She thought he sounded too interested. Rheada returned his stare. "Why did you change your mind?"

"It's my good deed for the day," he said, but without a smile.

He didn't seem the type to perform good deeds . . . at least not without a motive. Rheada skirted around the front of the Jeep.

"I thought you didn't want to cancel," he called out.

Rheada glanced across the street. People stood at their cars, preparing to leave—because she had let them down.

He idled the Jeep alongside her. "They haven't left yet," he said, as if reading her mind.

Rheada jerked her gaze to him and found his narrowed eyes considering her.

"Guess they heard your tour is worth waiting for," he said. "Are they right?" He smiled—that is, if the lazy softening of his eyes could be called a smile.

Once again, Rheada found herself staring into a gaze she recognized and understood. He had the look of men she knew who lived on the periphery. From his uncut black hair, to his keen eyes and weathered skin, his appearance eschewed the world of clocks and laws. His features were hewn by the harder survival beneath sun and stars.

It was an environment she knew well. An environment she loved. Even more, his gaze summoned a response from within her—that most elusive of responses and one she had resigned herself to live without: the merest of connections with another human.

The connection zinged through her, delivering—inexplicably—a new rush of pride and determination. She felt a smile spread across her face. "They're right," she replied. "It is worth waiting for."

For a moment, he seemed taken aback by her swift smile. His gaze darkened, not with menace, but something else. Then, before Rheada had time to place a word to it, the look vanished and his black eyes were once again void of expression.

The sudden change didn't startle Rheada, only confirmed her intuition: He was a careful one . . . which only made her want to know more about him.

"Rheada Samuels," she said and offered her hand.

He reached his hand through the window and clasped hers. "The name's Kee." Long fingers wrapped across her palm. His sun-baked skin was even darker than hers.

He withdrew his hand, reached for the gear shift, and swung the Jeep past her into the parking lot.

She had found a driver. She wouldn't have to cancel the tour and she could return the shard today. As Rheada watched him step from his Jeep, her thumb idly rubbed the place on her palm where she had felt his rough calluses.

And she wondered at her luck.

In the De-Na-Zin Wilderness, a badland of shale, clay, and sandstone conspired into turbans, towers, and labyrinths. Tourists journeyed there to gape at the contorted landscape, to wind through the mazes and climb atop sandstone slabs that looked like a mushroom garden. But Rheada didn't even slow the tour. Kee wondered at her decision to drive right past one of the most popular destinations.

It took another half an hour of negotiating mammoth potholes and merciless boulders before Rheada told him to stop. They were in a small, pink canyon in what seemed the middle of nowhere.

She led them down a rocky path, just a short hike from the van, and stopped. "In the short distance from De-Na-Zin, we have journeyed back nearly nine hundred years to the time of the Anasazi."

Before Rheada raised her arm, Kee had already spotted the small ruin clinging to the face of the cliff. It was well camouflaged: The contour of the dwelling, along with its pinkish stone, matched perfectly that of the canyon.

"Less than twenty miles away," Rheada said, "lay the center of civilization for the Anasazi in Chaco Canyon. They built fantastic cities, roads between their cities, and trade routes far to the west and south. They had a culture rich with beliefs and ceremonies. Then suddenly they abandoned it all and fled."

She paused, gazing up at the ruin. She had a faraway look in her eyes as if she were seeing something more than a precarious pile of stones. Kee couldn't help taking a step closer.

"It was the great exodus. They left behind the homes they had built, the huge community plazas, the irrigation systems, the roads, even their belongings and their buried loved ones."

She turned to face the group and Kee was taken with the glistening fierceness in her eyes, as if she were remembering some personal history.

"Many would have traveled through here more than eight hundred years ago. Men, women, and children, the elderly and the infirm, storytellers and traders, warriors and priests."

Kee listened as she breathed life into the lives of people long dead and an annoyance flickered to life inside him. To him, the word Anasazi was merely a label—a class of artifacts, a category of contraband. The word conjured images of specific pottery and mugs, yucca sandals and feather blankets, shell bracelets and turquoise pendants—and every item carried a price tag. He had never thought of the Anasazi as people; and he was sure he didn't want to begin now.

Yet, he couldn't help listening to Rheada.

She stared down the canyon and Kee followed her gaze, seeing a barren, harsh landscape hospitable only to spindly saltbush, sage, and skinny lizards. "They headed north, scattering into the cliffs."

"Why?" The question had come almost as a whisper from one of the women in the group.

"Did they just disappear?" asked a man.

"No, they didn't disappear," Rheada said. "Today's Pueblo Indians are descended from the Anasazi."

"So, why did they leave?" asked a young boy.

Rheada looked over at the boy, her mouth open as if she

were about to say something. Instead, she turned and walked toward the cliff.

The tourists followed her, their steps within hers, like obedient schoolchildren. Kee's annoyance grew.

She stopped at the base of the cliff and faced the group. "If you look carefully as you turn in one place, you can see a gentle rise of earth surrounding you."

People shifted, twisted their necks, and looked puzzled. Kee, however, saw the outline of a debris field.

"You're standing on nine hundred years of silt, Mother Nature's backfill, protecting the refuse area of these Anasazi."

Sounds of awe rose from the group. Some lifted their feet, as if now uncertain they should be standing here at all.

"You're right to be respectful."

Kee wanted to groan.

"And you should be a little afraid."

Kee jerked his gaze to Rheada.

"Perhaps it's the mystery about the Anasazi. Our questions about how they built their great cities, even *why* the cities were built. Or why they fled from the warm desert to cold, uncomfortable cliff dwellings. Who were their enemies? Perhaps because these questions haunt us, we have also given haunting powers to the Anasazi themselves."

She spoke to the group, but her voice sounded directed to someplace distant. Though Kee couldn't take his eyes from her, his gut churned with the effort to control his anger.

How dare she add to the mysticism!

"Rangers from different Anasazi sites tell of hearing voices, even seeing ghostly figures. There are rooms they won't go into after dark. And they all warn visitors from picking up and taking away any relics from the Anasazi. For one, it's illegal." She paused. When she spoke again, her voice was stern. "But the arm of the law is benign compared to the vengeful reach of the Anasazi. You can believe or not believe. The curse of the Anasazi will still find you."

A hush swept over the group and down the small rise where they stood, gathering momentum and silent volume, until a quiet filled the whole canyon. One by one, members of the group approached closer to the cliff, slowly, reverently, as if they were in the presence of a shrine to be honored.

Kee couldn't believe his eyes. He wanted to yell, *It's a ruin, for crissakes!*

It was nothing more than the crumbling remains of where someone had lived. It could be a migrant shack, or a run-down tenement, a cardboard box . . . or a hogan without water or electricity.

The vision leaped to his mind, a memory blurred by dirt and grit: a small adobe—more like a cave built aboveground—with an old Navajo woman standing outside, a hand shading her eyes as she stared into the distance. What she looked for—what they both looked for— was not there and would never return. Sarah had been seduced away, lured into the dark world where pot thieves ruled, where evil masqueraded in the guise of hero outlaws, where murder was the first resort. All because romantic tales of ancient peoples fueled a demand beyond the supply.

He couldn't stop a sharp jab of grief, a laser stab that pinched his heart.

He glared at the tourists—their eager steps clumsy, their faces stupid with delight—and he blamed them, their curiosity, their adolescent enthusiasm. More than them, he blamed Rheada because she had brought them here. She promised them an adventure. She filled their heads with legends. And she delivered it all with such style they couldn't help but be enchanted!

Kee gritted his teeth against the swift rise of anger and strode back along the path. Intending to put distance, if only the merest yards, between himself and the spectacle, he found himself at Rheada's tour bus—conveniently alone.

The bus had every possible convenience, every comfort, surpassing that of even the priciest cruising van. Every seat was a captain's chair, with raised back and a drink holder. Above the seats hung six television monitors mounted to the ceiling and wired to a tape player. He had had to listen to a video on the ancient people of the Southwest for the entire drive to this valley.

Most amazing was how this living-room-on-wheels navigated the punishing back roads: equalizing the ruts, rolling right over brutal desert ground like a tank.

Kee glanced over his shoulder and confirmed everyone's, including Rheada's, preoccupation with the ruin. Then, he crouched low to inspect the undercarriage. The shocks on this tour bus were nearly the size of ones on a diesel truck.

In all, these were mighty plush wheels for a tour business. Custom-made from the ground up, inside and out—and, according to Max, paid for in cash.

Kee stood up and blew out a breath between his teeth. *Where the hell did that young Indian get the money?*

She couldn't be more than twenty-three, yet she had the finances to put together a business? Or, maybe she had backing.

Kee gazed down the trail. Rheada stood at the base of the cliff, her finger pointing at the masonry of the ruin. The group huddled close, a semicircle of attentive faces, seemingly holding on to her every word.

Kee turned and leaned against the bus, his back to the ruin. He couldn't deny that she seemed to know her stuff—but that only added to her mystery. Where did she come from?

"A lot of wild country out there."

Kee jerked his head around. There stood Rheada, just a few feet away. How in the hell had she gotten so close without making a sound?

"Sorry. I didn't mean to startle you." She offered a smile. "Canyons give a lot of room to get lost in your thoughts," she added.

She widened her smile, a bit self-consciously. A tendril of her black hair broke loose from her braid and danced free, giving her an innocent, waiflike appearance.

Kee realized he was staring at her. He straightened and pushed off the side of the bus. "Ready to go?"

"Not yet." She glanced up the slope. "I gave them another ten minutes," she said.

She leaned her back against the bus and was quiet for a minute. Then Kee saw her shift to look at him.

"So, I'm guessing that you're Navajo," she said.

For the second time in two minutes, she had taken him by surprise. "Why?"

"Because of how you reacted at the ruin. Most Navajo don't want to be around the Anasazi ruins. Ghosts of the dead and all that."

Kee didn't know whether he was bothered more that she

had noticed his reaction or by the assumption he would give a damn about ruins. "My family is Navajo."

Rheada wondered at his short, cryptic answer. Then, he averted his gaze to the distance, and she realized the subject was off-limits. It was just one more way in which he reminded her of the men she knew from her years in the canyon—outlaws without a past, but with a whole lot of secrets.

"And you?"

His question brought her gaze up and Rheada found those keen black eyes studying her.

"A mix," she said, giving her stock answer. "A little of this. A little of that."

He didn't look satisfied with her answer. He shifted to face her, leaning his elbow on the hood, his gaze never leaving her face. Rheada had to fight the urge to duck and hide from his intense scrutiny.

"I think mostly Pueblo," he said finally.

The fact he was right didn't bother Rheada nearly as much as the uneasy feeling he had reached this conclusion after long deliberation. What did it matter to him what she was?

"What did you do before this?" He gestured to the tourists.

Rheada matched his forthright gaze and gave the same answer she had given since walking out of the canyon. "I traveled with my father. He was a miner."

His brow quirked in surprise. "Really. Gold or silver?"

"Both. But more turquoise than anything."

"Really," he said again. He looked at the bus and ran his hand over the hood. "I didn't know one-man turquoise mining could be so profitable."

"We did okay." Rheada left it at that. She had run across enough itinerant prospectors to know they were as close-mouthed as any renegade from civilization.

"Guess I picked the wrong line of work," Kee answered. "I'll never see the money in mapping to buy these kind of wheels."

"It was hard work. And it's not like my dad ever struck it rich. He managed to provide a life, was all." This came so close to the truth, Rheada had to look away.

"You didn't like that life."

His statement caught Rheada unprepared. She wondered what he had heard in her voice that had revealed so much.

"Some things I liked a lot," Rheada heard herself say. She hadn't meant to divulge even more to this man, but her heart wouldn't let her stay silent. She could almost hear herself describe her *own* canyons; how she missed their specific golden-orange at sunrise; or how the pungent scent of sagebrush after rain made her homesick. There *were* things she had liked and now missed . . . like having someone to talk to.

Immediately, her mind conjured up Tilly's face, her broad grin and mischievous eyes.

"But you left."

Emotions rose swiftly in Rheada and she had to swallow. "Yes." She pasted a smile on and glanced at Kee. She found him gazing at her with such interest that Rheada nearly forgot the role she needed to play.

Nervously, Rheada jammed a hand into her pocket. Her fingers brushed the shard—the one of the raven. Her pulse leaped.

"I've heard it's dangerous, too," he added.

"Yes. It can be deadly." The words slipped from her mouth before she could stop them.

She was thinking of what had happened to her father. She was thinking of her stubborn sister, refusing to leave the canyons. And she was thinking of this shard, the one she had to return to the Aztec ruin.

She didn't want to go back. Just the thought of the place made her uneasy, and she knew why. Her whole childhood had been a quest with her father to find the mask of Poseyemu—the two-faced kachina mask, half Anasazi and half Aztec. Her father had been obsessed with finding it . . . until the day Tilly found him dead. The mask, along with its powers, was hidden and safe, Rheada told herself. But still, she couldn't shake the sense that by discovering the ruin she had disturbed terrible secrets of the past.

Movement at her side made Rheada turn her head. She found Kee looking at her. In his dark eyes, she could see a depth, a wealth of experience of a man who had traveled far. Yet, there was also a loneliness. Just like she had herself. It was like looking into the eyes of a friend.

The image that filled her mind was how the very blackness of Kee's eyes, his intense, unblinking stare, reminded her of the only one who had guided her safely: Blackjack. The thought occurred to her that she had nothing to fear: The mask was safe where she and Tilly had hidden it. Soon, this shard would be safe, back where it belonged.

In that moment, she wondered if it might just be possible that she could make this life work.

Rheada's chest tightened in defense against the onslaught of emotions. Her hand closed into a fist around the shard, as if she could will herself strength.

"Go ahead and start up the bus," she said, though her voice sounded a little tight. She turned and walked down the path, and with each step loosened her grip on the shard.

"I have one more place to show you before we end the tour."

Kee could see Rheada in the rearview mirror as she addressed the group. The road out of the canyon was ungraded and washboardy, beyond the compensation of even the high-performance shocks on this bus. Yet, there she stood, effortlessly, in the middle of the aisle, not bracing herself on any chair or overhead racks—as if she herself were outfitted with some high-tech inner gyroscope. He had never seen anyone so balanced and light on her feet.

The same could not quite be said, however, of her demeanor. She had faltered when talking about her background. And she still appeared tense. He looked at her now, her arms crossed at her front. Something about how her shirt pulled taut across her small shoulder blades, or maybe it was the small closeness to her—her slightly veiled and distant demeanor—made Kee think she looked very much alone and guarded.

And since that was a condition he knew well, he had little sympathy . . . though much curiosity: What did *she* guard from the world?

"Our last stop today will be at a ruin only recently discovered as an Aztec Indian outpost."

The right front caught a pothole and jerked Kee's focus to the road. He gave a quick glance to Rheada's reflection and saw her still planted squarely in the aisle. Now, however, she was staring back at him, her brow furrowed, her brown eyes assessing, as if she knew he had been looking at her, maybe even pondering her, instead of watching the road.

Kee pulled his gaze from her and stared out the window, but what he saw were her intense eyes, the *knowing* keenness he remembered from the bar. Inexplicably, that quiet scrutiny provoked the same startling unease as when she had surprised him at the bus—as if she could sneak up on his thoughts as readily as she had tread silently over the ground.

"The site is southwest of Blanco," she continued. From the sound of Rheada's voice, Kee could tell she again had her back to him. "If you'll look at your maps and find Canyon Largo running south off Highway 64."

Kee heard the rustle of maps.

"Let your fingers slide to the east, toward Highway 44, a distance of only fifteen miles. Look closer at the area your finger covered. You'll notice there's only white space; no roads, not even any dirt roads marked on the map. Of course, we *are* on a road."

She paused.

"Hundreds of miles of roads in the Southwest are not on any maps. Though maybe your driver will correct that oversight."

Kee saw heads raised from their maps, looking toward him. Their faces were expectant, waiting for him to talk, to enlighten them. He glanced at Rheada and saw the same expression.

Is she testing me?

"Kee, you want to tell the group a little about yourself?"

No.

"I don't map roads," he stated flatly, not much caring to conceal his irritation.

He kept his gaze on the road ahead, hoping to effectively shut off any more questions. The silence swelled, filling the bus, straining against his neck, until finally it pushed the words out of his throat. "I map wilderness areas."

"Designated wilderness areas?"

He heard the pointed curiosity in Rheada's voice and wondered what she was thinking.

"Not necessarily," he answered.

"Interesting," she said, barely above a whisper.

Kee slanted a glance to her, but she wasn't looking at him. She had her gaze set on the passing landscape. Soon, she brushed past Kee and took her seat.

"In about half an hour, you'll come up on Blanco Wash. There should be only a trickle of water this time of year."

Kee nodded, his gaze ahead, but he could see from the corner of his eye that Rheada was staring out the window. She sat quietly—more quietly than he had ever seen her—and Kee wondered what could be consuming her thoughts.

"I'm sorry if I embarrassed you in front of the group. I just find your work interesting."

Her sudden apology surprised him—nor did he quite believe her sincerity. Shining the spotlight on him before had been a maneuver, he was sure: payback for his own scrutiny.

"What I find interesting," he replied, "is you."

He slanted his lips to a smile and glanced at Rheada. He was immediately gratified by the startled widening of her eyes.

"I'm impressed by how much you know about this area and its history," he added. "And to already be running such a successful business." He tapped his fingers on the steering wheel. "You must have gotten your degree at turbo speed." He kept the smile on and let his gaze linger.

She looked down for one beat. When she raised her gaze to his, Kee saw a flicker of determination, like the yellow tips of a flame that burned blue deep at the source. "No school," she said finally.

The smile on Kee's face felt suddenly cold and hard, as if he were smiling in the face of someone else's hardship. He had the absurd notion to apologize.

Either she was self-taught or she had apprenticed to someone. He didn't find it likely she had picked up her information from traipsing behind her prospecting father.

Kee stared ahead at the harsh desert. They traveled along a high, flat plateau. The vegetation was monstrous, heroic proportions of sage and juniper, as if survival here was rewarded. Rheada pointed the way with single directives and an occasional raise of her arm.

How did she know this area so well? There wasn't a mine within one hundred miles.

"That way," Rheada instructed.

Kee navigated around a cluster of giant sagebrush and saw the Blanco Wash ahead. It was near dry, as Rheada had predicted. On the opposite side, as if the winding creek bed proved a boundary, the sage were mere clumps he could drive right over—any semblance of a road having long disappeared into the sand.

They crested a rise and another valley spread before them, the sparse vastness punctuated by a solitary mound, dark against the yellow ground. He knew, without any further guidance from Rheada, that this was their destination.

He parked at the base, stepped from the bus, and peered up the mound to the rubble of stones at the top. In places, the slope skirted wide, then drew close again, creating natural terraces. It was nothing extraordinary. Yet his skin pricked with anticipation. He walked around the bus to where Rheada had gathered the group.

"One thousand years ago, one city dominated the landscape of the Southwest. It rose five stories from the canyon floor. Taller than any buildings on this whole continent until only one hundred years ago. That city, in Chaco Canyon, ruled a territory over hundreds of miles, for this was the center of the gods' pleasure."

She was gazing to the southwest, a faraway look in her eyes, as if she could actually see not only the distant canyon, but into the past.

"But it was also the center of a great power struggle. Warrior cults from present-day Mexico made their way to Chaco, intending to take over and create a huge empire of Indians. They must have thought the peaceful Anasazi would be easy prey."

Hatred simmered just below her words. Her passion drew Kee closer.

"But the Anasazi rebelled from the horrific rituals of sacrifice. Factions and fear overtook Chaco. Rumors of witches led to terror, then massacres, and finally to the destruction of a great civilization." Her voice was trembling. She took a breath and faced the mound.

"Today we have crossed over land through which the Anasazi fled nine centuries ago. You've seen one of the dwellings of these refugees, clinging high on a cliff wall. These people were farmers, used to living in communities spread across valley floors. But when they fled from their cities, they built on canyon walls, in locations that could only have made for incredible hardship in getting to crops and water. Why?

"The answer is that they went to every extreme for protection from their enemies." She glared up at the mound, her expression so fierce that Kee could have sworn the air stirred and the temperature lowered. "From these people."

A gust of wind swung her braid up from her back. The man next to Kee grabbed on to his hat. In just minutes, the sky had filled with an army of dark clouds that now advanced across the valley and raised the dirt from the ground into a dusty haze.

Kee looked back to the mound and Rheada was gone. She had disappeared. He walked to the crumbling wall of stones, peered into the room cavities. No Rheada. He stared down the slope. Still no Rheada. *How could she have slipped away so fast, so silently, so completely?*

A strange uneasiness crept over Kee, as if he should be concerned—not so much for her, but for something else he couldn't name.

His steps quickened. He found himself at the far side of the ruin and his ears picked up a low murmur, a soft hum. As he rounded the only towering wall, Kee saw her. She was ten feet below, crouched on a small, earthy ledge, her hands cupped together, her body rocking just the slightest along with the monotone song.

He stopped, so taken by the sight that he couldn't move.

She brought her hands close to her mouth and seemed to blow onto them. Then she lowered her hands, still cupped, to a hole in the ground. Kee saw a flash of white, black, and red drop into the hole. With the edge of her hand, she pulled dirt into the hole, then patted it firm with her palm.

What the hell is she doing?

She stood, brushed her hands across her jeans, and turned. Her eyes narrowed at the sight of Kee.

"What are you doing here?"

"That's my question, Rheada. What were you doing?"

"That's none of your business." She crossed her arms in front.

He walked toward her. "Why would my question bother you?"

"Because you don't need to know what I'm doing."

"This is public land, Rheada."

"I know."

"And you were digging on public land."

"Not digging. Burying."

Now she walked toward him, but Kee was not going to be drawn away.

"Burying what, Rheada?"

She stopped close to him. Her eyes were filled with the same determination he had seen earlier, but now much more than a flicker, and laced with something else—a slight desperation, as if she would implore him to drop the whole subject.

He wasn't about to do that. "Burying what?" he asked again.

She glanced at the freshly filled hole, then back to him. "It's nothing important. And it's nothing illegal. Can't you leave it at that?"

"No."

Kee strode to the new dirt and knelt.

"Wait! Don't."

She was at his side. Her hand stayed his arm from reaching the small mound. "I'll tell you."

Kee looked up over his shoulder. The anxiety in her gaze almost made him stop her. Almost.

"It's a pottery shard. Anasazi," she added. "A tourist from the first group I brought here took it. He returned the shard to me in the mail, along with a letter begging me to replace it where it belonged. Please don't dig it up. This is where it belongs." With a last glance at him, she walked away, leaving the choice to Kee.

Kee stared after Rheada. She climbed the slope to the ruin with ease, then disappeared around the corner. The landscape seemed to shrink in her absence, as if an integral component were now missing—an essential piece that made the land whole.

He looked to where she had replaced the artifact, and thought of her plea to leave it alone. *This is where it belongs.* Her voice had held the conviction of *knowledge*. She seemed to have a tangible connection to the land and all it comprised.

Kee sat back on his haunches, struck by the sudden notion that Rheada might be the very person he needed. She knew the land like no one else he had met, and she knew the prehistoric sites—the important sites that just might lead him to Raven. He'd be a fool not to stay by her side.

Chapter 4

KEE drove the next day and the one after that. Yesterday, he had taken a busload of tourists to the northwestern edge of Carson National Forest. Rheada had ignored the more popular Navajo Lake State Park—where recreational vehicles snuggled close like steel babies nursing at every curve of the mother lake—and had chosen instead a remote meadow.

Without benefit of a trailhead, let alone a path, she led them to a small creek and a surprise hot springs. Sunlight and steamy water had seeped into Kee, lapped against the cold recesses, warming, thawing, eroding the dark chill within him and melting bits of his rigid control. He had lain down on the spongy grass, rested his head against a sun-baked boulder, and watched and listened as Rheada weaved stories with names like "Why Bears Have Short Tails," and "The Boy Who Became an Antelope," and "The Tricky Coyote."

She whispered low at the moments of suspense, then her voice rose with passion at the height of drama. All the while, her eyes twinkled with the delight of sharing something special, maybe even precious.

A sudden pitch to the right brought Kee's thoughts back to the road he was driving. Today, Rheada directed him southeast of Aztec, into a maze of canyons off Carrizo Creek. The dirt road wound along narrow ground—hemmed in on one side by the creek and on the other by canyons. When the creek veered off, the road sputtered to a lonely stop at the base of looming sandstone cliffs. Erosion from the top of the cliffs sloped to huge *bajadas*—wide yellow skirts of land debris so high up the cliffs the mesas seemed in danger of being swallowed whole by their own rubble.

Dry arroyos cut the ground and snaked into the canyons; the land promised no easy way in and threatened no way out. The place looked wild, edgy, and suspicious—a place perfect for outlaws and thieves.

Kee's pulse jumped. He glanced at Rheada, who had already sprung from the bus, barely hesitating long enough to

allow the passengers to grab their binoculars and water bottles.
She had the enthusiasm of a child—boundless and contagious,
drawing the group after her in eager steps—seemingly oblivious to hidden dangers and the evil he knew lurked in canyons
just like these.

By the time he stowed valuables beneath seats and locked
down the steering wheel and the doors—precautions Rheada
never instructed and seemed to not even consider—he had
only plumes of dust on a faint path to guide him.

The trail held to a wash for several hundred yards, then
angled across the canyon to one of many rincons—the narrow
canyon walls offering only a slice of sky. The same relentless
sunlight he had baked in for two days was no match for the
towering cliffs. Shadows owned this territory, sinking fingers
deep within crevices and plunging whole fists of blackness
into yawning caves. The sunless crack in the earth beckoned
no one, and warned off any explorer.

Anticipation built in Kee. Before looking up the impenetrable walls, he knew what he would see. This canyon had
been home to the Anasazi.

His steps slowed, his eyes focused on telling details. He
could see hand- and toeholds carved into the cliff face, angling
there, to that cave. He stopped just below and gazed up at the
cave. Confidently, he stared. Patiently, because he was in no
hurry. The shadows, more powerful than the sun, were no
match for him.

He let his eyes adjust to the darkness, the contours. As the
shadows retreated, the pueblo ruin Kee knew to be there
emerged, gradually—a thief cornered and defeated by Kee's
gaze. He saw the unmistakable masonry of an ancient dwelling—its crumbled walls maybe three feet high.

"There are more around the corner."

Kee jumped at Rheada's voice. He jerked his head and
found her standing just a few feet behind him, but lower, on
an incline. It was then he realized his blind steps had taken
him up a talus slope.

"Maybe you should wear a bell," he offered, letting his feet
slide ever so carefully toward her.

"Sorry. I seem to keep startling you." She offered a smile.
"I was a little worried. You were taking so long . . ." Her voice
trailed off, though her gaze stayed on him, unwavering.

He had never met anyone so forthright yet shy, like the ruin behind him—there for anyone to see, yet built with the hope no one *would* see it. The comparison appealed to Kee and he smiled.

He stopped alongside her. "I was locking down the bus." He slanted his gaze to the ruin. "You could learn something from these Anasazi, Rheada."

Her brow rose, and she looked expectant, awaiting some exciting revelation.

He leaned close to her. "They never assumed anything, Rheada. Least of all their safety," he said, a little teasingly. "I don't think they much trusted the next guy."

He expected a laugh. He had hoped to see that glint of amusement in her eyes. Instead, her gaze darkened and he swore he saw a flicker of fear just before she turned and walked away.

Kee stared after her, mulling over what he had just witnessed. She had closed down, drawn the shades. Why?

What did she have to be afraid of?

He followed her around a jagged corner of the canyon wall. One of the group stood, binoculars to his eyes, gazing up the cliff. Some had walked far ahead, while others scrutinized the opposite cliff face. For a moment, Kee couldn't pick out Rheada. A slight urgency increased his pace. He wanted to see her eyes. Her behavior before was a mystery and right now he was compelled to figure her out.

He spotted her talking with two people just beyond a copse of tamarisk trees. She was facing him. Kee knew she would see him approach and, for some reason he couldn't name, it was important he see her reaction.

She glanced at him over the shoulder of the man she spoke to. Though the look was quick, furtive, he caught a trace of the haunted woman he had first met in the bar. Somehow, over the past three days, he had forgotten that dark, veiled gaze. It had receded beneath the layers of the sunny days and her enchanting stories . . . so much so that now, this guarded glimpse was as unexpected, incongruous—and suspicious—as the sudden appearance of shoe prints in pristine sand.

Brusquely, Kee pushed aside the spindly branches of a tamarisk tree. She kept her focus on the other man, without a glance to Kee, as if deliberately ignoring him and his noisy approach. All of which only made Kee that much more intrigued.

"Now over here," she said, walking to the cliff and away from Kee, "are early Anasazi petroglyphs."

She pointed to a cluster of etched figures on a particularly smooth expanse of the cliff wall. The bodies of the figures had broad shoulders and tapered to a point. Stick arms bent out from the shoulders and ended in drooping, elongated hands.

"Because scientists need to label and categorize, these are called 'anthropomorphs.' "

She turned and smiled at her listeners. "Of course, we would call them human. And these," she said, pointing to a group of three, two large and one small, "we recognize immediately as a family."

The sharp call of someone down the canyon drew everyone's attention. One hundred yards farther in, two of the group had hiked to where the cliff wall curved inward to form a low ground-hugging cave, and sheltered within the rock was a prehistoric home.

Rheada ducked beneath the overhang and into the cave, followed by the rest of the group, stepping gingerly over low eroded walls.

Kee dismissed the site with a glance, and let his gaze drift across the cliff face, his eyes sharp. The Anasazi had been clever, not always building within caves, but sometimes on ledges, crafting their sandstone blocks to blend nearly imperceptibly with the canyon walls.

He caught sight of a marked regularity in the sandstone, and inched his way closer, probing for obstacles with his boot toe so as not to take his eyes from his quarry. Finally, standing just below, Kee looked upon the most perfectly preserved Anasazi dwelling he had ever seen.

His gaze scanned the cliff wall for access to the cave—the faintest trace of a path, possible ledges, anything. He took a few steps back for better vantage and spotted a vertical crevice not more than twenty feet from the cave. Leaving behind the group and Rheada, he maneuvered through a dense growth of saltbush straight for the cliff wall and started to climb.

The crack in the sandstone was too narrow, too tight for him to squeeze into and reach all the stone-cut holds. He had to improvise, using the Anasazi holds and stretching for the merest outcrop of sandstone with his fingers and boot toes, all the time gauging his progress in relationship to the cave.

Leveraging himself on the merest edges of rock, he angled to the side and up, his hands gripping tenaciously to the cliff face. When he finally reached the ledge of the cave, his gasp came not from the struggle but from the reward.

The small, square building's walls reached to the ceiling of the cave in a solid sandstone masonry of nature and man. He stared, amazed that vandals had not knocked down the walls in their search for bounty. How had they missed such a find?

Kee straightened and walked into the cave. Cool air from the core of the canyon breathed over him, evaporating his perspiration, raising gooseflesh on his arms. Anticipation skidded down his spine. Over and over, the thought ran through his head, *This place is too perfect.*

The walls of the pueblo sealed off any sunlight. Kee pulled a small flashlight from his back pocket and flicked it on. Its bright yellow beam cast the sandstone bricks in an eerie golden hue.

He followed the spread of light from the floor of the cave up the walls of the dwelling. Suddenly, he realized that what looked like one room from the front was actually three, extending back into the recesses of the cave. Kee's heart pounded with an inexplicable certainty.

He found the doorway and, crouching low, bent beneath the stone-slab header and entered the first room. He shone the light on the walls and across the floor. Sand and silt covered the floor and had accumulated in small drifts in the corners. There wasn't a single shoe print.

He let the flashlight's beam search every inch of the building. In the center of one wall was the doorway to the next chamber. He peered inside and found a smaller room, this one with a swept-clean appearance as if the inhabitants had only just left for a stroll.

Now the ceiling of the cave sloped and Kee had to walk half-bent toward the doorway, and the last chamber. Crouching low, he inched into the room. When he raised the flashlight, its beam caught bits of yellow in the far corner. His pulse jumped. He crawled closer, stopped, and leveled the light again.

They were kernels of corn, maybe a handful, left in the deep curve of a metate. He fanned the beam over the floor, up the walls, across the cave ceiling. Damn if he couldn't find any trace of vandalism.

"Kee."

Rheada's voice echoed off the stone walls and plumbed deep into Kee. He didn't have to turn to know she stood right behind him, in the same room. Once again, she had appeared without warning, as silently and unexpectedly as the skittering of awareness across his skin.

"Kee!"

He swiveled on the balls of his feet to look at her. She was only a shadow in the doorway.

"Back out of here, now, Kee."

Her tone carried an edge—determination cut with almost a desperation, as if she would drag him out if he didn't obey.

He couldn't ignore her. Truth was, he didn't have any good reason to stay. He straightened—as much as he could—and walked to the doorway. She backed away, letting him through, though never taking her gaze from his.

Then she took the lead and Kee followed her out through the next room and into the front chamber, where she stopped in the doorway and turned toward him.

"What compelled you to go in there?"

"Just interested," he said. "Aren't you?"

Her eyes widened slightly. "That's not the point."

"What is the point?" he asked. "You bring people to these canyons. Surely you don't expect them not to explore."

"You shouldn't be in here." Her tone wasn't scolding, but rather breathless, as if the words were squeezed past a tightness in her chest.

"And shouldn't you have stayed with the group?" he asked.

"That's right," she said, without a pause. "Instead, I'm traipsing after you."

Her slender frame was an easy fit within the small entrance. It was the same scene as when he first saw her, standing at the threshold to the bar, the sun so hot-bright behind her she had glowed like an angel. This time, however, she couldn't have looked less like an angel.

Sultry canyon shadows held her close like a lover's hands framing her face, and sparking fire in her eyes.

Kee's pulse jumped.

"I can take care of myself, Rheada," he said, stopping within hand's reach of her.

She was silent for a moment. "I'm sure you can. And you've probably never had to think about anyone else. But I do."

That he *only* thought about someone else, that all he ever thought of was his sister and every step he took was driven by the image he carried in his head—that he would use his last breath to deliver her some peace—all of this jammed at the base of his throat and stole whatever he could have said to Rheada.

"Are you all right?"

The light touch of a hand on his arm may as well have been a gun jammed to his side, shocking his thoughts to the present.

"Fine," he managed.

He noticed her sideways glance just before she slipped from the cave onto the narrow precipice. He watched, absent-mindedly, his heart and mind trapped at a place deep inside. Then something about the ease with which Rheada descended the sandstone snagged his interest—slender fingers finding the slightest holds, her slim body hugging the sandstone—as if she were not human, but a desert creature with intimate knowledge of every jagged facet of this rugged cliff.

He watched, unable to look away; too involved with each choice she made, each seemingly effortless movement, to even begin his own descent.

She glanced up. "You're coming," she said, her tone a statement, not a question.

Her eyes narrowed on him with sudden, keen purpose. Her gaze alone seemed to shorten the distance between them and Kee knew the light-headed weakness of an instant loss of balance.

"Yes, I'm coming," Kee said and inched his way down backward. He glanced over his shoulder and saw her watch him for a moment, then proceed on her own.

He reached the bottom just after her, though with not nearly the grace. A slight wipe of her brow and quick brush of her hands were the only indication she had expended any effort. And when she spoke, she wasn't the least out of breath.

"I asked everyone to meet me near where we entered but on the other side of the canyon," she said.

Kee stared at her easy gait across the uneven canyon floor. For all the climbing he had done the past eight months, for all the countless times he had forced taut muscles to endure an hour followed by one more and one more, as he crouched in the shadows of a cave—he had thought himself as fit as anyone. He'd been wrong.

He watched Rheada approach the others, her braid swinging across her narrow back. He could hear her voice—pleasant, engaging, reaching out to each person as she neared her group. It was a tone at once inclusive, yet removed—the perfect balance of friendliness and authority.

She may have been a prospector's daughter, Kee thought to himself as he joined the rest, but she wasn't born for that solitary life.

"Over here are an interesting collection of petroglyphs." She drew the group close to the cliff wall to where a huge boulder, fallen from the crest eons ago, was imbedded deep into the hard-packed ground.

"In the foreground is the female *Yei* of the Navajo Night Chant, made obvious by her rectangular head and the stepped-cloud *tabletas* on each side," she explained. "But, in the background, if you look closely you can see faint handprints. These were made nine hundred years before by an Anasazi."

She pointed out the prints, tracing the silhouette of the ghostly images without, Kee noticed, ever letting her fingertip graze the etched rock art.

Still staring at the picture, she continued. "These ancient handprints signify a sacred place. Perhaps the Anasazi artist found special healing plants here. Perhaps this was a place where the Anasazi prayed to his, or her, god. Or maybe this was the site of an important religious event."

She paused and faced the listeners. Her haunted, fearful look had disappeared, and her eyes shone. Even with only the dim lighting, her amber eyes sparkled as if lit with some inner fluorescence.

"What do *you* think, Miss Samuels?"

It was the man in front of Kee. Rheada smiled. "Well, I think this place was important."

"Because it is Navajo and Anasazi together?" he asked.

"Because it is a Navajo masked god and Anasazi. And because the masked god is from the Nightway, a ceremony that includes all the first gods of the Navajo."

A little woman wearing a sun visor and sensible shoes stepped forward. "Did the Anasazi have masked gods?"

All heads turned to Rheada. She looked away, left and to the ground. "No," she answered.

Kee's instincts fired on the sideways glance of someone carefully choosing her words, the manner of someone hiding information. But why? What could possibly motivate her reluctance?

"That's all for this canyon," she said, her voice a bit too bright, her smile a touch too wide. "I have a few more sites to show you in another canyon before we head back for Aztec. That is, if we can make good time." She let her gaze scan across the entire group, and though she didn't pause at Kee, he sensed her words were aimed at him.

Two stragglers were obviously reluctant to leave. They lingered at the petroglyphs, comparing the etchings with catalogued entries in a journal.

"You heard Miss Samuels," Kee said, stepping between them and the boulder.

The woman shot Kee a perturbed glance. "Just give me a moment. I don't have this drawing in my collection."

He didn't know if it was her clipped British accent, or her tone that left no doubt she wouldn't be dissuaded, or the fact that she was gathering drawings of Anasazi art like so many tombstone rubbings that set Kee's jaw.

"Take a picture."

Her mouth dropped open. "Well! I—"

"You don't want to be left behind, do you?"

Kee didn't wait for her response, but walked ahead, his mood as dark as the gathering gloom in the canyon. He didn't know where the sudden impatience had come from, and he realized Rheada would not appreciate the fact he had offended two of her customers.

That thought annoyed him all the more. He shouldn't give a damn *what* bothered Rheada, whether it was him investi-

gating a ruin or someone else asking questions she apparently
didn't want to answer.

He stopped. The thought brought his gaze up from the
ground to straight ahead, down the canyon, in her direction.

Why *did* she give a damn about what he explored or what
questions people asked?

He thought of the trace of fear he had seen in her eyes
when he had joked about danger in the canyons . . . and he
thought about the hint of desperation he had heard in her voice
when she found him inside the ruin. It was as if she already
had firsthand knowledge of danger within the wilderness, and
yet had elected herself as some sort of guardian and protector.
What kind of person had such a passion for these ruins?

Oh, he knew plenty with their own brand of interest, but
their passion ran along the vein of greed. Her passion had the
power of devotion.

He heard the woman and her companion approach, her mut-
tering about the "extraordinary good fortune to see a Navajo
mask. Now, you see Aztecan masks in southern New Mexico.
There's an absolute plethora of those at the Three Rivers site."

They passed Kee and he slid a sympathetic glance to the
man who had no escape from this woman's boring lectures.
But the man looked interested—the attentive tilt of his head
to the woman, the concentrated furrow of his brow—and
Kee's sympathy evaporated to disgust.

"But to see this!" she said loudly, as if for Kee's benefit.
"Such a treat. And her comment about no Anasazi masks does
raise questions, don't you think? Though she does seem to be
certain."

Kee could hear her annoying chatter even after they were
yards ahead, but it was her last words that rang in Kee's ears.
Rheada *did* seem to be certain—certain in the way of someone
who knew a secret, as if anyone should care whether there
were Anasazi masks or Martian space helmets for that matter.
Any speculation about the beliefs of these dead-as-dust people
was a waste of time.

Kee slid a dismissive glance behind him to the boulder and
its array of rock art. When he turned to leave, from the corner
of his eye he caught a flash of black and felt a rush of air
across his face. "Damn swallows."

A loud caw rent the canyon silence and raised the hair on

Kee's arms. He jerked around and there, poised on top of the
boulder as completely still as one of the carvings, sat a huge
raven. The bird stared back at Kee with beady, unblinking,
black eyes. Kee was only fifteen feet away, but the bird didn't
look the least concerned.

Kee turned and kept walking.

A swift breeze on his cheek and a loud flap of wings were
Kee's only warning. The raven swooped low over his head
and landed on the flimsy branch of a saltbush just in front of
Kee. The great bird's weight bent the branch nearly to the
ground.

Caw!

His shiny-black stare gave Kee the eerie sense this bird
was actually playing some sort of game.

Kee snorted in disbelief of his own imagination and stepped
around the bush.

The damn bird reached out and pecked his ankle!

"Son of a—"

The raven lifted, flew straight at Kee, so close that Kee
swore he felt the brush of a wing. He stumbled, and raised his
arm over his face.

Caw! Caw!

Kee swung around, his leg stinging from the attack. The
bird sat calmly on the boulder. Kee raised his hand—

"Stop!"

Footsteps ran up beside him. "What are you doing?"

He faced Rheada. But she wasn't looking at him. She was
staring at the bird. For a second, Kee had the absurd, tilt-of-
reality notion she actually had been *talking* to the bird.

Suddenly, she yanked her gaze from the bird to Kee. Her
eyes were too wide, her lips slightly parted, worry etched her
brow. Involuntary heat rose in Kee with such sudden intensity,
he shifted his gaze to the bird.

The raven opened and closed his mouth, but didn't utter a
sound. Then he gingerly inched up and over the top of the
boulder and disappeared down the back side. Rheada stepped
around the back, shaking her head. Kee could have sworn he
heard her mutter, "He shouldn't be here."

He followed her gaze to where the huge bird now strutted
across a mound of earth. Rheada drew in a breath, then turned
quickly away. "We need to get going."

Her urgent tone skittered across his skin like a sudden chill raising the fine hairs on his arms.

Brawk! Brawk!

The bird screamed, and furiously flapped his wings. Kee couldn't resist. He took a closer look. At Kee's approach, the raven folded his wings and sat still except for repeated bobbing of his head.

"Kee!"

It was a command, not a request, but Kee's focus was on the mound. Thick stands of serviceberry partially obscured the full length, but when Kee pushed some aside—one eye on the raven who merely fluttered once, but stayed put—he could see that the mound stretched behind the slab along the edge of the cliff for at least seven feet. Thick carrizo grass climbed the sides and crawled over the top, the bright green mat in sharp contrast to the stark desert ground, like a cozy blanket laid over a grave.

This mound was too uniform, too evenly rounded to be a natural heap of earth. This was manmade, and not recently.

Kee's instincts fired, seeking connections. You didn't see Anasazi burials, at least not in the open. Was this a refuse pile?

A firm hand on his arm stopped Kee. He looked over, found Rheada staring at him.

"This shouldn't be bothered, Kee."

"This shouldn't even *be* here."

Her eyes narrowed on him and Kee realized he had just admitted knowing more than he should have.

"You're right," she answered quietly. "Neither should we."

But Kee couldn't walk away and pretend disinterest. The suspicions he'd had from the moment they arrived that this canyon held secrets now whispered eagerly in his ear, traveled through his blood on a rush of certainty that he was on to more than discovering Anasazi secrets. This place just about screamed pot thief haven.

He shook loose of Rheada's grip.

"It's illegal to disturb sites."

Her plea didn't even scratch his surface. "Then maybe you want to go back to the bus."

He walked the edge of the mound, pushing aside serviceberry, studying the ground for any disturbance. The raven now

sat at the far end, stepping from one foot to the other in some
agitated bird dance.

Kee walked to that end.

"Shoo!" Rheada yelled.

The black bird stayed put.

"Shoo!" she screamed, her tone so desperate Kee looked
up and saw fear in her eyes. His heart stopped on the look—so
vulnerable, so desperate. He nearly reached out to her, though
not understanding what could have scared her.

Brack!

The bird screamed right at his ear. Kee nearly jumped from
his skin. He jerked his head to the raven, and there, to the side
of the black bird, where the mound creased to the desert floor,
Kee saw the nearly indiscernible signs of disturbance. Small
bits of deep pink sand stood apart from the lighter sand of the
canyon floor. He swiped a hand at the nearest serviceberry and
it fell to the side, roots exposed. It had been stuck back in the
ground, covering the dig.

Instantly, his gaze went to the surrounding area, searching
for prints. Now he noticed the slightest of horizontal tracks,
probably from some sort of sand brush, sweeping the area
clean.

Such careful, near perfect work.

His chest tightened in an electric heart-stopping jolt. Could
it be her? Had he finally stumbled onto one of Raven's sites?

He would get his equipment, come back tonight. Maybe
his luck would hold and she wasn't through here. Kee stood,
his muscles taut, his body a rush of excitement. His mind was
already hours ahead, setting up the sensors. His pulse was
alive, beating heartily with the determination he would catch
her. This time she wouldn't get away!

He turned and nearly plowed right into Rheada. The
stricken look on her face stopped him dead in his tracks. She
looked from him to the mound to the raven. Her eyes filled
with an emotion he recognized.

Why would she look as if that damn bird had betrayed her?

Chapter 5

SHE knew Kee watched her, but Rheada was too stunned, too confused to think, to talk, to take a step away. A part of her wanted to reach out and caress Blackjack's shiny feathers, give her fingers what they had missed and now ached to do. She yearned to hold Blackjack close, press her nose to his soft neck feathers, let him chortle softly in her ear.

Oh, how she had wanted him at her side these past six months; and when she had heard his unmistakable call her chest had expanded, filling the cavity around her heart with joy. She had run back to the canyon, answering his call.

Except he had not been calling her.

He had been talking to Kee, drawing Kee straight here, presenting it to him, even urging him to look closer at the site—this *burial* site.

Rheada had recognized Tilly's work the moment the clumps of carrizo grass fell away from the mound. Her heart still beat at her throat. Tilly knew better than to dig at a burial. Blackjack knew better. Why hadn't he stopped her?

Rheada stared at Blackjack, her head dizzy with questions and a turmoil of emotions.

Suddenly, she was aware of an acute silence, and she knew that if she glanced at Kee, she would find him looking at her, wondering why she was frozen to the spot and staring at a damn raven! She had to leave this canyon, leave Blackjack, walk away now. "We have to get back to the group," she said to Kee, perhaps too quickly, but she didn't care.

She started down the canyon with a glance over her shoulder and was glad to see that Kee followed close behind. He looked up just then, catching her gaze, and in the fraction of a second before he shot her a quick smile, Rheada saw the same veiled, guarded look as when she had first met him. What was he thinking?

Suddenly, her heart pounded at her ribs with the painful urgency of an immediate threat. She tried to force calmness with each step, slowing the rhythm of her racing heart with each deliberate footstep.

He's a mapmaker, she told herself, not a ranger or a detective for the BLM. She knew the local agents of the Bureau of Land Management—at least by name and reputation—and he didn't resemble any of them. At worst, he was a concerned citizen and would report the site disturbance.

But she knew her silent assurances to be foolish, because the worst he could be was a pot thief and Blackjack had just delivered to Kee a site Tilly obviously was working.

The anxiety struck again, full force, a streak of pain stabbing across her chest—so sudden and acute she barely controlled a groan. Her fingers drew into fists—resisting the urge to press a hand to the pain—and she made herself think past the chaos of emotions.

She had to find Tilly, warn her to stay away from this place. As soon as she finished the tour, she would ride out to find Tilly. She would make Tilly listen, convince her sister to quit, leave the unlawful life behind once and for all . . . before it was too late.

Kee couldn't believe his luck: finding a trace of the elusive Raven while he drove a tour group. He could barely contain the furor of his emotions: impatience to set up his sensors; anticipation of what he would see; the hope that his hunt might be nearing an end—that his prey could finally be within reach.

His gaze flitted from the road to the landscape, searching the canyons they passed for any likely haunt of hers.

Could she be camped in there? Down that ravine? Up in that cave? Just over that rise?

His blood surged with a furious need. His heart pumped with the certainty that this time he was closing in on the most notorious of all pot thieves—and the one who held the answer to his sister's death.

He wanted to thank Max for urging him to drive. He wanted to thank Rheada for taking him within striking distance.

He glanced at her staring out the window, her gaze on the canyons. Her small, slender frame was but a mere breath of weight on the bulky seat. Despite the hot air, she had the window rolled down. Tendrils of black hair floated free and intimately across her cheek. One slender arm rested on the upholstered sill of the window; then Kee noticed her hand drawn into a fist. Her eyes glistened—an intensity Kee took for passion.

It struck Kee that she matched the land she gazed at: wild, strong, yet also vulnerable. She would hate anyone who took advantage, who scavenged and sold, who vandalized and profited . . . who corrupted and murdered.

She would appreciate his quest. She would understand his hatred. She would approve.

His mind froze on the concept. Would she approve? Could anyone accept what he had done in the name of justice? For that matter, accept what he might *still* have to do? What he had thought himself capable of just eight months ago had been only the foul surface of the black, fetid depths into which he was now willing to sink.

No, he thought, Rheada couldn't approve. No one could. Not even himself.

He stared ahead, hoping the end was in sight—and knowing, when all was finished, he would have his own hell to face.

Kee pulled into the tour company lot and parked. Rheada opened her door, slipped from the front seat to the ground, and started for her front door, so quietly and without her usual enthusiasm, that Kee paused and watched.

Passengers offered their thanks, said their goodbyes, yet she barely acknowledged them—a half-smile here, a small wave there—and headed straight for her building, walked in, and shut the door behind her. It just then dawned on Kee that she didn't lock her business, but left it open for anyone to wander in. Was she so naïve, so trusting of the world?

Kee shook his head. He would correct this lapse of security right now.

He locked up the bus and strode to her door. There was a keyhole in the knob and another for a dead bolt. Both looked fairly ancient though adequate, and the door was plenty sturdy. It just needed to be locked, for crissakes.

He walked through the entry room, past the racks of brochures and pencil drawings of artifacts on the walls, and knocked on the door leading to her office.

"Rheada?"

No answer.

A glance through the large window confirmed her office was empty. Kee saw that the door behind her desk stood open. He walked into her office, skirted her desk, and peeked through the doorway down a hallway that obviously led to her living quarters.

"Rheada?"

Still no answer . . . nor any noise at all. Where had she gone?

He opened a door and found a bedroom—probably for guests, since he didn't see any personal touches, like photographs. He passed a linen closet, a bathroom, and then found himself in the kitchen. Looking back down the hallway, he realized there had *been* only one bedroom—that sparse room was Rheada's. Odd that such a vibrant woman, so full of life, should keep her surroundings so bare.

The sputter of an engine drew Kee's gaze to the window where he saw Rheada edge an old Jeep out of the detached garage. As quick as she had covered ground into and out of her house, she now inched the Jeep along at the pace of a snail. A fraction slower and she would be at a dead stop.

The next instant she *was* at a dead stop, having killed the engine for lack of any gas. With a staggering lurch, she brought the Jeep back to life and continued the excruciating crawl.

Kee pressed a hand to the screen door—a part of him registering that this door plus the heavy oak one were unlocked, just like the front—and watched her creep the vehicle into the backyard, where it died, again.

She ground the gear shift into first—the loud noise sounding like a scream for help from the beleaguered machine. Kee took a step from the house just as Rheada turned in her seat. She jerked her head toward him, her face a mixture of surprise, frustration, determination, and helplessness.

For a moment, Kee was left speechless staring at her wide amber eyes and a flush of pink to her brown-skinned cheeks.

"Where are you going?" he asked, taking the back steps two at a time and striding to the driver's side.

"I—" She glanced away, back again, then swallowed. "To report the site disturbance," she finished.

She looked so upset—and all because of that burial site for people long dead. It dawned on him just how much she cared about these ancient sites.

It also dawned on him he couldn't let her report the disturbance. He leaned on the window frame and glanced at his watch. "Offices are closed now."

"Oh. Yes, you're right."

Truth was, Kee thought, she didn't look at all sure about anything.

"I'm just going to take a drive," she said finally.

He smiled. "You won't get far the way you're driving. I can see why you hired me. How did you ever get a driver's license?"

The pink in her cheeks rose to red. "I'll have you know I've been driving since—" She stopped, her lips flattened to a thin line. "I just don't *like* to drive," she finished.

"Well, that's good, because you also don't seem too good at it."

All the emotions on her face coalesced to a glare, aimed at Kee. "I'll be fine once I'm off-road."

A smirk tugged at Kee's lips. "Smarter for everyone, I would think."

She shot him a pained look.

Kee started for the back door, then stopped and faced her. "Do you know where the keys are for your doors?"

"The keys? Why—?"

"You have got to start locking up, Rheada. You can't run your life here as if you're still in some remote prospecting site."

Her eyes turned immeasurably sad, as if his words had dashed a fervent hope of hers. Suddenly, Kee wanted to apologize, restore her belief in a safe world.

Except it wasn't a safe world.

"Lock the doors, Rheada. It's a dangerous world with dangerous men."

He was walking proof of that.

Dusk came early to the canyon, but Kee couldn't risk even the dimmest glow of a flashlight. He would just have to work faster.

He laid the trowel alongside the duffel, then reached into

the bag. He gave a wistful glance to the sledgehammer, but shoved it aside to grab the anchor. Already, he had set three sensors and the camera at the mound, digging them into the ground with brute strength as his only tool—he couldn't chance the echoes of metal on metal.

Mounting them at the cliff dwelling had proven more difficult, with his only choices bedrock in the cave or talus slope below. He had opted for the base of the slope and a sensor on each side of the vertical crevice—the only route a climber had to the cave.

He had one more sensor to place, then he had to position the camera—his last one. He was expending a lot of equipment on these two sites—it had to work.

Kee shoved the anchor into the hole he'd just dug and starting twisting, screwing the metal into earth. His shoulder muscles screamed; his thighs, knees, back . . . they were already numb from kneeling at impossible angles.

A bead of sweat slid from his brow to his eye, the salt instantly stinging. He swiped his forehead across the top of his arm, but kept turning, turning, turning on the anchor, until only the top one-eighth of the black rod remained aboveground.

With practiced hands, he slid the joint of the sensor box into the top of the rod. Holding the two steady with one hand, he took the last screw from his mouth, and pushed it through the hole on the anchor rod. Then carefully, patiently shifting the rods ever so slightly to align the holes, he worked the screw through the sensor.

All that was left was the video camera, the most important component of the trap. He had to choose carefully where to place it.

He scanned the canyon floor area and saw several places protected from the elements and nocturnal life, but also worthless for usable video: At best, the lens would capture the bottom half of any intruder. The camera had to be aimed from above.

His whole body stiff and tense, Kee stood, dragging the duffel along, then slinging it onto his shoulder. Blood drained in a dizzying rush from his head. He stumbled back a few steps before catching his balance. He hardened his focus on the cliff face, refusing the dizziness any grip on his senses, and started to climb.

He felt for grips—scraping knuckles and palms against jagged sandstone—and inched higher, one hand- and foothold at a time. He risked his weight on an edge of rock. The next instant, the edge sheared off. He slid, grabbing at the wall. Ragged stones sliced through his skin clean as razors. His feet and hands fought for purchase, frantic to end the free fall.

Suddenly, the side of his boot caught a ledge. He clung, spread-armed, to the cliff face, his heart wild, pounding in his chest.

The tide of adrenaline subsided, dragging an aching prickliness down his scalp, across his chest, over his arms—leaving acute points of torture in its wake.

Pain speared through him, like the stabs of foot-long needles. He could smell his own blood, oozing from myriad cuts. He ran his tongue over dry lips and tasted the metallic-copperiness of his bleeding wounds.

From a short distance away, he heard a sharp caw. In minuscule movements, he adjusted his position, pressing his body closer to the cliff, securing his weight. He eased his head to an angle and gazed up to the cave, then beyond to the mesa top and a juniper tree. There, in the near dark, he spotted the raven.

Here he was, nearly seventy-five feet off the canyon floor, in a remote canyon, with no one around but the damn bird—the very namesake of the criminal he sought. If he had fallen, the next one to find him would be that very criminal and his life would have been at the mercy of someone with no compunctions about killing.

A bubble of manic laughter rose in his throat. Swiftly, he gritted his jaw to choke down the sound, but not before a hiss of air broke through his teeth.

The raven answered with another *caw*. Shiny black cut the night sky and the bird landed only feet away, balancing effortlessly on the smallest margin of an edge. He cocked his head, stretched his neck out and chortled, all the time staring at Kee. Then the raven climbed the vertical wall to a narrow shelf of rock just four feet above, where he stood, his neck craned down, his eyes on Kee.

Kee followed the black bird, stretching his whole body, his

arms and fingertips, to reach the ledge. As Kee pulled himself up, the bird stepped gingerly to the side, then continued up the wall to the next ledge. Right behind the black bird, Kee made his way to the cave.

With a soundless flap, the raven flew to the ruin and settled on one of the masonry slabs.

Inexplicably, Kee thought of Rheada, the silent ease of her steps. He imagined her rising up the cliff wall as gracefully as a plume of smoke, as readily as one of the Anasazi who'd engineered this precarious dwelling. She had the slender build, and obviously the keen attention to surroundings. In many ways, she was a better fit for this job.

He swung the strap of the duffel over his head and off his shoulder. He pulled out the camera and its mounting, let the bag slide to the ground, then walked to the back corner of the cave, opposite the ruin. He wedged the mounting into the rubble of cave debris—a jumble of sandstone pried from the roof of the cave by the natural cycle of contraction and expansion of freezing, then thawing water seepage. He stood back and scrutinized the placement, satisfying himself that no one would notice the camera, or even look back here.

"Now all I have to do is sit back and wait. And pray I'm right about this site." He paused. "And pray I'm right about Raven," he muttered.

Kee glanced to the raven and found the bird staring back at him, his head cocked to one side as if considering what Kee had said.

He thought of the legend of Raven: the pot thief guided by a black bird to special sites. Some said her raven was the oldest of all ravens, that he had soared over these lands for hundreds of years. He knew all. He saw all. And he remembered. And the only one he shared his knowledge with was Raven.

Some said that proved she was a chosen one of the ancients: They had chosen the raven and the raven had chosen her. That was why she had never been caught . . . and never been harmed by the so-called Anasazi curse.

Kee had thought that the legend of a curse on any Anasazi relic had probably been the idea of a particularly enterprising pot thief. He had found it amusing that anybody would believe that pieces of clay held danger.

That was, until he had met Rheada and witnessed her burying the potshard. She obviously believed in the myth—but then she attached meaning to every bump in the landscape, every animal in the desert, every scratched mark on a cliff wall. It seemed everything was inherently significant to her, with an accompanying story and a special name.

She weaved history and botany together with Indian stories into a tapestry more colorful than these arid, stark canyons deserved. Max was right; Rheada gave an interesting tour.

Kee sat at the edge of the cave. He looked out across the opposite mesa, to the first stars of twilight, but what he saw was the sunshiny day in the meadow. What he heard was Rheada's parable about the Antelope Boy, an Indian fable of morality. He thought of her stories about the Anasazi, their suffering, their triumph, and defeat, and through it all, their endurance. And just today—had it only been a few hours ago?—her tales of the ruins and the petroglyphs. She spoke as if she were a chronicler. She provoked and enchanted—a mistress of the canyons.

Kee blinked, shook his head. Why had his thoughts drifted to Rheada? Since when did he ascribe anything romantic to this land or to the barren lives of its inhabitants?

He stared into the chasm until the darkness once again filled him, until what he saw was what truly existed—nothing but a blackening abyss that swallowed the lives of young girls, seducing them with tales of adventure and *goddamn* legends.

Raven had been the seducer and his only sister the victim.

He felt a light touch at his cheek, a sudden weight on his shoulder. Kee jerked his head to the side and found himself staring at the giant bird, his shiny feathers the only delineation of his silhouette in the enveloping nightfall.

Wafts of pine needles and fresh air—the scents gathered by wings cutting the sky—came now to Kee, resting on his shoulder. The powerful wings lay quiet against the raven. His dangerous talons were gentle on Kee's skin, barely penetrating the denim, as if the bird knew the strength he harbored and *chose* restraint.

Their black gazes met and held. The raven stared solemnly, unblinking, as if the choice of Kee's shoulder should be no surprise.

The raven shifted, jumped to the ground, then flew to a pile of stones. The sudden absence of the big bird's weight was disconcerting. In that moment, a longing swelled within Kee, an ache to fill a void. But as the longing grew, so did the void within, a hollowness too big to fill, an ever-deepening abyss over which he stood, teetering on the edge, no shred of hope tethering him.

His body jerked, terror-stricken, the jolt of awakening from a nightmare. He stared at the canyon below, the consuming blackness beneath his dangling legs, and he knew what scared him. He knew what he feared more than anything, more than the evil he courted, more than the hatred he nourished: He feared failing and never exacting revenge.

He glanced aside, caught the gleam of the raven's feathers in the moonlight, and his hatred coalesced.

"I *will* catch you," he said, staring into the night.

Chapter 6

THERE is no silence like that of a canyon in deep night. It is alive, breathing—a nocturnal predator, stalking on soft pads.

Your nerves rise to your pores, millions of antennae tense. Your ears strain for the slightest noise, until you believe—*you know*—you can hear the smallest rock falling, the merest breath of wind tangling in sagebrush. Your mind immediately calculates the distance, grappling for perspective, for depth, for any point of reference to anchor you in the void . . . because all you can see is blackness.

Your eyes stare long and hard, trying in vain to pierce the night. And because thoughts grow more powerful in the dark—with fangs and claws sharp enough to tear a man's soul—the canyon, finally, delivers images, whether or not they're real.

Kee stared into the night—an utter darkness like that in a coffin . . . or the deathly black at the bottom of a dirt hole.

The image of the man in the pit leaped to Kee's mind. He shuddered. The jolt traversed up his spine and across his scalp. He squeezed his eyes shut, opened them wide—neither way saved him from the consuming darkness and its nightmares. An urge possessed Kee: throw open the Jeep's door—jump out, walk away, leave the confinement, escape the images.

A mechanical click raised the hair on his neck. Kee jerked his head to the window, half expecting to see a gun a second before the bullet put an end to his nightmare.

But there wasn't a gun. There was no one there.

Kee realized he had made the noise. His fingers still gripped the door handle in a death vise. Kee forced himself to relax, loosen his hand, ease the door shut. His chest hurt with the effort to breathe deeply.

Since when had the darkness become his enemy, plaguing him with hallucinations? The night was his companion, his soul mate, his partner and coconspirator. The night hid him, as a friend would offer refuge . . . except now his friend, the darkness, was a betrayer, taunting Kee with his sins, sins Kee had committed *within* the night.

His hand swept the seat beside him. He grasped a black box—the lifeline to one of the sensors—and, in the darkness, he ran his thumb over the box and felt the strip of tape. Kee glared into the darkness.

He would pay for his sins. He didn't expect understanding or forgiveness . . . and he demanded the same fate for the one he sought. The night *owed* him as much.

For hours Kee sat unmoving: his gaze straight ahead, the box forgotten in his hand—his fingers had long since gone numb in their frozen clutch. He hadn't moved; not even to turn his wrist to press the backlight on his watch. He could last as long as the night—in the same way as the night: silent, relentless, uncompromising.

Suddenly, a green pinpoint of light glowed in the darkness—a tiny globe of life in the dead of night. The signal came from the box in his palm—from the remote activated by the sensors at the cliff dwelling.

Kee smiled.

In the next instant, one hand flipped the switches activating both cameras, the other turned the key in the ignition, starting the Jeep. Sitting four canyons over, at least a mile away from the sites, he wasn't worried about noise or even the headlights. He *was* worried about making time.

Five minutes later, he was in the main wash. The headlights caught the mouth of the canyon ahead. Kee slowed, cut the lights and the engine, and let the Jeep drift to a stop.

His steps careful on loose rocks, he walked toward the canyon, flicking on his flashlight for mere seconds to navigate. He crossed the open ground at the entrance, and found his way to the narrow arroyo, then stopped, realizing he hadn't seen any vehicle.

For a moment Kee paused, puzzled. Raven couldn't have driven into the canyon—the cliff walls sloped to a sharp vee slicing down to the canyon floor. But then, maybe she had a horse. Kee had never considered Raven on a horse; she left sites with barely a trace of her trespass—no shoe prints, and never any horse prints.

He stared ahead into the depths of the canyon, though he

may as well have had his eyes closed for the pitch-black night surrounding him. A sliver of doubt worked itself into his thoughts: How could he possibly snag Raven if he couldn't see her?

But she can't see me, either. And she doesn't even know I'm here.

Anticipation soared through Kee, pulsed through his veins, drew his muscles taut and ready. He raised his nose and caught scents on the slightest breeze. He stood just a moment longer, picturing the canyon in daylight, burning each detail into his brain. His gun in his hand, he walked guided by keen, hot instincts.

His eyes, now sharper than ever, caught the outline of a boulder at his feet, then a tamarisk tree dead ahead.

He was a predator, tracking his prey.

At the second bend in the arroyo, he stopped. Just over the ridge of the arroyo should be the first site—the mound near the canyon wall.

He climbed up the mud wall and crouched, his gaze lasered on the spot just twenty feet away. He listened for the merest untoward noise. Only the cold breath of night filled his ears.

Taking no chances, Kee hunched close to the ground, and stole to the cover of one sage then another, narrowing the distance, until he stood near enough to strike.

He rose by inches, his breath held in his lungs. There was no one there.

Satisfied, Kee headed deeper into the canyon. He retraced his path to the arroyo. Quicker this time, he followed the winding wash, his sights set on the cliff dwelling, his mind racing ahead, his thoughts flying over the cliff wall he still had to climb, his heart pumping with the deadly certainty he was closing on his prey, cornering her with no escape.

Cold, murderous intent settled at the base of his skull. His fingers flexed and gripped on the handle of his gun.

Fully ten minutes had passed by the time he reached the place which he estimated to be near the base of the dwelling. Again, he crouched and listened, his ears straining. As before, he heard nothing.

He dragged himself up the mud wall of the arroyo and slid over the top on his belly where he lay perfectly still. He couldn't see the twenty feet to the cliff, but instinct told him

the crevice was straight ahead. He pulled into a crouch and
trotted to a copse of tamarisk—the very same group of trees,
he realized, from where he had watched Rheada talking to
some of the group.

The image filled his mind so completely Kee felt the warming heat of day on his neck. For that whole time he'd worked
the crew, infiltrating Crow's band of thieves—living with
them, becoming one of them for all those months—he didn't
remember any daylight. There had to have been days with
sunshine, even in the deep forest of the Gila Wilderness. But
he only remembered the darkness.

Now here, deep in the canyon night, he should feel the
warmth of sunlight?

He not only felt the sunlight, but also Rheada's presence,
as if she were here, as if the canyon were possessed by her
. . . here, where she worked her magic with stories.

He saw the slow smile of her lips, as if she were gazing
on something precious. He saw the passion in her eyes—the
sunlight in her amber gaze—when she looked at the petroglyphs; he heard the love in her voice for the land and the
people who had wandered here.

Kee never would have believed himself capable of any interest in Anasazi stories, let alone to have his thoughts haunted
by the *storyteller*. He would miss those stories and Rheada's
enchanting voice.

The thought stunned him. Kee shook his head, refocused
on his mission, but an eerie disorientation plagued him as he
approached the crevice and started to climb—the disconcerting sensation of going down the wrong path.

Kee checked one sensor, then the other, to confirm they
were intact. Then he scaled the cliff, his fingers awkward,
unsure. Twice he nearly slipped, reaching for grips he couldn't
find, his arms and legs strained with the effort. He thought of
how easily Rheada had climbed, her body hugging the wall,
her hands and feet working in unison. The image stayed with
him. Before Kee knew it, he had reached the ledge leading to
the cave.

He stopped there. His heart pounded from the effort. His
lungs ached to gasp air, to breathe deeply. He set his jaw
against the urge, pressed himself against the cliff face, and
listened, his body poised for attack.

Moments passed. He heard nothing. Instincts told him no one was there, but his mind wouldn't let go, argued for possibilities. She could be deep in the back room of the ruin where he wouldn't hear her.

But he knew he was only fooling himself—just as he knew that particular sound of silence breathed from the cave.

She wasn't here. Not anymore.

Still hoping—though telling himself he was only being careful—Kee edged to the opening of the cave. He sank to his hands and knees and crawled silently around the front of the dwelling and through the doorway. Hugging the walls, he made his way through each room an inch at a time, listening, until he was in the last room and faced his defeat.

A part of him wanted to scream, let his anger echo across the canyon to her ears. She would *know* he had come close, that he was right behind her. He wanted her afraid of him . . . just as his sister should have been afraid of the infamous Raven.

Rage pounded at his temples. White sparks of hate fired across his eyes. He spun, thrust a fist into the adobe wall. Ancient mud crumbled. Kee stared at what he'd done, acknowledging the damage . . . and an urge raged through him to cause *more* damage, knock down the walls, turn these ruins into dust, obliterate the enticement, destroy the means of the pot thieves . . . destroy them.

The Anasazi lived in these rooms, raised their children. All the time fearful of something, of someone.

Rheada's words washed over Kee, prying his thoughts loose from the murderous stranglehold on his emotions. His urge to do violence ebbed, and drained to the aching hole in his gut. In the wake of the anger flowed rational thought.

What had Raven sought in this dwelling?

He scanned the room, the walls, the floor, searching for any sign of digging. His gaze settled on the grinding stone, now lying flat on the ground. Hadn't it been leaning against the wall?

Kee jerked his head, and the beam of the flashlight, to the corner where the metate had rested this afternoon. He walked closer, hunched beneath the natural slope of the cave ceiling. The light rippled over golden stone bricks and brown sand. There wasn't any obvious disturbance, but then Raven would have made sure there wouldn't be . . . except someone had moved the metate.

He stepped back to get a wider view and then saw a definite discoloration in the sand: a slightly darker color, like that of sand unearthed, threaded within the dusty top layer. He crouched close to the ground, his gaze following the pattern of sand granules scattered out and away from the corner.

She had dug right here. He knew it.

He pulled a trowel from his pocket and dug into the earth. No more than six inches down, the tip of the trowel struck something hard. He shoveled away sand, scraping across the top of what seemed to be a sandstone slab imbedded in the ground. He uncovered an edge to the stone, worked his fingers around it, and pulled. The stone lifted easily into his hands . . . too easily. Kee knew he had just retraced the steps of the thief.

He set the stone on the ground beside him, then shone the flashlight back to the hole. More stone lined the inside of the hole and solid rock ran across the bottom, the bedrock of the cave. Kee realized the slab he had pulled off was the lid to an ingenious stone box built by an Anasazi—a small cache to hide things.

Had there been turquoise bead necklaces? Or shell bracelets? Whatever trinkets the Anasazi had hidden were now gone, raided by a scavenger . . . probably just within the last hour.

A hiss of air escaped between Kee's teeth. He could care less about the belongings of some long-dead Anasazi, but he would sure like to know what had been hidden here. If this was the only cache in this ruin, there had to have been the possibility of more than jewelry for Raven to even bother. It was too small a hiding place for any sizable piece, though more than jewelry could have fit—like fetishes or a figurine. The last could certainly have been worth Raven's attention.

Kee stood and walked to the other corners, scrutinizing each one, but saw no sign of any disturbance. He returned to his dig, replaced the stone "lid," and, as thoroughly as he could, re-covered the area with the displaced sand. If Raven returned, he didn't want to tip his hand. Still, as carefully as he worked, he was all too aware that he couldn't re-create the site as perfectly as she had with her practiced hands. Frustration itched across his scalp. Why couldn't she be like the hundreds of other careless, greedy pot thieves who had more luck than intelligence?

He rose and inspected his work. Amazingly enough, his attempt quite nearly equaled hers.

He left the chamber and closely inspected the other rooms, even though neither of those held enough sand or earth to cover much of anything. When he emerged from the ruin into the cave, Kee was surprised to see the night's blackness had faded to a dark gray. He checked his watch and realized he had been inside for nearly two hours. He gazed across the opposite mesa, wondering how far, or how close, was the elusive Raven. His hands flexed, eager to have her once and for all in his grasp.

That would come soon enough, Kee told himself. He glanced in the direction of the camera and smiled. She had no idea just how close he was.

Kee strode to the back of the cave, and knelt beside the camera. He pulled a screwdriver from his pocket, loosened the casing, and then slipped the camera from its mounting. He pressed the rewind button and waited. The mechanical whir tingled his fingers, and resonated through his veins, building on his anticipation. At the finishing quiet click, Kee raised the camera to his shoulder and his finger depressed the play button, his breath held in his throat as the static cleared and the camera found its focus.

He stared at the black-and-white image of the ruin, the picture so static he could be looking at a photograph. Minutes elapsed. If he opened one eye, he could see the lightening of the night sky; he could hear the morning trills of mockingbirds; he could smell sage and cedar, their scents carried on the crisp morning air.

But all of that was of the here and now . . . and meant nothing to Kee.

He watched a colorless, motionless picture—the weight of the camera on his shoulder forgotten in his taut muscles, air to breathe forgotten in his tight chest.

So caught within the picture he watched, Kee jumped when a hand appeared on the ledge of the cave. He nearly dropped the camera and leaped to his feet to grab her.

He held steady. Another hand pressed to the edge. A shoul-

der and the crown of a head followed. She pulled herself onto
the ledge, one knee at a time, then stood. She brushed off her
hands, swiped long hair behind her shoulder, then walked to
the doorway of the ruin, her strides as silky and graceful as a
mountain cat.

He was staring at the infamous Raven, caught in the dead
of night.

Every one of Kee's nerve endings fired in a lightning ma-
trix of impulses across his skin, provoking a shudder down
his spine.

The next moment, she bent beneath the threshold, and disappeared into the dwelling. The sudden absence of her image
slammed against his chest.

He punched rewind, stop, replay—his fingers ordered by
his brain in an instant reflex.

He watched the tape again and again—her every movement, her easy carriage, the lightness of her footsteps. Each
time he noticed another detail: a bulge in her back pocket that
was possibly a flashlight; a strap across her far shoulder that
was probably a backpack.

He stared, imprinting every second of the video on his
brain, then let the tape proceed.

He was again staring at the dwelling. It could be a black-
and-white still life if not for the intermittent twinkle of a distant star. Even that seemed more a mirage, a false brightening
forced by his intense focus. As the time stretched out, seemingly endlessly, his imagination took hold—bred by his consuming, dark need to nail Raven and by the niggling doubts
he ever would—and his mind started questioning whether he
had ever really seen her. Had his eyes been playing tricks?

He had the absurd, yet nearly overwhelming urge, to follow
her into the dwelling, catch her in the act . . . when, of course,
all he could do was sit here, his eye pressed to the camera.

Minutes turned to a quarter hour.

Her reappearance through the doorway startled Kee to his
toes. His gaze darted to her hands, where she cradled something. She slipped off the backpack, crouched, balanced the
object in her lap as she opened the bag, then placed whatever
she held inside.

She stood and Kee prayed she would turn toward the camera.

"Give me a look," he muttered, as if he could will her image to obey.

She did.

Kee's breath caught in his throat. He stared at her shadowed face, desperate to see her features. The glance lasted less than a second, then she turned and started for the ledge.

His finger found the stop button, almost pressed, but then something in the way she moved away from him, something in the movement of her hips . . . something in the way she slipped effortlessly over the edge of the cliff wall and disappeared, stole the breath from his lungs.

He *knew* that walk.

He knew the way she brushed sand off her hands, and the way she swiped the hair from her forehead.

All the details of her that were collected in his brain tumbled into place, into one particular person, into such an impossible identity Kee shook his head, not believing, not wanting to believe.

The truth slammed against Kee with the force of a fist in his gut.

It was Rheada.

The camera fell to his lap. He stared from his dark corner in the cave to the outside and the mesa top beyond. The mouth of the cave framed the dawn. Clumps of cedar and juniper caught the first morning rays in their crooked branches and cast twisted, mangled shadows. The gnarled landscape seemed to stretch to the horizon. But that was a deception, a trick on the untrained eye. In fact, rugged canyons slashed the mesas to bedrock, trapping the unknown in narrow, winding chasms.

You couldn't trust your eyesight here. You couldn't trust assumptions. You *only* had your instincts.

Kee knew that. But instead he had denied his instincts, ignored them, in favor of amber-eyed beauty and enchanting stories.

Emotions welled within Kee: disbelief at his lapse of judgment; frustration for the time he had wasted; shame for his stupidity; but above all, anger—anger for his weakness, anger for forgetting his hatred . . . anger for letting slip his iron mask of purpose.

He knew better. Raven knew better.

Rheada sure as hell knew better.

Never once had she let her mask slip. She played the consummate tour guide—knowledgeable, passionate, the guardian protector of the canyons—all the time scouting for new sites.

He remembered her first words when she found him in this ruin.

You shouldn't be in here.

Damn if he hadn't bought her innocent act!

She had convinced him of her honesty, integrity; fooled him with traces of fear and vulnerability; weakened him by degrees. Then seduced him with artful displays of spirit and childlike purity.

He had ascribed the haunted look in her eyes to some hurtful past, a wound still healing. He had actually believed her guileless and uncorrupted!

God, she was good. Evoking every man's fantasy to protect and possess.

All of the hatred he had brought into the night while searching for Raven, chasing after her as one might chase after wisps of a legend, drove through him like a spear. The guilt he bore for not being there for his sister, the hell he had endured, and the evil he had tolerated—and, God help him, embraced—all this bled from a wound in his gut. His hatred, now fired red-hot as tempered steel, lanced straight to the open wound, searing it shut in one caustic stroke.

Kee's heart pounded hard with newfound strength.

He disengaged the camera and dismantled the mounting, hauling it all with him for use at another site, but left the sensors in place at the base of the cliff. He doubted that this ruin offered any more interest to Rheada, but he didn't want to take a chance.

He walked deeper into the canyon, searching other likely sites, but came up empty, and so retraced his steps and continued to the mound. He didn't have to dig far before he was rewarded. Beneath loose dirt, his fingers brushed against wood. He worked his hands around it, and pulled loose what looked like an effigy, no longer than eight inches. And within the grooves were bright grains of sand the same color as that in the cave ruin.

Kee sat back, realizing he had unearthed the relic that Raven had just stolen and then reburied . . . in an Anasazi burial. He didn't care about the Anasazi, their homes or their burials. But Rheada claimed to. She talked about them with reverence, convincing anyone who listened that these ancient sites were to be honored. She had even had him believing! She would have had no trouble in convincing a naïve fifteen-year-old.

His hands gripped the effigy and it was all Kee could do not to hurl it against the canyon wall. Instead, he placed it back where he had found it, then replaced dirt and grass on the mound, careful to cover all trace of his disturbance. Unbidden, the vision of Rheada returning the shard to the earth leaped into Kee's mind. Her cupped hands filled the image, with her lips close, blowing onto the relic just before she placed it in the hole.

He had believed her. He had *let* himself believe her. He had let himself be enchanted by her stories, by the reverence in her voice, by the look in her eyes, that haunted, veiled gaze.

He had connected with that gaze, believing it as the same he knew from the inside—a weariness, an *aloneness* he had immediately understood.

He jogged to his Jeep, then drove out of the canyons, trailing a plume of dust. He didn't head back to Aztec, though. He drove to the ruin where Raven had buried the shard, arriving there as early morning light cast a pinkish glow over the canyon. He found the freshly turned earth and knelt. His hands lunged at the dirt, digging fiercely. When his fingers touched the shard, he pulled it from the dirt. He brushed it clear, and the image appeared: a raven.

He strode to his Jeep, his heart pounding violently in his chest, his hand gripping the shard. His foot weighed on the gas and the Jeep flew down the highway. The landscape blurred. The images of Rheada dissolved in the whipping wind and Kee was left with one thought only: Rheada might be good; he would have to be better.

He pulled up to Rheada's building in a spray of gravel and dust, and jumped from the Jeep. Kee had every intention to continue driving, and watch her every move.

Several customers were gathered out front. A part of him registered how odd it was they weren't waiting inside. He also noticed their quick glances as he strode through the door.

Rheada wasn't in her office. She wasn't in the room beyond, either. He threw open doors in the hallway, strode to the very back, into the kitchen, where he found himself looking at the empty garage.

A sick feeling spread from his gut. Had she bolted? When he last saw her, she was driving off in her Jeep. His brain fought through his frustration to picture her face, examine the memory. Had she known *then* who he was—known it before he had even discovered her identity?

Kee jogged to the garage, hoping he was wrong, but the Jeep was gone. He walked back inside, paced the kitchen. What the hell was he going to do now?

"Should we just come at the same time tomorrow?"

Kee jerked his head around to see an older man standing at the threshold of the kitchen. He looked apologetic, then wary. When Kee faced him, he took a few steps back.

"What?"

"For the tour," the man said. "The note says it's postponed until tomorrow?"

Kee brushed past and practically ran to the front door. He ripped the paper from the windowpane.

"I am sorry to have to cancel all tours for today," Kee read. "Please return tomorrow when you will receive a longer tour for the same money. Or I will gladly refund your money. I am sorry for this inconvenience."

Kee stared at the note. His pulse pounded at his temples. Was she telling the truth? Would she be back? Or had she disappeared? Again.

"So we should just come back?"

It was the man again. Kee looked up from the paper. The man had a hopeful look on his face.

"They say she's the best," the man said.

Kee crumpled the paper, let it drop to the ground, and walked to his Jeep. "They're right," he muttered.

Chapter 7

ALL day, Rheada drove canyons looking for her sister. There were only half a dozen or so hideaways close to Aztec that the family had used. Tilly had to be close by. At least that's what Rheada kept telling herself, as concern—then desperation—built inside her to find her sister.

The concern wasn't for herself—though Tilly had certainly put Rheada's new life in jeopardy by digging in one of Rheada's "tour" canyons. But Rheada had the whole Southwest in which to take groups. She could always move on to other canyons.

No, the panic she felt was for Tilly. As impulsive and fearless as Rheada knew her sister to be, Rheada still couldn't believe that Tilly would dig at a burial! What could have possibly compelled Tilly to take such a chance?

Rheada drove south of Aztec, taking one dirt road then another, searching the canyons, and was frankly relieved not to find Tilly there. At least Tilly had followed the cardinal rule of any smart pot thief: not to camp anywhere close to her digs.

She left New Mexico and headed for the Colorado border and the western reaches of the Ute Mountain Indian Reservation. Pink bald-rock mesas hugged Mother Earth like helpless, abandoned newborns clinging to the green-fringed skirts of the higher plateaus. She entered tribal lands along the Marble Wash, winding back into the canyons cut by runoff from Sleeping Ute Mountain. Rheada covered a lot of ground in a few hours, but still found no sign of Tilly. She had only one place left to look: the canyons of their childhood haunts.

By nightfall, she reached the outlying reaches of the Grand Rincons, a wild, labyrinthine country. No one ventured into the maze—unless they were foolish, or lost. No one, that is, except for those who called this dangerous area home—just as she had for over twenty years.

She drove down one canyon, turned into another, then turned into yet another, going deeper and deeper. She maneuvered across washes and over the rough terrain almost without thinking, guided by the inner radar any child would have to her home.

Led by instincts and her memory, she drove to one encampment after another—some where the family had stayed for months, some sites that had been only a stop for the night years ago, yet she found them.

But she found no trace of Tilly.

Fear for her sister skittered down Rheada's spine. She shuddered, then gripped the steering wheel fiercely.

Deep, black night settled on the canyon; still Rheada searched. She didn't need daylight to maneuver through her old home territory. She could find her way blindfolded. To guide her, she had her other senses, now enlivened and fully engaged in a way she hadn't felt in months.

Waves of familiarity flooded over her. Smells she knew played with her senses, seducing her, evoking memories, and finally provoking a knot of emotions in her throat.

This had been home. Here she had not been alone. She had had Blackjack and Tilly. They had owned the days and the canyons.

Here, she hadn't worried about her every step or what she did. She hadn't been concerned with what she said or what anyone might think about her. When she found a ruin, she had only Tilly or Blackjack to answer to. Now, she felt as if every movement of hers were under scrutiny.

Here she had known who she was and what she had to do.

The Jeep idled to a stop and died. Rheada let her gaze rise to the towering cliffs. They were cloaked in blackness, indiscernible in the night, but Rheada *knew* their presence. Her heart could see their jagged silhouette against a turquoise sky. These cliffs had been the boundaries of her childhood, her sanctuary, her fortress and home . . . and home for the Anasazi.

They had shared their home, provided for her, given her a way to escape these canyons and start a life.

Now, she almost felt as if she owed an apology, that she had somehow betrayed them.

A reassuring voice inside her whispered, *This is where you belong.*

Rheada's heart constricted around a sob. Was it true? Was

she doomed to stay here, incapable of finding happiness past these cliffs?

The image of Kee filled her mind, his keen black eyes gazing at her, and she stared in the way she wanted to whenever she was with him. She held the image, looking deep into him, letting herself fill with the *power* of him that she knew was there.

Her heart fluttered. Her pulse beat faster. Her body came alive as if suddenly aware of something new and wonderful.

Urges quickened within her. Her heart gave a small lurch like that of a horse yanking on the reins in a burst of energy when he catches the promising smell of home territory. Home that was *not* here, but in the world beyond.

She glanced back up the canyon walls. Like an overprotective parent, the massive cliffs spread wide, enveloping arms. That she had ever escaped the grip of these canyons was a miracle. The odds were against her, the law was against her, the canyons were against her, even her sister had been against her. The day Rheada had left, Tilly had told Rheada she would be back.

Now she was.

But she was *not* back to stay.

Rheada crouched on the ledge, her gaze set on the ravine below. A low mound, bunched in the middle, hugged the ground. She recognized the unnatural, manmade shadow as a sleeping bag. At the same time she registered the shape as a sleeping bag, she realized it lay on open ground far from the protective wall of the canyon.

She studied the shape, the contour of the bag, and knew, with a small measure of relief, that it wasn't Tilly's.

Yet her heart still skipped beats, leaping excitedly within her chest. Tilly was here. Rheada knew it. Which meant that bag belonged to someone else, someone who was traveling with Tilly . . . someone who wasn't very smart.

The concern she had for her sister, the anxiety she had tried to deny, all the loyalty—and love—she harbored for Tilly, now surged within Rheada, bringing all her senses to life and aimed dead-on at that sleeping bag. Whoever was in that bag was the reason Tilly was taking chances.

Rheada eased off the ledge and down the cliff face. She

moved over the rocks like the night, slipping darkly, soundlessly, ever closer to the sleeping bag. An icy prickling of foreboding spread through her veins.

"What are *you* doing here?"

Rheada whirled at the sound of Tilly's voice. Her arms flew open wide, ready to take Tilly into a huge hug. Tilly stared back, for one beat, then two, before walking into Rheada's embrace.

Rheada pulled her sister close, pressed her arms across Tilly's back. Her heart burst with love, breaking through a wall she hadn't known she had built. Until that moment, she hadn't known how very lonely she had been without Tilly. She wanted to tell her, but she couldn't speak past the knot of emotions in her throat.

Her hand ran up and down Tilly's back, remembering countless embraces, evoking every protective urge in every fiber of Rheada's body.

Tilly pulled back. For a second, Rheada couldn't believe it, but then Tilly pushed away.

"What are you *doing* here?" Tilly demanded.

Rheada's heart staggered. For a second she couldn't think past the darkness she faced in Tilly's gaze. She also saw a tiredness—her youthful sister's face was now thinner and carried worry lines across her brow. How could Tilly look so much older in the span of only six months?

Rheada said the first thing that came from her heart to her lips. "I've missed you so much." Her lips spread to a smile.

Tilly stared back. "You shouldn't have come. You shouldn't be here."

Rheada's breath drew in at Tilly's harsh tone. Before Rheada could find the words to respond, Tilly said, "You should go."

"Tilly, I've spent nearly an entire day looking for you. I've been worried about you."

A trace of pain flashed across Tilly's eyes as if Rheada's words had touched some soft, vulnerable spot. Quickly, Tilly looked away.

"No one asked you to," Tilly said.

The words cut straight to Rheada's heart. Something was wrong. Terribly wrong. Rheada reached a hand to Tilly's shoulder. "Tilly, you're my sister. We don't have to ask each other. We just know, remember?"

Over Tilly's shoulder, Rheada saw the sleeping bag move and a shadowy figure emerge. Apparently, Tilly saw the same thing. She faced Rheada.

"You have to go."

With that, Tilly pulled away from Rheada and started to walk away.

Fear for her sister sliced through all the other emotions. She grabbed Tilly's arm. "Tilly, talk to me. What's the matter?" With an eye on the approaching shadow, Rheada held firmly to her sister.

Tilly slanted only the briefest glance to Rheada. "Please, Rheada, go now." Tilly spoke barely above a whisper, but Rheada could hear the panic.

The next instant, Tilly broke free and walked away. In that horrible moment, as confusion and raw emotion slammed within her chest, Rheada caught the glint of a gun in Tilly's hand. The sight startled her—not the presence of a gun, but the sight of Tilly holding it. Carrying the gun, protecting Tilly, was Rheada's duty. The stark evidence of her neglect was right there, in Tilly's young fingers wrapped casually around cold steel.

She should never have let Tilly stay behind. She should have forced her sister to come. All the arguments, Tilly's obstinacy, her vehemence, came rushing back to Rheada. She had told herself that Tilly was old enough to make her own choices, that she had no right to force her sister. No one had the right to dominate someone else's will.

But she had been wrong. She should have made Tilly leave. Rheada was the oldest. She was responsible. And she had left her sister. She would correct that mistake right now.

Her sister was nearly to the campsite. The other person had stopped after a few paces. Rheada could now see it was a man, barely taller than Tilly. He glanced from Tilly to her, back and forth, as if unsure what to do.

Rheada ignored him and strode straight for Tilly.

"Raven, what's going on here?"

That her name came from *his* lips jolted Rheada. She jerked her head to him, but found him looking at Tilly.

"What—" Rheada started.

"It's my sister, Orin," Tilly interrupted.

"You never told me you had a sister."

His accusing tone grated against Rheada. What business was it of his, anyway?

"She has her own life." Tilly spoke firmly as if to end any more discussion. Then she glanced to Rheada. "Away from here."

Rheada caught the hint of a warning in her sister's voice. Warning her off? Or not to interfere? Rheada couldn't tell, and right now she didn't care. She wanted time alone with her sister.

Orin took a few steps toward Rheada. "Well, does your sister have a name?"

"Rheada," Tilly said, a bit quickly.

Orin looked from Tilly back to Rheada. "Raven and Rheada."

Rheada stared at Tilly. What was going on? Why was he calling Tilly *Raven*? She wanted to call out to Tilly, but now she feared to even use her sister's name. Inexplicable panic took hold in her gut, a sudden terrible sensation of the world tilting.

Orin closed the distance to Rheada, stopping only a few feet away. "Rheada and Raven," he said again.

The way he murmured their names sounded sinister.

"Sound alike," he said. He took a long, assessing look that made Rheada's skin crawl. "Even look alike."

"But we aren't alike." Tilly walked away from Orin, drawing his attention after her. She stopped at the cold, blackened remnants of a fire. "In fact, we couldn't be more different, could we, Rheada?"

Rheada didn't know what to say. She felt caught in a game for which she didn't know the rules.

Tilly shifted, glanced at Rheada over her shoulder. "Why don't you tell Orin what you do?"

"I give tours."

"She gives tours," Tilly mimicked.

Then she laughed. The sound raked over tender memories in Rheada.

"Don't be so modest, Rheada. I've heard the hype about your tour company. I also heard about your discovery of the ruin."

Tilly faced Rheada. "See, Orin, my sister doesn't just give tours to any old place. She takes people to ancient ruins in canyons they wouldn't normally go."

"You discovered a ruin?"

"No big deal, right, Rheada? You've been doing it your whole life. Except now you lead groups to those ruins. You take them to hidden places, don't you?"

Rheada flinched inwardly at Tilly's derisive tone.

"What a great scam! That has got to be the perfect cover—a pot thief as a tour guide."

"She's not a pot thief, Orin. Not anymore."

He didn't seem to hear Tilly. He was already walking toward Rheada. "So, what did you find?"

Rheada couldn't miss his excitement, the greed.

"Don't bother, Orin. She didn't find anything for us, did you, Rheada? You only share with your tourists, or with the *authorities*. You know, you've put a real crimp in my style."

"She what?"

"She's crossed over, Orin."

Rheada couldn't find her voice. She stared at Tilly, standing only ten feet away, but Rheada had never felt so distanced from her sister.

Tilly leveled her gaze on Rheada. "Tell me this, dear sister, how do you keep those ruins safe now that everyone knows about them? Have you forgotten your promise to the Anasazi?"

Rheada stared, speechless. This was her sister? The one Rheada could always confide in? The *only* person in the universe who knew the importance of their pact with the Anasazi? The one who now continued looting? How could Tilly throw their solemn pledge in Rheada's face?

Tilly's words had the brutal impact of a blow only a loved one could deliver with perfect aim.

Anger overwhelmed the disbelief. Rheada strode to Tilly. "You made that pact, too. Have *you* forgotten?"

Tilly flinched.

"Sounds to me like maybe your sister's jealous. Kind of hard to live up to the legend of the great Raven," Orin said.

"I imagine it is," Rheada said, staring at Tilly. "So hard, in fact, that Raven *herself* stumbles sometimes."

Tilly's eyes widened as if warning Rheada not to say another word. But Rheada wasn't finished. Tilly had always been the one wanting to play games, to take chances. But using the name Raven was beyond taking chances—it was dangerous.

"Raven doesn't stumble. Raven is a legend. Aren't you, my little black bird?" The man wrapped skinny arms around Tilly.

Rheada wanted to yank him off her sister—and not out of jealousy or spite. Orin wasn't honoring Raven. He was laying *claim* to her.

"Raven isn't a legend. She's human. And she makes mistakes. Like your last dig? I've never known *Raven* to dig up a burial."

"How did you know—" Orin stopped. His eyes narrowed on Rheada. "If you're thinking of blackmailing us—" His fingers slid down Tilly's arm and encircled the gun.

Rheada flashed her hardest gaze on Orin. "You idiot. I don't want your loot—"

"That's right. It's my loot."

Suddenly, Rheada understood. She saw it in his eyes: the glint of stupid pride. "Carrizo Canyon was *your* idea, wasn't it, Orin?"

He smiled. "Oh, I don't need to take credit. Raven and I are a team."

Rheada looked at Tilly. "You've got to be kidding."

Tilly stared back, unblinking. "You're the one who walked away."

It was the truth . . . but none of this was supposed to happen. "I begged you to come with me. You still could."

"Oh, I don't think so," Orin murmured. He actually kissed Tilly's cheek.

In that moment, his lips pressed to her cheek, his gaze on Tilly, Rheada caught a glimpse of an emotion other than greed. Could it be that he truly cared for Tilly?

No. Everything about him—every instinct in Rheada—told her he only cared about himself. Raven was simply a means to his end.

She gripped Tilly's arm. Orin jerked his attention to Rheada, but she didn't let loose. "Come with me now. I need you. I'm *scared* for you."

Tilly's eyes flitted sideways to Orin, then back to Rheada. Rheada again saw the trace of fear. Her heart drew her hand tighter, to pull Tilly close, protect her. But Tilly's eyes then went hard.

"You always scared easily, Rheada. It's because you only saw things from two sides: safe and unsafe, good and bad, right and wrong. Did you ever even consider that the world might not be so narrow? That what matters is our intentions?"

Rheada stared back in disbelief. "You can say that to me, knowing what we *both* endured in order to get out of here? We did what we had to in order to survive, in order to get *out*. That was the intent, that was the goal. Remember?"

Tilly's eyes slanted with a knowing look. "And you're still beating yourself up for what we had to do, aren't you, Rheada? You think you have to redeem yourself."

Tilly's words found home—that place in Rheada where the truth lay in wait: a monster poised to attack any hope she held for herself.

I lived as a criminal. I am a criminal . . . no matter what I do.

"But you *didn't do anything wrong*," Tilly said.

The guilt lunged for Rheada's throat, squeezing tight, forcing stings to the back of her eyes.

"And neither did I," Tilly continued. "We did what we had to then, just like I am now, for my *own* reasons. Whether you like them or not."

Rheada found strength in the only shred of hope she had for her own salvation. "We had no choice then. But you *do* have a choice."

"Maybe I don't," Tilly said.

Her words, her conviction, rang in Rheada's ears like a hammer striking bedrock.

"As for choices, Rheada, if I'm so wrong—if *I'm* the one betraying the Anasazi—then why is Blackjack with me and not you? I'll tell you why." Tilly slid from Orin's embrace and stood alone. Right before Rheada's eyes, Tilly seemed to gain strength. "He stayed here because this is where he belongs. It's where I belong. And so do you. *You're* the fool if you think you can really walk away."

Tilly's words descended between them like an impenetrable wall.

"You don't have to do this. There's a world out there,"

Rheada said quietly. "Just waiting for you. It's the way we dreamed it. Don't you remember, T—"

Tilly's eyes flared at Rheada's near mention of her name. "What I remember is an older sister who lectured and nagged, and I had to listen. I don't have to listen anymore." Tilly's eyes were fierce with barely controlled emotion. Her lips drew tight in a thin line.

Rheada wanted to plead with Tilly—or just drag her away. Maybe in full daylight, far from here, she could talk sense into Tilly. There had to be a way to reason with her, to turn the conversation around. If she could just start over, turn the clock back, back to when they depended on each other, to when they believed in each other.

Rheada's mind raced, searching for the right words. She only had to find them, speak them. This was her sister!

Rheada looked to Tilly, sure that this was a nightmare, and when their eyes met, the spell would evaporate, everything would be right again with the world.

But it wasn't Tilly who stared back. It was someone else— someone who hadn't shared a lifetime with Rheada, someone who had forgotten they had only each other.

Rheada's heart beat wildly; she was frantic, desperate— already aware of a mortal wound.

"I think you better go."

The finality in Tilly's voice nearly undid Rheada. She denied the rush of emotion, swallowing hard for composure and for strength—just for another moment, for Tilly.

Rheada walked to her, wrapped her arms around her sister, and pressed her lips close to Tilly's ear. "You're not Raven. Raven is a myth. You're my sister. Please stay safe."

Tilly couldn't watch Rheada leave. She turned her back and headed into the canyon.

"Where are you going?"

"For a walk," she said over her shoulder, not caring whether Orin heard.

"You want to tell me what that was all about? Why did she come here?"

"She's my sister, Orin. She goes where she wants." Tilly kept walking.

"Raven!"

The name I stole from my sister.

Her gut twisted. She did *not* want to talk to Orin right now. Tilly's gaze flitted from the sky—now light blue with morning—to the cliff walls, to the canyon. All of this, as far as she could see in this vast outdoors, had been hers and Rheada's. Together.

God, how she had ached to see Rheada, to feel her big sister's arms around her. In that moment, she had nearly been defeated, nearly confessed her plans to the one person she could trust. But if she had, she would have been placing Rheada's life in danger, too.

She saw Rheada's eyes, the pain that Tilly *herself* had caused her own sister. Tilly's throat clenched around a terrible, silent cry.

She heard Orin's fast steps behind her and she swallowed the grief inside her. The next instant, he had a hold of her arm.

"Why would she come here, Raven? Why now?"

Tilly heard the concern in his voice. She stopped and faced him, saw the crease in his brow and the need in his eyes to be reassured. He was worried about their loot, about being found out, robbed, turned over to the BLM before they could complete the big deal. Bottom line, he might even be afraid of losing her, his golden goose.

Poor Orin. He didn't have a clue he already was with the wrong sister.

"We just got a little close to her stomping grounds, Orin. That's all. She worries too much. So do you," Tilly added.

"Really? Your sister shows up in the middle of the night at our campsite, just when we're about to pull off the biggest score of our lives. How the hell did she find us, anyway?"

Tilly's gaze lifted to the mouth of the canyon. There was no sign of Rheada, just as there had been no warning of her arrival.

Because she's the best.

Acute loneliness rose within Tilly—a void that grew, consuming her. Right now, she had never felt so burdened.

"Answer me, Raven."

She glanced at Orin and saw him studying her, his gaze narrow, speculative . . . suspicious. Suddenly, Tilly was worried for her sister. Just how much of a threat did Orin consider Rheada?

"She just got lucky, Orin."

He looked down the canyon. "I don't like it. I think maybe she knows something."

"She knows plenty, but not about this," Tilly murmured. "She doesn't have a clue. Trust me."

"Meanwhile, we're sitting ducks here."

"She's not going to bring the troops down on her own sister, Orin."

"Maybe. But then maybe she was followed. We have enough. I say we make the deal now."

She knew he was greedy, and not particularly smart. Those were precisely the traits she had counted on when she agreed to the alliance. He hungered to believe any tale she told, and with such blind avarice that she had easily manipulated him.

But he was also impatient. With every haul she made from ruins, he had become more nervous, more excited, and more anxious to deliver the goods and get the money.

Tilly wasn't in it for the money. She had her own agenda— one that had started to form when Orin confided Crow's obsession with the mask. The more she heard about Crow, the more Tilly had wondered if Crow could be the one, the man she had seen on the cliff above her father's body.

Soon, she would know for sure. And she knew what she would have to do.

Tilly looked Orin straight in the eyes, and lied. "I'm not going to let anything happen to you, Orin. You're with Raven, remember?" She leaned close. "When this is done, *you're* going to be a legend."

Inwardly, Tilly smiled. Rheada would like that irony. Even more, she would appreciate the ultimate twist of fate that Tilly was about to deliver . . .

. . . though Tilly wondered if she would ever have the chance to tell her.

Chapter 8

As Rheada drove away, she tried to focus on the terrain, but her heart offered image upon image of herself and Tilly: the two of them always together, forever, against the world.

You're the one who left.

Tilly's words drummed at Rheada's forehead, an accusing finger meant to push at Rheada's guilt. Instead, Tilly's pronouncement, her *judgment,* stirred sibling contentions, provoked old emotions simmering deep in Rheada—a hot brew of anger and frustration that steamed through her mind, forming one clarified thought.

You left me no choice!

Tilly had insisted on one more deal, just one more, and one more. Then, she had heard of Crow's rich dealer contact in Germany and was determined to steal him away. Rheada had finally understood that Tilly would keep them in the canyons forever.

But that was *not* a choice for Rheada, and she had left, making Tilly promise she would join Rheada later. Rheada had always been *sure* that Tilly would eventually join her. Their plans had been for a life together, a legitimate life, one where they didn't live in fear, where they could hold up their heads, do honest work.

Instead, Tilly had taken the name of Raven.

That name was to have died when Rheada left the canyons! She had sacrificed her honor, integrity, her own self-respect, for that name. She had lived in fear for herself and Tilly, both surviving as orphans in the canyons, at the mercy of unconscionable thieves—and she made that name notorious, fearless, a force to be reckoned with. She had built a reputation as the best pot thief in the Southwest . . . the Raven . . . all for the right to *someday* bury that name and that life and walk away.

Now Tilly kept that name alive!

Anger and frustration boiled to a fury in Rheada. She saw

everything she had worked for, all that she had sacrificed, be for nothing . . . and Tilly didn't care.

In her anger, Rheada wondered, maybe irrationally, even desperately, whether Tilly had ever cared.

She thought of her winsome sister, cavorting seemingly weightless through the canyons, unfettered. Tilly seemed sometimes to have been *born* fearless, ready to take on the world, or anyone who stood in her way—including her own sister.

The rush of anger lodged in Rheada's throat with a taste of betrayal. Her heart jumped in her chest, as if to escape the thought, flee from where Rheada was going.

But it *was* a betrayal; a betrayal of what they had meant to each other, of the promises they had *made* each other.

Rheada set her jaw against the tide of emotion pushing past the knot, but she couldn't stop the instant blur at her eyes, or the mortal ache at her heart.

She was losing her sister.

The saddest moan escaped from her lips. The sound, though barely a whisper, had the strength of a sharp knife prying loose the knot in her throat, releasing the watershed of emotion.

Rheada let the Jeep drift and die. She lowered her head to her hands still gripping the wheel.

How had this happened? How had she become so estranged from the only person she cared about? And what was she to do now?

She could keep driving to Aztec, to her business—the place that conjured the precious glint of hope, where she had a *chance* to make things right, pay back for all the wrongs committed by herself and her family.

Or she could turn the Jeep around, drive back into the canyon, rejoin Tilly, revert to life in the night, stealing pots . . . and betraying the Anasazi.

A sharp pain arced across her chest—as if she were cutting out her heart.

God, how she wished she had someone to talk to! Someone to whom she could confide, someone who could bear the truth of the dark life she had lived.

Unbidden, Kee's face filled Rheada's mind. His sudden appearance in her thoughts startled Rheada—and yet she didn't want to let go of the image. He looked back at her, his gaze contemplative and unreadable, a careful man. His features were shadowed—no matter that she had spent days with him in the sunlight—just as they had been when she first met him, when she had sensed his gaze on her from the darkest corner of the bar.

She had not been able to resist that gaze. The *gravity* of his gaze had drawn her to him, compelled her steps across the floor to his table. She had had no more choice in her direction than a compass arrow magnetized to true north.

She may not have had a choice, but she realized she was *glad* she had hired Kee. He had proven to be a good driver, even a good companion. From the first day, she had felt an ease in his company, a mutual quiet, a shared understanding—strangers to each other who fell into step on common ground.

He had secrets. She knew it. She had known that from the moment they met and had seen it within his eyes every day since—the way his eyes narrowed when he gazed into the distance, as if he must squint to shut out where he was, even where he had been, and focus only on where he was going.

That thought pulled her head up from her arms. She didn't know where that insight should come from, yet she *knew* it was true. Something drove Kee forward. That same something would certainly drive him right out of her life someday. In fact, he may have already left, given she had not shown up at her business for a whole day.

Rheada's insides gave a small lurch as if momentarily losing their footing. That reaction was even *more* disconcerting.

She straightened in the seat, stretched her arms rigid to the steering wheel. How foolish of her to be contemplating Kee!

And yet she couldn't dispel his gaze, his quiet *sureness*, from her mind—and one thought emerged . . . she too had a purpose. To return to Tilly would be Rheada's own betrayal, of herself and the Anasazi.

Her hand slipped to the key and she brought the engine to life. Her arms locked and she forced the Jeep ahead, her heart breaking, cracked beneath the truth that she would truly be alone—without the comforting *caw* of Blackjack, without even the hopeful image of Tilly beside her to make her feel whole, loved, right.

Rheada's gaze focused on the lightening eastern sky and

she aimed the Jeep in the only direction she could go, forward and away.

"She was born June 9, 1985, near White Rock Village in the northern res. She weighed six pounds, seven ounces. She hardly ever cried." The words droned from Kee, one after the other. His thumb ran back and forth across a photograph. "I carved a turquoise bear for her. It took me a week. I cut my thumb." These were the facts of Sarah's life as he remembered, an accounting . . . a habit. It was the exercise he used to keep himself awake, alert.

He said the words by rote, but not allowing himself the actual memories, the images. That would be too much to bear.

"She watched me from her cradleboard when I swept. Her eyes were big and brown. She had a funny smile."

Kee pinched the bridge of his nose to relieve the incessant stinging at his eyes. *God,* he was tired.

"When she was three hundred and forty-five days old she said her first word. *Shash,* she called out to me from her cradleboard.

"She called me Bear." The stinging raced across his eyes. "And when she grew older, she loved to wander the canyons behind our home."

Kee closed his eyes. He pressed his first finger and thumb against his eyes to rub and was surprised to find wetness.

It was exhaustion, he told himself. He had divided his time between the canyons and here, waiting for Raven to show. He was vaguely aware of an ache in his bones, a numbness in his brain. His body was telling him he had pushed himself hard. Damn his body! Damn any weakness!

Kee opened his eyes and stared hard at Rheada's building, letting his hate build, bring him strength, rejuvenate him.

His gaze followed the dim outline of the sidewalk up to the white window boxes full of flowers, all just now emerging in the dawn's light—though he didn't need any light. Each detail was already burned into his brain, along with the floor plan, the rooms inside, the spare furnishings, her meager possessions. He could recount every item on her walls, in her drawers . . . in her closets.

His jaw set against the instant replay of excitement he had experienced when he discovered the boxes of shards. He had thought he had her. The notorious Raven, meticulous, careful, uncatchable, had actually *stored* her loot in her house!

But then he'd found the letters from tourists and Raven's detailed itemization of each piece, including when she had received it and from whom. Some entries noted the date of when she had returned the piece to the site. But most said "site unknown," and cross-referenced boxes organized by type of shard.

A spot check confirmed the shards mentioned were indeed there, many still in their original padded mailing envelopes. He even found a file with copies of the letters to the tourists.

She hadn't missed a beat. Anyone, including any authority, would think Rheada Samuels not only ran a legitimate business, but was a valuable asset—a good little soldier—in the war against the looting of artifacts.

Kee had searched her home, hoping for an advantage: an insight into how she thought, maybe even a hint to what she might do next.

Instead, he had discovered just how cunning an adversary he faced.

Oh, he had known she was intelligent and calculating. She had managed to outsmart every cop, park ranger, detective, and every other BLM special agent who had ever pursued her. But Kee had never really appreciated her talent for strategy.

Here she was, not only living the very demanding life of the consummate pot thief, but simultaneously the unbelievable parallel life of a legitimate businesswoman—and again the *best*. She not only provided great tours, tailored to her clients. She carried out the role past all expectations. She created a whole persona, complete with conscience and moral duty.

The task she had set for herself was staggering, daunting, brilliant . . . and ruthless. Only the most amoral person could pull off both—the best thief *and* the best citizen.

This time, though, Raven had met her match, because Kee also didn't give a damn about conventions or expectations. And he didn't give a damn about the law, not when it came to Raven.

Kee looked down at the photograph in his hand. Sarah gazed back at him. Her fifteen-year-old eyes were narrower, though that may have been from the flash of the school camera. He didn't know. She also wasn't smiling, but then she might have wanted a serious picture for the yearbook. He didn't know that, either.

For all he knew, this might have been her usual expression—a bit wary, a bit sad.

If only he had visited more the last few years. Hell, if he had visited at all, he would know how she looked. More important, he would have known what was going on behind those eyes.

What was on her mind when she sat for this picture? Could she have been thinking of a boy, wishing he liked her? Or some high school intrigue between friends?

These should have been the thoughts of a teenager, shouldn't they?

Kee thought back to his own youth, but he couldn't conjure *any* thoughts—of girls, or friends, or even schoolwork. It was as if none of that had existed; certainly none had been important enough to leave even the slightest imprint of a memory.

His only strong memory was of an emotion: frustration. Frustration for being born on the res, at the northernmost reaches of the res, in a place so isolated that time itself didn't bother to pass through.

Everything stood still in White Rock Village.

The frustration was so keen in his mind that he could still taste it—as bland mutton stew and dry corn tortillas; as the bite of burning juniper or the headachy reek of gasoline in the kerosene heaters; and as dirty sand, the constant grit at the back of his mouth.

Frustration alone, however, would never have gotten him off the res. There was a whole Indian nation full of drunks whose frustration took them only so far as the next bottle.

Hatred was Kee's salvation. It started at the back of his throat, like the burn of too-hot green chile after the first bite, after you've swallowed and you think you're fine, you think you can deal with it. But you're wrong. The chile bites your throat, claws its way back into your mouth, a flash of fire that consumes your tongue and your lips and you can't taste anything but the burn, you can't feel anything but the pain . . . and you can't take one more bite.

Kee stared at Sarah. He didn't see fire there. She had always been quiet, always kept to herself, mostly to the canyons that spread from White Rock—almost as if she would stay out of everyone's way. But there had been *something* going on in her mind.

He realized now that they had never *really* talked. Had he even told her how much he loved her?

He must have. He thought back, searching every memory, frantic to remember. But something told him he was hunting in vain. He had been too angry, too full of hate for any love. Then he had left and abandoned Sarah.

He'd left her to the thoughts only she knew; to the needs that drove her to explore the canyons . . . to where she finally disappeared.

The guilt rose swiftly inside him. If he had been there, he could have given her a way out—a legitimate way. But Sarah had been on her own and the path she had chosen had taken her to pot thieves . . . to one particular pot thief.

Kee still didn't understand: Why choose to be a criminal?

He imagined his sister, young, innocent, gullible, searching out Raven, drawn by her legend, seduced by her stories, *brainwashed* into believing that Raven actually *cared*!

Sarah's only communication had been a single postcard to her mom that said the raven had found her. After that there wasn't a single word and all Kee had to go on was that she had disappeared—until he infiltrated Crow's crew.

The man was obsessed with a pot thief named Raven. And when he lost one of his biggest buyers, seduced away by Raven, Crow went crazy. Crow cursed her—her ingenuity, her luck, her success—with all the vehemence of a driven man. People believed in her legend, he ranted in a drunken rage, as if she were a damn chosen one. Just how much of her legend would be destroyed if people knew she had murdered? Murdered a young girl, he said, looking at Kee.

Kee felt his grip tighten. He looked at the photo, saw the crease made by his thumb. He forced himself to set it on the passenger seat.

He pulled his gaze from that of his sister and stared out the window, across the street to the small, unassuming adobe—Raven's home, where she slept and ate, ran a business, pretended to be an upstanding, law-abiding citizen. She had built a house of smoke and mirrors, where the unsuspecting were confused, disoriented, and finally lost track of the light. She had bankrolled that tidy life on lying, stealing, maybe even murder.

God, even he had believed her!

A pulse throbbed at his temple, sending a murderous red to the back of his eyes. He glared hard, willing her to appear, pull into the dirt drive of her home, the place where she felt *safe*.

Just then he heard the downshift of gears, the unmistakable rumble of a Jeep, and with a slow, measured blink, his gaze slid from Raven's house to the street to the approaching Jeep.

It was her. He knew it in the instant response of his body, the kick-start to his pulse, the eerie fading of all other noise and all other scenery to just that Jeep.

Kee opened his door, stepped to the street, and raised his hand to a wave. When she turned her head to him, Kee blew the air from his lungs, took a deep breath, slipped his mask into place, and let his lips curve to a smile.

Let the battle start now.

She slowed the Jeep and pulled alongside him. "I'm so glad you're here," she said. She actually smiled at him.

"Why wouldn't I be?"

She glanced down, then away. "Because I didn't show up yesterday."

Kee studied her face. Now with the side view, he could see beneath her sunglasses. The hollow of her eye looked dark, as if she hadn't slept for days. "So where have you been?"

"I had some things I had to do. I'm going to make it up to the customers who had to wait."

She looked back at Kee. Her lips drew together with purpose, then she pulled her sunglasses off. Kee found himself staring straight into her eyes. They were tired, too, and glistening. "I'm sorry," she said. "I'm back now."

He didn't believe his ears. She sounded sincere, as if she truly *were* sorry and needed him to understand. He almost laughed.

"Glad you're back," he said, and he had no trouble making himself sound sincere. He *was* glad she hadn't flown off.

He backed up a few steps to let her curve into the driveway, and followed her down the path to the back of the building. He noticed the spray of dirt on the vehicle's back end and up the back window. Yellow mixed with a more coppery color.

She had covered some territory over the past day.

Questions raced through his mind. Had she been finishing up some digs? Or rendezvousing with connections?

He reached the Jeep just as she lurched it to a dead stop in the garage. Kee opened the door for her, used the opportunity to look beyond her to the backseat, where he caught sight of a bedroll and a backpack.

"You want some help with those?"

She glanced over her shoulder, then back to Kee and shook her head. "No, I leave them here." She stepped out and slammed the door. "Never know when you might need camping gear, right?" she said, looking up at him.

Kee had to back up. "Right."

Her brow rose slightly, but then she continued past him out of the garage. Kee cursed his lack of control. She must have heard something in his voice. He had better get a grip. He followed her to the back door and into the kitchen.

"Make yourself at home. I just need to clean up a little," she said over her shoulder. Then she stopped at the doorway to the hall and turned to him. "Can you make a decent pot of coffee?" She smiled. Her eyes warmed with familiarity, as if glad to share this morning routine with him.

"I can make coffee. Can't guarantee the *decent* part." Kee forced his lips into a smile.

She tilted her head and considered him. "I really am glad you're here, Kee." She said the words barely above a whisper, and her brow creased as if she were pinched on the inside. Then she turned and disappeared down the hallway.

Kee stood there, staring, after she had disappeared into the bathroom, even after he heard a rush of water. His mind tried to analyze what he had just witnessed, that lapse in her usual confident self.

When he added up the obvious fatigue on her face, her quietness, her hesitant conversation, and now this pained, almost vulnerable expression . . . under other circumstances, with anybody else, Kee might feel sympathy.

But this was Raven, the master imposter.

Yet as much as he looked for the deception in the way she had behaved, he couldn't see it. She certainly couldn't pretend the exhaustion. Perhaps all the rest came from that—the quietness, the sadness. Sleep deprivation was hell on keeping a level head, that he knew firsthand.

His instincts, however, didn't buy that she was just tired. Something was wrong. Kee was dying to know what that was.

Trouble in *Raven*'s world could be good—or bad—for Kee, depending on the type of trouble. He wouldn't mind a few frustrations added to her life—people could do stupid things when they were frustrated.

What he didn't need, however, were any major conflicts that scared her or threatened her and forced her underground again. He needed Raven to feel safe.

Kee realized the rush of water had stopped. At the same time, he remembered his promise of coffee. He didn't see a coffeemaker on the counter, so he started opening cabinets, one after the other. Finally, on the shelf with the pots and pans, he found an old aluminum percolator, the kind you would take camping. This one had seen its share of campfires—and of hard-packed mess kits—considering the streaks of black reaching up the dented sides like cold flames.

He thought of the instant coffee—or, at best, the cowboy coffee cooked strong in a saucepan—that he and Crow's men lived on. Here was the notorious, elusive Raven, rattling around canyons with an actual percolator. Kee found the image so absurd, he couldn't help a sound of disbelief.

"I didn't know a coffeepot could be amusing."

She was in the kitchen, right behind him.

Kee schooled his features to casual amusement. "Most aren't." Still in a crouch, he swiveled on the balls of his feet toward her. "But then most don't look ready for last rites and a funeral pyre."

She was smiling. "But it makes the best coffee," she protested.

Kee raised a skeptical brow.

She laughed. "Okay, it makes coffee the only way I know how."

Her black hair, slick and shiny from the shower, was smoothed back from her forehead. He could see the comb marks. A bead of water clung to the end of a strand hanging close to her neck. A slender line of wetness marked the front of her crisp white shirt. It was the first time he had seen her hair down. He wondered how long it fell in the back.

Suddenly, Kee was annoyed. He stood, walked to the sink, pulled the innards out of the percolator, and filled it with water.

"I have an idea for a trip." She stood next to him, arms crossed, her gaze out the small window over the sink. He wondered just what was going on in that scheming mind of hers.

Kee shut the water off. "Really? Where?" He busied himself with the filter and coffee she had placed on the counter.

She pushed off and paced to the other side of the kitchen and back. "I just don't know if I can pull it off."

Kee's heart jumped. For a second he had the sense she was confiding in him, discussing her next dig. He knew that was absurd, and yet this morning she had created an atmosphere of intimacy, familiarity. He turned slightly to find her leaning against the far wall, looking at him.

Kee made his lips curve into a smile. "I'm sure you can do whatever you set your mind to."

Her gaze slid to the side in the manner of someone unsure. Once again, her reaction surprised him. Kee found himself ever more curious about what weighed so heavily on her mind—because something obviously shadowed her thoughts.

"What kind of tour do you have in mind?"

"A trip," she amended. "A four-day trip to northern Arizona. Hiking, horseback riding, campfire stories." Her voice and demeanor brightened with every word. "Days in some of the most beautiful canyons. Nights under the stars." She was grinning now, not even looking at Kee—her gaze far away as if already on the road to this adventure.

Kee, however, was locked on the question of why she was suddenly interested in Arizona. "And guided tours of some prehistoric sites?" he asked casually.

"Oh, I don't know." She shrugged as if she hadn't thought about it.

Kee repressed a snort of disbelief.

"There don't have to be ruins, right?" She was looking at him. "I don't promise only trips to ruins in my brochure. I mean, there is so much else out there worth doing."

Her gaze held Kee's. He could have almost sworn that he saw conviction in her eyes, a *need* to believe her own words ... that is, if he didn't know better.

He poured himself a cup of coffee, leaned his hip against the counter, and watched. She certainly was full of surprises.

"You don't think I can do it."

"What—?"

"I know those canyons can be dangerous, Kee. And I know I would be responsible for the people for several days."

She crossed the kitchen and stood right in front of Kee. He looked down at intense amber eyes.

"I want my tours to be about more than ruins, more than petroglyphs, or legends. I'm tired of everything being about the Anasazi." She stopped. Her mouth fell slightly open, as if she couldn't believe what she had just said.

For a second, Kee thought she might apologize.

"I didn't mean that. I just meant—" She broke off, turned and walked across the room.

The notion that Raven would apologize to the very people whose existence she lived off of, took advantage of, vandalized and robbed . . . the idea that she felt guilt or regret had never occurred to Kee.

And he didn't believe it for one instant. How dare she act as if she had a conscience!

Kee set down the coffee, careful to control his urge to slam it down on the counter. "I'm sure whatever trip you come up with will be worth it," he said. "For everyone," he added.

She smiled at him. "Thanks, Kee."

Kee could have said that she better make it worth it, because he had every intention to make sure she didn't give many more.

Chapter 9

BOUGAINVILLEA cascaded down the hillside to the white beach in a tumbling riot of red and pink. Cecilio had never seen such a gaudy display of color. Certainly not in his home in the desert mountains of northern Mexico, where color was shy and dressed in muted, respectable shades . . . and certainly never *tumbled*.

He heard the *shoosh* of the sliding doors behind him and knew Alfonso had joined him on the balcony. Cecilio didn't turn from the view. He wanted one more moment of the brilliance before he heard the sobering news.

"The northern pueblos are backing Zamora." Alfonso breathed a deep sigh.

Cecilio squinted at the ocean. Dazzling white danced on the waves. A man could be blinded by such effervescence if he stared too long. He turned to face Alfonso, and saw his campaign manager's downcast gaze on the flimsy sheet of paper he had just torn from the fax machine.

"Does Orozco say why?"

"He's a stupid man," hissed Alfonso. "He says the Alliance is better served by one from the north. He uses the excuse that the tribes are better organized in North America. A leader from there will have the strength to pull all the indigenous people together from both continents. Liar." Alfonso spit the word out.

"Orozco is just looking out for his own."

"I'm talking about *Zamora*, Cecilio. He has seduced the northern pueblos with his lies. You have to do something. In your silence, the lies grow."

"The lies will catch him."

"But what he claims is impossible to verify!" Alfonso paced across the balcony. "There are no records of lineage from the Anasazi. And now the pueblos are standing behind him!"

"His claims are also too spectacular to be ignored by the media."

Alfonso stopped pacing and faced Cecilio. "Perhaps. That is if they decide to show the least bit of interest in this campaign. And will it happen in time to help us?"

That was the question. Looking across Alfonso's shoulder, Cecilio could see their reflection and that of the sparkling ocean view within the glass of the sliding door. As if playing some trick on his eyes and mind, Cecilio could also see *beyond* the glass, into the villa, an opulent residence that just a year ago he never would have imagined occupying. The two images, comfort and pleasure, superimposed one on the other, produced one blurred image both intriguing and unreal.

The dizziness he had experienced before now returned. And the thought crossed Cecilio's mind that things were much too precarious. What if he should lose? What then?

"Cecilio."

Cecilio heard the concern in Alfonso's voice. He felt the touch of Alfonso's hand on his arm. He laid his own hand on Alfonso's and squeezed. "You worry too much, Alfonso. The northern pueblos are well organized, that is true. But there are millions of Indians here and in Central and South America. The people will know who is best for this job."

"*How?* Zamora has ten times our resources to get his name out. It seems he has workers in every barrio, every remote village. They *know* his name, Cecilio."

Cecilio couldn't look at the ocean, or at the tenuous images in the glass, or even at Alfonso, who looked ready to throw the lounge chair off the balcony. So, he stared at the terrazzo, the solid ground beneath his feet. Beneath this terrazzo was earth, from where all things grew. He was, after all, a farmer.

"How can you be smiling?"

"I was only thinking that we have come a long way, but even this is temporary." Cecilio shared his smile with Alfonso.

But Alfonso wasn't amused. "*History* is not temporary, Cecilio. This is the first international alliance of indigenous peoples."

"Yes," Cecilio interrupted, "and it will still be historical no matter who is elected."

"Not the witch Esteban Zamora!"

For a moment all was silent—as if all earthly creatures held their collective breaths at the damning pronouncement.

"You won't use that word, Alfonso."

"I'm not afraid to call him what he is." Alfonso paused. "You should not be, either."

Cecilio leveled his gaze on his friend, his confidant, the one man who had always believed in him and in the reality of a union of Indians. "I refuse to win the election by using rumors and slander."

Alfonso didn't blink. "You will not win at *all,* if the *witch* has his way. Will you let this moment in history be defamed by the likes of Zamora? *Then* you will see interest by the press! They will say the Indians got what they deserved!" His eyes glowed with inner fire.

"They will say what they want, Alfonso. I won't give them the words. And neither will you." Cecilio stared hard. "Do you think that one man—no matter how bad, or how *good*—" Cecilio held Alfonso's gaze. "That he could change who we are? Do you think we are so weak and malleable? One man cannot change our destiny."

"Really? What does he believe is *his* destiny? Assume for one moment that Zamora is who he says he is, a direct descendant from the Anasazi, that great northern tribe that lived before all others. They conquered and *ruled* with an iron fist. Does the blood of those warriors, of their terror and dominion, run through Zamora?"

"How dramatic you are! This is an election, Alfonso, not a war—"

"He has no fear, Cecilio! If Zamora is not of Anasazi descent, he doesn't fear lies. He doesn't fear scandal. If he *is* Anasazi, he does not even fear the wrath of his ancestors for stealing from them! He's buying votes on the sale of stolen Anasazi artifacts, Cecilio. And now he is even using the discovery of that *ruin* in New Mexico in his campaign."

"It is an amazing discovery, Alfonso. To finally see proof that Indians from here were a part of the Anasazi Phenomenon."

A sharp, derisive sound came from Alfonso. "Don't you understand? That plays exactly into Zamora's hand!"

"Alfonso, it doesn't play into anybody's hand. It is simply a piece of history. In fact," Cecilio added, hoping to reassure Alfonso, "it gives power to the idea of an alliance of all indigenous peoples."

"Power that Zamora is using, not us. I'm afraid that this

recent support for him warns of a change in the tide."

Cecilio turned to the ocean. In the space of only the past few minutes the landscape of the water had transformed. The dancing white flashes were gone, as was the turquoise blue in the waves. The surface had turned slate-gray, a reflection of the dark clouds now gathered on the horizon, signaling a small squall far offshore.

As dazzling as the scene had been just moments ago, it was now somber, pensive, gathering its own strength in preparation for the onslaught of the storm.

Cecilio found it immensely tranquil.

Alfonso approached close enough to speak barely above a whisper. "Cecilio, Zamora would steal from the ancestors of the very people he claims to represent!"

"We don't have evidence of that," Cecilio answered, still looking at the ocean.

"Not yet." There was a promise in Alfonso's tone. "There is rumored to be a mask. The first mask."

"Yes, I have heard the legend of the first Kachina."

"The mask supposedly gave power to the Anasazi over their enemies."

"It's a story, my friend." Cecilio glanced at the worried man. "You need to get your mind off this, Alfonso. Think of other things. For instance, is everything in place for the debate in Santa Fe?"

"Yes."

Cecilio had to smother a smile at Alfonso's gloomy tone. "This will be a good debate," he offered, unable to keep a hint of consolation from his voice.

Alfonso paced across the balcony. He stopped at the far side and faced Cecilio. "Answer me this. Would you let a thief be elected if you had a way to stop him?"

Cecilio considered the loyal man standing before him. It crossed his mind that perhaps Alfonso should have been the man to run for office. Alfonso had more desire than Cecilio, who would be happiest right now to dispense with any more talk of intrigue and witches, scandal and thievery.

"No, Alfonso," Cecilio conceded. "I don't want a thief *or* a liar to lead. I am not *letting* Zamora be elected. But I also can't *stop* it, if that's what the people decide."

"Then we must see that they decide on you."

* * *

It took Rheada four days to prepare for the trip to Badger Canyon. She had to buy and pack supplies. She took the bus in for new tires and an alignment—Rheada didn't want to be stranded with eight tourists.

As another precaution, she filed her itinerary with the Navajo tribe, though it wasn't required and was seldom done even by the huge outfitters based in New York and California. Rheada, however, wasn't taking any chances.

She didn't know where this sudden urge to be overprepared came from. She had always been cautious and organized, but this time she knew she was closing in on obsessive.

She told herself it was for the safety of the tourists. She would be taking them as close to the middle of nowhere as you could get in a vehicle. They would also be exploring a canyon better described as a fissure to the heart of the earth. In some places, the opening at the top was no more than a narrow crack that a bird could step across. At the bottom, the canyon would be no wider than a hallway—a death trap in flash floods.

But it was mid-September, the end of the monsoon season in the Southwest. Now, at the beginning of fall, the colors of the earth rose to the surface, seeming to reach for the fading sun. Badger Canyon's swirling red rock dappled in broken sunlight made the canyon a place of wonder and reflection, a place to ponder existence.

She envisioned hiking deep into the magical canyon, so deep that only tranquility and stillness could follow. And maybe, Rheada thought, she could abandon the foreboding clinging to her, leave it behind with no way to find her . . . and emerge hopeful again.

Perhaps, Rheada considered, she should make this trip alone.

She raised her gaze to the window and saw Kee crossing the front yard, sleeves rolled above his elbows, his arms stretched to the handles of a camping-gear box, his effortless stride belied by his distended muscles. He bent and slid the box within the storage compartment beneath the bus, his shirt drawing taut across his back. When he straightened, arms now empty, Rheada noticed the resolute line of muscle still defining his forearm—the promise of strength now contained, but ready.

Unbidden, the image of Blackjack filled her mind—more specifically the ridge of muscle rounding the top of his wing. Her hands remembered the muscular power he harbored beneath the glossy feathers. He had only to spread his wings, and with a few graceful flaps lift and soar.

Kee harbored the same strength—the ability to rise above and see far. In him, she saw even more of Blackjack: a sureness, a purpose. With Kee beside her, Rheada felt able to try anything.

The squeak of wood resisting wood was followed by a *whoosh* of air as Kee pushed open the front door, and she gazed on the tall, dark length of him.

"Humidity has swollen the wood," he said as he pressed hard to again close the door. He wiped his brow on his shirt. "You sure this canyon's going to be dry?"

"The air's just saturated from the monsoons. I promise you, though, if there's any rain within ten miles we won't go down."

Kee stood there, his strong arms lax at his side, his long black hair pushed back from his forehead. His dark, keen eyes studied her . . . in the same way Blackjack would, his wise eyes never blinking.

Rheada shook her head to dispel the image, and the emotions growing within her. They were dangerous . . . yet so compelling. She returned her attention to the box she was packing.

"This is the last one," she said, for no other reason than to distract herself from Kee.

I should go by myself.

The thought popped into her head with such clarity, Rheada wondered for one horrible second if she had spoken it aloud. She glanced up at Kee, found him still watching her, his features slightly stiff as if he were silently mastering an acute pain. It was an expression she had seen a lot on him the past four days . . . and one that so closely mirrored what *she* felt inside that Rheada couldn't help but conjecture about some personal suffering he too endured.

"So, is that it?"

His voice surprised her, as if almost conjured from her

thoughts. "Yes . . . I think so." Rheada forced her mind over her mental list.

Kee reached for the box just as Rheada remembered. "Oh, wait. Almost forgot."

She disappeared out of her office and into her house. Kee heard the creak of the back kitchen door. A few minutes later, she reappeared, the backpack Kee had seen in her Jeep now slung on her shoulder and a folding camp shovel held in her other hand.

He reached a hand out. "Just lay them on the box and I'll carry them out," he offered.

"That's okay." She skirted him. "I can fit these up front by me." She headed for the door, only breaking stride when, with both hands on the knob, she had to lean her weight back and yank to pull the door open.

Kee followed, his mind speculating what would be in the backpack: the flashlight he had seen her pull from the bag on the video; perhaps even her own personal maps, marked for special digging sites. He paused beside the bus, pretending to balance the box, and watched her through the windows as she stuffed the backpack under her seat. Maybe it even held a notebook with the names of her contacts—a piece of evidence he would love to get his hands on. Right now.

He *knew* she was Raven. He could nab her where she stood.

He shoved the box into the storage compartment, but it jammed against the duffel holding the tent stakes. He pushed the box aside, stretched his arm and most of his torso toward the duffel, muscling it farther back, all the time cursing this whole goddamn plan. He might not have the evidence he needed to put her away forever, but he could put a stop to her illegal trafficking—at least for now . . . except then he wouldn't find out what he had to know about Sarah.

Frustration took hold of him with the power of an electric current, zapping urgent, desperate energy through his veins.

He gave a violent punch to the bag and caught his knuckle on the metal tip of a stake.

"Damn it!"

"Kee! What's wrong?"

He grabbed his hand and pressed against the wound, but already he could feel the throbbing. He lay there, wedged between the boxes. For the time being, he didn't want to move in any direction.

A hand touched his leg. "Kee?" She gripped harder and started to pull. "Kee, answer me! Are you all right?"

He didn't like the concern in her voice, the *worry* he heard in it. "I'm fine." His voice sounded like a growl echoing in a dark tunnel.

He eased out and crouched at the side of the bus, where he took a closer look at his hand, except what he could mostly see was a lot of blood.

"Oh, my God!" She took his hand in hers. "What happened?"

"Jammed my hand into one of the spikes." Kee started to pull his hand back.

Her grip grew firm without causing him any pain. "Let me see." She supported his hand with her own, and with her other hand straightened his fingers out with the slightest of pressure.

"Kee, can you move your fingers?"

A part of him was amazed at how he barely felt her touch. "They're fine. It's just my knuckle." The annoyance was clear in his voice. This time he succeeded in pulling his hand away.

"Come on. Let's wash it off and see what we've got."

"I can wash it off, Rheada." The last word came with extreme effort.

"I'm sure you can. And you've probably got some manly *dirty* rag in your pocket just perfect for wrapping it up, right?"

Kee heard a chuckle. When he looked down at her, he was even more annoyed to find her smiling.

"I'm not trying to be *manly*—" he started.

"Good. Come on."

She had him by the elbow and was walking for the door before Kee could think of any good reason *not* to go inside and take care of his hand. She got him into the kitchen, where she gestured to a chair. She pulled a cotton cloth from a drawer, went to the sink, turned on the water, and let it run over her wrist until, apparently satisfied with the temperature, she filled a small bowl. Next minute, she was back at his side with bowl and rag. She slid her hip onto the table, and bent over him, obviously intending to clean his hand.

Kee grabbed the rag. "I told you I can do this."

She started back, then smiled. "Okay. I'll get the medicine." She scooted off the table and was gone down the hall-way.

Kee dipped the rag in the water, squeezed out the excess, and laid it across his knuckles. The warmth soothed the throbbing. He worked the cloth the length of his first two fingers and over his knuckles, wiping off blood. When he reached the fleshy part between his fingers, he felt the sudden sting of water on wound. The stake had sliced through the skin and nearly into his knuckle. White bone peeked from beneath torn tissue. He was going to have a hell of a time setting up sensors for a while, or climbing down into canyons . . . let alone driving the bus.

The thought brought him back in his chair. What if Raven decided he shouldn't drive?

"Damn it!" The expletive came on a hiss of frustration. He pressed the cloth hard to his hand and stood. Raven was in the doorway.

"Where are you going?"

"To finish packing."

"Forget that. Have a seat."

Kee walked toward her, intending to keep right on going down the hallway. "I've had worse, Rheada."

She stepped in front of him, blocking his path. "I can't afford a sick driver, Kee."

"I'm not sick. It's just a scrape. Now, let's get on with it."

"Kee, we're not going anywhere until you let me see that hand."

He knew that tone in her voice. It was the same one she had used in the pueblo ruin, ordering him out. His frustration and annoyance jumped a notch. He was *not* taking orders from Raven! He faced her, ready to tell her to go to hell.

Instead, he found a worried face and beseeching eyes. In one hand she held bandages. In the other she held two small white jars. They were exactly the same as those his mother would pull from the cabinet—her *remedies,* she called them.

The sight provoked memories: comforting hands; the quiet, reassuring murmur of Navajo words; all enveloped by the scent of the medicine—pungent pine and soapy aloe that bit the air upon the release of the jar lid and then filled his nose and lungs so completely that the world smelled reassuringly of juniper, piñon, and yucca for days.

He smelled it now. He felt the coolness of the lotion on his hand.

"Have a seat, Kee."

He was so caught in the memory that he barely registered that Rheada was practically toe-to-toe with him.

She stepped closer. Kee backed up; his legs touched the chair and he sat down, resigned.

Rheada planted herself between his knees, determined that he wouldn't bolt on her again. She held his wrist firmly, prepared for his flinch against the first sting of the medicine, as she spread the first fingerful of salve on the wound.

He didn't move. In fact, she could have almost sworn she detected a relaxing in his shoulders. She couldn't be sure—she couldn't see his face. His hair hung forward, straight and long—the shining black hair of an Indian. An insight dawned on her: His body knew this medicine.

As she cut a small piece of padding, Rheada found herself wondering about Kee's background, where he was raised. Had he been born off the res? Or raised there and then left? If so, why had he left?

He never talked about himself or his past. Neither did she. Rheada had appreciated his reserve—it had limited the number of times she had to choose words carefully or, for that matter, lie outright. In no small measure, Kee's unforthcoming nature had suited her, matched her own need for anonymity.

But now, the idea of anonymity, of having *no one* know her, seemed more like a curse than a blessing.

"This is an old Navajo medicine," Rheada said. The words came without forethought, a betrayal of her mind as she immediately realized it was her subconscious attempting to reach out.

She set his hand down, suddenly embarrassed by her own vulnerability. Covering her lapse, Rheada set about cutting a small piece of padding.

"Yeah, I know," Kee answered.

Rheada was startled, then pleased, that he had admitted even that much. Carefully, Rheada placed the padding between his fingers. "Hold this," she instructed. She held her finger there until Kee complied, pressing just the tip of his own finger to the padding.

"So was your father Navajo?" he asked.

"No," Rheada answered.

Rheada was unwinding gauze and looked at Kee. She caught the curious raising of his brow. "We would come across Navajo in the canyons. My father would make friends with them, with almost everyone." The ache of loneliness, of missing him, welled up within Rheada. She caught Kee's curious look and forced a smile. "You know these old prospectors. They collect anything they think might be of use."

Rheada placed the end of the gauze under his hand, held it against his palm, and started to circle.

"And your mother?" he asked.

So, he had been speculating about her heritage. She paused, then said, "She left when I was young. I actually never knew her."

Kee shifted and Rheada knew he had looked away. She didn't mind his withdrawal. The moment of silence suited the subject—she had no more to say about her mother. Rheada had never understood her mother. You don't just abandon your family.

Except, that was exactly what Rheada had done when she left Tilly.

A sudden blur filled her eyes. She couldn't see what was right in front of her, but she *could* see Tilly's eyes, her gaze set on the distance, past Rheada. As much as Rheada wanted Tilly here with her, Tilly was just as determined to go her own way.

She felt the weight of Kee's hand in hers. She thought of the people she would take on the tour . . . with her.

Rheada lifted her chin, and forced the emotions down inside herself. She finished the wrap and secured it with bandage tape. "There," she said, with a final gentle smoothing of the bandage.

She replaced the lids on the jars, and gathered the rag and bowl. Kee had already stood and started for the door, but then paused. Rheada could feel his gaze on her. In her mind, she could see his dark, somber eyes considering her, just as he might an unreadable terrain as he decided on the best way to proceed.

She liked that aspect of Kee—his careful, calculated approach.

Rheada slid from her perch on the table and chanced a look

to him. Just as she had imagined, Kee's eyes were narrowed and focused on her.

Then he turned and strode away. "Thanks," he called over his shoulder, raising his bandaged hand in a sort of wave.

Rheada was left with the dark scrutiny of his eyes. Once again she was reminded of Blackjack, a creature who really could see all.

The raven and the mapmaker . . . now there was a natural combination.

Chapter 10

KEE could see her in the rearview mirror, talking to her group, making comments on the scenery as he drove them west on Highway 64 into Navajo country. His right hand lay useless in his lap, though it now caused him no pain and the throbbing had ceased. In fact, he hadn't given the hand much thought after the awkward and inept attempts to grip the steering wheel. He had to admit that Rheada's salve, and her bandaging, had made the difference.

It made sense she would be handy with first aid, having lived deep in the canyons, alone, isolated.

I never knew my mother.

Her voice had held little emotion, as if just stating a fact. But then he had seen a stillness come over her, and a sadness had claimed her eyes with the swiftness of a new wound. The next moment, she had regained control—the instantaneous response of someone who *had* to be strong. He had watched, been *compelled* to watch, her brave struggle.

Inexplicable anger bubbled up inside Kee. What did he care of her struggles? She didn't have a corner on hardship. Was he supposed to now feel sorry for Raven, this motherless child?

He flicked a glance to her. She was bent, pointing out some landmark to the group, her face the picture of the consummate tour guide: enthusiastic, helpful, dedicated.

His mind latched on the word "dedicated" and the comforting hatred returned. She was dedicated, all right—dedicated to a life of crime. And she was goddamn good at it. So good that she had spawned a legend—a legend that had drawn his own sister into the night.

He didn't care how *desperate* Rheada had been, she had still had a choice. Everyone had a choice between right and wrong.

Kee's own gut twisted, a sickening stomach-wrenching churn as if his body were rebelling against something rotten deep inside.

The sudden blare of a horn brought Kee's attention back to the road. He checked the rearview mirror and saw a white four-door straddling the center lane, its headlights flashing on and off. He edged the bus toward the right to give room for passing.

The car sped from behind, but then pulled alongside the bus. The passenger window lowered. From the height of the bus, Kee couldn't see into the car, but he could see the frantic gesturing of the driver's arm. Kee guided the bus onto the shoulder and stopped. The other driver followed, parking his car at an angle across the front of the bus.

A man jumped out with a bedroll and backpack, and ran back to the bus, barely pausing to check for oncoming traffic.

"I'm not too late, right? I want to go on this trip very much."

Kee looked down at a narrow, olive-skinned face with close-set eyes. Mexican probably, Kee figured from the guy's broken English accent, and maybe early twenties. "You nearly drove me off the road."

"I've been trying to get your attention for the past three miles."

"So you force me off the road?"

The Mexican grinned widely. Kee ran out of patience. "Move," he ordered, his hands on the wheel. He shot a glare to the Mexican—who hadn't moved and was still smiling, but now Kee saw that the smile was aimed past him.

"Kee, what's going on?"

Her voice drifted across his cheek. She was standing right behind him, leaning toward the window.

"You are Rheada Samuels?"

"Who are you?"

The man reached a hand into the window and Kee had to lean back. "I'm so glad to meet you, Miss Samuels. Please, you can take one more on this trip, right? You see I would not take up much room." He stepped back with a flourish and a self-deprecating smile.

What Kee saw was disheveled black hair, a wrinkled shirt, stained khakis, and really old tennis shoes. The kid looked as if he had driven straight from Mexico without stopping. Kee wanted to know why.

"We're full—" he started.

"Why do you want to go on this trip?" Rheada interrupted.

"Because you are the best! Everyone knows that."

Again the smile—quick, perfect, well practiced. Kee wondered who the hell this man was.

"Well, thanks—"

It was Kee's turn to interrupt. "How did you hear about this trip, Mister . . ."

"Please, Miss Samuels. I near the end of my American visit. I am looking *forward* to this trip."

Kee didn't buy the broken English act. He saw intelligence in the man's eyes and downright cunning in his attention to Rheada—to the exclusion of Kee. He had also noticed that this guy had never once answered a question.

"How did you say you heard about this trip, Mister . . . ?" she asked.

It was as if she had read Kee's mind. Of course, Raven was anything but stupid.

"You are too modest, Miss Samuels. Everyone knows of the woman who discovered the ruin."

"We're not touring ruins on this trip."

Kee was surprised by the determination in her voice. He nearly glanced over his shoulder to her.

"Okay, no ruins," the man said agreeably. He started to walk around the front of the bus.

"Wait just a minute!" Kee called out.

"He doesn't seem for real, does he?"

From the corner of his eye Kee could see she had shifted to sit on the arm of the passenger seat. Her arm stretched to the back of Kee's seat, bridging the distance between them. She was talking to Kee, asking his advice.

"No, he doesn't seem real," Kee finally answered, without looking her way.

The man stood in front of the side doors, obviously waiting to be let in. Kee gave a sharp turn to the steering wheel, intending to pull away, but at the sound of tires scrunching on the gravel, the man yelled.

"Wait!" He pounded on the door.

Kee inched the bus around the back end of the car.

"Okay, okay! I tell you the truth!" He ran to the front of the bus, planting himself in Kee's way. "Miss Samuels, listen to me. I work for *Southwest Adventure* magazine. I am a

writer! I will do a wonderful article on you and your trips."
He grinned.

"You want to do an article?"

Kee heard the concern in her voice. He could just imagine
what Raven was thinking—an article about her, in a national
magazine. So much for remaining anonymous. Kee stopped
the bus and leaned back into his seat. He couldn't wait to hear
her response.

"An article," she repeated.

Kee could almost hear the desperate race of her thoughts
as she bought time.

Kee couldn't resist. "This is your chance to put your company on the map, Rheada."

Rheada looked from the man to Kee, her stomach tight-
ening. She knew he waited for an answer, but Rheada's
thoughts were pinned on the man's mention of the ruin. She
had thought this trip would be an escape.

How could she turn down this reporter without drawing
questions from him and from Kee? She glanced over her
shoulder at her busload of passengers and found every one of
them watching her with rapt attention.

Rheada turned back to the window. "I'm very flattered,
Mister . . ."

"Carlos Sisneros, journalist," he supplied with an exaggerated bow.

"Well, Carlos, this is quite a surprise. A nice surprise," she
amended, trying to sound intrigued, though her stomach was
now in a knot. "I'm flattered," she said again. "So please don't
get me wrong, but I don't know how everyone would like
having a journalist along."

Kee shifted in his seat, gave barely a glance to her and
faced the passengers. "What do you think? Shall we let the
writer join this trip?"

Heads nodded. People smiled enthusiastically. Rheada
stood there helpless. They saw this as a novelty. Rheada, however, saw the trip change before her eyes—from a new adventure to a nightmare.

"So what do you say, Rheada?"

Kee looked at her. In his forthright stare, Rheada found
strength.

Rheada smiled at Kee—a grateful smile he wouldn't understand, but one that came from her heart.

"I say, why not?"

She saw a flicker of surprise in Kee's eyes as she bent across him to address Carlos through the window. "Glad to have you aboard, Carlos."

"Thank you!" He was already running back to the door.

"Your car!" Kee yelled out the window.

Rheada had opened the side door. Carlos was stepping in. "He's right," Rheada said. "You can't just leave your car here. Not if you want to see it again."

"It's just a rental." Carlos shrugged.

"You still can't leave it here," Kee said. "You can follow us."

Carlos looked from Rheada to Kee to his car, seeming to weigh the decision. Rheada couldn't imagine anyone even *considering* leaving their car in the middle of nowhere, even if it *were* a rental. His eagerness to be on the bus, with her, just didn't seem natural.

She nearly changed her mind right there, then Carlos grinned and said, "You are right, of course. I will just follow you!" He jumped off the bus, shaking his head as if not believing his own lack of sense.

Rheada closed the door and watched him walk to his car, where he stopped and looked back, seemingly focusing right through the front window on Rheada. "You won't regret this," he called out.

The midday sun bore down on his face and reflected off his shiny black hair. His teeth gleamed. His eyes shone. Everything about him was too bright, too severe—like a blinding flash of lightning, warning of a change in the weather.

They camped in Wild Horse Canyon, along the shore of the Navajo Creek tributary leading to Lake Powell. The tents were the only strong color in an otherwise pastel world. They were also the only touch of green. Pink bluffs slid gracefully beneath calm turquoise water in a perfect Southwest still-life painting. Nothing moved or disturbed the placid landscape—not a tree kissed by a breeze, or even a hint of grass. They could be looking at a photograph, a favorite snapshot from a vacationer's album.

Rheada unpacked the fishing gear and collapsible camp chairs, and got her group comfortable down by the water—all except for Carlos, however, who wouldn't leave her alone.

"So, now they're settled. Can I ask you some questions, Miss Samuels?"

"Rheada."

"Rheada," Carlos amended with a smile. He pulled a pen from his pocket. "So—"

Rheada headed for the bus. "Right now, I have to set up camp."

"I can help with that," he said, trailing her and Kee back to the bus.

"Thank you, Carlos, but that's my job. And Kee's," she added with a glance to Kee, whom she could have sworn had a slight smirk on his face. She gave a tug to a cooler and Carlos immediately stepped up to help. Kee, on the other hand, now had his back to her.

"So, tell me, why this place for a tour?" Carlos asked, walking backward across the slickrock.

She would have shrugged, if not for the weight of the cooler. "It's beautiful. It's different. Thought it would be a nice change."

"But there are no ruins." He made it sound as if she had committed a terrible mistake.

"Oh, there're ruins." It was Kee. He had a tent bag under one arm and balanced another on his shoulder.

Carlos set down his end of the cooler. He pulled a small spiral notebook from his shirt pocket. "Anasazi?"

"I couldn't say. But I'm sure Rheada would know."

She wished Kee wouldn't encourage Carlos, not that the guy needed any encouragement with his incessant questions. She set down her end of the cooler. "Yes, there were Anasazi here."

"Where?"

She watched Carlos scan the landscape.

"Down there," she said.

"What do you mean, 'down there'?"

Rheada nodded to the water.

Carlos took a few steps toward the edge. They stood on a wide apron of sandstone, the lap of the bluff—its fat pink knees bent, and graceful limbs slipped into the water.

"In the lake?" He shook his head. "I don't understand."

"Before the lake, there was only a river winding through the canyons. And within those canyons there are hundreds, even thousands, of prehistoric ruins."

Rheada's father had talked about the sites. She could hear him now, reminiscing at the campfire about the caches of pottery, the riches of jewelry, the virgin burial grounds just waiting to be discovered. It was a damn crime, he had said, when the government flooded the whole area, forcing the pot hunters into other areas.

Of course, he wasn't being sentimental. It was a crime against him and other men who hunted relics of the Anasazi.

"Man, this must really piss you off. What a shame to lose all that history."

If Rheada squinted, she could almost see *just* the wild landscape, in its primeval natural state. She imagined a ribbon of water leading clans of Anasazi on their migration. They had made homes and raised families here.

Now all was drowned· and forgotten in a huge, watery grave.

It looked eminently peaceful to Rheada.

"Not at all," she said. "At least this way, down there, the Anasazi are safe, protected."

A raven's caw drew Rheada's gaze to the sky, where she found him circling in lazy spirals, then finally landing on an outcrop of sandstone only thirty feet away. He jerked his head to her and stared. Rheada couldn't help a smile as she walked back to the bus.

Kee stared after Rheada, questioning what he had heard, what game she could be playing. She had actually sounded sincere, though he knew that was an act. No self-respecting robber of grave sites could be happy if those sites were effectively placed beyond their reach. Even assuming she had calculated her words for the benefit of Carlos, wouldn't it make more sense for a tour guide—one who purported to *love* the Anasazi—to be outraged by some *white* man's selfish need for recreation? She could certainly have justified righteous indignation for the tragic disrespect.

Instead, she had taken their side. She had made it sound as if she would like the whole Southwest flooded.

Her response confounded Kee and plagued him for the

whole time he was setting up camp—until, as he was driving
a stake into bedrock, he heard her laughter. It was a carefree
laugh that skipped along the sandstone and the thought suddenly occurred to him . . . maybe she *didn't* care if all the old
sites disappeared. What if Raven had decided her time was
about to run out and she had better retire, start a new life as
Rheada?

He stopped, sledgehammer in midair, and stared across the
pink rock at her, casually talking with some of the group. Did
she think she could just walk away, suffer *nothing* for the
crimes she had committed?

Did she seriously believe she could escape the conse-
quences?

Kee had the nearly overwhelming urge to stride over to her
now and tell her she would *never* escape. No matter what kind
of life she lived now, the wrongs she committed existed. They
would catch up, claim her, and exact their punishment.

He heard the screams from the dark hole in the dead of
night. His heart raced in the instant replay of the nightmare—
that moment of truth when he'd understood just how much of
his own humanity he was willing to sacrifice, the price of his
own soul he was willing to pay . . . that he would *have* to pay.

He would make sure Raven paid, too.

The juicy sizzle of beef fajitas still lingered in the air and
wafted across the bluff on the smoke from the fire Kee stoked.
Dinner had been good; the best he'd ever eaten over an open
fire. But then Raven would have had plenty of practice at
cooking outside.

"Great fire, Kee."

He glanced through the flames and saw it was Marjorie,
the lawyer from New York. Her husband, Stephen, was a psy-
chiatrist. They made at least two trips a year to the Southwest
for hiking, fishing, and "rejuvenation," as Marjorie called it.
They had to be in their fifties, but they were in damn good
shape. Kee couldn't help liking both of them, despite his sus-
picion that their trips here fed some highbrow concept of "connecting," another one of Marjorie's words.

"No problem," he said. He brushed the black ashes off his
hands and pivoted, intending to stand and retreat to his tent.

"So, Kee, tell us something about yourself. I've been wondering what brought you to this job."

She had a beatific smile on her face, as if she were talking to one of her daughter's friends.

"The usual," Kee muttered, but he gave Marjorie a small smile.

"Kee's actually a cartographer," Rheada said, walking up.

"A mapmaker!" exclaimed Marjorie. "How interesting out here in all this wild country."

Kee saw Hans whispering to his parents, no doubt translating as he had for the whole day.

"So you draw maps while Rheada leads tours?"

Kee glanced back to Marjorie. "No."

"He bailed me out on a tour when my driver didn't show." Rheada was across the fire from Kee, a cup of coffee in her hand. "It was lucky I found him. And that he's stayed for this long," she added. She caught Kee's look and held it.

The fire glowed amber on her face and shone in her large eyes, giving her an untamed, waiflike appearance—like a wide-eyed deer visiting itself upon a strange, dangerous world.

Rheada's gaze softened and she smiled at him, at Kee—the most dangerous one of all.

Kee's pulse jumped. He looked away.

"And what about you, Rheada? What made you start in this business of giving tours?"

"I wanted to give back—"

She stopped.

Kee jerked his head toward her. There was a pained look on her face. Then she seemed to draw a deep breath.

"I meant, I wanted to share my knowledge of the desert, of the people who have lived here."

"Well, my dear, word of your knowledge has certainly traveled. But you're so young. How did you come to know all you do?"

"I grew up in the desert."

"You grew up outside? How cool." It was Mack. Everyone looked a little surprised. It was the first time Mack had lifted his head from his hand-held computer game. Kee thought the kid had a permanent green glow on his face.

"Cool, huh? I never thought of it that way."

"Was it hard?" The kid had actually lowered the game and was leaning forward.

"Well, it's really all I ever knew."

"You never had to go to school?"

"No schools in the canyons, Mack."

"Man, were you lucky."

She looked at the fire, her gaze on the red-hot embers. "Maybe. I never had a choice. My father simply taught me what I needed to know." She stated it as a fact, without sadness, without pity.

For a moment, all were quiet, the only sound the intermittent crack of the fire.

It struck Kee that this, maybe, was a piece of truth. *Maybe*, in the beginning, she didn't have a choice, any more than he had being born on the res. And maybe she saw a chance now to choose a different life.

As far as Kee was concerned, she had made this choice too damned late.

"So what did your parents do?" Carlos leaned forward. "Were they missionaries?"

Rheada chuckled. Kee heard a wealth of irony in her laugh. "My father was a prospector. We traveled all over the Southwest, following rumors to the next turquoise lode."

"He was a dreamer," Stephen said.

"Not hardly." Her eyes hardened to black flint. Then it was gone, leaving Kee to wonder what he had witnessed.

"Just a man trying to make a living and raise his kid," said Mack's dad. "That's hard enough to do in a city."

"Well, none of us have a choice where we're born or how we're raised," Stephen said matter-of-factly. "But when you sit out here, under this big sky, you can't help but believe in endless possibilities."

"How did you come to learn so much about the Anasazi?" Though Carlos didn't have his notebook out, Kee could practically see his mind scribbling notes.

Rheada jerked her head to Carlos. There was that deer-look again in her eyes. Kee sank slowly, quietly, to his haunches and watched.

"My father would tell us stories around the campfire," she finally said. "We didn't have computer games." She smiled at Mack.

"What kind of stories?" Carlos asked. He was staring at Rheada, with more than curiosity in his eyes. Kee thought he saw a purpose in them.

"Oh, the legends. Fables, you might call them. They were our bedtime stories. I mean, for my dad and me." She shifted, giving her shoulder to Carlos.

Kee didn't miss the gesture of blocking Carlos off, and his instincts fired. Just what bothered Rheada in talking about these stories?

"Why don't you share one now, Rheada?" Kee asked.

She looked at him across the fire. He saw concern there. But then, as her gaze settled on Kee, the concern disappeared.

"Okay," she said quietly. Her gaze softened again and she gave a small smile, as if if she could do what he asked.

Something flickered across Kee's stomach—his skin tightened, drawn by a quickening sensation. He had to look away. He focused on the black nothingness not ten feet beyond the circle of light of their little camp. The more he stared, the deeper the blackness grew, until he was a part of it, enveloped, invisible, alone, and comfortably numb . . .

. . . except he heard her voice.

"I'll tell you a story about the 'Man in the Maze.' The petroglyph drawing shows a circle maze with the figure of a man at the top opening. It was drawn by the migrating clans. It is a map of the right way through life. The man will lead you to the safe place."

The same quickening raced across Kee's abdomen, drawing the tightness lower—and with the sensation, the blackness ebbed, defeated by a damn singsong voice.

Kee stood, shook out his legs, and strode from the fire to his tent. He heard the abrupt quiet, caught the turn of heads at his departure, and heard the smattering of goodbyes, but he kept his silence—he *needed* silence, the cold silence of not giving a damn.

Chapter 11

RHEADA sought the sun. She stood alone at the edge of the bluff, her gaze on the eastern horizon. Faint blue shimmered above the red hills, as if dawn were in a mighty struggle to wrest the blackness from the sky. It was the longest night— and the most restless one—she could remember.

She hadn't been able to clear her mind from thoughts of Kee, from his strange behavior at the campfire. He had been the one to ask her to share a story. But then he had left before she had barely begun, striding off to his tent without even a glance behind. What thought had yanked him from the ground and pulled him away?

She had wanted to go after him, ask him to share his troubles, his secrets. She would listen. She could help, she told herself. She understood secrets and the relentless energy needed to suppress them.

For the whole night she had thought about Kee. She wished he had heard the story of the "Man in the Maze." He could be that hero, she had thought. His keen, strong gaze would be able to find the safe place. He *was* a safe place.

Every time she looked into his eyes, her heart jumped as if in recognition—just as it had the first time she'd met him in the bar. How amazing he had been there in her time of need. And so many times since, when just the thought of him, of his keen, black gaze, had brought her strength.

He was a safe place *for her*.

The thought had pulsed through her—a quickening at her heart that flowed through her and throbbed deep inside. She wanted him. It was that simple. And he was only yards away from her, in his tent.

But just when a surge of courage would jolt her upright and bring her hand to the tent zipper, an equally strong force had stopped her as surely as if a solid wall had sprung up all around her. How could she think she could help him, when she was a prisoner of her own secrets?

What kind of fool was she? Did she seriously think she could *hope* for something with Kee?

The answer had kept her awake all night.

"Beautiful day for an adventure!" Marjorie's gusto filled the air. Rheada couldn't help a smile. "You're right. And how did you sleep last night?"

"Heavenly," Marjorie breathed out on a stretch. "Though I had the strangest dream. I was caught in a house of all hallways and couldn't get out. Then I saw Stephen." She laughed. "He is calling himself my 'Man in the Maze.' " She leaned toward Rheada. "I think it's so romantic."

Rheada smiled at the wonderful woman. "I think it is, too."

Movement caught her eye and she turned her head in time to see Kee emerge from his tent—one long jeaned leg, then the other. He straightened, dwarfing the small tent behind him. His bandaged hand hung at his side.

"Curious that he has kept driving for you. Do you think he's found something more interesting than mapmaking?" Marjorie gave Rheada a wink over her shoulder as she walked to the campfire.

A flush of heat rose in Rheada. She couldn't do more than offer the woman a smile. She let Marjorie walk away, for the moment stuck to the spot. Suddenly shy, she couldn't look at Kee.

Instead, she skirted the campfire and walked to the metal folding table she had made into the kitchen. She opened the camper stove, lit the burners, placed biscuits in one skillet and bacon in another. Her head bent to the task, she could hear the camp coming to life: the Kleigels talking in German, Stephen and Mack's dad sharing a joke, Marjorie humming, the coo of a mourning dove . . . and beneath it all, Kee's low voice. He was talking quietly, and though she couldn't hear his words, she could *feel* the deep timbre, in the same comforting way as reaching out in the darkness and touching something solid.

She looked up, her gaze drawn to Kee. He was talking to Mack. He had one leg bent, his foot resting on a large rock, his forearm resting casually across his thigh, his full attention on the electronic game Mack held. Mack handed the game to Kee, and without even hesitating Kee started punching buttons, his thumbs moving rapidly and adeptly. Mack let out a whoop. Kee shrugged and laughed. He handed back the toy and clapped Mack on the shoulder. Rheada couldn't take her gaze from Kee's huge smile. It transformed his face, brightened his eyes. Laugh lines radiated across his still-unshaved cheeks with a rough ease.

Rheada raised her nose, breathing in air that had traveled from the mountains. She didn't smell rain. The big yellow sun globe rose slowly, reluctantly, peeling itself from the horizon. Perfect blue spread before the promise of a warm day. Every natural sign of the earth and sky told her she had nothing to worry about.

An hour later, Rheada descended the rope ladder down into Badger Canyon. They entered from a mere crack in the bedrock. From there, the canyon looked like no more than a shadowy, narrow chasm serpentining across the hogback mesa. But with each step down, the wonder of the canyon unfolded.

A rainbow of reds, oranges, and yellows surrounded them—walls of color that beckoned them deep into the heart of the earth. At the bottom, a flat ribbon of clean white sand wound around a corner and out of sight.

They walked, their pace naturally slow, no one speaking—a line of worshipers winding through a cathedral.

Mack was the first to break the silence. "Awesome, man. It's like the labyrinth in BeastMaster."

All Marjorie whispered was an occasional, "Oh, my."

Rheada could hear only echoed murmurs from the German couple. They were behind and around the corner. Their voices reverberated into unintelligible sounds. Carlos was at the very end of the small troop. Kee wasn't here at all.

He had driven the bus along the top, following the fissure to the place where Rheada had decided they would emerge. There, they would enjoy lunch.

Rheada wished they hadn't made those plans. She wanted to see his face, see him smile. He would have to be smiling. No one could walk through this sanctuary of rock and color and not be moved.

Now more than voices echoed between the narrow rock walls. From behind, Rheada could hear the rapid click of cameras, as silent awe finally gave way to the need to capture this and carry it home.

With a glance over her shoulder, Rheada saw Mack crouched at the wall, along with his father. They were inspecting a particular swirl in the rock.

"Now this is cool," she heard Mack whisper to his dad. Rheada's smile widened at the utter delight on his face.

She walked ahead, slowing her pace even more, letting her fingers trail over the rough sandstone. The path widened to more than ten feet, inviting a leisurely stroll. Close on one side, the wall jutted out low to the ground, forming a natural ledge. Instinct drew Rheada's gaze up the side and there, at what would have been the uppermost reaches for the arms of a small Anasazi, was an etching in the rock. A spiral accompanied the small outline of a hand.

Rheada stepped onto the ledge, and hoisted herself up, her throat tight with anticipation, just as it was every time she discovered another trace of their existence.

"What's there?"

She looked over her shoulder to Mack, his dad, and Stephen. "It's a migration symbol. It was this Anasazi's way of saying 'I came by here.' "

Rheada stepped down and gave them room to see for themselves. She scanned the rock wall ahead and saw more etchings: a long, winding line that led to a squared maze. It was another depiction of emergence and migration.

The rest of the group caught up. Rheada walked, pointing at more petroglyphs. A swarm of encircled crosses soared upward; handprints "walked" over the rock face; there were spirals and even an etched parrot. All signified a special honor for this place.

The numbers increased, spreading to the other wall, in a veritable *excitement* of messages. Only a few times had Rheada seen such a proud display, each drawing adding to more and more in this exclamation from mankind.

She rounded a corner, having to slip sideways between the now-narrowed walls. Hot air washed over her in a rush forced by the funnel of the chasm. Suddenly, there were no more petroglyphs. She thought it must be the narrowness of the path, leaving so little room to maneuver. She almost stopped and turned back. She knew, though, that the canyon ran for miles and they had hiked only half a mile at most.

Rheada glanced over her shoulder at her intrepid band. "Everyone game to go on?"

"Yeah!" Mack's yell reverberated in the chamber. His dad grimaced, holding his ears, but he nodded. The Kleigels, Marjorie, and Stephen looked just as eager. She couldn't see Carlos.

Rheada inched her way around the jagged wall. As the canyon path turned, sunlight found the opening above, and bright rays slanted to the sandy floor. Glancing up, Rheada couldn't see any opening. The walls bent and closed, blocking a view. Rheada craned her neck to see, and thought she saw a trace of white against the rusty-red rock. Angling closer, she realized it was an etching of a lizard, caught in the motion of scuttling up. To his left was another lizard. Both had tiny claws extended from their feet, as if desperately gripping the wall.

Then she saw a long, dark line, running horizontally just beneath the bottom lizard, a full six feet off the canyon floor. It wasn't an etched line, but neither was it part of the rock, for it stayed perfectly parallel to the ground.

Suddenly, Rheada recognized the brackish line of a flood. She looked away, but in her mind she saw the lizards, scampering up the wall. She knew that every etching had a meaning. Some marked a sacred spot. Some related an event, or served to remind the artist of a story. Lizards, known to move easily over and between rocks, were mostly used to show a path. The need for a path here, at what had to be a most difficult part of the canyon, not only raised questions for Rheada, but also concern. She decided not to point them out to the group.

Then, just ahead, scratched into the rock face close to the ground, Rheada saw the unmistakable jagged body of the water serpent, complete with horned head. Her gaze went between the snake and the lizards—underground serpent below, representing water; scrambling lizards above.

Not ten steps farther on, Rheada saw the sign that confirmed her suspicions. Three stacked triangles with straight lines extending below and a jagged line piercing the top—the drawing could be confused for a small mountain range with rivers running from the bottom and a single sun ray shining on the top. Rheada knew better, however. It was the picture of dense clouds with lightning and rain—a blessing on the desert ground above, but a horror for anyone stuck in the canyon.

The message could not be clearer.

Taken together with the snake and the lizards, the cloud symbol completed the message: If you were caught in a flood from sudden rain, the lizards showed the way out. If she was right, there would be hand- and toeholds above the lizards. It was a map to safety, as clear as any modern road map.

Kee would appreciate this, Rheada thought. Again, she missed his presence. She wanted to share this with him.

The thought spirited her past the ominous etchings. With the others not far behind, Rheada followed the sandy path. She turned the next corner and saw the red cloth attached to a metal collapsible ladder. It was what she had given Kee to drape over the top of the canyon. She gazed up, knowing he was there, waiting. A gratefulness filled her, absurdly out of proportion to his simple act of doing as they had agreed. Still, her chest filled with an eagerness to see him, share the adventure.

For now, though, she had to stay below, holding the bottom rung taut against the rock face, until the last of her group had ascended out of the canyon, and she was alone.

She could hear Kee greeting each person. Their voices were vivid and enthusiastic. Rheada climbed, full of a keen yearning.

He saw the crown of her head, black hair shining; then her eyes, big, glistening, gazing up beyond the wall of the cliff straight to him; then her mouth, spread into a huge grin. All the features combined to an image of utter joy, settling totally on him.

It was so disconcerting that Kee missed offering his hand to her to help her over the top. Not that Raven would need any help, he quickly reasoned.

"Oh, Kee, you need to see the canyon," she said.

She was still standing there, looking up at him. Every one of the group had said the same thing to him upon climbing out. But her voice held the intimacy of a secret passion confided by a friend. It was as if she had carried the wonder of the canyon within her, toting it to the top, as a child would some precious discovery.

He smiled at her.

In the same instant, his brain tripped over the emotion that had provoked the smile and a swift rush of guilt, followed by anger, surged through him, and turned him on his heels.

"Lunch is on!"

His invitation came more as a barked order. From the corner of his eye, he saw Marjorie startled from the animated conversation she had been holding with Mack's dad. Kee inwardly cursed his own lack of control. He strode to the table, intending to pull out the cooler of drinks, but with every step his anger increased, pounding through him. By the time he reached the lunch table, he had the near overwhelming urge to sweep everything onto the ground and keep on walking.

What the hell was he doing here?

The question beat at his temples, demanding an answer.

His gaze scanned the barren, slickrock mesa. Nothing broke the monotony of the landscape—no landforms, not even a tree to help judge the distance. A man could lose all perspective out here.

Just what the hell *was* he doing?

He had single-mindedly sought Raven, his only conscious goal to find out what had happened to Sarah. He was no closer to that goal now than he had been ten days ago, before ever meeting Raven.

He faced the bus and the happy group of hikers. There, in the middle, was Raven, her small form easy to spot from anywhere. She raised her face, seemed to spot him; then raised a hand and waved.

Enough was goddamn enough.

He gave a nod, then jerked his attention elsewhere. He saw Mack and Hans far off, walking along the crevice of the canyon, stepping over it and back again, their strides casual. Two young men, maybe sixteen, without a care in the world. He had never felt that way.

As he stood and watched, Kee realized a deeper truth—that he would probably *never* feel that way. His eyes narrowed and his jaw set in satisfying purpose. When he looked back at the group, he could stare at his prey, comfortable with his destiny.

* * *

Rheada watched Kee cut across the mesa in the direction of Mack and Hans. The two boys were already so far in the distance, they resembled Anasazi stick figures drawn on a pinkish rock. As the others finished lunch, they also wandered off to walk the rim of the canyon. Stephen and Mrs. Kleigel went in the opposite direction and Rheada watched them look down upon the canyon path they all had traveled. Marjorie had stepped across the crevice and set up an easel. Only Hans's dad and Carlos remained behind, which Rheada found curious since they were each limited in how much they could communicate.

Rheada covered the fruit bowl, and wrapped the tortillas. There was no rush to pack—she had allowed for a two-hour lunch break here. It pleased her that everyone seemed to enjoy this trip. This afternoon should also be fun. She would take them to a nearby launch at the lake where she had rafts waiting. Next trip she would bring the rafts herself, and then be able to embark from an even more remote area. She knew a wonderful spot in southern Utah, just west of the Grand Rincons. After a day of hiking in the wilderness, they could relax for a scenic float.

She froze at the thought. What the hell was she thinking? She couldn't take *anyone* to that area. What if she stumbled on someone who recognized her?

She stared at the open cooler, a bag of lunch meat in her hand, for a moment confused.

"At last we are alone."

Rheada's pulse jumped at the surprise. She recognized Carlos's voice and bent out from under the table, schooling her face into a smile. When she glanced up, she had to squint against the blinding sun framing Carlos. She couldn't make out his face and she had the immediate sense of being at a disadvantage—a ridiculous notion.

"Hi, Carlos." Rheada stood and noticed that Mr. Kleigel had left. "You still have about an hour, if you want to enjoy some of the scenery."

"Those migration signs you pointed out. Were they made by the Chaco or Kayenta Anasazi?"

"The Kayenta," Rheada said, surprised Carlos knew there were different tribes of Anasazi. "The Chacoans didn't live this far west. So you have studied the Anasazi?"

"There is much interest in the Anasazi in Mexico."

"And this is what your article will be about?"

He rubbed his chin as he looked off, as if trying to sort out his thoughts. "So the Chaco Anasazi lived just in the area of New Mexico?"

"The center of their civilization was in New Mexico, in Chaco Canyon. But their influence reached tens of thousands of square miles. There are Chacoan outliers in what's now Colorado and Utah."

"And the descendants of the Anasazi? They are among all the Pueblo Indians?"

"Well, the Hopi claim direct descent from the Kayenta."

"No, not the Hopi." He paced a few steps, then turned, and faced her. "But there *are* direct descendants?"

"I suppose."

"How do they know this?"

Rheada shrugged. "Oral history would be the only way."

"Stories," he muttered.

Rheada heard his dismissive tone, but her thoughts were embracing the wonder of her father's stories at the campfires. "Stories capture the imagination," she said.

He walked to one of the camp chairs, appeared to be ready to sit, but then kept walking. "So the stories form the linkage to descent," he said thoughtfully. He paced back to her. "And, for anyone claiming descent, there would be a chain of stories leading back to the Anasazi."

Rheada couldn't figure out what he was getting at. "Are you interested in today's Pueblo Indians or in the Anasazi?"

"And just as true," he continued, ignoring Rheada, "is that a *lack* of that story chain would *disprove* any ancestral claim." He paced a few steps, nodding. "Yes, that is logical." He faced her, a smile on his face. "The truth is in the stories."

"Well, it's not quite that simple. There may be a nugget of truth, but Indian legends are mythical, multilayered, and serve a lot of purposes. The storyteller may want to make a point to children, for instance, and so will embellish a legend, or change it entirely to suit the situation.

"These stories also leap from clan to clan, tribe to tribe. The hero figure changes names, though usually to something similar. His abilities change, grow, become mythic. That 'chain' you're looking for," she said to Carlos, "would be more like a spiral, ripples circling outward."

"The legends take on a life of their own," Carlos said thoughtfully.

"Whether they're true or not," she pointed out.

"And what would you think of a man who claimed a direct descent from the Anasazi?"

"That would describe a Pueblo Indian, Carlos—"

Carlos interrupted her. "But this man is *not* a Pueblo Indian. He is *mestizo*. A Mexican Indian." Carlos stood right in front of her.

"I don't understand," Rheada said.

He was staring at her, his gaze grave, intent. "How could a *Mexican* Indian descend from the Anasazi?"

The intensity in his eyes was disconcerting. "I—I don't know," Rheada faltered.

He leaned across the table toward her. "The ruin you found. That was built by Indians from Mexico, yes?"

Rheada braced a hand on the table. "Yes."

"They coexisted with the Anasazi?"

"I'm not sure we would call it 'coexisting.' "

Carlos quirked a small smile. "You think they were enemies."

Rheada leveled a stare at the Mexican. "Yes. I think they were enemies."

"And what if they were not?" he countered. "What if the high priests of Chaco were in league with Mesoamerican warlords? A potent mix of religion and terror that *built* the Chaco empire!"

Tremors ran through Rheada. She had the trembling sense of walking blindly toward something frightening.

She took a step away from Carlos, but he grabbed her arm across the table. "What if they were *both* the enemy, Miss Samuels?"

The tremors grew to shudders, coursing through her veins. *Not my peaceful Anasazi.* "No," she said, but the word was barely a whisper.

Carlos rounded the table. "Do you know the legend of Poseyemu?"

Rheada jerked her gaze to Carlos's. The last person to utter that name to her had been Tilly when they found—and then hid—the mask. She saw knowledge in Carlos's eyes and knew she couldn't pretend ignorance. "Yes," she admitted. "It's another of the legends I talked about, Carlos. Just a story."

"With a nugget of truth," he reminded her. "The story goes that the daughter of a Chaco priest married an Aztec warlord—"

"Was forced to marry," Rheada corrected.

"And their son," Carlos continued, "would rule the empire—"

"But he was killed, because it was a union the Anasazi didn't want." Rheada faced him. "You can't make something good out of something bad."

As soon as the words were out of her mouth, though, the shudders within Rheada grew to full-blown quakes, as if her own body were reacting to a lethal threat.

From far away, Rheada heard a low, nearly indiscernible rumble. Carlos didn't seem to hear it: He was still staring off across the slickrock. Rheada shaded her eyes, searching the horizon. She couldn't see any clouds.

Then came another rumble, again so low that she *felt* it beneath her feet. The fine hair on her arms rose. Rheada lifted her chin, drew in a breath of air, and caught the scent of water.

Rain. She couldn't see it, but she knew that smell as surely as if the drops were falling right on her. For her to feel the rumble, the storm must be within ten miles, probably in the foothills of Lake Powell. Thank goodness, they were no longer in the canyon.

Rheada walked to the crevice and followed with her eyes its winding crack across the top of the bedrock. She could see Stephen making his way back. Behind him were the Kleigels and Mack's dad.

She turned and scanned the terrain in the opposite direction, but she couldn't see Mack, Hans, or Kee. Kee knew the itinerary for the afternoon, she told herself. He'd be back with the boys soon. A chill swept over her skin, like a shadow passing over her—and with it a terrible foreboding.

She walked to the chasm, and her eyes scanned the distance, searching every detail of the terrain. Still, there was no sign of Kee and the boys. At her feet was the ladder, still slung over the side of the canyon. She knelt and pulled on one of the metal stakes, realizing as soon as she did that she would never get it out by herself. Kee had driven it into the bedrock. She lay on her belly and reached over the side for the top rung, intending to at least pull the length of the ladder up to the top.

Her eyes caught a flash of light at the bottom of the canyon. She scooted farther over the edge. The light disappeared. She angled her head and the squiggle of light reappeared, a tiny ripple, as if moving, yet still staying in one place. Intrigued, Rheada moved farther forward; the light disappeared. She realized it was her shadow causing the disappearance. The sun was reflecting off something, except Rheada couldn't figure what that might be. It wasn't a can or bottle, not with the ripples of light.

Rheada sat up, and stretched her foot to the top rung, then started to climb down, her gaze focused on the canyon floor. She descended a few steps, then bent, one hand holding tight to the warm metal.

Before her eyes, the sliver of light widened, doubling, tripling, moving fast. Suddenly, her brain registered. It was water—a trickle, growing quickly into a stream, covering the canyon floor.

In the same instant, another rumble coursed through the earth. This time she felt it within her hand gripping the side of the ladder. Her pulse jumped. Her feet, without her conscious demand, started up the ladder.

Then she heard the yell.

It echoed against the canyon walls and out. She jerked her head above the rim and saw it couldn't have been any of the group. Which meant it had come from within the canyon. Rheada held her breath and listened. There was another yell. Then a deeper voice called out. It was a voice she recognized—Kee.

Her heart leaped to her throat. He and the boys were in the canyon. Her mind raced ahead to what she could do, as she listened hard, trying to gauge their distance before they were swept by. Rheada glanced down at the swirling water that was already two feet deep.

"Throw me a rope!" She screamed to carry her voice over the rim.

Stephen's face appeared at the edge. "What—?" Then he

looked past her, and his eyes widened. He reached a hand to her. "Come on!" he yelled to her.

"No! It's not me!"

The yells of the boys echoed around them. Rheada saw in his eyes exactly the horror she had to avert. People died this way. They got pulled under, bashed against the rocks, and finally dumped into the thick, soupy silt at the mouth to the lake.

Stephen disappeared. Rheada could hear yelling coming from above. She couldn't wait. She didn't have the time. She went down five more rungs, until her feet were in the water. She slid one leg over the rung, so that she was straddling it. She wrapped her foot around the side of the metal ladder, trying to anchor herself. She thought of the metal stakes Kee had driven and prayed they would hold.

There was another yell. It was Hans and he was closing in. The next instant, Hans came whirling around the corner. She could only see his head. Then she saw the tips of his shoes. He was holding his legs straight in front of him, riding the flood like a body toboggan, just like a pro.

"Hans!"

His eyes jerked to her. Her legs wrapped tight around the ladder, Rheada let her body hang upside down. With all her weight on her legs, she reached out for Hans with both hands, and caught his boot in her arm. Her hands skimmed clothes and grabbed frantically. A huge weight slammed into her, knocking her head into the cliff wall, bringing stars to her eyes. She held tight, looked down, and saw she had Hans by his upper body.

"Climb over me!" she yelled above the roar of the rising water.

He grabbed onto the rungs and planted a foot on a step. She watched a second, saw arms stretched to him from above, and turned her attention back to the canyon. In less than a breath of time, she saw both Mack and Kee careen around the bend. They too had their legs pointed downstream. Kee held Mack across the chest. She saw blood on Kee's forehead. Her eyes locked on Kee's. He nodded. She bent again, stretching, throwing her body weight as far as she could. She caught Mack's legs. The violence of the water, and their forward momentum, pulled her down, but she didn't let go. With every bit of her strength, she held tight and dragged him close.

"I'm okay, I'm okay." Mack coughed, and pulled himself over Rheada.

She felt an arm grab her, lift her back to the ladder, and she was looking into Kee's eyes. Rheada gasped a breath. "You're all right." She heard the relief in her voice. An emotion she couldn't name raced across his eyes. Abruptly, he looked away.

A roar filled her ears, the sound of a wall of water exploding over them. She had only a second to grab a breath. Water rushed over her head, up her nose. The power of the water ripped her loose from the ladder and into the fury of the flash flood. She flung her arms out, fought to find the surface.

Think. Don't react.

She forced her body to straighten, her legs to stiffen. Her face emerged and she gasped for air. Her body rode the water like a stick. Her mind raced ahead, searching her memory of the cliff walls for ledges, handholds. She craned her neck to see ahead, but what she saw drove her heart to her throat. Not twenty feet ahead, the canyon walls narrowed to a funnel. She was going to die here.

As if time slowed, her mind filled with the images of Tilly, and Blackjack and Kee . . . and she didn't question the vision of him. Somehow, it was right.

At least I saved his life.

Suddenly, the etchings came to her in a flash. Rheada jerked her head up. She recognized the approaching bulge in the cliff wall. She rolled her body slightly, angled her arm like a rudder, and aimed her toes toward the wall. Seconds later, she muscled her arms out of the water and flung herself toward the wall. Her feet fought for measure in the sand. Her knuckles, then fingers, scraped hard rock, gripped, lost the hold, and gripped again.

Rheada looked up and saw the lizard, his limbs splayed across the rock face, his claws sharp. She dug her fingers into the rock, dug the rubber of the shoe soles against the cliff, and worked her way up. She found a solid ledge to plant her feet on. She wrapped an arm around the bulge of cliff. She glanced down to the water, below her now; she wasn't going to die.

Then she saw the sweep of an arm, a dark face emerge. It

was Kee! She reacted before her brain could scream at her to stop.

"Kee! Here! Angle your body!"

She crouched, gripping the wall with both knees and her arm. She stretched her other arm behind her, toward Kee. His boot slammed her hand against the wall. Pain shot up her arm. She grabbed at water, frantic to catch him. Her fingers grazed cloth and she yanked. With every ounce of strength left in her, Rheada held on to Kee and the wall.

His head came up beside her, then his shoulders, as he pulled himself up the rock face. Rheada dragged him next to her, close to the wall, and planted herself between Kee and the water, pressing herself to him.

They stayed there for a moment, the water rushing around their legs, clutching at them, but Rheada knew they were safe. She could feel the promise of life pumping in her, and through to Kee, and back again. Their hearts beat violently, relentlessly. Gradually, her heart calmed.

On a deep breath, she leaned back a fraction. Her face was only inches from Kee's. Watery blood trickled from his brow. His dark eyes met hers. His breath fanned her skin.

Rheada's pulse leaped, as if pulled by some invisible cord. The next instant, her lips were on his. The shock of his wet lips against hers jolted through her, scrambling her thoughts. Her heart jumped, dancing erratically in her chest. She couldn't have been more electrified than if she'd been struck by lightning.

Just as swiftly, she pulled away, her mind yanking back her body. For a second, before she opened her eyes, she hoped she had only imagined the kiss. She *couldn't* have been so bold!

But a glance at Kee told her the kiss had been real. His eyes were dark, full black, stunned . . . and menacing.

"I'm sorry," she muttered.

She inched away, and started up the wall, suddenly so drained, so void of any energy, she didn't know if she could climb one more inch. Heaviness weighed within her, dragging her. She set her gaze on the lizards, the map to safety drawn by an Anasazi. A rod of steel wrapped across her back and under her arms. She thanked her inner strength, and reached one hand over the other, climbing the rock face, her fingers finding handholds. Brute strength pushed her, angled her higher, over the lizards, to the top.

Only when she pressed her arm to the rim, willing the power to lever herself over the top, but found that nothing remained in her, not a drop of energy, did she realize that the strength she had thought was her own, was Kee's. The rod of steel at her back was his arm. And with one muscular heft, he hauled her, and himself, onto the dry bedrock.

Chapter 12

RHEADA didn't want to open her eyes. She didn't want to look at Kee. She didn't want to face the judgment she was sure would be in his gaze.

How could she have kissed him?

He had nearly drowned on her tour. My God, three people had almost drowned . . . and she would take the opportunity to kiss Kee?

From the distance, she could hear the voices of the group approaching. She wanted to slip over the edge of the chasm and disappear. But she couldn't. She owed everyone her apology. She owed Kee an apology.

She levered herself up on her palm, then saw an outstretched hand. It was Kee's. She placed her hand in his, and he lifted her from the ground, seemingly effortlessly. She saw the taut muscles in his arm. She remembered the power of his arm across her back, the sense of strength he had evoked within her.

"I'm sorry," she said. "I'm sorry for everything."

She chanced a glance to his face and anything more she would have said stuck in her throat. The intensity of his gaze seared straight to her heart.

"The important thing is that neither of us drowned." His voice was tight. "By the way," he said, looking away from her, "how did you know that way out of the canyon?"

"It was a map."

His eyes narrowed on her, as if her answer were suspect.

"Drawn by an Anasazi," she finished. "In fact, I had wanted to show it to you. I thought you'd find it interesting."

"Handy."

Rheada smiled. "Yes. But I don't know if I could have made it to the top without your help."

"Oh, I'm sure you would have."

She heard a trace of sarcasm in his voice. Suddenly, the emotions swirling within her funneled to pure shame: It was true. She would have gotten out. She had spent her entire life climbing out of canyons; this one would not have stopped her.

"You're probably right," she responded, and she couldn't hide the shame from her voice. Would she *ever* live enough, repay her past deeds enough, that she would not feel shame for what she knew, for who she had been?

Rheada started across the slickrock, preparing herself to face the wrath of the group.

Hans and Mack were ahead of everyone, running toward her and Kee. "You guys all right?"

"We're fine," Rheada called out.

"Man, what a ride, huh, Kee?"

"Are you both okay?" Kee asked.

"Some scrapes. I've still got water up my nose." Mack laughed. "Who knew? In the middle of the desert!"

Rheada appreciated his lighthearted perspective, but it only heightened her sense of failure. "I'm sorry, Mack. Hans." She looked from one to the other. "Are you sure you're both okay?"

"Good!" Hans smiled.

"It was scary at first, but worth it!"

"What do you mean, 'worth it'?" Rheada asked.

"He went down to look for more rock art." Kee's voice came from right beside her.

From the corner of her eye, Rheada could see his glistening black hair. She could feel the vapors of his wetness mingling with her own—a cold wetness evaporating in the sun's warmth. An urgency gripped her to bridge the distance expanding between them. But how? If only she had told Kee earlier how she felt and not surprised him. If she had been honest. But then, honesty had not exactly been her strong suit.

"And that's not all!" Mack's excitement was palpable. "I found these." With a rip, he pulled back the velcro flap on his pants pocket, and brought out four small shell beads. The white conch had been hand-ground to circles and hand-drilled with holes . . . just like the shell beads of the necklace Tilly had once given Rheada.

With her finger, Rheada turned a bead over in Mack's palm. Her hand remembered the feel of the beads between her fingers. Her skin remembered their rough texture against her neck. Sensations flooded her with a bittersweet ache.

"They're old, right?"

Rheada pulled her gaze to Mack. He was staring at her—more precisely, at her throat. Rheada realized her hand was at her neck. Casually, she lowered it to her side. "Yes, Mack, they're old. They were ornamentation for an Anasazi. Probably part of a necklace."

"I knew it!"

"Mack, you can't keep them. They don't belong to you."

He gave her a stunned look. "They don't belong to *anybody* now. I leave them there, someone else will take them, or they'll get lost in a flood. There used to be more beads, right? Most have already been lost."

"And so another young person gets seduced by the lure of the Anasazi."

Rheada jerked her head to Kee. What was it in his voice, in his eyes, that sent a chill through her?

She faced Mack. "The other beads aren't lost, Mack. They're out here somewhere. They're still part of the land their owner called home."

Carlos, Mack's dad, and Stephen reached them. Mack's dad laid his arm on his son's shoulder. "What do you think about those beads, Rheada? How old do you think they are?"

"About a thousand years."

"Amazing, isn't it? Quite a souvenir there, son."

"I was just telling Mack that he should let me put them back."

For a second no one spoke. They looked between her and the beads. Mack's father had the look of a man who couldn't believe she was making such a huge deal out of such tiny things. Rheada didn't care. She *did*, however, care what Mack thought. Here was a young boy, probably tasting his first adventure. What would be the lesson she sent him home with? That it was okay to take what he wanted, no matter how small?

She edged closer to him. "Mack," she said quietly, only to him. "It would be stealing. It's as simple as that."

She saw Mack's dad pull him close. "He didn't *steal* them. He found them. In fact, he could be *saving* them from thieves."

Rheada couldn't help a chuckle. "That was exactly the rationale museums used to loot."

"So now you're calling museums thieves?"

Rheada leveled her gaze on him. "They certainly started out that way. *They* were the first vandals, digging through sites to haul off whatever they could find. The first pot thieves were *hired* by museums. The museums *created* pot thieves."

"That was a hundred years ago. Besides, who appointed you the guardian?"

"I did," Rheada answered quietly.

Mack's dad made a noise of disbelief.

Carlos pushed forward. "So you don't condone *any* kind of digging for relics? No matter the reason?"

"No matter by who?" Kee's voice was as cold and rough as the wet clothes now dragging on Rheada. And his question weighed just as heavily.

She wanted to shed them, lose the weight of them, be warm again. She wanted to walk away from the pointed questions and from her own irreconcilable answers.

She thought of her own life. She had known only one way to provide for herself and Tilly. She hadn't had a choice, but that hadn't made it right. She had known that then, just as certainly as she knew it now. The truth was, though, she would do it all over again.

Which only went to prove she might *never* atone for 'her sins.

Her stomach clenched, fighting against the words she had to say. "No, it doesn't matter." Her gaze went from Mack to Kee. She *needed* to tell him a truth from her heart. "It's still stealing. No matter what the reason or by who."

He stared back, his brow furrowed, his keen black eyes studying her.

Rheada knew what she was doing. She was damning herself. If the day ever came that Kee discovered the life she had led, he would have her *own* words to throw in her face. Yet, she couldn't lie and she wouldn't look away from him. She *needed* him to remember that she hadn't looked away.

Right before her eyes, his gaze changed. Confusion clouded the keen directness she knew. His mouth opened, as if to say something. Abruptly, he looked away—but not before Rheada caught a glimpse of defenselessness, a spark of awareness that had matched her own for him. The look, so small, was so powerful—Rheada could have grabbed him, right there, in front of everyone, and kissed him again.

The kindling of hope she nurtured resparked within her.

Maybe, just maybe, she really *could* navigate her life toward a new beginning.

She smiled at Mack. "So what do you say, Mack?"

He turned his hand over and let the beads drop into her palm. Rheada went back to where she and Kee had climbed out. She eased herself over the edge and down, using the ancient handholds. At the lizards, she pulled out her knife and dug into the cliff wall at an angle, catching pieces of the rock face in her other hand. She made a hole tucked down and out of sight, and placed the beads back into the earth. Here they could rest until the end of time.

Rheada's hand stopped. She stared at the spot where she had buried the beads and thought of the thousands of relics she and Tilly had found, and the thousands their father had sold, and the hundreds she had sold in order to survive. How many *beads* would she need to return, how many pieces of pottery before she could bury her own past?

For a moment, she was overwhelmed with futility and—worse—with hopelessness. She was just one person in a huge, nearly unfathomable landscape, replacing relics one by one by one. Meanwhile, thieves looted and sold artifacts by the truckload . . . thieves like her sister.

There had been a time when Tilly had helped return relics. Together, they had hidden ancient pieces safely in the cave. Rheada thought of the most sacred piece of all. Deep in the Grand Rincons, resting in a dark chamber, was the mask of Poseyemu. It was a piece any pot thief would literally risk his life for. But only Rheada and Tilly knew where it was.

Rheada's heart gave a small leap. She wouldn't, Rheada told herself—Tilly wouldn't sell the mask. She and Tilly were the guardians. They had made a vow.

But then it wouldn't be the first promise Tilly had broken. Could Tilly decide the treasures were hers, just as she had decided that, with Rheada gone, the name Raven was now Tilly's?

"You okay down there?"

Rheada jerked her head to Kee's voice. She couldn't see him. She could only hear him and he sounded so far away.

"Fine. I'm fine," she managed. She jammed the remaining big chunks of rock into the hole.

She climbed up and he was there, just as he had been before, with his outstretched arm, offering her his bandaged hand. As he lifted her from the gorge—making her heart pump at the easy, weightless moment—Rheada decided she would take another trip to the canyons. This time, though, she wouldn't be looking for Tilly. She would check their cave, make sure everything was there.

Kee settled her on the ground. Rheada kept hold of his hand and turned it over. "How does it feel?"

"Fine."

That's all. Just "fine." Rheada smiled. "How about we change the bandage?" She headed toward the bus.

The sun shone on the side of her face. Heat emanated from the baking slickrock. Here, on warm, high ground, there wasn't a trace of the distant storm or the flash flood.

One could almost imagine none of it had ever happened.

It occurred to Rheada that she could do the same with the relics she and Tilly had collected. She could haul them off, make them disappear forever, seal off that part of her life.

"Does your opinion of stealing extend to Pueblo Indians?"

Rheada started at the question. Carlos was right at her side, appearing from nowhere, dogged as usual.

Rheada sighed. "They can't steal something that already belongs to them, Carlos."

"And what if they were selling what they dug from sites?"

"That's a weird question. I don't know any Pueblo pot thieves."

"So you *do* know pot thieves?"

Rheada wished she'd kept her mouth shut. Out of the corner of her eye, she could see Kee. His strong presence shored her. "Anyone who lives or works in the wilderness long enough stumbles across desecrated sites, and sometimes across the vandals."

"I see." He was scribbling in his notebook again.

Rheada quickened her steps to the bus, but Carlos kept pace with her. "Would any of these criminals be willing to talk with me?"

Rheada laughed out loud before she could stop herself.

"Well, could you find one of them and ask?" Carlos asked.

"Carlos, they're criminals. They don't usually schedule interviews with reporters."

"I could make it worth their time."

A swift, cold chill flooded Rheada.

Oh, God, what have I walked into? What does Carlos really want?

A hand on her arm brought her to a stop. Carlos's eyes were hard and fast on her. "You have a profound respect for these artifacts. Don't you want to stop these thieves?"

Kee stopped alongside her. Rheada had the near overwhelming urge to slip her hand within his. Instead, she jammed them into her pockets.

"If that's your intent, Carlos, why in the world would any of them speak to you?"

"They don't have to know that."

Rheada started walking again, shaking her head with disbelief.

"They would know, Carlos," Kee said. "They may be criminals, but they're not stupid."

Rheada smiled inwardly at Kee's assessment. Then she realized she was taking his comment as a personal compliment. Except he wasn't complimenting her. He was warning Carlos off the criminals . . . just as he would warn Carlos off her, if he knew.

A shudder rippled through her and dissolved the smile.

"Just answer me this, Rheada," Carlos called after her. "If there *were* an illegal pot dealer among the Pueblo Indians, wouldn't they want to know? Wouldn't *you* want to know? Wouldn't you want the chance to expose him? Make him pay for his crimes?"

Rheada stopped and faced Carlos. "If a Pueblo Indian is stealing and profiting from his ancestors, he has more to worry about than me or anyone else finding out."

Carlos blinked. Behind him, Kee stared at her, looking equally puzzled.

"What could be worse than being caught for betraying your own people and thrown in jail?" Carlos countered.

"How about what he's doing to his own soul?"

Though behind Carlos, Kee filled Rheada's frame, his dark eyes set on her. She swore she saw him wince.

"He could worry about that while he rots in a cell," Carlos muttered. "I don't give a damn about his soul."

"If a pot digger were Pueblo, Carlos, he's already in trouble with his own people—the Anasazi. And their punishment is worse than anything this world could exact." Rheada paused, then added quietly, "It's worse for *anyone* who dares the wrath of the Anasazi."

He took a step closer to her. "How great would be the wrath of the Anasazi if a thief stole the mask of the first Kachina?"

Rheada stared at him, unable to speak.

"You do know about this mask, don't you?" His eyes narrowed on her.

"I—" She swallowed, trying to ease the press of her heart at her throat. "There are stories," she finally managed. "Who knows what is true?"

Rheada pulled her gaze from Carlos and started to walk. It took every bit of control she had not to run. If she were still living in the canyons, she would be fleeing over rocks, leaving not a trace.

Tonight, after she returned the group home, she *would* run, but not to escape. She would run back to her canyons, to the cave.

The ride back to Aztec was quiet. Mack and Hans were sullen. They had wanted to continue the trip, including rafting on the lake. But the Kleigels were adamant about getting their son checked at a hospital, and Rheada had agreed. After packing up the campground, everyone had loaded onto the bus, except Carlos, who had long before slid into his rental car and driven out of sight.

No one spoke as Kee navigated the bus over the slickrock, then onto the dirt road. Even Raven sat quietly in her seat, without offering her usual animated travelogue. She had changed into shorts and a T-shirt, and pulled her long hair back into a braid, but the fresh, dry clothes and combed hair only accentuated the battering she had suffered in the canyon. Besides the cuts on her forehead and above her lip, Kee could also see bruises and cuts on her arms and shins. If she weren't Raven, he could feel sorry for her, for what she had just been through. She looked so tired . . . and vulnerable.

Not for the first time, Kee gripped the steering wheel with both hands, to keep himself from slamming a fist into the dash. The sharp, physical pain at his knuckle sent a satisfying rush of anger through him.

Damn his own wandering mind!

She *was* Raven, and didn't have a vulnerable bone in her body. He had never met someone so strong and fearless ... the way she had hung from that ladder and yanked Mack and Hans from the raging water. That had been an amazing act of courage. He could barely believe what he had witnessed. And he still couldn't answer why ... why someone with the heart of a criminal would take such a chance.

She had to, he told himself. Raven would know that incompetence was not suffered lightly in the wilderness: She couldn't have a death on her trip. If that had happened, the locals of Aztec would never recommend her. She would be put out of business. She would lose the perfect cover for her criminal life.

Unbidden, his mind replayed what she had said. *It's stealing. No matter the reason or by who.* Just before she uttered the words, he had seen fear in her eyes. Then she had looked at him, into his eyes, and a measure of strength had filled her gaze. *It's stealing.* She had admitted *to* him, as if determined he should hear this from her lips.

It was the same look she had given him last night at the campfire when he had asked her to tell a story. He had hoped to put her on the spot. Instead, she had smiled at him with confidence, willing to share because *he* had asked. She would do it *for him,* the look said.

He gripped the wheel against the new onslaught of tension. He was imagining it all, he told himself. Whatever was in her eyes, he was imagining. Or she was pretending. It was all the same—a role for her to play.

Except that didn't explain what she had said to Carlos.

It's worse for anyone who dares the wrath of the Anasazi.

The next moment she had pulled her gaze away, but not before Kee had seen a glistening in her eyes—the spark of truth hitting its mark. She was stating a fact. He knew it as he stared at her, every one of his instincts honed on her. Which meant that if she believed her own words, she was damned for what she had done ...

... or she had not done anything, and everything she appeared to be—a dedicated tour guide, devoted to the Anasazi—was true.

A pulse beat violently at his temple. She wasn't dedicated to anything but herself! What the hell was wrong with him?

But he knew the answer, because the image he had fought with every fiber inside now consumed him.

He saw her as she reached a hand to him in the canyon, her eyes wide with fear—for him. He could see the fierceness on her face as she fought to save his life.

She had risked her life to save him!

Kee remembered his rush of adrenaline, the surge of relief when he felt the grasp of her hand, and the flood of gratitude— all in the moment just before she lowered her lips to his. Her gaze had filled his sight; her eyes looking into his, deep into him, connecting—*goddamnmit!*—with something he couldn't name, didn't want to name!

A cord deep within him wound tight and drew tense the muscles in his gut and down his legs, forcing an ache that had no source, but spread, like a need he couldn't satisfy.

His knuckles blanched at the wheel.

How dare she kiss him! Was she stupid? Did she think he liked her?

Of course she thought he liked her. He had tried to portray just that. And he was now in exactly the position he had wanted: to have her confidence. So this was good.

Then why did he feel so damned confused?

"Are you okay?"

Kee jerked his head to her. He wanted to tell her to go to hell, but his insides leaped at her wide-eyed concern. His pulse jumped to his throat, and for a moment he couldn't speak.

He flexed his hand, hunting the pain, seeking the satisfying anger. Instead, his skin remembered the gentle coolness of her touch with the salve. His body remembered hers pressed against him in the canyon. His lips remembered . . .

And he knew he would be going to hell right along with her.

He positioned himself in the back corner of the bar and watched the door. This would be a place Kee Blackburn would visit. In fact, this chair was probably the one he chose—in the shadows, facing the front. The damn murderer would feel safe here—a nondescript little bar, hundreds of miles from where he had played his last role.

A racking, sickly cough rent the air. He let the cough consume him, run its course of poison through his veins. He welcomed the shooting pain in his chest. He indulged the terror, his body's battle to live. It reminded him of the night he had had only dirt to breathe. It reminded him of clawing his way out, fighting for air. It reminded him he was alive.

It reminded him of the man he would kill.

The coughs subsided in raspy wheezes. His chest ached. His heart raced. His mouth tasted the rotten pieces of his insides. His head was light, drained of oxygen for his dying lungs . . . but then, he had already died once. He didn't fear that anymore. Maybe he should thank Blackburn for the new perspective on life.

The thought produced a chuckle and another round of coughs. He threw back a gulp of the scotch. The raw sting ate through the cough.

First, he had to find the son of a bitch. All he'd gotten out of the snitch was that Blackburn hung out near Aztec. He hadn't even known what Blackburn's cover was. That twitchy informant had deserved to die for stupidity alone.

He downed another drink, and savored the pain as the liquor burned a path to his stomach. It didn't matter. He knew Orin hung here. There was another twitchy sorry ass, but he just might know something. He would also know where to find Crow.

There would be a nice little party with Crow and Blackburn—before he killed them both.

A mean pain shot to his head. He pressed the heel of his hand to his temple. With each throb, Blackburn's image pulsed in his head—as if tied to the beat of his own damn heart. He smiled to think he held Blackburn's life in his hands.

Chapter 13

KEE parked in the breezeway of the emergency entrance, and helped Raven shepherd the Kleigels, Mack, and his dad inside the hospital. Mack and Hans were still objecting to any exam, and both continued to share the excitement of their adventure with each other and with Raven. She gave hugs to the boys and reminded the parents to stop into the tour office before they left town. The next thing Kee knew, Raven was heading for the driver's side of the bus.

He started after her. "You're not going to drive."

"I'll take Marjorie and Stephen back to their car," she said over her shoulder. "It's only a few blocks."

He followed her around the bus. For the first time, Kee noticed a nasty bruise on the inside of her left leg and a gash on her upper right arm. She hadn't once mentioned her wounds.

Without a thought, Kee grabbed her arm. "You need to get looked at."

She looked at him, startled, as if he had suggested something she would never have considered in a million years.

"That cut." Kee nodded to her arm.

She stepped down from the running board of the bus and gave a cursory glance to her arm, then smiled at him. "This is nothing. I've had worse."

For a second, Kee stared dumbfounded. He knew enough about wounds to recognize one that would require stitches. In fact, of everyone in the group, she was in the worst shape. Yet she wasn't interested in any medical help.

Suddenly, Kee realized she *wouldn't* ever think to seek any treatment. He wondered how many times she had been injured in the canyons and had had to treat herself. Probably many.

Just as the thought settled, annoyance that he should even care swept through Kee. Simultaneously, he felt a gentle touch to his forehead.

"You need to get *this* looked at, Kee."

Raven's finger glided close to his temple.

Something jolted through Kee, splintering the annoyance to a thousand ragged pieces.

He couldn't breathe. He couldn't think. For an instant, he couldn't even react. Then he swiped her hand away. "No."

His voice was strained, foreign. And he knew his answer didn't make any sense.

He maneuvered around Raven and slid into the driver's seat. "I'll take Marjorie and Stephen," he said. He wanted to slam the door shut, but Raven stood in the way.

"All right," she said. "But don't bother with emptying the bus. We can do that tomorrow. Just go on home, okay? I'll call a taxi from here. And Kee, I . . ." She paused.

He had to look at her. Her gaze was on him with that same wide-eyed deer look, like some lost wild creature grateful to come across him.

"Just thanks," she finished, with a slight tilt of her head.

Kee's head nodded, an involuntary motion, as if he were tethered to her by an invisible thread. The annoyance thundered through him. He reached for the door handle. Raven stepped aside and he yanked it closed.

He turned the key, gave a glance behind him for other cars, then to the side to be sure she was out of the way. She was gone, disappeared, once again startling Kee with how fast she moved.

Goddamnit, she's good.

"She's right, you know."

Kee jerked a glance to the mirror and found Marjorie smiling at him.

"You should get yourself looked at, too, Kee," she added.

Of course. She and Stephen had overheard the conversation. Which meant they had also witnessed his reaction. He didn't like the glint in Marjorie's eyes.

Kee deliberately changed the subject. "Are you both heading right back to New York?"

"No," Stephen said. "We still have a day here since the trip ended early."

"Right." Kee glanced into the mirror and offered a sad smile. "Probably not what you expected," he added, allowing just a hint of disappointment into his voice.

"We had no idea!"

With satisfaction, Kee pointed out, "I'm sure you will get some refund."

A grand laugh brought Kee's gaze back to the mirror. Marjorie was beaming at him. "We don't want our money back. We had the best time!"

"Oh. Good."

"We'll be telling all our friends. Rheada deserves more business than she can handle."

"I'm sure she would be glad to know that," Kee forced out.

Marjorie laughed again. "Then again, maybe we'll be selfish and keep her our little secret."

Kee couldn't believe what he was hearing.

"I bet you agree."

It took Kee a second to realize Marjorie was talking to him. He looked in the mirror and found her smiling at him, a twinkle in her eye. She actually thought he liked Rheada! The notion rocketed through him on a blast of anger. He wanted to yell at Marjorie that she had been duped by the master imposter. Rheada was not what she seemed: She was not a wonderful, selfless tour guide devoted to the outdoors. Regardless of the fact that she had saved Mack's life, Hans's life, risked her own life to save Kee . . .

He pulled out of the hospital drive a bit too fast, bumping onto the cross road, and just missed a passing car. Kee imagined Marjorie and Stephen staring at him, wondering what the hell had gotten into him. He took a deep breath and forced his foot to lighten on the pedal. No one spoke for the rest of the drive to the tour office.

Kee pulled into the lot and parked. "We're here."

Neither Marjorie nor Stephen responded. Kee glanced to the back. He could see Marjorie and Stephen cuddled, Stephen's arm wound close over her shoulder. The late afternoon light was soft on them, but still provided no privacy. They didn't seem to care.

Their foreheads touched in relaxed intimacy, with no shyness, no apologies, no boundaries. Kee was aware he was staring, but neither of them moved to leave. Their quiet contentment warmed the van. Stephen brushed a kiss to Marjorie's forehead, so casually it was profound—the small gesture of a deep love.

For an instant, Kee thought he could feel a warmth inside.

His mind drifted to the meadow, the hot springs, Rheada's singsong voice telling stories. He could feel the sun on his body. An immense exhaustion spread through him, weighing on his eyes, his body. God, when had he become so tired?

"Tell Rheada thank you."

Marjorie's voice came from right behind him. Her hand squeezed his shoulder. The comforting, motherly gesture was too foreign to Kee—and so unnecessary.

"I'll tell her," he said, and moved to open his door, but Marjorie held firm.

"And thank you, too, Kee. You know, I would love to see one of your maps. I bet they're so carefully drawn, no one would get lost."

Lost was exactly how he felt right now. And what in the world did he say to this nice woman who believed his lies?

"Thanks." He shifted and looked past Marjorie to Stephen. "We enjoyed having both of you on the tour and we hope you come back." Kee heard himself say "we" as easily as if he truly were speaking for himself and Rheada. Just another lie, he thought. What did it matter?

"Oh, we'll be back." Marjorie's gaze settled on him. "And we expect to see both Rheada *and* you." She leaned close and whispered, "That gal deserves a good man at her side." She winked. With a chuckle, she turned to Stephen and stepped from the bus. He heard their pleasant murmurs until they closed their car doors. The sound of the car engine filled the twilight, then they were gone.

He wondered at his lack of annoyance with Marjorie for assuming so much. It was one thing for her to believe that he liked Rheada. It was the role he had played . . . evidently well enough for Marjorie to presume even more about his feelings for Rheada.

His mind stopped on the word. Just when had he begun to think of Raven as Rheada?

He gave a quick shake to his head. He was tired. His thoughts were muddled, that's all, and all of Marjorie's sentimental talk about Rheada had only played into his hazy state. The old woman was a romantic. Not what he would have expected for a lawyer, Kee thought. If he hadn't known Marjorie's occupation, he never would have guessed. The same could be said for Rheada, Kee admitted to himself. She was *definitely* not what he had expected.

He had pictured her so differently: rough, even crass, a female version of Crow, who shunned the daylight and could never get the dirt from under his fingernails. He had expected cunning, not thoughtful; mercenary, not charitable; hard-edged, not engaging.

He had not expected beautiful . . .

. . . or vulnerable . . .

. . . and he had not expected the betrayal of his own thoughts.

Kee opened the door for air, to escape. He had spent too much damn time close to her. That was it. She had gotten under his skin, just like the dirt under Crow's nails—there for good, no way to get clean, because Crow *was* dirt. He *liked* dirt.

Kee's heart jumped as if touched by a frightening truth: Did he *like* Rheada? Did his black heart now rule his mind, damning him to be drawn to the very person he hated?

No. It wasn't possible. He didn't give a shit about Rheada. *Raven*, damnit!

He slammed the bus door and strode to his Jeep. He climbed in, turned the key, and in rapid motion backed up, then pulled out of the lot. He sped through Aztec, intending to drive to his cabin. Ten minutes later, he found himself on the highway heading east. He saw the dirt road ahead and he turned, knowing now he was going to Largo Canyon, to the sites, to his sensors.

The Jeep bounced over the ruts, jogging him loose from his thoughts, from all his emotions. As the sunlight waned, the *real* Kee that he knew returned—the one used to the cold and dark . . . the one who deserved no more than that.

He drove straight into the canyon, not caring if anyone heard the Jeep rumble. He had no reason to be careful. She was back in Aztec, pretending to give a damn about two kids.

He wanted to grab her, make her tell the truth. He would look her in the eyes . . . those wide amber eyes . . .

His thoughts slammed against his conscience. Kee jumped from the Jeep, nearly before he had it to a stop.

Damn her! I can't wait for the moment to take Rheada down.

His gut tightened around the need. His whole body tensed with an indescribable ache. His ears thundered with the sound of his heart racing. He thought his head would explode from the pressure.

His steps ate the ground to the first site. What he saw brought him to a staggering halt: The burial mound lay open and empty. Piles of dirt surrounded the pit; shovelfuls dug and thrown haphazardly, probably in haste, definitely with no care or intention to replace. It was a hit-and-run, an amateur grab-and-go—not the work of a professional, like Raven. Not that he had even considered Raven: He had checked the sites right before they left on the trip and he'd been with her every moment since. That he had another pot thief on his hands also came as no surprise. The Southwest was crawling with them. He just wished this particular thief had picked another site to loot. This canyon would be dead for Raven now.

Kee skirted the site to retrieve his sensors and camera. He pulled the flashlight from his pocket and scanned the ground where he knew he had set the sensors. The beam spread across barren sand. Kee swiveled, searching the area. He couldn't even find the hole for the rod with all the site disruption.

He shone the light in the opposite direction where he had placed another sensor. It was there, but the sensor head had been smashed flat as if struck dead-on by a hammer. An array of dents on the extender bore evidence to the effort to knock the rod from the ground in the same way as the other sensor. Finally frustrated, the looter had simply leveled a blow. Kee walked to where he had hidden the camera, sure he would also find it destroyed. He found the casing in pieces, literally ripped apart at the seams. The camera wasn't there. He eventually spotted what was left of it lying at the base of the cliff. Six hundred dollars of equipment was trashed.

A professional would have dismantled everything, hauled it off, and had his own high-tech site protection. All he would need was the remote, which any electronic junkie could create. Kee choked down a laugh at the enormous stupidity of the thief.

He glanced over to the petroglyph Rheada had explained.

The man, woman, and child guardians of the mound stared back, helpless.

He started for the cliff dwelling in no great hurry, already sure he would find only more wreckage. Kee shook his head. This amateur son of a bitch had gone crazy. The idiot was probably lucky to have even stumbled across the sensors in the first place.

Kee stopped. His mind flashed to the sensors he had planted deeper in the canyon—not by any site, but at a narrowing of the cliff walls. He had set that camera on the chance Raven would trip it first and he would catch her red-handed at a site. He realized now, after witnessing Rheada scale the canyon walls in Arizona, just how pitiful that plan had been—Raven would no more use a path than would her namesake. But he would wager a bet with that camera and sensors that this moron had strolled right down the path.

Kee followed the dry wash back into the canyon. He could hear the caws of ravens from the mesa top above, talking to each other as they would from some high vantage point at the end of the day. He had heard the ritual a thousand times, for a thousand nights, no matter what isolated, pitiful corner of the Southwest he was in—there they were, too, surveying the terrain.

At times, when he had crouched for hours in a cave, his muscles screaming for relief, he had thought of the ravens, ever vigilant. They were harbingers of the night, drawing forth the darkness—the cloaked-in-black territorial spies, calling out warnings of intruders. He could recruit them, outfit them with tiny spy cameras.

Undercover ravens, lurking in the night, cunning and sleek.

His mind flashed to Rheada, her keen eyes on him. His heart jumped. His gut seared with a caustic, irredeemable pain. He tried to force her image from his head, but she stayed there, staring, her eyes wide now, as she reached out to him, risking her life . . . to save him. A need drove straight through him, pulling him tight.

Kee stopped, impaled on his thoughts, *damned* by his thoughts! His gaze jerked to the ground. He couldn't see two steps in front of himself. A crazy laugh escaped from his lips.

He *was* damned. And he was losing his mind.

He jerked the flashlight ahead. It took him two beats to

realize he was only a few steps away from the sensors. He pushed through thick stands of tamarisk and Russian olive trees that fought for hold on the wettest ground at the head of the canyon. The beam found clear ground, the level path that ancient Anasazi had surely used to climb down into the canyon from their swallows' nests above. A half-dozen more strides, and he reached the jagged outcropping of cliff wall that had been his landmark for the sensors. He scanned down the wall, toward ground level, and there, the reflecting shine of the metal rod greeted him.

He scanned the ground again for the rod, found it, and bent to check for damage. There wasn't any. He directed the beam toward the other rod. It too was just as he had left it. He could hope the same for the camera.

He walked several yards down the path to a cluster of juniper trees, and crouched at the base of the nearest one to the path. His hand skimmed the ground and touched metal. It was the camera, intact, though that still didn't guarantee he had caught anything on film.

Caw!

His pulse jumped. He yanked the light up. Glossy black feathers winked from the branch of a juniper. For a second, Kee thought he might even recognize this one as the same raven that had pranced along the mound and pestered him in the cliff dwelling. It was a goddamn conspiracy of ravens! Maybe it was Raven herself, watching his every move.

Another laugh, crazier than before, pushed up from Kee's chest and out his mouth. The raven blinked, but didn't move. Kee bent back to the camera, but had the unsettling sense his every move was watched.

With sure fingers, he unscrewed the casing of the camera from its mounting and pulled it from out of the shadows. With a glance at the cassette inside, he could see the tape had advanced. He just might have caught this stupid thief in action. Kee settled against the cliff wall, pushed the rewind button, then balanced the camera on his shoulder for the show.

A second of static signaled that the sensors had tripped on the camera. The picture cleared and Kee was staring at a black-and-white image of the path. A shadow moved in from the right and a coyote slinked into the frame. It nosed the

ground, then trotted off the path toward the arroyo. The tape
went to static.

Damn it.

Kee's finger hit the off button, and he lowered the camera.
A check on the tape, though, confirmed it hadn't advanced far
enough. There was still more to see. He turned it back on, the
static cleared, and the black-and-white still of the path again
filled the viewer.

This time, a beam of light preceded the form. The light
caught the camera and both Kee and the camera's eye blinked,
adjusting to the sudden brightness. The shadow following the
light was a man—a small man with a shovel in his hand. Kee's
eyes narrowed on the criminal, looking for anything familiar.

The man took a couple steps, then stopped. He looked over
his shoulder. Then he took another few steps, stopped, and
looked behind again.

"Yeah, you're being watched," Kee muttered.

The man stood there as if making a decision.

"But you just can't resist, can—"

Kee's question hung unfinished, for just then someone else
entered the picture. He first saw slender legs rounding the
corner. The legs stretched to slim hips and a trim waist. It was
a woman, and she advanced on the man, grabbing the light,
and shutting it off. A second later, the camera readjusted to
the darkness. The two stood there, obviously arguing. She still
had the flashlight in her hand, but then she reached behind her
and pulled forward her backpack.

Kee knew that backpack. He stared, not believing what he
was seeing. They were still too far away for Kee to see faces,
plus the woman was slightly behind the man. Then she
stepped from behind, rounded the man and strode forward.

Kee knew that easy stride. He watched lithe, graceful steps
that seemed to glide over the ground, straight for him. His
breath caught in his throat. His mind raced to rationalize the
impossible. It couldn't be Rheada. He had been with her. How
could she have possibly traveled to this canyon and back to
the campsite at Lake Powell? She couldn't. Yet, here she was,
on tape. In black-and-white. Irrefutable proof. Just as irrefutable as the other tape Kee had of her at the cliff-dwelling
site.

Indisputable . . . and impossible.

The image went static. The next moment, a clear picture of the path appeared. Kee saw her. She was walking back up the path. The man was obviously ahead, for he had again tripped the sensors. The pack hung low and full off her shoulder, and bumped against her small hip.

She disappeared. The picture ended. He turned off the camera and lowered it to his lap. Kee stared into the blackness, his mind hunting answers.

He didn't know who the man could be. In fact, he had never heard of Raven working with anybody, but then, everything he knew about her was hearsay, rumors, legends, some of it questionable, certainly exaggerated. Anyway, it was more logical that she would work *with* someone, than by herself.

Logic be damned! None of this made any sense.

Kee stood and paced. He stopped at one of the sensors and kicked it, intending to loosen it. His kicks came harder and faster.

This couldn't be Raven!

He had Raven already. He knew Rheada was Raven. His instincts weren't wrong.

He called up the memory of the other tape of Raven. He could see her every movement as if he were viewing the video; and she matched perfectly the person here. They were the same.

Except they couldn't be the same!

He strode to the camera, bent, and tried to yank the rod from the ground. It wouldn't budge. He had rammed it in, he could get it out, he told himself, but the rod didn't move. His hands slipped, unable to get a grip, unable to master the very thing he had devised.

Kee's temples throbbed unmercifully. His gut clenched. His whole body went weak. He could only crouch there. He stared at the ground. He could see every mundane, minute detail. Tiny crystals were laid over by small bits of white, then larger pieces of red, then slivers of green, and short rods of brown. He widened his perspective and the colors became sand, covered by pebbles, then rock fallen from the cliff wall, then juniper needles, and small branches.

Kee sat back.

The tape of Raven at the cliff replayed in his head. He remembered the moment she had paused on the ledge of the ruin. It was the moment he had gotten a full view of her face. He saw her eyes, narrowed, as if speculating on her next move, maybe considering just what she would do with whatever she had stolen. He realized that at no time in the past ten days had he seen Rheada look calculating or devious.

But I wouldn't! She's Raven, the imposter. The master of deceit!

The pounding at his temples doubled, tripled. Kee felt as if he were battling for every thought . . . and losing ground.

He saw the dreamy love in her eyes as she had woven her stories, enchanting the listeners. He saw her wide-eyed gaze at the campfire—the wild, yet curious creature. He saw the desperate flare in her eyes when she saw him careening on the water. And he saw the passionate haze in her eyes when she had kissed him.

He had wanted to kiss her back. He had *needed* to pull her tight against him and press his mouth hard on hers.

His body tightened with that need he had not wanted to name, but couldn't ignore. He sat back on his heels, the truth dawning on him—the truth nearly every bit of him had known—his mind, his instincts, his body—but a truth his heart had fought because he had *needed* to make Rheada *Raven*. He had needed to end the quest.

But she wasn't Raven. He grabbed the camera from the ground. This, he thought, holding the camera with its tape, this was Raven. He had just spent ten days focusing all his hatred on Rheada.

Kee walked out of the canyon. He walked the same ground as when he had first set the sensors, still tracking Raven, not knowing her as Rheada. He passed below the cliff dwelling where he had caught Raven on tape. His heart jumped with the memory of his certainty that she was Rheada. But with each step, his thoughts continued back on a time continuum: in that same dwelling, Rheada had demanded he leave, her gaze determined and protective. He walked past the bulge in the canyon wall where she had talked to the group, spiriting them away from the present into the past with just her heartfelt words. He retraced the steps he had taken with her, before he knew her as Raven, and he drank in the memories. Every one built on the one before, creating and re-creating, rebuilding the person he knew as Rheada.

She was the only child of a prospector, raised alone in the canyons, with no education. Yet she was wise. And she was fearless. She had bravely sought the world, though it must be so foreign to what she knew. But she couldn't have stayed in the canyons. She was too full of life. She was destined to be a part of this world.

He couldn't help but compare himself to her—leaving home, striking out on his own, determined to have his own life. There was a lot he knew about Rheada because he recognized it in himself. He realized that there was a lot more that he *wanted* to learn about her.

His chest tightened with excitement. He was anxious with an immediate need that claimed every fiber.

He wanted her.

The thought flashed through him with hot urgency and quickened his steps to the Jeep. His heart had fought this need from the moment he had first seen her in the bar. He had encased his heart in hatred, but now . . . maybe with her . . . He had seen the want in her eyes, too. She had gazed at him, unmasking her own vulnerability, not hiding her desire. She had seen *something* in him, something that attracted her, some-*one* she had wanted to share herself with. With Kee.

Chapter 14

A full yellow moon hung over Fremont Ridge, the eastern side of Dead Horse Canyon and Rheada's landmark for her descent into the Grand Rincons. She didn't want to go back to the canyons. She didn't want to go back to where she had lived. She didn't want to walk that ground, stir those memories loose beneath her feet, but she had to. She had to retrieve everything she and Tilly had collected and hidden. She should never have left the treasures alone in the cave in the first place. She should never have left the mask.

Of course, she hadn't thought she would have to worry about Tilly and her intentions. She had believed—because Tilly told her so—that they had the same goal and dream: to leave the canyons, leave the past behind, and lead legitimate lives.

But Tilly had never meant to leave. Rheada saw that now. She had seen the change in Tilly as far back as when their father died. It had broken Rheada's heart that Tilly had found their father. No child should be the one to stumble on that. And it had changed Tilly. There had been a haunted look in Tilly's eyes that scared Rheada.

Rheada talked even more frequently about leaving the canyons, and Tilly nodded—but Rheada could see that her heart wasn't in it. The once playful, spontaneous child turned serious . . . and then took on their father's quest for the mask. When they found it, Rheada thought her sister would finally be released from whatever spell she had been under.

But now Rheada wondered whether the spell of the mask could *ever* be broken. She thought of her father's warnings: that the mask had been the harbinger of doom for the Chacoans. A shudder traversed her spine at the thought of all her family had endured. And a very big part of her blamed the damn mask!

Even now, as she struggled to make a normal life, with no more skulking in the dark, no more fear, no more deceit . . .

here she was again, slipping into the night. Because of the mask.

No matter what she did, she couldn't seem to shake the hold of the past. If only she hadn't found that Aztecan ruin, because everything seemed to have gone wrong from there.

Everything, except for Kee.

Her mind filled with the moment in the canyon with Kee, when she pulled him from the flood, held him safe against the cliff wall. Then, she had felt *good*. Her heart beating furiously against him had made her feel alive, filled with purpose—as if she had been born for that moment, destined to be there for him. For that one instant, she had been at the right place, the *center* place, as a Puebloan would say. And she had been worthy.

There was no way she could have kept her lips from his. The kiss was her seal, her mark of life—her handprint on the canyon wall signifying emergence.

Only she hadn't known what the kiss would do *to* her. She had tasted the promise of more—more than *just* life. She had felt her own urgent rush mingling with his, the electric jolt of connecting to another living force.

She had never felt such joy. No discovery of any Anasazi relic had produced such a rush of elation. Not even when she and Tilly had found the mask, she realized.

She also realized that she had been moving toward that moment of connection from the first time she had laid eyes on Kee in the bar. She pictured him again, a dark figure in the shadows. She would have been repelled . . . if not for his eyes. They stared with unblinking conviction. They held fast with unflinching character. They gleamed with purpose. And she could have sworn she saw a flash of need in Kee's eyes.

His eyes hid secrets, but they couldn't mask his integrity. She had wanted no more, right then, than to have those eyes gaze on her and reflect those same qualities. She wanted him to *see* her.

Her breath caught as if faced with a sudden threat . . . and she knew what that threat was. Just as certainly as a deer *knew* when he faced a hunter that his life was at risk, yet he couldn't move. He stared, eyes wide, his swift hooves impaled on the spot, because *this* predator was different from the rest, and he couldn't run.

A thousand needles of adrenaline skittered across Rheada. From this predator, Rheada couldn't run. Kee was foreboding. His mere presence warned of a risk. Yet she could not stop staring; and she could not . . . stop . . . wanting . . . his eyes on her.

She wanted more than for him to see her. She wanted Kee to believe her worthy. She wanted him to *know* her.

The need rose from her heart. Heat rode on her veins and arteries, pulsing through every part of her, rising to her skin, through her pores, dissolving the icy pricks of fear. It was like sunshine in the dead of night, bathing her in warmth.

This was what she had left the canyon for. This was what her heart yearned for—not just the goal of a decent life, but the *love* of someone for *her,* for Rheada, the good and the bad.

Her mind stumbled, swerved away from that thought. She couldn't let Kee know about the bad. She could *never* let him learn of her past. But if she succeeded tonight, this would be the last secret she would have to keep.

Her heart clutched at the thought and she focused on her mission. She was already deep into the wilderness. Her thoughts of Kee had bridged the distance, shortened the road, brought her closer to her destination. She wished she could tell him that. But, of course, that was impossible.

She drove toward the moon on a nonexistent road, her body remembering the terrain, her mind slipping into role with each primitive mile that only one at home with the night and the moon could travel. She would let the role consume her, this one more time, in order to keep her promise and retrieve the precious treasures she had vowed to protect.

The night and the moon obliged, providing cloudless, bright light deep into the wild canyons. Rheada navigated the labyrinth, taking one turn, then another, and another, homing in on one cave among the tens of thousands. Seen from above, she would look like a mouse in a maze.

The notion provoked a crazy bubble of laughter. She *was* in a maze, but she now saw a way out. That way was not only in keeping her vow to the Anasazi: Her way out was finding love, finding someone who loved *her*.

It was possible, she told herself, hope building on every word. She was a person of honor, of integrity. She had made a promise and was keeping it. She would bring the treasures home with her, including the mask. They would be safe. Her past would be behind her and the future ahead.

She might even get Tilly back. When her sister found the relics gone, she would come to Rheada, and Rheada would never let her go.

Rheada pulled into a nondescript side canyon. At the entrance, the opposing cliffs were more like small hills, their sandstone walls a crumbling slope of talus debris. Heavy erosion like this had occurred over hundreds and hundreds of years. Even an amateur Anasazi aficionado would know at a glance that this canyon held no promise: There wouldn't be any slick walls with Anasazi art, let alone any sturdy limestone caves for an Anasazi family to call home.

Rheada herself had made the same assumption and had, at first, ignored Blackjack's calls to follow him into the canyon. But Blackjack made ignoring him impossible—in fact, painful. She winced at the memory of the searing pain at her scalp where Blackjack had grabbed hair and tugged, his wings flapping powerfully, as if he would drag her into the canyon.

She had followed him, her impatience growing with each step into the unremarkable canyon. When she came to the dead end of the box canyon, and Blackjack was nowhere in sight, Rheada had known she'd been had by the wily bird . . . until his cawing had drawn her gaze up the wall and Blackjack appeared, as if emerging from solid rock.

He had appeared, in truth, from a hole in the rock face, though she only discovered that by climbing after him—in response to his incessant squawks.

She stood below that hole now. She craned her neck to stare high up the cliff, though she could see the hole no better today than the dozens of times she had been here before.

Her heart, though, knew the spot: there, to the right of a deep crevice that cut the cliff wall in a perfect vertical gouge from the mesa above straight down to the ground. Within the crevice was an ancient staircase—steep, narrow blocks of stone carved right out of the cliff. The work was painstaking and perfect—too perfect. The steps looked almost pristine, as if they had never been used. Yet they were the obvious way to ascend, and exactly what she had attempted her first time here.

Blackjack had gone completely nuts. He had swooped down on her with a screech and hovered right in her face so that she had to back away. Eventually, she had found hand- and toeholds farther down the cliff.

With a glance now to the much easier steps, Rheada continued on to the carved-rock grips and started the precarious climb up the sheer cliff. This way was much harder and senseless, given the proximity of the steps, but Rheada never questioned the wisdom of Blackjack.

She pulled herself up, scaling the rock face, her pack hanging limp and nearly empty against her back. The holds had been carved to take the climber in a gentle curve toward the shadows. Gradually, the outline of the hole became clear. For all her trips here, at different times of the day throughout the year, she had never seen the hole in sunlight. After what she had found inside, she was sure that the eternal darkness was the reason for the Anasazi to have picked the spot. She had known too that this was the place to hide the most special of the relics.

She could see the rim of the hole now. She half expected to see Blackjack on his perch and to hear him urging her onward. She wished he *were* here. He would approve of her plan, she knew it.

She gripped the edge of the hole and pulled herself into the tunnel. The passage curved downward—a tube carved of solid rock leading deep into the cliff. She always felt as if she were crawling into something intimate and sacred, like the legendary *sipapu* opening through which the ancestors of the Pueblo Indians—the Anasazi—had emerged into this world. Rheada knew the Anasazi could not have carved this tunnel. The earth had given birth to this channel, a secret passage that led to the recesses of the mesa. Perhaps this *was* the *sipapu*. In the darkness, hugged close by the inside of the mesa, Rheada could believe it was true.

In the darkness, her thoughts slipped back to her father's stories. Her surroundings forgotten, Rheada was at the campfire listening to her father as he spoke of the origin of the Kachinas. He sat across the fire, his hand holding an ancient staff out to his side. The fire glowed eerily in his eyes, and Rheada could imagine him as the high priest of Chaco, leaning upon his staff of power, as he related the event that had spelled doom for the great Chacoan civilization.

Tilly knew the story. She had been there. Rheada could feel her presence now, sitting alongside her, hanging on their father's every word. She had glanced at her sister and seen the image of the staff and the reflection of the flames dancing around in Tilly's eyes. Her heart ached with a loneliness like she had never known.

As she neared where the tunnel ended at the innermost chamber, Rheada thought of each piece that she and Tilly had squirreled away. Eagerness skittered down her spine to again see these most special relics, to remember each moment with her sister. She would first find the necklace Blackjack had given her, and slip it around her neck—just for while she was here, Rheada promised.

The tunnel dipped, the walls receded, and Rheada knew she had reached the end. She slid from the passage to a sitting position and pulled the flashlight from her pack.

She flicked it on and gasped. The chamber was empty, completely and totally empty.

Rheada couldn't believe it. Everything was gone: the black-on-white pots, the thick mugs, the rare cylinder vessels. All the relics she and Tilly had found and hidden from their father, saving them from being sold, had now met that very fate. How could Tilly have done it?

She swept the light back and forth across the ground, her mind and heart refusing to believe what her eyes saw. She walked around the small room, hoping from the bottom of her heart that Tilly had left the mask. She wouldn't take the mask. It had been the only piece here when Blackjack first showed Rheada the hidden chamber. This was the mask's home. The mask belonged here! It wasn't for Tilly to take and sell! She had promised Rheada, on the very night they had learned what their father did. Now Tilly would betray her?

Rheada's heart pounded against her rib cage. Shudders grew inside her to quakes, as powerful as if the ground beneath her were rumbling and sending tremors through the soles of her feet, up her legs, through her body, and centering on her stomach, twisting and churning.

Rheada fell to her knees, the flashlight forgotten in her lax fingers.

My sister would betray me.

The thought lasered to her heart and wound tight in a grip of searing pain that doubled her over, forced an agonized moan deep from her soul. The moan surrounded her, echoed back across time, reaching for her sister, for the love Rheada had believed in. She rocked forward and back, her arms wrapped around her middle, squeezing her chest, desperate to calm her aching heart—more desperate to feel again Tilly's embrace.

Rheada didn't know how long she sat there, swaying, the tears flowing. She became aware of cold arms, numbed legs, sore chest muscles racked from sobs. Slowly, her thoughts coalesced to a safe place, a step back from the abyss. Her heart searched for solid ground.

Tilly had taken her own path, Rheada told herself, stiffening her back. Tilly had her own life now. Apart from Rheada.

A sob caught in her throat. The need to have Tilly back, to have everything as it was, threatened to overwhelm Rheada again. She straightened, trying to force the need deep inside.

Rheada rubbed her arms forcefully against a growing chill. An emotion clutched at her, driving the sob higher. It was fear. Fear that she really would be alone now.

"Tilly can go her own way!" Her words echoed in the chamber—a chamber emptied by Tilly, and the despair grew within Rheada. She had taken everything, not to keep safe as they had promised each other, but to sell. Tilly wasn't just going her own way, she was a constant reminder to Rheada of the sins they had committed . . . and the sins Tilly would still commit.

Emotions flooded Rheada. Wave after wave assaulted her—anger, fear, grief—until finally, with a near mortal blow, guilt. She should be there with Tilly. None of this would have happened if Rheada hadn't left. She should have stayed, taken care of her sister.

Except the only way to care for her would have been to continue with their crimes. Her stomach clenched violently. She *couldn't* have stayed! She would rather have died!

"Am I to take care of my sister?" she yelled out, frantic for an answer. "Or am I the guardian of my promise?"

The anger within her won against the grief, pulling her from the ground, railing against everything unjust.

"Can I ever be just a person? Someone worthy of a good life? Will I ever escape?"

Fear sluiced through her on open veins . . . fear that she couldn't make this life work, that she would never escape the horrible life she had led.

"Will I ever have my own life?"

Her pleas echoed, resounding through her on shock waves that plumbed to the core of her fear: What was her own life?

Rheada stood there in suffocating silence, the question pounding at her temples until the answer slipped from her lips.

"I don't know who I am anymore."

Uncertainty trembled through her. She stumbled. She shot her hand out for balance. Her fingers grazed the inner wall and she grabbed and clung. It was rock-solid—like the cliff face in the canyon, like the steely hold of Kee's arm helping her from the canyon. Her body remembered the feeling of his arm against her back. Her fingers remembered their desperate hold on the climb . . .

Her hands remembered reaching for Kee, pulling him from the water, close to her, pressing him to the canyon wall. And her *heart* remembered Kee's unflinching gaze. He was looking at *her*. Just before she lowered her lips to his—he was staring straight at her, confusion flaring with need in his eyes. She wondered now why he had looked confused.

Maybe she had looked confused and *he* was wondering why. Laughter—effervescent, translucent—cascaded from her mouth. She *was* confused. But not when she was with Kee. She remembered feeling strong and purposeful. Had it come from him?

She knew the answer. Her mind was already leading her out of the cave, pulling her through the tunnel, out of the dark recesses. To Kee.

The need to see him simmered low in Rheada—a slow burn, hot embers, that Rheada didn't want to extinguish. She walked back to her Jeep—barely needing the flashlight for guidance—and she drove out of the canyons, with Kee's keen, unwavering gaze drawing her. She drove, seeing him in her mind's eye as clear as if he were an image just beyond the windshield, keeping pace ahead as she navigated the back roads as fast as she could. For the first time in her life, Rheada wanted speed. She wanted to eat the ground, consume the

miles, devour the distance between her and Kee. She needed
to see him now. She needed him to look at *her*. She needed
to see herself in his eyes.

Rheada saw the first sparse lights of Aztec in the distance. She
was almost there. Her pulse jumped so suddenly, she pressed
a hand to her chest. Her insides were jumpy, excited. At the
same time, sharp pricks, like needles at her neck, were a warning.

She had had the same sensation the first time she had entered Aztec after leaving Tilly. She had driven through town,
hoping she looked as if she belonged; scared to death and
hungry for life, all at the same time.

It was the sense of nearing a place of great risk . . . but even
greater reward.

Her lips spread into a smile.

Then it dawned on her that she had no idea where to find
Kee.

She knew he lived in a cabin, but where? She drove aim-
lessly around Aztec, down countless dirt roads to dead ends
and back again. She didn't know what she could be hoping
for: that he would be standing in front of his cabin, waiting
for her?

She racked her brain for an idea and remembered the bar.
Of course! Max might know! She could hardly get back to
town fast enough.

The edge of town was always dark, but she didn't remember it as this dark. She also wondered at the total lack of
traffic. She pulled in front of the bar, stopped, and jumped
out. A part of her registered that she had parked on the wrong
side of the street, facing oncoming traffic, but she didn't care:
She was staring at a dark, locked bar. Did bars close?

Rheada stood there, unmoving. She didn't have another
plan. She hadn't planned any further than to find Kee.

It occurred to her suddenly, as if delivered on the breath
of a sadistic god, that she hadn't planned any further when
she dreamed of leaving the canyon. Yes, she had thought of
the tour company. She had saved money. She had bought
newspapers when they were in towns and read the advertise-
ments of other guides. She had dreamed of a different tour
that would take people into the past.

She thought she had planned, but she knew she hadn't. Just like now, she had set off, convinced that determination, drive and desire were enough. She was like a child wanting something, no matter that it was out of reach.

Rheada walked back to her Jeep, turned it on. The rumble was out of place on the dark, lonely street. Drops of rain hit the windshield, startling Rheada, then brought a sarcastic laugh from her as the rain increased to huge splotches, then to a shower, then to a downpour, as if the sky had opened up right over Rheada and delivered an unexpected, unseasonal rain.

She drove home, her hands steering, her mind empty, her gaze bleary through the watery glass. The uncertainty, the fear she had felt in the cave crept over her again. She had so little energy to fight them.

She rounded the corner to her street, and saw the street lamp in front of her home, her business. The lamp's light—refracted by the Jeep's headlights and the rain—formed bands of concentric circles. It was an illusion: Light wasn't constrained to defined circles. Yet, it was real. She was sitting right there in her Jeep and seeing it, while everyone else had their eyes closed.

She pulled into her lot, parked in front of her home, and smiled. She *had* gotten this far, even without much of a plan.

She stepped from her Jeep into the pouring rain. It soaked her hair, ran down her neck, under her collar, trickled down her back. She raised her face and let the water splash. It was cold, yet electrifying, evoking shivers of life. She laughed out loud.

That's when she heard the door slam.

She jerked her gaze to across the street. A man was approaching. Her mind caught, but her instincts took in his particular gait, the way one hip swung out when he walked. She knew that stride.

Rheada's heart caught on the sight of Kee walking purposefully straight for her. She met him halfway, her gaze on him. His hair hung long and wet behind his shoulders. In the glow of the street lamp, his eyes glistened.

She didn't know what she would say. She didn't even know if she could speak. She couldn't take her gaze from his face, from his eyes.

She saw him raise his hand. He swept a wet strand of her hair behind her ear. The touch of his finger at her temple sent shock waves through her. She could feel her heart thumping in her chest. She could be running through the canyon, for the way her heart raced. Instead, she was standing still, merely looking into Kee's eyes.

She laid her hand along his jaw, drew him closer. Kee's eyes flared, as if a flame burned within him. He lowered his head. Their lips met. Cool, smooth, wetness.

The embers in Rheada burst to life.

Chapter 15

KEE stared into eyes that wanted him. Her hand pressed his head down. Her lips sought his. Her mouth opened, wanting more of him, and Kee felt a rumble quake through him.

This was why he was here.

When he had left the canyon, sure that Rheada wasn't Raven, he had driven straight here, pulled to her. He had been powerless *not* to come here, as powerless as he had been the first time he met her in the bar and couldn't take his gaze from her. She had made him look, made him wonder. And every day since, the wonder of her had only increased, *despite* his belief that she was Raven.

He had thought himself damned. Only the most loathsome excuse for a human being could be attracted to the source of his hatred. Hatred had eaten him from the inside—hatred for *her*. She was a witch, a sorceress, who had cursed him, enchanted him, *claimed his soul,* and condemned him to a living hell.

But this was not hell. *This was life.*

His arm slid around her back, holding her tight, holding *himself* upright, taut, against her. Urgent throbs pulsed through him. His fingers drove through wet hair to the back of her head, pulling her closer still.

Shock waves of desire jolted through Kee. His arms stiffened, every muscle pulled tight. Rain cascaded over them, sliding down his face, her face. Sheets of water slickened them, surrounded them, covered them as intimately as if they were in bed.

Kee's blood raced at the thought. That's exactly where he wanted to take her.

He pulled back to look in her eyes and found Rheada gazing at him. Rain slid down her forehead, dripped from her brows. Wet, black tendrils of hair clung to her jaw. She looked just like she had in the canyon right after pulling him from the deadly water . . . right before she had kissed him.

His gaze went to her lips, swollen from his kisses, slightly parted. Her tongue licked rain from her top lip. Kee bent to those lips. He wrapped his arms tighter around Rheada, pressing her to the ache growing in his body. He angled his mouth, wanting more of her.

He felt a touch at the juncture of their lips. He thought it might be the rain, so gentle was the sensation, but the touch curved *up* across the arc of his lip, then down again to where they joined. It was her finger, exploring, tracing their lips, as she opened her mouth wider to him, offering her breath, and Kee took it, with no power to stop for the life of him.

He felt pressure at his chest. For a second, he thought it might be his heart, it was pounding so hard. The pressure stayed, increased. She pulled her head back from him. The withdrawal brought his ache to a hard throb. He looked down at Rheada, trying to focus.

"We can go inside," she whispered. Amber eyes, golden in the streetlight and full of passion, looked back at him.

Desire surged through Kee. He didn't need a bed. He didn't need to lie down. They had the rain.

Kee reined himself in, laid an arm across her shoulder and turned her toward the front door. Her arm wrapped around his hip and she walked with him, matching his strides. At the door, she turned the knob, and pushed through.

Rheada's hand slipped within his, drawing him inside. Kee brushed his other hand behind him, closing the door. A part of him registered, again, that she hadn't locked the door and also how easily the door slid open—the rain should have made it tight—but the thought was lost as Rheada turned, pinning him against the door, just as she had pinned him against the canyon wall, placing herself between him and the raging flood.

She would save my life.

The thought pounded through him and Kee held fast, wanting to believe. His pulse leaped. His hands sought her, framed her face, pulled her to him. She rose up his body, dragging across his legs. Her hips met his.

Kee's blood surged. He felt himself swell against his jeans, pushing toward her. Her body stiffened, her arms tightened across his back, pulling him close with an urgency that matched his own.

Her arms bent up his back, her fingers tugged at the back of his jacket collar, as if she would peel it right off him. The wet denim clung to his shirt. She swung her arms to the front. Her fingers moved down the buttons, loosening them. The next moment, warmth splayed across his chest. His heart thumped, drawn to her touch.

She slid her hands up his chest, over his muscles, then his nipples. Kee gasped. Passion drew him tight as if her fingers pulled on a cord straight to his groin. His tongue sought hers, tangling, dancing. Her fingers circled on his chest, dragging across his skin, drawing a moan from inside him.

Suddenly, his clothes were too heavy, too constricting. He slid a hand to his buckle, began to unfasten it, when he felt her fingers trailing across his, finding the keeper. She slid the leather out. Kee laid his fingers between hers, felt her maneuver the button from its hole. Their hands went together to the zipper, pulling it down, releasing him, where he swelled impossibly more against her warm palm.

Kee drew a sharp breath for control. He dragged his mouth across her cheek to her ear. "Rheada," he whispered.

She arced to him, pressing her ear to his lips, as if she craved his breath. She wanted him—this woman of the sunlight—she wanted *him*.

The notion weakened Kee to his knees.

She pulled her mouth from his, weakening him more with the absence. She slid lips down his neck, his chest. Her breasts caressed him as she moved. Her fingers trailed to his back and stopped at his hips. He felt a tug as she pulled his shirt free. Warm hands glided up his back. Her fingers played across his bare skin, sending tingles down his spine, bringing every nerve in him alive.

Then her hands slid over his back to his sides, toward his chest, and the tingles turned to a rush of anticipation as fingertips climbed. Her thumb found his nipple. Her hands circled, slightly trembling.

Each fluttering motion brought every one of his senses alive—more alive than he had ever felt. If she continued, he wouldn't make it past this door. If she stopped, he might just die right here, right now.

A small moan escaped him. "Rheada." Her name was dragged from deep inside him, as if it had been there forever, buried deep within, waiting for him to bring the word, her name, to life.

God. I want her.

As if reading his mind, Rheada slid her hands up his belly, to his shirt, to the collar of his jacket, and she pulled him with her to the floor.

Warm air brushed his chest. It was the breath from her mouth. Silken coolness followed—her thick hair trailing over his skin. Lips touched his skin, fingertips kneaded his back. She was taking possession of him and Kee could barely breathe.

He didn't remember when he had been wanted like this, touched like this. A part of him—the lonely part, used to being alone—tried to pull back, fearful of being drawn out of the shadows. It might be lonely and cold there in the darkness, but it was safe. Better to not want more. Better to accept his fate.

That dispassionate, judgmental voice nearly had him, when Rheada's mouth found his lips and the damning voice scuttled away, no match for the light she promised or the hope she kindled in him. She breathed air into him. The heat in his belly fanned to flames, melting the coldness he was used to. Tingles of new life spread through him, up his back, down his arms.

She would save my life.

The thought repeated, a whisper of truth that rode his blood, pulsed through his veins, and provoked a shudder of need from deep at his core. He breathed Rheada's name on a ragged, desperate sigh into her ear and followed her down to lie on the floor.

All of Rheada caught on the sound of her name, on the passion in his voice. Her eyes fluttered open to find him looking down at her, his gaze keen and sure—on her. Her heart stilled. She didn't want to breathe. She didn't want this moment to end. She wanted that gaze on her forever, seeing *her*.

His hand slid from around her waist to her chest and his finger traced the undercurve of her breast. Rheada drew a breath, staring at him. Kee stared back at her, unblinking, his gaze full of passion, as his fingers gently circled, ever closer.

Her eyelids slipped closed. She felt his lips on hers, pressing her mouth open. His tongue slipped inside as his hand closed around her breast. His fingers circled, dragging the wet shirt across her nipple. Shards of desire spiked through her.

She arched, drawn to him, craving his touch. Another sound pushed from her throat and filled their mouths, rolling between their tongues.

Her hands went, without volition, to her shirt. Her fingers stumbled over the buttons. Kee's hand lit on hers, warm, strong, sure. He slipped the buttons free, peeled the clothes off. She arched to undo her bra. His hand slid behind her back; their fingers entwined, freeing the strap together, and the next moment, she lay bare before Kee.

He bent and kissed her lips gently. She didn't want gentle. She wanted his hands on her, his mouth hard on hers. Instead, he lifted and moved down, trailing kisses down to the vee at her neck, trailing his damp hair over sensitive skin, evoking trembles of desire throughout her. His hand cupped her breast, kneading as he kissed, producing an aching need that pulsed deep within her—a demanding need that his every touch only escalated.

She reached for him, drove fingers through his hair, not to pull him away, but to do more, something else, something to answer the craving that grew and grew.

She felt his hand at her jeans, cupping her between her legs, massaging her.

Yes! There!

His lips closed around her nipple, his tongue circling, drawing on her as his hand pressed and moved between her legs. Urgent sensations burst through her, drawing a cord tight within her. Though his every movement came closer to this *need* that now thumped hard within her, it was not enough.

Her hand slid to her jeans, where her fingers unsnapped the button, pulled on the zipper. He raised his head from her chest. His gazed flared, unblinking, and Rheada's heart skipped, but her fingers didn't falter. She drew strength from the look in his eyes, the honest *want* in his eyes. She pushed at the waistband, wanting no material, no barriers. She felt a tug. He pulled on the denim, freeing her.

He bent back on his elbow and gazed down at her, taking all of her in. His sultry gaze slid from her eyes to her lips to her body, now fully exposed. His gaze enveloped her, warmed her. When he pulled his gaze back to her face, his eyes so sultry and consuming and *strong,* the heat from his eyes spread straight through her.

He slid a hand up her leg, slowly, over her knee, up her thigh. Muscles clenched, pulsing within her, aching for that very hand. She pulled his head to hers, his mouth to hers. She *needed* his touch, if only his lips, his tongue.

His hand stopped between her legs. His palm cupped her. He moved, circling, kneading in a rhythm that matched the hard throb inside her.

Rheada gasped. She was at the cusp of something, a precipice she couldn't see, but knew was there. *There.* But, oh God, even this wasn't enough.

She arched, her body pleading for more. Kee's finger slipped inside.

Her breath broke. All thought fractured. She heard herself moan, *felt* the moan be pulled from her depths. Her body moved on its own, in a rhythm she had never known, yet it was there, organic, awakened by Kee.

Right now, she wanted nothing more than to feel all of him.

Her hands pushed at the top of his jeans, dragging them inch by aggravating inch over his hips. Her fingers sought flesh, found the band of cotton and she slipped beneath, flesh on flesh, her hand trembling slightly against him.

Kee shuddered, a trembling quake that matched her own. She ran the backs of her fingers down and up. She felt his stomach clench against the back of her hand. Her fingers touched wisps of hair she knew would be black as night.

He pulled in a deep breath. His body stilled.

Rheada paused. She realized that her hand held him, her thumb rested on the tip of Kee. She could feel his pulse at her finger, his lifeblood throbbing against her. Her finger traced the ridge of him that seemed to grow right beneath her touch.

Kee released a deep moan into her ear. He slid to her chest. His lips encircled her nipple. His finger worked inside her.

Blood surged through Rheada. Her heart beat at her breasts and at the spot where Kee's finger probed. The pulses were rapid, urgent, driving to a pinnacle. She slipped the cotton band down over Kee, releasing him into her palm.

Kee's groan reverberated through her.

Suddenly, he stopped. Rheada's eyes opened to see him working free of his jeans. Then he reached behind him. She couldn't see what he held, or what his hands were doing. The next moment, he leaned over her, his eyes on hers. She felt his hand at her head, lifting her to him. She rose, seeking his mouth, his lips again on hers. Instead, he slipped something behind her head, then lowered her gently. She found a soft bundle beneath her, as if Kee had pillowed her shirt.

Why? she thought. But she didn't have time to ask. His lips met hers, his tongue slid over hers. With his arms wrapped around her, he angled himself between her legs. His hips moved, and she felt him against her where his palm had kneaded, where his finger had probed. The pulse within her jumped, seeking *more*.

Suddenly, her mind stilled, caught on one thought.

Should I tell him this is my first?

Rheada looked up at a gaze that made her heart vault, leap *to* him. His eyes, always keen and narrowed, were even more so, with fierce lines of focus right on her. He wanted her. This man who seemed to always be looking into the distance toward a purpose, had found a purpose right here, with her. Emotions pushed at the base of her throat—emotions without words.

He held her gaze as he slid within her slowly, stretching her, pushing higher. Her thoughts fled. Her eyes closed. Every pulse in her body merged into one aching, relentless, overpowering throb just beyond where he reached, *begging* him to reach there.

Her hands skimmed his sides to his back. She could feel his control in the steely muscles ridging his spine. Let go, she wanted to say. *Give me all of you.*

She dragged her hands to his waist, to his hips, pressing, pushing, *willing* him deeper.

He pushed higher. But it was still not enough—it was as if there were a barrier. Instincts lifted her hips, angling herself higher, wider, bringing him deeper.

A sharp, tearing pain seared through her, catching at her throat, wresting her breath. Splinters of light rent the blackness. It was like *feeling* a shooting star break across the night sky just for her.

The pain dissolved to wonder, like a shower of stars raining down upon her. She felt joy beyond what she could ever possibly describe. Was this what making love was about?

Kee had stopped. She opened her eyes, wanting to see the reflection of the wonder in Kee's eyes. Instead, he was staring back with alarm. She could feel his pulse within her, but his face was tight with control. Something was wrong.

"Kee—" she whispered, her voice breathless, slightly trembly.

His brow pinched. "Rheada—"

Her name came out choked as if he were in pain. Anxiety raced through her, tripping her heart. She laid her hand on his jaw. "Kee, what's wrong?"

"Are you all right?"

"Am I—" The question startled her. "I thought you were hurt."

"Not me. You. I hurt you."

She felt him tense within her and start to withdraw. Her anxiety for him rocketed. "No. I mean, just for a second. I saw stars," she added, hoping to share her wonder with him.

"Stars. You saw stars." Concern deepened his gaze.

"A shower of them." At the memory, her skin tingled. She felt her lips curve to a smile.

He didn't smile. He stared back, the concern still there, but something else sparked in his eyes, as if he were seeing something new and unexpected in her. His eyes glistened—a light flickering far back in the depths of their blackness. It struck her that she had brought something to life in Kee, something vulnerable. She was *responsible* for that light.

She ran her hands up into his hair, resting her thumbs at his temples, and stared into his eyes—that gaze that had been dark, fathomless, opaque as a mask, protecting him. But now they glimmered . . . because of her.

"Don't stop," she whispered.

His gaze flared. He lowered his mouth to her neck, then he kissed her ear, capturing the fleshy lobe between his lips. He trailed his tongue along the ridges of her ear. His tongue slid within at the same moment he pushed deep between her legs, and Rheada's mind was lost on the sensations exploding through her. Her muscles clenched, pulling him deep inside to know every part of her . . . every part of her.

He drove in deep, measured thrusts that forced her breath from her lungs. The world spun—a spiral of ever-heightening peaks, where she would climb and climb, air knotted at her throat, sure that the pinnacle was *there,* only to find another slope, another ascent, another pinnacle just beyond reach.

She wouldn't make it. She thought she couldn't stand another climb, only to find herself—again!—rising, driving herself higher.

This time, the stars exploded. There was no gentle shower. It was a burst of light, an electrifying bolt that rent her body, drawing her to one last tightness, before escaping on a small, unheard-before sound.

Her heart thudded in her chest, racing ahead of her breath. Gradually, her pulse slowed. Blood drained from where it had surged, leaving her light-headed, light-limbed, yet more full of *life* than she had ever felt. A last shudder resonated through Kee, through her. She wrapped her arms across Kee's back, wanting to lie like this forever.

Kee didn't want to move. He wasn't sure he *could* move. Never before had he felt so spent. It wasn't just the sex. It wasn't just that he fit her perfectly, that her body felt *made* for his. Though, at the thought, he could feel himself throb inside her. His heart beat at his ribs. He had to take a deep, controlling breath.

No, it wasn't just the sex.

He was drained, emotionally, as never before. And it had happened when he learned she was a virgin. But it wasn't the knowledge that he was the first that had slammed into him, immediately stopping him. It was that she had *never had another.*

He had seen her as wild, free. She had been raised in canyons, unfettered, uninhibited. It was as if he had been holding one last assumption about her, one final dark judgment from when he thought she was Raven: that she possessed a witchly power.

Instead, she was truly an innocent. The realization had cracked the last of his defenses. Such a small thing: sex with Rheada, except she had shattered his *own* barrier that he had so carefully constructed . . . and Kee didn't know how to pick up the pieces.

The thought produced a streak of anxiety across his chest, as if gentle hands with profound strength had reached his heart. His heart jumped, provoking another throb where he still joined her—as if his body couldn't separate his mind from his heart and would take her, again, now . . . ignoring the danger he risked.

He *was* in danger—of losing himself in her, of losing himself in hope. As if there *were* any hope for someone like him. As if she could possibly want to still be with him if she ever learned what he was capable of.

God. What had he done?

He felt her hands trail up his back to his head. Fingers tangled in his hair. She kissed him on the cheek.

She was an innocent. And he was the devil.

Emotions knotted at his throat, stung at the back of his eyes.

She shifted, seeking his mouth. Kee was powerless to withstand, incapable of saving himself, protecting her. He took the kiss, slid his tongue between her lips, and caught her gasp in his mouth. Her air flowed into him, warming him, breathing into him as if he really *could* be saved.

Her kisses pulled him from his thoughts to her, to only her, and, once again, he pounded with life.

God help him, at this moment, he wanted to hope.

Kee lay with his arm around Rheada. He had awakened this way, with her tucked at his side, her black hair fanned across his chest, weightless yet comforting, like cool, black silk. His finger trailed up and down her slender arm, an easy motion that matched his languid mood. He didn't know how long he had lain here since waking, and he didn't care except to hope that he could lie here, like this, for a lot longer.

Lips brushed his chest and Kee looked down to see Rheada placing another kiss. "Good morning."

She laid her cheek against him and sighed. "Yes, it is," she said.

Her breath caressed his skin. The easy intimacy enveloped Kee. He could spend a day just like this. "Should we be worried about a tour group showing up?"

"Not today. There's one tomorrow, though."

"Maybe I can move by then."

She chuckled and the sound resonated fully through him, finding no barriers. "Or we can just give them one of your maps and send them on their way."

His maps. His lie. He'd forgotten.

Kee felt the mattress move. Rheada rose up on her elbow and looked at him. "I would love to see one of your maps."

He looked into eyes that trusted him. For the past night and this morning with her, he had forgotten what she believed him to be. "I don't have any of the finished maps." It was a lie, but could it also be a first step toward the truth?

"Oh." She looked truly disappointed.

"Someone else actually makes them, Rheada." The wedge of truth was getting wider.

She considered him, her head tilted. She smiled. "They should at least give you free ones for all your work."

She slid back to his side. "Tell me of some of the wonderful places you've seen."

He hadn't seen any wonderful places. He hadn't seen any place he would ever want to be in again. Except here. His heart lurched at his chest. "There's nothing to tell. Just back roads, hard terrain, lonely canyons."

"I love the canyons," she murmured into his side. "The hidden places nobody knows about. To stand in a box canyon, in the middle of a labyrinth of canyons, and to know that I'm one of a few, maybe the only one, who knows of this place, it makes me feel, I don't know, small."

Kee laughed aloud. "Small?" Kee thought she was heading toward a sense of wonder.

She angled her head to gaze at him and the wonder he had imagined was there on her face. "Yeah, small," she said.

Kee stared, intrigued.

"I would lie on the canyon floor at night and stare up at towering cliffs. I thought they looked like overprotective parents, standing over me, keeping me from the world. I couldn't wait to get out."

She was staring past him, into the distance, back to the canyons.

"And so they made you feel small," Kee said.

"No. Yes." She yanked her gaze to Kee. "I mean, that was one part of it, but now it's different. I feel small in a *good* way."

Kee must have looked confused. Rheada focused right on him. "While I'm here, those cliffs are still there watching. The canyons are still digging deeper, without any preplanned purpose. Rivers are cutting wider, finding their own meandering course. There aren't straight lines. They know the meaning of patience, of trying a different route. Really, they *are* like every parent should be: sturdy, patient . . . honest."

Her voice trailed off on the last word. A sheen misted her eyes. He watched her defeat the rising emotion. She gave Kee a quick smile.

"In all that great space," she said, "the land knows there is room for mistakes. That's the *good* part of being small."

The mist in her eyes cleared, revealing a light as if cast by a flame deep within her—a flame that burned inside her with conviction. It was a belief that kept her going, more than would mere hope.

Rheada didn't just *hope* for something. She put all of herself behind it and went for broke, even if that meant making mistakes, because ultimately, what she hadn't said—but what Kee could see deep in her gaze—was that she believed in forgiveness.

Would she believe in forgiveness for him, too?

His heart thumped at his ribs. He felt her hand, warm, alive, press at his chest, right over his heart, as if drawn to exactly where he needed her. Cool hair swept across his skin, bringing tingles of life to him. Kee reached within her cool hair and brought her close. "I *like* that meaning of small," he murmured into her mouth.

He breathed deeply of her, slanted his lips to hers. The urgency of wanting her pounded through him again. This time, it was more than wanting her; he wanted what was within her, he wanted to believe as strongly as she did. He wanted to take deep breaths and not fear the cold ache in his gut.

He wanted his quest in the darkness to end.

Once he learned the truth about Sarah, he told himself, then maybe he really could walk away. Once he caught Raven . . .

The thought fingered into his mind, finally gripping him: He still had to catch Raven. Which meant he had to quit as driver for Rheada. Which meant he would not be spending his days with her, or even his nights.

The thought crawled through him, clenching every muscle. Kee wrapped his arms tight around Rheada and rolled her to her back, his thigh resting across her hip. He slid his leg across her, straddling her, and stared down into eyes reflecting his own passion.

For right now, he wouldn't let her go.

Chapter 16

MAX washed out a bar glass, but his mind was on the stranger. The man had resumed the same spot as yesterday—the dark corner with his back against the wall. Max didn't have to glance in the mirror to check. Sickly coughs punctuated the air, finally stopping on another gulp of scotch. Max had endured the sound for nearly twelve hours yesterday until closing time. The man hadn't moved even to go to the john. He had sat there, facing the door, in the same chair Blackburn always chose.

There was something else about the two men that Max had noticed: They both had the look of predators.

Max knew that look. He had perfected it himself for far too many years not to recognize men on the hunt. It was all in the eyes—the ability to observe without showing any intelligence, to stare without blinking, to crawl within and pull the mask over one's face.

For a moment, the present dropped away and he was in another time, another place. His heartbeat slowed, his mind quieted, his temperature even dropped a few degrees. A beat longer and he could be mistaken for a statue, his body able to keep this position for hours, and yet ready to spring with deadly precision.

His heart lurched, fighting the descent. His focus jolted from the darkness back to the inside of his bar. He stared, uncomprehending, at the glass in one hand and the rag in the other, and forced his hands into cleaning motions, until his mind could catch up. Lastly, he felt the dryness at his eyes, and he blinked.

Afterward, he was still left with the lingering hollowness from that loathsome existence. He placed the glass on the counter, picked up another, and rubbed hard, reminding himself of his new life. It had been a long climb out of that hole, a climb many others just couldn't make. It was common knowledge that if you stayed under too long, you never got out: You were either killed, turned, or you forgot there even was a world on the outside, in which case you were better off being killed. Without hope, you might as well be dead.

Max thought of Blackburn. There was a man who had been under past the limit. Of course, Max was assuming Blackburn was law, but then Max had stayed alive by knowing where a man's heart was. Max was damn sure that Blackburn was law. He was also a man too close to the edge, but not gone—yet. Max had seen the look in Blackburn's eyes when the Samuels woman walked into the bar. It was as if Kee had seen an apparition, the way he stared at her—an apparition that had brought the faint glimmer of hope to his eyes.

That was the difference between Blackburn and this man, and it was what kept Max's cautious attention on the stranger—because there wasn't even a prayer of hope in his gaze. His eyes held one purpose: murder.

The front door opened, cutting a swath of morning light across the wood floor. The coughs ceased, though Max hadn't seen the man lift the drink to his mouth. It was as if he were holding his breath. The air was charged with electricity and Max's annoyance rose. That son of a bitch was staking out *his* bar and Max wasn't happy about it. He lowered his arm, his movement casual, and touched his gun on the shelf below the bar.

The door closed and a young guy in rumpled khakis walked to the bar counter. He was Mexican and looked as if he had been in the same clothes for days. From the corner of his eye, Max saw the stranger lift the drink to his mouth, as if he were no longer interested in the new customer. Max still kept his fingertips near the barrel.

"What will it be?" he asked the Mexican.

"Corona."

Max reached for the beer in the small refrigerator, and set in down on the counter.

The man slid onto a bar stool instead of walking away to one of the tables. The way he sipped and played with the label, Max knew the guy wasn't working on any thirst, he was working on a question.

"This place looks like it's been here a while."

Max shrugged.

The Mexican gave a cursory glance to the bar, smiling as if in approval. "Nice bar." His gaze hit the corner and the stranger, and he gave a start, obviously just noticing now that they weren't alone. The Mexican's eyes came right back to Max. "How about you? You been here long?"

"It's home," Max allowed. Max went back to the glasses, waiting.

The Mexican took a sip, and gave a quick glance over his shoulder. "I bet you get all kinds here in the bar." He was leaning toward Max, as if he weren't one of the "kinds" he was talking about.

"Yeah. All kinds," Max answered. The kid was after something or, more likely, someone. He wasn't a cop. He was too young to be a detective, and way too young to be undercover. He could be a claims adjustor or a reporter. He seemed just sneaky enough, though not exactly sharp. "How about you?" Max asked, picking up another glass. "You sightseeing or just passing through?"

The guy sat back in his stool and grinned. The bright white of his teeth glared in the bar. "Actually, I'm a reporter," he said, clear as day and loud enough to carry to the farthest corner.

Max was about to chuckle out loud at his own brilliant judgment of this amateur when he noticed the slight shift in posture of the stranger. He took a gulp of beer to wash down the laugh choking his throat. "Is that right?" he managed. "And what are you reporting?"

He took a swig of his beer. "I'm researching an article for *Southwest Adventure* magazine." He swiveled on his stool toward the dark corner. "About Anasazi artifacts."

It was as if he were directing his conversation to the stranger, but they couldn't know each other. The man in the corner could chew this guy up and pick his teeth with his bones.

What the hell was this guy up to? Max shouldn't care, but he couldn't resist a puzzle. "What about the artifacts?"

"I'm more interested in the men who *deal* the artifacts." He was facing the mirror. He took another long, slow swallow.

He was talking about pot diggers. Max knew it as sure as he knew this guy's gaze was on the stranger's shadowy reflection in the mirror.

"Men who *deal* artifacts don't usually do interviews," Max

said. He was starting to feel a certain responsibility for this asshole.

"You're the second one to tell me that."

"Well, whoever the first one was, he was right."

"She." He tipped the beer to Max. "It was a *she*. Rheada Samuels."

Everyone in Aztec knew the tour guide who had discovered the ruin. Max knew more about her than anyone, and he had his suspicions about what he *didn't* know. So far, though, she was doing just what she said: building a business. "Miss Samuels knows what she's talking about."

The Mexican crossed his arms on the bar and leaned toward Max. "I think she knows *more* than what she's saying."

The bar was quiet, too damn quiet. Max realized he hadn't heard the stranger cough since this guy started talking. "That's probably true. Not many people like talking to reporters."

There was that flash of white teeth again. "Including you."

This time Max chuckled. "Don't bother me none. I'm not digging pots."

"But I bet you know people who are, yes?"

Max could feel the charge in the air coming from the corner, but this guy didn't even seem to notice.

He braced his hands on the counter and leveled a stare at the Mexican. "Listen to me, kid. There's a reason why this article has never been written. People don't *want* it written." He held the stare a beat longer, hoping to get his point across.

His best glare left the Mexican unfazed.

"That's where you're wrong," the reporter said. He threw back the last swallow and set down the empty bottle. "People are paying a lot of money to have it written. And I'm paying a lot of money for information." He stood and faced the corner for a moment before walking out.

Instincts told Max he was looking at a dead guy. Damn if that didn't bother him.

Kee sat in the cave. He was somewhere in southern Utah. He didn't know where. Right now, a part of him didn't even know why.

He had left Rheada mid-afternoon with the excuse that he had to contact the map company about his next assignment. He could still see the look on her face: first the surprise, then the dawning realization that soon he might be leaving for good, then the sadness at her eyes, just before she leaned up and brushed a kiss to his lips.

I'll be back, he had thought.

He realized that she would be without a driver for her next tour, yet she hadn't asked when, or even if, he would return. She had folded up and tucked away the sadness he had seen, if only briefly, and she had simply kissed him goodbye.

I'll be back.

He stared across the black oblivion and the words repeated inside his head with the force of a promise.

It occurred to Kee that he hadn't had the same conviction when he had left home so many years ago. Even in the face of his mother's sorrow, he hadn't even *thought* of returning. If he had returned, though, Sarah might still be alive.

He could feel the guilt gnawing at his gut. Soon, the strength of that guilt would pound through him, like a hammer on steel stakes, impaling him to the spot. It was how he endured.

Except this time it didn't happen. He hunted down the emotion, but it had dispersed, leaving instead Rheada's face, the wonder in her eyes. He would feel her lips on his, her breath in him, the promise of hope and life. He imagined her hands on him, and his heart jumped. And his body, always strong, turned weak. He wanted to be with her, to have her warmth. How in hell was he to endure this dark, cold night?

For the first time he could remember, fear fissured through Kee. He hadn't been afraid when he left home. He hadn't been afraid when he crawled underground, hunting the murderer of his sister, even *knowing* he might not survive. But at the thought of not being with Rheada, he should feel fear?

As if in answer, his chest tightened with enough force to take his breath.

How had she become so important?

Would he trade his sister for the arms of a woman who didn't even know who he was? Would he abandon his sister yet again? Had he lost all his humanity?

Rheada's face filled his mind: the wide-eyed look of a wild creature drawn to him, trusting him. Her eyes, glistening with more than passion, were on *him*.

He breathed deep, filling with the smell of night air and

pine. They were the smells Rheada had grown up with.

The land knows there is room for mistakes.

Rheada's words swirled through him. He had made plenty of mistakes. And he *was* trying to make right.

The cliffs are there watching. They know the meaning of patience, of trying a different route.

He could try a different approach. Why search canyons on the mere hope of finding Raven? Why even bide his time until Crow was ready to move again? Kee already had someone who knew all the canyons. She also knew pot diggers. He had seen the look on her face when Carlos questioned her. She had been afraid. She hadn't wanted to answer. But maybe she would for *him*?

He wouldn't have to tell her why he sought Raven. Rheada hated pot thieves. She hated what they did to the sites and the loss of the artifacts.

He recalled the boxes of carefully packed relics in her office. She might even have what he could use to bait the infamous Raven.

Kee's thoughts coalesced to a plan and pounded through him, delivering new strength. He would be using Rheada, but it was to right a wrong, a wrong that she would also abhor. Once it was over, she would understand. She would approve. And Kee could leave behind the night, once and for all.

He climbed down out of the cave.

In Aztec, the streets were quiet. Kee glanced at his watch, saw it was nearly two in the morning, but still drove straight to Rheada's place. She would be asleep, her black hair cool on her shoulders. When she came to the door, and she saw him, her smile would be dreamy in her still-sleepy eyes. He imagined the kiss, her body still warm from bed. He pulled into her drive, killing the engine with his abrupt stop as he leaped out, his body eager, already anticipating.

Several knocks on the door didn't bring her. Kee strode around the side of the building, stopping once to pick up some pebbles. He felt like a schoolboy. Hell, he felt like Romeo, calling upon his dark-haired Juliet, except, of course, there was no scheming family, no curse upon them, no tragedy to unfold.

He reached the window and realized he didn't need the stones. He could walk right up to the chest-high panes. Romance aside, it made more sense to knock. Besides, he didn't want to scare her to death. He dropped the pebbles and tapped on the glass. Nothing. More taps, and she still didn't respond. It didn't seem Rheada's nature to be a sound sleeper. Kee cupped his hand to the glass and peered inside, but all he could make out through the gauzy curtain were the shadows of the furniture. He tapped louder while watching and didn't see the slightest movement.

Kee stopped and listened. The night was still, too still—as if all noise were captured in a held-breath hush. He thought first of checking to see if Rheada's Jeep was here, but a tangled mess of juniper blocked the way to the back of the house. Kee walked back around to the front. Every step, the sense of something wrong grew in him. If Rheada wasn't here, where the hell was she?

Instead of rounding the building to the drive leading to the garage, Kee went to the front door, and turned the knob, expecting to find it unlocked as he had every time before.

The door didn't budge. A part of him was proud that she had finally learned to lock the front door. But why the hell had she chosen *now* for security? He took a step back, caught for a second by her unexpected behavior.

Kee didn't like the unexpected. He walked down the drive, the crunch of his boot heels on gravel grating against the looming silence. The sense of something wrong grew, an intangible feeling like that of knowing he was being watched. He even stopped abruptly once and turned, his eyes narrowing on the darkness.

There was no one there, of course. There was also no Jeep in the garage. She was gone. That was all he had sensed, he told himself. But as he walked back up the drive, his steps angled to the back door. Something pulled him to check inside.

He prepared himself for a locked door, and nearly fell inside when it pushed open beneath his weight.

She had locked the front and not the back?

He moved through the kitchen, down the hallway. He thought of the time she had run out the back to her Jeep. She had done the same this time, was all.

Despite the logic, Kee couldn't ignore the pricks of warning that skittered down his spine. His body was tensed for danger.

He didn't know why, and he didn't ask himself why. He had depended on his instincts too many nights to question them now.

He reached for his gun and remembered he had disarmed back in the canyon. It lay useless under the seat of his Jeep. He stopped and considered going back for the gun. Silence pressed at his back, like a palpable force pushing him forward, racheting up an inexplicable urgency inside him. He walked the hallway, barely summoning the patience to pause at her bedroom and peek inside.

She's not here.

Logic teased at him, but his instincts wouldn't listen. Rheada's name pounded in his head with each violent beat of his heart. Adrenaline swept over his skin, demanding he go faster, face the threat. He had to force his impulses to obey, take one step at a time, listen hard, control breathing. But with each step, Rheada's name rang louder in his head. Something was wrong here. Something had happened.

Kee gritted his teeth on a prayer that it hadn't happened to Rheada.

He reached the end of the hall. The door separating her home from the business stood partially ajar. Kee toed the door open. Light from the street lamp shone through the window and across the floor—the floor where they had made love just the night before. A vision replayed: her hand at his neck, her eyes on him as she pulled him down to the floor. The image filled with just her lips and the sound of a small moan.

Did he actually hear a moan?

His thoughts slammed against the present. His pulse took off and beat at his temples as he tried to make sense of what had just happened.

Had he heard a moan or just imagined it?

Kee jerked his gaze to one side and the other. He turned on the balls of his feet and faced the back corner and the storage room. He heard another moan.

Rheada! He knew it was her.

He was around the desk and at the door in the same instant that her name materialized in his head.

"Rheada?"

There was a louder moan, then, "Kee?"

His heart leaped to hear the pain in her voice, but he

couldn't see her. He took a step inside and his boot hit something. He remembered the boxes stacked everywhere. Kee stopped. He didn't want to knock any down on her. "Don't move, Rheada."

He stepped out, ran his hands along the wall, and found the light switch. He strode back to the closet, but came to a halt at the sight. The neat stacks were now piles of torn-open boxes, with bubble wrap, tissue, and pottery everywhere.

"Rheada!"

"Here."

Kee saw the flutter of newspaper and forced his way through the mess. Rheada pushed up from beneath some cardboard.

She's fine. She's moving. His urgent need to pull her into his arms, to see that she was all right, battled with the side of him that said move gently, easily. Kee threw debris to the side and crouched beside her shoulder.

"I'm here," he said. Kee reached an arm behind her and lifted carefully.

Her low moan of pain went straight to his gut. She grabbed his shirt and levered herself up, into his arms.

"It's okay," he whispered, running a hand down her back, soothing her, checking for wounds.

Her hand gripped the back of his jacket as if she wouldn't let go. He didn't want to let go, either. "It's okay," he repeated. "Are you hurt?"

"My head," she murmured into his shirt.

His hand went to her head. His fingers caught on stickiness at her temple. She drew in a sharp breath.

He leaned over her and saw the deep red of coagulated blood. The gash looked maybe an inch long. Kee's gut twisted fiercely. Anger leaped from that dark hole inside him—anger that turned his vision black.

For a second, he couldn't focus. He couldn't think past the emotions driving through him.

"I'll be fine. It's okay, Kee."

Her soft voice yanked him in. With all his will, Kee summoned his dispassionate side. "Let me take a look."

He sat her back a little bit. Gently, he moved aside some strands of hair. Dark, clotted blood covered her temple, but he could see the wound wasn't that deep. She'd been struck with something blunt, maybe the butt of a handgun. From the look of the wound, the blow had come from the front and above. The trauma of the blow itself must have knocked her out.

A new emotion surfaced, flooding him. It pumped through him with an urgency to pull her close, protect her. It wasn't anger. It wasn't something he had ever felt—it was more the haunted thoughts of a man realizing he'd almost lost something precious. His heart pushed at his throat.

"How bad?" Her fingers reached tentatively to her temple.

"Not so bad." His voice was choked. Kee swallowed. "Nothing a few stitches won't help."

"No—" She started to shake her head, but drew a sharp breath at the movement. "No stitches," she finished raggedly.

She would need to go to the hospital, but Kee wasn't going to argue about that now. "How about we start with getting out of this closet?" he asked.

She moved to rise, but Kee already had an arm behind her legs. He pushed up on one knee, holding her in his arms. Her gaze flew to his and he thought the independent Rheada might argue to be put down. Instead, she laid her head back against his chest. The jam of emotions at his throat threatened to break through, overwhelm him. He rose to his feet, with her barely a burden at all.

He turned her sideways, kneeing boxes out of his way. His boot crunched on pottery. He felt her grip swiftly tighten on his back, but not for support; to turn her head and look behind them. He heard her gasp, as if the sight of all the destroyed relics hurt her more than any physical pain.

Kee settled her in the overstuffed office chair and went to the bathroom to get a rag and the same salve she had used on his hand. When he got back to the office, she was still staring at the storage room door, her eyes filled with a hurt that came from deep inside.

Who the hell had done this? And why?

Kee knelt beside her and applied the warm, wet rag to her temple. "Can you tell me what happened? Who did this?"

"He—" She stopped. "I was surprised."

"It was a man?"

She closed her eyes, as if drawing up the image. She nodded slightly.

"You found him in here?"

She looked back to the storage room. "He was going through the boxes. Tearing them apart like an animal." A flash of hate streaked across her eyes.

"Did he say why? What he wanted?"

She shook her head, but Kee couldn't tell if that was in answer to his question. "He didn't have to do this. There's nothing there to sell. Nothing worth what he—" She broke off. The hatred had hardened in her eyes, hatred Kee could see as if it were tangible . . . hatred for a particular person.

Suddenly, Kee realized he hadn't asked for a description. "Did you see him, Rheada?" .

She pulled her gaze to his, a stricken look in her eyes. She had that look as if she couldn't believe this had happened. But Kee wondered whether that disbelief was because of *who* had done it.

"Rheada, did you recognize him?"

The stricken look grew. Was it someone she knew?

Good. I can find him and kill him for this.

The violent thought plumbed from the place where Kee was capable of murder. Now more than ever.

"Kee?"

His pulse pounded at his temple. Kee jerked his focus to her. Her eyes were wide, staring at him. Kee forced the anger down. "Do you know who did this?" He barely recognized his voice.

She stared for a beat, her eyes shiny with tears. Then she closed her eyes, as if pulling up the image. Kee was sure he would hear a name. And then the son of a bitch was history.

"It was dark," she said, her voice barely above a whisper.

He waited, hoping there was more to come, but she remained silent. Kee dabbed the rag at her temple, trying to be careful, though she didn't even seem to notice. She was looking down at her hands, rubbing her thumb over her palm, back and forth.

"It's okay, Rheada. We'll find him." Though Kee knew he shouldn't promise. Whoever did this was probably long gone with whatever he had stolen. He'd be a fool to try to sell the pieces in Aztec. In fact, he was probably some low-life pot thief who had heard about the relics, and figured it beat digging in the desert.

He saw a drop of wetness on Rheada's jeans. Then another. She was crying. Kee pulled her close. "Let it out, Rheada."

"He didn't have to do this," she said again. "He didn't have to."

Kee held her. God, he was glad he had found her. If he hadn't come in, hadn't followed his instincts . . .

His thoughts went to the empty garage. Did she even know that her Jeep was gone? He didn't want to mention it, but he also knew this might be the only way they would catch the asshole.

He squeezed her shoulder in comfort. "Rheada, did you know the Jeep is missing?"

He felt her become still at his chest. She didn't say anything.

"Can you give me the license plate number? I'll call the station."

"It's not worth it." Her voice was low and quiet.

"That's not true. This is your best bet for catching him."

She tensed and pulled back from Kee. "No. It's not worth it," she said, more firmly this time, but Kee heard a wealth of despair. It worried him that she was so affected by what had happened.

Kee shifted and took her by the shoulders. "Look at me, Rheada."

He lowered his head to catch her gaze. Slowly, she raised her eyes to his.

"Listen to me, Rheada. You don't want to let him get away with this. That's not you. That's not what you stand for."

Instead of the strength he had hoped to engender, Kee saw an immense sadness take over her and a hopelessness in her gaze he could hardly bear to see.

"Please, Kee, just let it go." Tears refilled her eyes.

Words squeezed from his heart. "Rheada, I'm not going anywhere." He pulled her close and felt her tears soak into his shirt. "I'm not going to let anything else happen to you," he whispered into her hair.

Chapter 17

RHEADA knew she wouldn't last another minute. She couldn't bear one more sympathetic look from the officers, or endure one more of their sincere, thoughtful questions. She had walked through her house with them; she'd shown how she had been surprised; she even reenacted the struggle; she had done everything they asked . . . except provide a description of the attacker.

It was too dark. I couldn't see him clearly.

When all the while, all she *could* see was Orin's despicable face, the greed in his eyes as he ripped through the boxes of artifacts.

She would love to give them Orin. She could make an intelligent guess where they would find him. He would be in handcuffs by sunrise . . . but then so might Tilly. As far as Rheada knew, the two of them were still together, though Tilly couldn't have had anything to do with this. She *wouldn't,* not to her own sister.

Rheada's heart clenched so hard she had to grip her sides with her arms.

"Are you all right?" It was one of the officers, looking at her with true concern.

Both the officers had been helpful. They seemed to truly care.

They had believed every word she said as she piled lie upon lie until she wanted to scream.

"I'm fine," she managed.

Her gaze went to the open door. She couldn't do this. She couldn't pretend for one more second to be a clueless victim. She wanted to slip into the night, disappear into the canyons, find Orin herself, demand her own answers.

Then she felt the touch of Kee's hand, the weight of his arm across her shoulder. She knew he meant to comfort her, reassure her, but the urge to scream only increased. He meant to help *Rheada,* someone he thought to be decent and honest

. . . and that wasn't her. She was lying to the cops. She was lying to Kee.

"You're doing great," he whispered into her hair. The concern in his voice clawed at her conscience.

Kee's arm pulled tighter, drawing her close to his side, as if he would keep her there always. Except he wouldn't. If he knew that all this had basically been called down upon her from her own dark past, he wouldn't be here any longer than it took him to reach that same open door.

A rush of anxiety made her lean against him. She yearned to feel once more that precious sense of security as when he had lifted her in his arms. His hand rubbed up and down her arm, caressing, soothing; but no amount of his warmth and closeness could dispel the dread growing within Rheada that the ground beneath her feet was shifting, crumbling away, swallowing her and burying her alive beneath her lies.

A shudder ran down her spine. Kee held her closer. "Come on. I'm getting you out of here." He moved them both toward the door.

One of the officers stopped them, but Kee handled him easily. The next moment, they were outside, beneath the stars where she could breathe. The night air rejuvenated her, cleared the fog of emotions that had been suffocating her. Out here she could think, and she knew her next move had to be to find Orin and Tilly.

But Kee was guiding her to his Jeep. She pressed her hand to his chest. "Thanks for everything, Kee."

"No problem." He smiled down at her, but didn't slow his pace.

She saw a purpose in his gaze, and she had a feeling that purpose had something to do with medical attention. She really couldn't endure another situation of being treated like a victim. She stumbled to a stop. "Kee, I'm okay now. I think I'll just get a room for the night."

He faced her. "Rheada, you need that forehead looked at."

"I'm fine. Really—"

"At the minimum, you need stitches."

"No stitches, Kee. And no hospital. I just want to crawl into bed." She stared up at him with what she hoped was her most unrelenting gaze.

He stared back. The hard purpose in his eyes softened. He

raised a hand and trailed his finger across her forehead, gently moving her hair aside. Oh, God, his touch could melt her own resolve.

"You really are something," he murmured.

Her heart lifted to the sound in his voice—the sound of wonder; the sound of a lover's voice. His hand cradled the side of her face. The pad of his thumb moved across her cheek. He stared deep into her eyes and every bit of Rheada rose to meet what she saw reflected in his gaze, to what he *believed* to be good and true about *her*.

His gaze never leaving hers, his eyes unblinking, he bent ever closer, until her focus blurred, the boundaries between what she saw and what she felt dissolved; and as their lips touched—as Kee wrapped his arms around her, pulling her close—all Rheada knew was that what he believed about her was exactly what she felt *within,* as if his belief brought what was good and true in her to life.

They walked across the lot, away from the cops, away from the destruction, away from her lies, and toward Kee's Jeep. He opened the passenger door, then walked around to the driver's side and slid in. When he started the engine, and Rheada knew they would drive away, she could feel her resolve to hunt down Orin fade. She didn't care anymore about why he had ambushed her, attacked her, destroyed the relics. His reasons were far away and of another life. Now, she realized, she would even have agreed to visiting the hospital, but when Kee turned the Jeep around in the street and headed toward the outskirts of Aztec, she realized he had also changed his mind about the hospital.

She sat back in the seat and waited to see where he would take them both. Rheada would not have stopped him if Kee had chosen to just keep on driving.

Her breath caught on that very notion: the two of them, driving away from Aztec, from the canyons, from this whole part of her life. They would never look back, she thought, just toward the future.

An abrupt bump brought Rheada's attention back and she saw Kee had left the highway and was guiding the Jeep over a rutted road. Just past a stand of cottonwoods, he pulled off the dirt trail and stopped. The headlights shone on an old wood cabin.

"It's not much, but you can rest here tonight, Rheada."

Kee's home, she realized.

Moonlight walked across the desert yard, up the front steps, and over the humble porch to a door with one window on each side, like dark eyes watching. The place was small, contained, isolated.

Had she driven past here when she was looking for Kee the other night? If so, how could she have missed seeing this cabin? How could she not have known Kee would live here?

She followed Kee up the steps, already picturing the spartan interior. He would have only what he needed, no more. He would bring here only what he had to . . . and he had brought her. She knew, without being told, that no one else had been to his home.

Her boot heel crunched on dirt. That one small sound brought Kee's glance, just as he too stepped and his boot ground dry earth against wood. His arm shot out to stop her as he went to the door. He had his keys out, but his hand was already at the knob, turning it, opening it.

This wasn't right. He wouldn't leave his door unlocked, Rheada was sure. Rheada's hand went to his arm, to pull him back, but he was already walking inside. She ignored his gesture to stay put and followed, stopping only because he still hadn't turned on a light. She could hear him crossing the room, his boots grating on dirt, and the sense of something very *wrong* rasped through her. Then she heard him stumble.

"What the hell?"

"Kee? Are you all right?"

"Stay there, Rheada!"

She wouldn't stay there. She widened her eyes to pick up the faintest light as if she were in a canyon, and she proceeded slowly, toeing forward just as she would on new terrain. Her shin brushed up against an object. She sidestepped, but again met an obstacle. And though she tried to make her way around, she kept encountering barriers. There seemed to be no way to get across this room.

She heard the clatter of wood against wood as Kee obviously shoved furniture aside. She took another step, impatient to see Kee, to be at his side. Finally, he turned on a light.

Kee stood maybe ten feet away, but between them was a calamity of furniture: chairs overturned, a small table on its side, legs jutted into the air. No wonder she hadn't been able to find a path. It looked like the aftermath of a tantrum—the rampage of a frustrated burglar, stupid destruction just for the hell of it.

Instantly, her mind went to Orin. She saw the hateful sneer of his mouth when she wouldn't cooperate; she saw his eyes, vacant of any intelligence, holding only a vicious gleam right before he knocked her out with his gun.

Fierce anger clogged her throat. When he hadn't found what he wanted at her place, he had gone to Kee's, somehow learning where he lived. She had brought this on Kee!

Tears of rage sprang to her eyes, blurred her focus. All she could think was that she had somehow caused this. If Kee had been here, would he now be lying hurt on the ground? The thought yanked a sound from her throat.

She heard steps. She felt Kee's hand at her arm. "Are you okay?"

Kee's deep voice resonated through her. She managed a nod, though evidently not one that convinced Kee. She felt his arm go to her shoulder. Instead of being calmed, Rheada shivered, as if his good, honest embrace were squeezing something sickly from her core, something contagious and deadly that infected anyone she got close to.

The shivers spread, like a virus claiming every part of her, and she had no defense. She broke free of Kee. She had to put distance between them! She stumbled toward a hallway, mumbling about a bathroom, pushed open the first door she came to, and reached for a light switch. The same moment, she heard Kee call out, "No, not that door." But she was already inside and staring at a huge pile of dirt.

For a second, she thought she must be seeing things. It was too bizarre, like a monstrous anthill growing from between floorboards. The rest of the room was almost as odd, with no furniture and only packing boxes scattered around. One had a metal rod driven through it as if to impale the box to the ground—the act so obviously violent her stomach turned.

From another box spilled some sort of equipment. Rheada thought she saw remnants of a camera in the smashed pieces. Why had Orin destroyed all this? Why had he taken out his anger on Kee?

She stumbled toward a box. She could clean this up, make things right again.

"Don't."

The harshness in Kee's voice cut through Rheada, raking across her already exposed emotions. He didn't want her help. Somehow he *knew* she was partly to blame. A flutter of panic rose in her chest.

"Kee, I'm—" But her words died at the look on his face.

He had the stark, frozen stare of a man coming face-to-face with a nightmare. Rheada went to him, striding quickly around the pile of dirt to reach his side. She touched his arm with her hand. "Kee?"

He was staring at the dirt, as if he half expected a monster to emerge. "I'm sorry," she said finally.

He didn't answer. He didn't move. He didn't take his eyes from the pile. His skin was growing pale, as if every moment longer that he stared, life was draining from him.

Panic rose in Rheada.

I'm going to lose everything.

The thought sprang into her head full force, making her gasp.

He glanced at her with a gaze so haunted and distant that Rheada's breath stumbled. Suddenly, his hand gripped her arm tight and he was forcing her out of the room, out the front door, down the steps and toward the Jeep.

"Kee, please. Talk to me."

"It's okay, Rheada."

But his voice raised her panic. She recognized that edge of despair. It was the same edge she had just stepped back from not an hour earlier when she had contemplated disappearing into the night, tracking down Orin. It was the sound of a desperate person hanging on by a mere thread of control.

In her mind, she was once again lying to the cops, schooling her features, while all the while her heart raced with a need to face Orin. No, not even so much to face Orin as to flee. Only Kee's strength, his sure gaze, his certain hands, had kept her grounded. How could she give that same strength to him? Rheada's anxiety doubled.

He pulled the Jeep back and away from his cabin, shifting gears easily, his actions fluid, unhurried—the quiet movements of a man who had already made a decision.

She shifted in her seat to look at Kee. In the dim light of the dash, she could see his tight jaw. His stony silhouette was like that of a cold statue. Anxiety raced through her, as if her own lifeline were slipping through her hands. She wanted to say something to him, maybe apologize again, anything to bridge the growing distance.

Then he looked at her. "It's all right, Rheada."

But it wasn't all right. *Nothing* was right. Nothing was true anymore. She knew who had done this, yet she couldn't say a word.

His hand settled on hers. "It was just someone's idea of a joke."

He was trying to reassure her, so she wouldn't worry—when *she* was the one keeping secrets! She wanted to apologize. She wanted to tell him everything, let the truth into the open. But the words hardened in her throat, and the hardness spread over her like a shell. She was the *only* one who could explain what had happened, yet she would be the last one who could help him understand. She was damned no matter what she did.

She thought of Tilly's taunt. *You're a fool to think you can escape.*

She felt the hardness enclose her, shutting her off from Kee. Her heart gave one last frantic leap as if she were stepping into a cell and hearing the click of a jail door.

In the recesses of her mind, she thought she could feel the brush of a human hand on hers. She almost cried out, but she sat silent, her hands clasped tight in her lap, her mask now ironclad.

Kee felt a coldness in Rheada's hands. He glanced at her and his concern rocketed, not for any fear he saw in her face, but for the utter *lack* of any emotion. She was staring out the window, her face devoid of any expression as if she almost weren't even there, but had withdrawn in shock to someplace far away, someplace safe.

He had brought this on her. After what she had already endured tonight, and then he had made her walk into this. She probably thought she had some monster not only after her but after everyone she knew.

She was right about the monster part, Kee thought. It was like a horror movie come to life. He kept telling himself it

wasn't possible. Miguel was dead, buried alive. But Kee had
known he was wrong when he saw the pile of dirt. It was a
message from Miguel, a message that the murdering asshole
knew Kee would understand: Miguel had risen from the grave
and he knew where to find Kee . . . which meant he also knew
where Kee had been lately.

Realization slammed into Kee: Could it have been Miguel
who attacked Rheada? Kee's gut twisted violently. He thought
of Miguel attacking Rheada, cracking her head open with a
gun. That cowardly son of a bitch had attacked a woman just
to make a point.

I brought this on her.

The thought pounded through him like fists beating at the
door of his inner dungeon. It was the cold, black place where
he hid away all the evil he had committed. He had almost
forgotten it existed. Because of Rheada, he had almost believed he had a chance. Damn if he hadn't even begun to hope.

He was a goddamn fool! Miguel's presence was the proof
of that. Kee hadn't escaped anything. His destiny had been
hiding quietly in the shadows, waiting patiently for the time
to strike, for the exact moment when Kee was vulnerable.

He glanced at Rheada. She was still staring ahead, allowing
him to take her where he would, *trusting* him and his judgment.

His gut gave a violent, near mortal twist. Kee barely contained the sound wrenched from inside himself.

God, how could he have let this happen?

Because he was a fool. He had forgotten what he was
about. That would not happen again. By whatever strength he
had, he would *not* let another person he was close to get hurt.
He would find Miguel, put him back in the ground for good.
That monster didn't have a prayer.

His blood ran hot, fueled by hatred, powered by the evil
he knew he was capable of. The hinges broke on his dungeon
door and the door came down.

Kee parked the Jeep in front of Max's bar. He opened the
Jeep's door, but stopped and turned to Rheada. "You stay here.
I'm going to get a key to one of his cabins."

She looked toward him but didn't focus on his face. She
had the detached look of someone who barely cared. The glim-

mer in her eyes was gone. That flame of life that he had always seen there, that he had yearned for, breathed from her lips, had vanished, leaving her gaze as distant as the night sky.

Because of me.

It was as if he had breathed the life right out of her.

He was desperate to coax the embers within her back to life. He leaned over and kissed her temple. Her scent rose and filled him—the scent of outdoors and wonder, the promise of daylight and laughter.

For a moment, he couldn't move, he couldn't pull away.

Before another day passed, he promised himself, he would make her world right again, make her world safe . . .

. . . which would mean he would have to leave.

He inched back from Rheada, rubbed the place on her temple where he had pressed his lips. "It's going to be okay," he whispered. His heart lurched to his throat with a need he could barely manage.

She seemed to force her face into a smile—and the smile scared him more than the stony expression she had before because it was fake. She was pretending. She had climbed into herself and was letting him see only a veneer. Before his eyes, she had withdrawn from him. She didn't believe it was going to be okay. She didn't believe he could *make* it okay.

He wanted to wrap her in his arms and make her believe . . . but then he would have to confide everything, including *why* Miguel was after him.

And then he truly would lose her.

Suddenly Kee had the sense of knowing what was to happen and being powerless to stop it—like peering ahead as he walked a dark hallway, knowing that something terrible lurked behind a closed door, something that *would* destroy him, and yet he was *compelled* to face his doom. It was a living nightmare from which he couldn't awaken or escape. He was delivering his own defeat.

Anger rose in him unbidden and swift. The face that appeared in his mind was that of Raven, his nemesis. Raven was the one who had begun his descent. Raven was the one who would pay for this nightmare.

His body filled with a keen hatred. His hands clenched to fists. Then he heard a gasp and he yanked his head to Rheada. She was staring at him, then she looked at the dash, and Kee realized his fist was on the dashboard. He didn't remember raising it. He didn't remember hitting anything, but he must have from the look on her face.

He lowered his hand. "I'm just frustrated," he said.

She nodded, as if understanding. But Kee saw a sheen fill her eyes.

Goddamnit. Now *I'm* scaring her!

The hand he had raised in violence, he now laid gently against her face. "I'm sorry. I—"

"No, Kee. Don't apologize," she interrupted. "*I'm* the one who's sorry." The sheen threatened to spill from her eyes. "All I wanted was a chance—"

She stopped and looked out the window. Kee watched her overcome the emotion and his chest tightened with her own effort.

"Never mind," she said abruptly. "It doesn't matter."

The defeat in her voice sliced through Kee. She couldn't give up. Not Rheada. He gripped her shoulder. "This is all going to go away, Rheada." His conviction rose like blood from a fresh wound.

She slowly turned her gaze to him. "Yes," she said. "It will go away."

He gave her a smile as his hand went to the door handle. But something in her clear, determined gaze stirred the dread inside him.

Chapter 18

MAX barely heard the knock above the newscast on the radio. At first he thought it was the dark stranger, back at dawn for another day of taking up space in the corner. He strode to the front, anticipating his pleasure in telling the asshole to find another bar to haunt, and peered through the peephole.

"Son of a bitch." Max unlocked and yanked the door open.

"We need a place to stay, Max."

Max heard Kee, but he couldn't take his gaze away from the gash on Rheada's forehead. He had heard on his police-band radio of the break-in at Legendary Tours, but that had happened two hours earlier. What had they been doing in the interim?

"What you need is a hospital," Max said. Kee knew better, Max was sure, than to drag her around in the night.

"No hospital," Kee said.

Rheada gave Kee a quick glance of appreciation. Her message, however, was wasted on the man. Kee never noticed. His eyes were cold.

"We need a cabin," he said. His voice was a flat demand. He stared ahead, past Max, to something beyond. He had the haunted look of someone with only one last chance.

For a moment, all thought was lost in Max—he could have been staring at himself . . . a dreaded memory of himself.

Sensations overtook Max, flooding him—the sense of being driven and lost, all at the same time. A chill ran through him and his hand nearly slammed the door in a desperate defense against the assault on every fiber of his body.

"Do you have a cabin or not?"

Kee's demand refocused Max. He looked back at two people in trouble and he knew he couldn't turn them away.

"I have a cabin," he managed to say as he stepped back from the doorway.

He watched Kee place an arm around Rheada and guide her inside. She leaned into Kee with an intimacy Max couldn't miss, and he suddenly realized that a lot had happened between these two since the day they had met in his bar.

Max walked behind the counter to the wooden peg-board that held the keys. He pulled one down and slid it across the bar to Kee who pocketed it. "This is for Cabin Five. The one at the end. It's the most private."

"Thanks," Kee said. He still had his hand at Rheada's back and started to guide her away.

"I heard about the break-in at your place," Max said quietly. "Any idea of who or why?"

Rheada shook her head without looking at him.

"Do they have any leads?" he asked.

"He took Rheada's Jeep."

"He stole your Jeep?" Max looked at Rheada with sympathy. "At least he didn't take the bus."

Rheada backed off a step.

"The plate number should be helpful," Max said.

He caught a flicker of *something* across her eyes.

Kee's arm slid to her shoulder and pulled her close. "A lot of lowlifes around."

Max saw a quick flinch at the corners of Rheada's eyes. Her reaction was as swift as if she were pinched with pain at Kee's words.

"They'll catch him, Rheada."

He meant to comfort her. Instead, her expression turned stricken. Max looked to Kee and his gaze froze on the icy hate flaring in Kee's eyes.

"Yes. He'll be caught." Kee's voice was a low rumble, like that of a far-off train bearing down, delivering his promise, at any cost. He was a man obsessed.

God help him.

"Maybe we'll go find that cabin." Kee started for the door, his arm still around Rheada.

"In news from Aztec," said the radio reporter in a somber voice, "a body was discovered in Canyon Largo."

Rheada's gaze shifted to the radio. Kee's arm dropped from her shoulder.

"According to the authorities the man was shot in the head. The man, Carlos Sisneros, was a Mexican national."

"Carlos." Rheada breathed the name out. "Kee, it was Carlos."

"Son of a bitch." Max slammed his hand on the bar counter.

Now he wished it *had* been the stranger at the door. Max would have had his hands around the asshole's throat until he confessed.

"Max?"

It was Rheada. Max realized that both she and Kee were staring at him. "If it's the same kid," Max said, "he was in here yesterday, spouting off about an article he wanted to write on pot thieves." Max shook his head in disbelief. "I told him thieves weren't likely to do interviews."

Max looked at Rheada. "In fact, he mentioned you, Rheada. Said you told him the same thing. But he obviously wasn't listening. He was too busy talking. The stupid kid was practically asking to get killed."

"To who?" Kee had left Rheada's side and was facing Max.

"What?"

"*Who* was he too busy talking to, Max?"

Kee stopped right in front of the bar and Max found himself locked in Kee's black stare. "Only one I know of," Max said, "is the man who was sitting here in the bar when Carlos came in."

"What did this man look like?"

Kee was staring at Max with the cold look of a man from whom deadly predators should flee. Even Max was caught for a moment by the snare of Kee's eyes.

He leveled his own stare on Kee. "He looked dangerous," Max answered quietly, as the realization dawned on him that he could just as easily be talking about Kee as he was about the stranger.

"You mean he looked like a criminal."

"Yes," Max said.

"Like the kind of criminal Carlos was after? A goddamn pot thief?" Kee's eyes narrowed on Max, demanding his information.

"Yes."

"And Carlos mentioned Rheada," Kee confirmed.

"Yeah. He mentioned Rheada."

Max shifted his gaze to her and found she had backed away, toward the door, her face a mixture of alarm and dread.

"What else can you tell me about this stranger?"

Max pulled his focus from her to Kee. "Only that he's been here for a couple of days."

"Here in Aztec?"

"In this bar," Max corrected. "Right there in that chair." He nodded his head to the back table, never taking his eyes from Kee. Instincts told Max to watch for a reaction, but Kee only slanted a quick gaze to the dark corner where *he* always sat, facing the door.

Then his eyes shifted and looked past Max to a distant point, like that of a predator homing in on his prey. It was the same look Max had seen in the stranger's eyes. Hell, it was the same look he had seen from the inside of himself staring out—like that of a laser locked on a target.

If Max had one last doubt that Kee *wasn't* who he said he was, that doubt fled. Kee wasn't a cartographer. He wasn't some simple working man caught in a bad situation. He *was* a bad situation. He had murder in his eyes . . . and more: His black gaze also held the decision that one more death didn't matter.

"Goddamnit," Max muttered.

Kee flashed a look that could freeze a heartbeat. "Goddamn *what,* Max?"

Max didn't flinch from the stare. "I was only thinking about how fast a life can end. Makes you appreciate just how precious your own life is." Max's gaze was hard and strong, delivering a message he hoped Kee didn't miss: that *Kee's* life was the one he was playing with.

Kee didn't even blink. "For some it doesn't end fast enough," he muttered.

Kee's eyes were narrowed on Max. The two men stared at each other, Max looking for a way to help Kee, but seeing no way past the razor-sharp black in his eyes. The next moment, Kee turned and walked to the front door. "I'll drive the Jeep around," he said over his shoulder.

Max stole a glance at Rheada. She was staring at the slowly closing door, her expression filled with a great sadness. As the door clicked shut, he heard her take in a breath, as if to draw one last bit of air—as if the door were closing *on* her, like a jail door, or a coffin . . . or as if she were witnessing her own lifeline being severed.

For all the sadness in her eyes, however, Max could still see a great yearning. He knew then that he was right about his guess that a lot had happened between these two. Suddenly, he saw a way to perhaps reach Kee. Maybe *she* could make the difference. If she was important to Kee, maybe he wouldn't be quite as careless with his own life.

Max laid a hand on her shoulder. "He's in a bad way."

She gave half a nod.

"You could help him, Rheada."

"You don't understand—" she started, but let the words drift off.

The morning news on the radio was the only sound in the bar. ". . . first presidential race for the Alliance of Indigenous Peoples of the Americas has been plagued with reports of scandal. Front-runner candidate Esteban Zamora is accused of financing his campaign through the illegal trafficking of ancient Indian artifacts. While Zamora has remained silent against the charges, he does claim direct descent from the Anasazi, ancient Indians of the Southwest United States. In two days, the candidates meet in Santa Fe for their next debate."

"Pot thieves and politicians." Max shook his head. "Should have known it wouldn't be long before those two criminals found each other."

Rheada was staring at the radio, her brow furrowed as if she were pinned on one thought. Then her eyes went wide as if she'd been struck with a revelation. The next moment, she turned and walked away from him and out the door.

Max ran after her. "Rheada, you need to talk to Kee."

"There's nothing to say."

He caught her arm and stopped her just outside the door. "Whatever is driving him right now is taking him straight over the edge."

For a second, she didn't say a word, then she looked up at him, her gaze clear and strong. "You're right."

Max's heart hurt from the ache he saw there on her face and from the defeat he heard in her voice—as if she were to blame for everything wrong.

She started to walk away from him just as Kee pulled the Jeep to a stop in front of the last cabin. She raised her head and her gaze settled on Kee.

She stopped walking. She seemed to be holding her breath, her eyes steady and bright on the tall, lean Indian. The air around her was charged with electricity—a taut connection between her and Kee. Max's own heart gave a start as if caught in the line of her keen focus.

She's in love.

The thought came to him, pure and simple.

His gaze jerked to Kee. He was walking with purposeful strides to the cabin door. He hadn't even looked over at them. His focus was set on something else when it should have been set right here, on what was directly in front of him. Max had the nearly overwhelming urge to run over and grab Kee by his collar, make him stop, take a look, before he lost sight of what was *really* important.

Max gazed down at the woman beside him. "Does he know how you feel, Rheada?"

She gave a start, yanking her gaze from Kee to the ground, but Max saw her incredulity—that he would have guessed the secret? Or that he would have the bad manners to voice it?

His hand still at her arm, Max made her face him. "He doesn't know, does he?" He couldn't believe his own presumptuousness. Still he didn't apologize.

Rheada looked from his hand to him. He half expected a rebuke. Instead, her eyes were sad. "I hope he doesn't know," she said.

"Why?" His question came on a whisper.

Her eyes filled. She looked away and gave a shake to her head, as if to regain her composure.

"Rheada—"

"Don't." Her voice was choked.

Max didn't understand. Why wouldn't she tell Kee? Why hesitate to tell him how she felt?

His heart beat fast with urgency, as if he were saving his *own* life. The sensation was absurd, beyond reason, yet he couldn't let go of Rheada.

"Rheada, you *have* to tell him." He made her face him. "You just might be his last chance."

Her brow furrowed in confusion. Then she gave a small laugh, as if Max were truly befuddled. "It was the other way around," she said. She slipped free of his hand, then turned around and walked in the opposite direction, away from the cabin.

"Rheada!"

She paused and glanced over her shoulder. "Tell Kee . . ."

She stopped and shook her head as if to find the trail of her own thought.

"You're leaving?" Max walked to her. "You can't. Don't you see—"

"I do see, Max." Before his eyes, her expression filled with strength. "Thanks to you." She gave him a smile. "Tell Kee thanks, but I have to take care of this myself." With that, she disappeared around the corner of the building and was gone.

Max stared after her, trying to make sense of what she had just said.

A lonely train whistle blew far off. Max pulled his gaze to the distance where he knew the rails took the train along the outskirts of town to another, predetermined destination. The train would slow, but it wouldn't stop; nothing could deter it from its goal.

An immense sorrow built within Max. He had the sick feeling inside that he was watching two people bound and determined toward goals that would end in disaster . . . and he was helpless to do anything.

He looked from the empty sidewalk back to the cabin and its open door. Kee was in there, sure that Rheada was coming. What the hell was Max going to say?

He reached the cabin door and found Kee on the edge of the bed, his head in his hands. Kee stood up and started talking as soon as Max entered.

"Rheada, I have to go back to my place. I forgot some things—"

Max interrupted. "Rheada's gone, Kee."

"What?" He strode to the door and looked outside, then back to Max. "What the hell happened? What the hell did you do?"

Kee advanced on Max, the rage in his eyes promising bodily harm. Another man would have fled—or at minimum backed away. Max heard the train whistle again, closer this time. He stood his ground. "The question, Kee, is *who are you?*"

Kee's eyes flared. "What?"

"You're not a mapmaker. You're not a *driver* for a tour company. Who are you?"

"You're crazy. What the hell did you say to Rheada?"

"Straight to the offense. Good training. You could be a detective, but I'm betting federal."

Kee didn't blink. He had a go-to-hell look that clicked into place for Max.

"Fed, I think," Max said. "But are you FBI or BLM?"

Kee stared at Max, his eyes narrowed to black shards of jet. Suddenly, his expression changed, softened, and he actually smiled. "You look worried, Max. You got a reason to worry?" Kee's voice was quiet steel slicing the air.

For a split second, Max was caught off guard. *This son of a bitch is good.* Faced with the truth, Kee could still act cool, detached, disconnected. It was all so familiar, so cold. Max's gut twisted, clenching against the sudden chill.

"Yeah, I do have a reason," he answered. "You remind me of someone."

"Really? Who?"

"Me."

It was Kee's turn to be surprised, though he recovered fast. "Too bad for you, Max." Kee brushed past him on his way to the door.

"How long have you been under, Kee?"

Kee hesitated on the threshold, then kept walking.

Max followed. "A year? Two?"

"You don't know what you're talking about."

"Or have you lost count?"

Kee didn't slow in his strides to the Jeep, but Max could feel the tension emanating from the man. If he pushed him too far, could Max stand up to the young, better-fit Kee? He considered backing off. It would be the smart thing to do, the sane thing to do, not to mention the healthiest.

But Max couldn't. A need impelled him—a need that came from deep inside, from the place where he had buried his own fears. He understood Kee. Hell, at one time he *was* Kee. And that time replayed in his memory so clearly now that he could *feel* the chill spreading through him. And with the cold came the darkness surrounding him, enveloping him in a stifling black world that had nearly swallowed him whole—past where he had forgotten the warmth of day to the point where he almost *dreaded* daylight.

Max shook his mind loose of the nightmare and saw Kee was already at his Jeep. In two strides, his legs propelled by his heart not his head, Max stood between Kee and the car door.

"Move." Kee's command was amplified by the challenge in his eyes.

Max angled himself, deliberately closing the space between them even more. "Or what, Kee? You have it in you to kill me?"

A look that promised just that flashed in Kee's eyes for a fraction of a second before he got it controlled. "You have an active imagination, Max."

"And you're lying to yourself. Are you lying to Rheada, too? Of course you are. Or maybe you're so far down you don't even know the truth anymore."

"Back off, Max."

"My name isn't Max. What about you, Kee? Is that your real name?"

Kee was just staring back. Max took the advantage. "Maybe you've forgotten. Before Max, I was Al. Before that I was John. Max is as good as any other, though, don't you think?" Max paused. "Especially since I can't remember the damn name my own mother gave me."

Max pressed closer. "I didn't care. I was glad. It made me the *best* at what I did: pretending to be someone else. In fact, I was so damn good at pretending that I turned into what I was hunting."

Kee didn't say a word. His face had frozen rigid, leaving the only sign of life a vein pulsing so hard at Kee's temple that Max thought it might burst from the effort of pumping life through near solid stone.

"How about this, Kee? Do you even care that Rheada loves you?"

Max saw a flash of pain in the man's eyes before an obvious herculean effort turned them cold again. "Then she's an idiot," Kee murmured.

"*You're* the idiot, Kee. You would throw away the only lifeline you have."

"I don't need saving, Max. Not by Rheada and certainly not by you. Now get the hell away." He reached his hand around Max for the door handle.

Max didn't move. "Kee, whoever you're after, he's not

worth it. He's not worth dying for. Worse, he's not worth you losing your own soul to."

Kee's lips pulled to a thin, vicious line. "Go back to your bar, Max." The words hissed from between clenched teeth. "Go back to your safe world with your pretend name. *You're* the one who was defeated."

Max closed his eyes to the words. They were too close, too frighteningly familiar. Kee shoved him aside and Max didn't bother to struggle. "You son of a bitch," Max said in a low voice.

"That's one thing you *are* right about."

Max opened his eyes to see Kee give half a smile, as if accepting a compliment. Then he drove away, leaving a dirty cloud in his wake.

Miguel yanked back from the doorway as Blackburn sped past. He ran to the front of the bar and watched the Jeep turn onto a side street. He was outside and, in less than a minute, had his truck on the same street following Blackburn. A sound came from behind his seat and he slammed his gun onto the small mound at the head of the bundle.

Silence.

He touched his jaw where the little bitch had connected with a hard fist. He thought he had caught her off guard—her head bowed, she had looked lost in thought, staring down at the sidewalk as she walked. Shit, she had reacted fast.

He started to wonder if he had made a mistake in nabbing her. The idea that she might come in handy had struck when he saw them both together at Blackburn's. Now he was thinking that she just might be more trouble than she was worth. He sure as hell hadn't figured on dealing with two, let alone this wildcat.

He watched the Jeep speed ahead, barely stopping at cross streets. Blackburn sure was in a helluva hurry.

The Jeep careened around a corner, turning onto a street Miguel had traveled several times the past few days.

"So, he's going to your place. Damn if I wasn't right. Blackburn's got himself a girlfriend. Now won't he be surprised when he finds out where you are?" he said over his shoulder.

The bundle was motionless and silent, but that didn't stop

him from imagining the sexy thing bound inside. His imagination fired. He pictured the torture on Blackburn's face as he was forced to watch.

The image brought a laugh straight from his gut, followed by a series of racking coughs. Miguel grabbed the bottle from where it was rolling on the floor, unscrewed the cap with one hand, and threw back several gulps. The coughs increased. He doubled over and his rib screamed in reminder of where she had kicked him.

The little bitch. She would pay and then Blackburn would pay.

He'll beg to die.

Chapter 19

KEE slammed the Jeep to a stop within an inch of Rheada's garage. He jumped out and strode to the back door, not bothering to waste any time on the front entrance. She never locked the back. Despite what he'd said, she seemed incapable of believing the worst about humanity. She just didn't see there were bad people, dangerous people . . . evil men, like himself.

The judgment pierced his gut in a familiar, comforting stroke of pain. He was evil, and he had brought all hell down on Rheada.

Rheada loves you.

Max's words slipped within Kee's brain like sunlight sliding over the horizon. For a moment, Kee was helpless against the words, against the *warmth* they promised. His heart lurched, as if in a frantic reach to grab and hold on to the light.

But the darkness inside was swifter, more sure, yanking him back and slamming the doors shut against the gentle fingers of daylight.

She doesn't love me. She doesn't even know who I am.

Or maybe she did.

Maybe she saw through his lies. Maybe she had *seen* the danger in him and that's why she had left him behind at Max's.

Good, he told himself. Good, that she should be afraid. Better yet if she didn't want to be anywhere near him. He just had to get her away from her place to somewhere safe, that was all. After he had Miguel, she could go back to her life. And he would go back to the darkness, hunting Raven.

He took the back steps two at a time and, in one motion, put his weight to the door. It didn't budge. He cupped his hands to the window and peered inside to a dark, empty kitchen.

Goddamnit. Where was she?

The events of last night descended on him. He saw her lying helpless in the closet. He saw the blood on her forehead.

For a second, he couldn't breathe, he couldn't focus. Urgency ripped through him and he stopped himself a moment before punching his hand through the window.

He took a step back, forced logic through the dense emotions knotting his thoughts. It hadn't been *that* long since she left Max's. Maybe she wasn't even here yet.

He grabbed the railing, jumped down the back steps, and walked up the drive. Out at the sidewalk, he looked down the street. No Rheada. The street was empty, save for a junked-up utility vehicle parked about fifty yards down.

Kee walked back to the building. She had to be here . . . and she had to be okay.

He reached the front and shoved on the door, but it too was locked and the office was dark.

Where the hell was she? She didn't have anyplace else to go. This was it. Unless she had simply hitched a ride out of town, gone back to one of her canyons, already knowing she had to put as much distance as possible between herself and Kee. Maybe she was running from *him*.

His gut twisted violently and sent a wave of weakness through him. *Oh, God, how I've let her down.*

Defeat pounded through him, jarring loose the last of his control. He could feel himself caving in, close to dropping to his knees.

Get a grip, Blackburn. But he couldn't peel himself away from the building. He couldn't think of what to do next. He was impaled to the spot, his thoughts frozen on Rheada.

Rheada loves you.

Max's words coaxed the truth from Kee. *And I love her.*

The words pounded through him, battering at his defenses. Kee took a deep, harsh breath, driving down his emotions.

I just want her safe, goddamnit.

He staggered back from the door, repeating the words. *I just want her safe.*

Goddamn her independence and self-reliance. Why the hell wasn't she here?

Because away from me is where she should be.

Then why did it feel so damn wrong? Why were his insides in such a knot and his legs incapable of moving?

Because he really was a son of a bitch. Max was right: Kee would drag her down with him, just to have her beside him, just to have the feeling that he *wasn't* doomed.

When the truth was, he was already in hell . . . and, somehow, Rheada had seen that.

He took a step back, then another, gradually finding the strength to back away. He heard the sound of tires on gravel. His pulse jumped. It was Rheada coming back!

He knew the thought was irrational. Even as he swung around, his instincts warned of trouble and his mind was telling him that it couldn't be her: She didn't have her Jeep and the tour van was here.

Still, his heart beat at his throat, anticipating seeing her.

He didn't have a chance against the utility vehicle. It slammed into him, the left front punching him in the ribs, throwing him to the ground. As he fell back, Kee's last sight was the face of the man driving into him . . . and his last thought was to thank God Rheada had gotten away.

Sharp, breath-robbing pain stabbed through Kee. Another wild bump jolted pure agony up his body. Kee slid his eyes open slightly and confirmed he was sitting in the backseat of the utility van. They were obviously traveling some back road and with every pothole his chest muscles screamed against sore ribs.

He forced his breath slow and shallow, but another pain grated at his wrists. When he tried to move his hands, the pain jolted to torture shooting straight up his arms. Pulsing numb fingers had just enough feeling to trace the tight cords of rope binding his wrists. Miguel had tied him up—so tight that Kee worried about the use of his hands when he finally did get free.

If he could just reach the knot . . .

He shifted slightly. The wave of agony nearly overwhelmed him. He couldn't even be sure that he hadn't groaned. He peeked his eyes open farther, praying Miguel hadn't heard or noticed anything.

But it wasn't Miguel driving. Kee registered the long, shiny black hair and Rheada's slender silhouette at the same instant he saw the gun pressed to her temple.

He squeezed his eyes shut, praying it was a hallucination, while his mind simultaneously raced over choices, a plan of action. But only one thought pounded clear in his head: *God, what have I done?*

"I think our boy's awake. And none too happy with the situation." Miguel laughed.

Kee opened his eyes fully, gave a cursory glance to Miguel, but no response. Instead, he shifted his gaze to the rearview mirror where he caught Rheada's eyes looking back at him. His heart caught on the relief in her gaze as she stared back at him. "Are you okay?" he asked.

She nodded. Her eyes shone with fierce courage.

Kee's pulse jumped with an indescribable fear. *Dear God, let me get her out of this.*

"So I was right."

The silky evil in Miguel's voice pumped hot blood through Kee. He saw the flicker of sick intent in Miguel's eyes. The realization struck Kee that Miguel was talking about Kee and Rheada.

Kee's fingers tingled with life . . . and with the deadly purpose to wrap themselves around Miguel's neck.

"She must be awfully understanding," Miguel said. His eyes narrowed with malice.

With the certainty of a man facing a speeding bullet, Kee knew what Miguel was about to say, and he was helpless to stop him.

Kee stared back, forcing his face to remain placid, as he worked frantically on the knot.

"I mean," Miguel continued, "how many women would want to be with a murderer?"

Kee locked his gaze on Miguel. He couldn't look at Rheada. He couldn't stand to see himself through her eyes. He tugged at the knot, and pain shot through him. He turned his wince into a stiff smile. "Not a murderer," Kee forced out. "Not *yet*."

"That's right. You failed." Miguel stared across the seat, his lips curving into a smile. "I'm *still alive*."

His pronouncement obviously struck Miguel as funny. He laughed—a harsh, mirthless laugh that turned into a series of racking coughs.

"Alive, barely," Kee said. "You're dying as you sit there."

Miguel still hadn't gotten the coughs under control. He lifted a nearly empty bottle to his mouth and threw back several gulps. All the time, Kee noticed, Miguel kept the gun tight on Rheada.

Miguel wiped his mouth. "Yes, dying." His voice was choked from the coughs.

The next second, the gun went off. The noise exploded in the car. Kee's heart stopped. He was sure that Miguel had killed Rheada.

With a primeval scream of rage, Kee threw himself toward the front seat. He would kill the son of a bitch. He didn't know how, but Miguel was a dead man.

Metal struck his brow. Kee saw sparks of light and felt himself fall back onto the seat. He felt the barrel of the gun jammed at his forehead, right between his eyes. Kee opened his eyes and was staring at a madman.

"That was just to get your attention. Yeah, I'm dying, because of you, asshole. Now you know I've got nothing to lose."

"You never *were* anything. Crow didn't miss you for a damn second. Even *he* knew you were nothing."

Kee thought he caught Rheada's sharp glance in the mirror, but when he looked, she was staring straight ahead.

"And won't Crow be surprised." The hate doubled in Miguel's eyes, like two black holes of hell, consuming the man from the inside. Kee had the sudden thought that Miguel might actually have a plan for vengeance on both of them. If that were the case, maybe he and Rheada had some time.

At the thought of her, he wanted to *look* at her, see that she was all right, but he couldn't break the stare with Miguel. More, a part of him was *afraid* to see what her eyes held now.

Miguel stared back, studying Kee. His gaze became speculative. "Yeah, you're a smart one. I don't think I want to worry about you."

Kee saw intent in Miguel's black gaze. He saw murder there, and all Kee could think was that Rheada would be all alone with this sick asshole. In that same split second, Kee threw himself forward in a desperate attempt to bash his own head into Miguel's.

Miguel raised his hand with the gun. The car swerved, throwing Miguel to the side against the window. He fought to right himself. Kee saw Rheada jerk the steering wheel to the side, tossing Miguel back again. He realized she was helping him—the knowledge pumped through him with power.

Kee dove for the front, but Miguel was already on the offense. Kee knew he didn't have a chance.

He felt the full weight of the gun smash against his temple. He was a dead man. Right here and now. And all he wanted was a last touch of her hair, a last gaze into her eyes. As he slipped into the blackness, he wanted to scream, to rail against the dark.

Max was right. He was right.

Tilly tried to fold up her bedroll but Blackjack wouldn't move from where he had planted himself in the middle. She gave a flip of her wrist. The bag floated up and settled, with Blackjack still attached.

Caw!

He strutted across the bag, his claws leaving sharp indentations in the nylon. She recognized that determined glint in his beady eyes, and she dropped the bag to the ground before he got close to her fingers with that skilled beak of his.

"Quit hounding me, Blackjack!"

He had been pestering her all day. Or maybe it was her own nerves that made it seem that way. In just a few hours she would put her plan into action—a plan no one knew of but her and that she alone could execute. This moment had driven her, consumed her thoughts and dictated her choices. Now it was finally here: the chance to avenge her father's murder.

Tonight she would face Crow. She would ride into his camp as Raven. And after tonight, there would be no turning back.

She wasn't afraid for herself. What she did fear was not succeeding. She wished she had someone to talk to, someone she could trust. She sat down on the bag.

She heard the velvety *shoosh* of wings just before Blackjack landed near her.

"Yes, I know I have you," she murmured, and reached for him.

But Blackjack didn't want to cuddle. He flew to her and grabbed some of her hair in his beak and tugged hard, his wings flapping as if he meant to haul her down the canyon.

"Ouch!" Tilly swept him away. "Damnit, Blackjack!"

He hovered in the air, staring at her from just a foot away, his beak open, his eyes fierce, as if he would actually attack. He rarely got this agitated ... only when he perceived real danger nearby.

A rush of anxiety swept across her chest and up her neck, and she had the urge to turn and run. Not even when she was a child—and she would nearly always ignore Blackjack—had her instincts been so triggered by this damn bird.

She had the fleeting thought that maybe she should listen to him this time. Just as strong, however, was her need to see this night through. Rheada would, if she were here.

She turned her back on Blackjack and returned to the sleeping bag. His squawk rang in the air, but Tilly ignored him. She heard a wild flap of his wings, punctuated with more squawks. She threw her hands up to cover her head—for the first time in her life, she feared Blackjack's intentions.

"Goddamn bird!"

Tilly looked over her shoulder to see Orin swinging his arms in the air. The raven's wings were a flurry of black.

"Blackjack!" Tilly called out.

The raven flew straight at her, then swerved, his great wings cutting the air and sending a breeze over Tilly. He landed on her bedroll.

"That bird is a goddamn pest."

Orin's voice held a threat. Tilly glanced back in time to see Orin pull the gun from his waistband.

"We don't have time for this," he said as he walked closer, raising the gun.

"Don't, Orin." Her command usually worked on the weak-minded crook. This time, though, he didn't stop.

"He's loud and he's obnoxious." Orin advanced, the gun raised.

Tilly stood, planting herself between Orin and Blackjack. "Put the gun down, Orin." Tilly told herself he wouldn't shoot her: Orin believed she was Raven, his golden goose, his ticket to the big time. But she had also seen a change in him in the last day. He was bolder ... and more irrational.

"Move aside." Orin pointed the gun at Tilly.

"Or what, Orin? You won't shoot me."

He was staring at her and something seemed to snap in his

eyes. They flared with a desperate madness. "You and that goddamn bird." His voice was low. "Why shouldn't I shoot him? He's worthless. When the hell is he going to lead us to the mask?"

"When I tell him to. When it's time."

He gave a sharp, crazy laugh. "We're fucking *out* of time! The deal is tonight." He narrowed murderous eyes on Tilly. "Tell him to do it now, Raven."

Tilly drew up all the courage she had, though her stomach was in her throat. She had to fool Orin one last time, or her scheme wouldn't work.

"I have a better plan, Orin." She forced her lips into a reassuring smile.

Orin snorted. "If you're thinking of crossing Crow, you're already dead."

Tilly's gaze hardened. "Are you saying he's better than me, Orin? Better than Raven?"

Orin hesitated.

Tilly took the advantage. "I can get us more money."

"Crow doesn't bargain. You know that."

Yes. I know that.

The memory of that night flashed through Tilly. She could hear him arguing with her father, Crow's voice lethal. He hadn't bargained then, and neither had her father. And it was Crow she knew, she was sure—she had had eight years to think about it—who had come back and killed their father.

"Did you hear me, Raven? Crow doesn't bargain. You won't get more money. You'll just get us killed."

"He won't kill us, Orin. Not until he gets the mask in his hands."

"I don't like it."

"You don't have to. This is *my* game, now." She brushed past Orin, confident he was distracted from Blackjack, and walked to her backpack. "You coming?" she said over her shoulder.

"Crow's expecting *me*, Raven. Not you. Just me and the stash of relics."

She casually lifted her pack from the ground, slipped it over her shoulders, and faced Orin. "We're not *taking* the haul to Crow." She smiled inwardly at the surprise on his face. He really didn't have a clue what she was planning.

"This is your plan? For *you* to show up, without *any* merchandise, and demand *more* money? You're crazy." He paused. "But I'm not." His face sobered.

He raised his gun.

God, he is so predictable.

Tilly prayed silently that Blackjack would also be reliable. "Blackjack?"

He fluttered, but didn't fly to her.

"Blackjack!" she ordered, though her heart was pleading. *Please obey me.*

A black blur flew past her to Orin. His mouth fell open a second before razor-sharp claws gripped his shoulder. His screams of pain echoed against the canyon walls. Orin tried to point his gun at the bird, but Blackjack caught his hand in his beak and held on, strong black wings flapping, as Orin struggled frantically to get free.

"Get him off me!"

"Drop your gun, Orin."

He did. "Call him off!"

Tilly nodded to Blackjack. He loosened his grip on Orin's hand, but kept his talons firmly locked on his shoulder. "Listen to me, Orin," Tilly said calmly. "You have two choices. Take me to Crow or tell me where he is. I don't care which."

"You show up without me," Orin choked out, "he'll know I told you where to find him."

"That's likely."

She stared at Orin, letting his imagination of Crow's anger fill the silence.

"He'll kill me." His words were almost a whine.

"That's likely, too." Tilly shrugged. "Or you can take me to Crow and leave the talking to me. You'll see why Raven is the best there is." She waited, breath held, praying he would go along—not that she needed him, but she didn't trust him left behind, and she had enough to worry about without looking over her shoulder for Orin.

Orin stared back, defeated. With only threats and talk, she had convinced him. It dawned on Tilly that he really *did* believe she was Raven and could do anything.

Warmth spread inside her at the thought of her sister. Rheada *could* do anything. She had proven that, time after time. For a second, Tilly wished she were here. With Rheada at her side, Tilly knew she could pull this off. But then both of their lives would be at stake.

She took a deep breath of renewed determination. No, this was for her to do alone. But she made a silent promise to her sister that, no matter what the outcome, Raven finally *would* be put to rest.

It was late afternoon when Rheada was sure of their destination. She had tried to convince herself otherwise. She had kept hoping that Miguel would direct her to make a turn, take them in another direction. Instead, he ordered her relentlessly on toward Fremont Ridge, the gateway to her canyons.

Why here? *What is happening?*

Only hours before she had known what was going on, she had had a plan to end the trouble, and she had had a name to put *with* that trouble: Orin.

All that had been before Miguel kidnapped her, before he ran over Kee . . . before Kee mentioned Crow.

How could he know of Crow? Could she have misunderstood?

Once again, her gaze darted to the rearview mirror, praying he was conscious—needing to *see* him, to see the answer in his eyes.

She had to have imagined Kee saying Crow's name, Rheada told herself. Or there was another man named Crow—not the notorious pot thief. Kee *couldn't* have been talking about the same Crow.

Her thoughts tumbled, one after the other, with no logic attached, as she simultaneously pretended to be ignorant of the landscape. She had to force herself to concentrate on *not* knowing the road, though her body remembered every rut, anticipated every boulder . . . and all the while she could see in her mind the looming darkness of the ridge; she could feel the dark power of the canyons pulling her closer. Her heart thumped harder with every mile. Miguel was taking her back to where she had never wanted to return.

And along with Rheada, he was taking Kee.

Her gaze cut to the mirror, desperate to see him, but she could make out only the silhouette of his body, still slumped in unconsciousness.

In her mind, she replayed over and over that last awful

moment in the car. Though unfocused and stunned by the blow, Kee's gaze had stayed on her. As he'd slumped to the floor, his eyes had filled with what she could only describe as remorse, and she heard his last word: *Rheada.*

With all her strength, she *willed* him to move, to open his eyes and look upon her once more. She needed to reassure herself with his strong, keen gaze—the sureness of his eyes, his *raven* eyes that could see to her heart.

That same heart jumped in her chest. Oh, God, he would see her here! How could she hide her true self from him while in this very place? Here—where she had been a criminal? Where she *was* Raven.

Or did he already know? Did he already know of her past?

The vehicle careened over ruts, out of her control. From the corner of her eye, she saw Miguel bounce wildly on the seat, hitting his head on the roof.

"Goddamnit! You drive like a beginner!"

She wanted to shout back that she had been driving *most* her life, right in these very canyons. She knew them better than he did. Did he think he was taking her to someplace remote? She wanted to laugh in his face at his ignorance. What the hell *was* he thinking? Why was he taking them here?

Suddenly, she wanted to scream at him, demand answers. Insane emotions welled within her. A turmoil of anger, desperation, and fear churned in a hot roil.

Oh, God. How could this be happening? How could she be here . . . with Kee.

You can never escape, Rheada.

Tilly's words pounded at her temple, over and over, as if to drive home that truth. And as Rheada drove into the canyons, deep into the labyrinth—a maze of wilderness where you could get lost—she saw how Tilly was right. For Rheada there was no way out.

Movement, followed by a groan, lifted from the backseat. It was Kee, sitting up. Rheada stared into the mirror, watching, drinking in every bit of him as he emerged into view: the breadth of his shoulders; his disheveled jet-black hair; the strong line of his jaw. Her breath held on the moment she would see his eyes.

The vehicle bumped into and out of a rut, and when Rheada looked back to the mirror, Kee's gaze was on her. He stared, his eyes filled with a heartfelt relief and then longing.

Whatever she had been thinking flew from her mind. The tormenting grip of emotions suddenly eased, and she felt weightless, set free. Joy like she had never known rose inside her. She could feel her lips curve into a smile.

"Are you okay?" His voice, low and intimate, made her heart skid.

"I'm fine—"

"Shut the fuck up and drive. Take this path."

Rheada obeyed, her hands steering the wheel while her eyes stayed at the mirror.

Kee's gaze held hers—for what must have been only a second, but felt like minutes—then cut sharply to Miguel. The change in his eyes was heart-stopping: cold, fierce, deadly—in such stark contrast to how he had been looking at her that Rheada winced at the thought of facing that hateful stare.

"You little coward." Kee's tone challenged Miguel.

"Shut up," Miguel said, without even turning in his seat. He was staring ahead, deep in concentration. It occurred to Rheada he might be lost.

"You don't have the guts to pull this off," Kee hissed.

"Shut up!"

Rheada noticed a shift of Kee's shoulders. He looked at her, then tilted his head to the right, his eyes filled with purpose. Suddenly, Rheada understood: He was signaling her to pull off.

She gave a slight nod of her head. But in the same instant, Miguel's arm shot out and grabbed her.

"Stop," Miguel ordered.

She swerved the car. Kee came across the seat, his hands at Miguel's throat. He pushed Miguel forward, slamming him into the dash. Rheada tried to grab for Miguel's gun, but both Kee and Miguel tumbled out the door. As she opened her own door, gunfire split the night.

"Get up!"

Rheada didn't recognize the voice. She jumped out her side, ran around the car, and came to a stumbling halt: A stranger held an automatic rifle on both Kee and Miguel. He motioned for Rheada to join them.

"Well, what do we have here?"

"It's me. Ortiz."

"I don't know an Ortiz."

"I have something for Crow." Miguel started to pull himself from the ground. Rheada thought she saw the glint of metal.

"And I don't know a *Crow*. But I've got something for you." The man aimed his rifle at Miguel's temple. In the same second, Miguel raised an arm and Rheada saw the gun in his hand.

"I think you do know Crow. And you're going to take us to him."

The man looked from the gun to Miguel. "You're a dead man," he said.

Miguel only grinned. "Yeah," he said, smiling.

The man's eyes flashed with fear and she saw him make a choice. He lowered his gun, and started up the dry wash.

"Follow him!" Miguel ordered Kee, at the same time grabbing Rheada's arm.

She stumbled into step, frantic for time to think. She could trip Miguel, break free. But the stranger could easily fire on her . . . or Kee.

She raised her gaze to him, as if she could find the answer to what she should do there, in his strong presence. But what she saw was a bowed head, a trudging walk. He looked defeated, as though he were being led to an executioner.

Rheada's thoughts tumbled in a free fall, and for the first time it occurred to her that they might actually die out here.

That possibility sparked against something inside her, like flint against her stone-hard determination. No, they wouldn't die! Not when she was this close to knowing what it really *meant* to be Rheada, not Raven.

They rounded a corner and a canyon wind lifted her hair. Undistracted, Rheada stared ahead and her eyes, fully accustomed to the twilight, immediately discerned people ahead—three that she could see standing. One of the three straightened, nearly imperceptibly, but Rheada's focus was locked. She could *feel* his stare, and she knew he was the leader. Her trained eyes scanned the area and she saw two others crouched.

The gust shifted. Rheada caught an unnatural motion, like long hair floating on a breeze. The movement struck her as familiar. Her heart skipped, triggering her mind: It was Tilly!

Chapter 20

RHEADA couldn't take her eyes from her sister. Tilly looked different, older, as if she had aged several years in the few days since Rheada last saw her. She was so thin. Her face was drawn and tight. She was too *young* to look like this.

What has happened to my little sister?

A sudden, hard grip on Rheada's arm yanked her up short.

"Stay back." Kee hissed the order under his breath.

Rheada had not even been conscious of walking forward. She had been so driven by the need to help her sister, she hadn't given a thought to Kee or anyone else here.

"Surprised to see me, Crow?" Miguel strode confidently from the group—blocking Rheada's view of Tilly—and stopped right in front of the tall, lean man.

Rheada's gaze locked on the man.

"Surprised you're still so stupid."

You're so stupid.

She had heard those same words, spoken by the same man to her father. Rheada's heart thundered. Suddenly, she was fourteen, watching *this* man argue violently with her father.

"That's what you thought, wasn't it?" Miguel said. "That I'm stupid. I was smart enough to live, though. You hadn't counted on that."

Miguel moved and Rheada could again see Tilly, staring at Crow. What was Tilly doing here? Rheada was afraid the answer was right there on Tilly's face, her thin features lined with a hateful determination. Even as Miguel's voice rose, confronting Crow, and the armed men circled closer, Tilly's focus never wavered, and Rheada stared across the thirty feet to Tilly, her senses acute, silently *pleading* for Tilly to look at her—but her sister never looked over. She seemed determined *not* to make eye contact with Rheada, keeping her head angled, her gaze averted, her face shielded. But nothing could bar the intense, *desperate* emotions that bridged the distance, and arched straight to Rheada's heart, pulling tight as a cord.

Tilly was in trouble. Rheada knew it to her core.

Kee pulled her close and leaned into her. "Rheada, you've got to get out of here," he whispered.

"I can't—"

"Yes you can. Just take slow steps backward."

How did she explain that she couldn't leave without Tilly ... when Kee didn't even *know* she had a sister?

Without waiting for her response, Kee gripped her arm and started to pull her back one step, as if to get her started.

"No." She stood her ground. She glanced up and saw a great need in his eyes that she listen to him, and do as he asked. "Kee, please, I won't leave."

He gazed back, his eyes filled with emotions as if his heart would speak to her. For a second, she thought she even saw love there.

Oh, God, what will he think, what will he feel, when the night is over?

"You *have* to." His grip was fierce on her arm.

She would do *anything* to be able to obey him, turn and freely walk away, as if none of this had anything to do with her.

Except it had everything to do with her ... and she had no idea what to do. She had the sudden sense of being swept over a ledge, out of control.

There is no way out.

The knowledge settled on her, seeped into her with the calming force of a deep breath. It was true: There was no way out. Her past had come back—just as she should have known it would.

Her hand closed over his and squeezed. He didn't respond. Rheada looked up, past his shoulder to his face. It was fierce, hard. His eyes stared straight ahead. He was a warrior, set on battle, his fears hidden beneath an impenetrable mask. He looked ready to die, right here and now.

Rheada's heart seemed to lift within her chest, reaching out to the man who would actually want to protect her. She raised a hand to his stone-hard jaw. She didn't know what she meant to say, until the words pressed from her heart. "I love you."

He blinked. His jaw drew tight, impossibly rigid, as if he were clamping down on all his emotions. The next instant, he looked at her, but Rheada's heart froze at the pain she saw in his eyes.

"Don't."

Don't? Don't love him? That was impossible.

"You'll be sorry," he muttered.

Before Rheada could say anything, the man with the gun jerked Kee from where he stood, shoved the automatic at his back and pushed him toward Crow and Miguel.

She wanted to yell after Kee that she would never be sorry for loving him, but the words stuck in her throat when her gaze caught on Tilly. Her intense anxiety was palpable and roared through Rheada on a rush of dread. Rheada had to do something.

She followed Kee toward the group, pretending to be an ignorant observer, an ordinary person snagged into a terrible situation. "Who's in charge here?" She hoped that the fact that her voice was choked with emotion only enhanced her pretense of being a scared, innocent bystander.

Waves of intensity aimed at her by both Kee and Tilly nearly stopped Rheada in her tracks. She forged ahead. She planted herself in front of Crow. "Are you in charge? I demand to know what's going on. This man kidnapped me." She slapped Miguel's arm.

She really didn't have a plan. She was only hoping to create a distraction—so that somehow, they could all get out of here.

"You little bitch." Miguel whirled at her, his fist raised.

"No!"

It was Tilly. She jumped in front of Miguel. His blow glanced off the top of her head and sent her spinning into Rheada's arms. Rheada staggered back and caught her. Her arms around her sister, she couldn't withhold a hug—a quick one, she told herself.

Tilly pressed a hand to Rheada's chest and pushed away. "I'm okay." She said it aloud so that everyone could hear, as she stared hard into Rheada's eyes. The message was clear: *Be quiet!*

Just as swiftly, Tilly turned her back on Rheada and faced Crow. "Get them out of here. Or you can forget—"

Crow laughed. It was a humorless, evil laugh that came with a promise of ruthlessness. "Well, well. What have we got here?"

Crow strode to Rheada, stopping only inches away. His stench of dirt and sweat made her stomach clench. He grabbed her chin and lifted her head, his eyes studying her. "Uncanny. Could almost be twins."

Rheada saw the realization in his gaze. She yanked his hand away from her face and stepped back, stalling, frantically thinking, as if there were anything she *could* do to stop what was about to be revealed.

"So this is Raven's sister," Crow said.

She heard Kee's breath, swift and sharp. She stole a glance at him and her heart stumbled, teetering before the intensity in his eyes.

"You're *Raven*'s sister?"

Kee's condemning tone sliced clean into her, stopping at the hard knot of lies. She couldn't move. She couldn't speak. It was as if she were impaled on a spear and a step in any direction meant her life.

"Interesting," Crow said.

"Remember I brought her to you, Crow."

"Shut up," Crow ordered without looking at Miguel. His gaze was fixed on Rheada and then Kee. "I see you found her," he said to Kee.

Rheada's gaze jerked to Kee. What was Crow talking about?

"This proves me out!" Miguel continued. "He was trying to get the goods on Raven."

The goods on Raven?

Rheada's heart faltered.

"How better than to get involved with the sister?" Miguel strode to Kee. "Pretty fucking smart for an undercover agent. Just not smart enough."

Rheada's heart stopped. It wasn't true. It *couldn't* be true. Kee wasn't undercover. Miguel had to be lying. She looked at Kee, knowing his eyes would reassure her, but he was staring at Tilly, his gaze stunned, confused, studying her as if comparing her to some files in his head.

"You thought you'd never be found out, didn't you, Blackburn? Well, you got lucky the last time."

"And you have no more proof than the last time." Kee's voice was low, threatening. He was on the offense, and Rheada was sure she would hear *his* truth, finally.

"Wrong again." Miguel smiled. "Orin?"

The weasel stepped forward, his beady eyes darting from

one gun to the next. He handed a short, black rod to Miguel, then stepped back into the shadows, this time closer still to Crow. Rheada immediately recognized the metal shaft as an anchor for a sensor. She suddenly remembered where she had seen metal rods: in the boxes of equipment in Kee's cabin.

"Recognize this?" Miguel waved it in front of Kee, then showed it to Crow, without handing it over. "It matches the one I showed you before, Crow."

"That proves nothing," Kee said.

"Oh, but it does. It came from Canyon Largo. From a site you staked out."

"Or maybe *you* staked it out," Kee countered.

Miguel stepped up to Kee, facing him from only inches away. "*I'm* not the one who scouted out the canyon, pretending to drive a tour there with *Raven*'s sister."

"That's right," Orin said.

From the corner of her eye, Rheada caught Tilly's sharp look at Orin. She also noticed that Orin had inched closer to Crow.

"Your luck has just run out." Miguel's eyes gleamed with certain victory.

Rheada staggered back, suddenly weak, powerless, all her life draining from her, her mind able to grasp only one thing: betrayal. Everything Kee had said, everything she had thought to be true about him, was a lie.

He wasn't a mapmaker. He was undercover. And he was after Raven . . . he had been hunting *her*.

God, was it true?

She looked at him, sure that she had to be wrong. She found his gaze leveled on her, his eyes hardened.

Rheada stared back, ready to hate him, wanting to hate him, but then she saw his brow furrow suddenly, as if he fought the pain of a great internal wound.

She felt the same pain, at the same instant, as if his wound were also hers; as if they were bound by an unyielding, *unbreakable* cord.

Rheada realized she couldn't hate him.

"Interesting," Crow said again. He shifted, turning his back on Kee. "Very interesting." Suddenly, he whirled, landing a fist in Kee's gut.

Kee doubled over. Rheada reached for him, but one of Crow's men jerked her back.

Miguel had Kee by his collar. "Now it's your turn, you asshole. Time to see how smart *you* are at defeating death."

"Shoot him," Crow ordered.

No!

"No."

For a second, Rheada thought she had spoken aloud.

"No, Crow," Miguel continued. "I want to see him breathe dirt." Miguel sneered at Kee. "I want to see you claw your way out of a grave."

"There's no time for this," Crow said. "Shoot him, Miguel."

"You're not giving the orders, Crow." Miguel glanced to the side. "Orin?"

Orin was now right beside Crow, with a gun at the pot thief's head.

The next instant, Miguel swung the metal rod, cracking it against the head of one of Crow's men. He grabbed the gun and faced the group.

Rheada's gaze shot from Orin to Tilly. What the hell was happening? But Tilly looked just as surprised.

"Did you think I would forget who *put* me in that grave, Crow? Or maybe you thought I was the forgiving kind." He leveled the gun to Crow's chest. "I'm not."

"You're crazy if you think you can get away with this." Tilly's voice rang out clear and strong.

"Orin, shut her up."

"You mean kill me," Tilly said.

Rheada's heart jumped. Her hand went to Tilly, but Tilly had already stepped away, toward Orin. "That's what he means, Orin. Kill me. Kill *Raven*."

He looked uncertain.

"You don't want to do that, Orin. What about our plans?"

"You mean the mask?"

Both Tilly *and* Rheada jerked their heads to Miguel.

He chuckled. "Yeah, I know about the mask. But y haven't delivered, have you, *Raven*? Orin has *other* plans Starting with both Crow and Raven dead!"

He shifted, turning the gun on Tilly. His lethal inter the air from Rheada's lungs.

"No! She's not Raven." Her words came out as a gasp. Rheada took a deep breath of the canyon air as she stepped in front of Tilly. "I'm Raven."

For a moment, no one moved, no one said a word. And Rheada wondered what she was going to do now. All she had known was that she couldn't let Tilly die.

"No you're not," Orin squeaked. "You can't be."

"How do you know that, Orin? You know only what my sister has told you."

He edged a step from Crow, still holding the gun to him, but looking past Rheada, to Tilly. "You *pretended*?"

"Don't listen to her. She's lying." Tilly stepped from behind Rheada.

Rheada grabbed her, stared with eyes pleading for Tilly to be quiet. Tilly's eyes carried the same plea—each sister desperate to save the other one. Rheada had to win this struggle, she had to prevail. She *had* to save their lives.

She hardened her gaze on Tilly. "Prove it."

Tilly didn't hesitate. "They already *know* I'm Raven," she said smoothly. "Why should they believe you?"

Rheada's mind raced, and when she came up with only one idea, she hoped she could make it work. She prayed that she knew her sister well enough, that Tilly couldn't have changed enough to have betrayed the one thing dear to both of them.

She faced Orin. "Only Raven would know exactly where the mask is. Has *she* shown you the mask?"

"No—"

"That's because only *I* know where it is."

"That's not true. I have the mask—" Tilly started.

"You told me you didn't," Orin said. He was looking at Tilly with real doubt. "You told me that damn bird had to show you where it was."

"She's been pretending all along." Rheada hurried ahead. "Without my approval. Which means any *deal* she negotiated, you need to renegotiate with me. There is only *one* Raven." She faced Crow. "You *know* you're looking at her." Rheada ~~ew~~ all her courage up into her eyes and leveled her gaze at ~~w.~~

~~e~~ was aware of Kee's steely eyes staring at her. She ~~arely~~ withstand the pull of his gaze. She yearned to ~~glance~~ to him . . . but she knew what she would see:

She could *feel* the pulse of his emotions directed straight at her.

He hates me.

Her heart buckled. She couldn't do this! To win, to convince Crow, was to lose everything—more than everything, for she had never dared hope for the love she had found with Kee.

Kee's hatred, his anger, coursed through her—an infusion of icy cold she could *feel* in her veins, pumping to her heart. She thought she would die, when something strange happened: The very *purity* of his hatred gave *her* strength, a clarity that she had never known. Yes, she was Raven. She had never asked for the role, but she had been damn good at it. And because of her, tonight, she just might save the lives of those precious to her.

"You're a little confused, aren't you?" asked Miguel. "You want to talk about deals, you talk to me."

Rheada stared at Miguel, making her gaze as fierce and hateful as possible. "I don't negotiate with undercover."

"You bitch. I'm not undercover. Blackburn is, and you know it. Everyone here knows it."

Rheada let his accusation hang in the air until the tension was crisp in the utter silence. "If Kee is undercover," she said quietly, making everyone listen to each word, "why would *I* be sleeping with him?"

"Don't ask me. Maybe you're desperate." He laughed, but he was the only one laughing. When his laughter turned to raunchy coughs, Rheada just stared, schooling her face into pity for this *pathetic* man.

"You're the one who's desperate, because someone else had *also* fingered you as undercover—"

"What—"

Rheada strode to him, her mind working fast. It was amazing how rapidly the lies came to her, how easily she had slipped into her role. She had dealt with criminals like Ortiz all her life. She wasn't going to lose to this one. "Have you forgotten about the reporter?"

"He was investigating pot thieves!" He turned to Crow. "He was asking questions, getting close. I did what *you* would have done!"

It was all true, Rheada knew. She was betting her life—

and Tilly's and Kee's—that Crow didn't know the facts. "He was getting close, all right. He knew about the sensors you planted in Canyon Largo, didn't he? You *had* to shut him up."

"She's making all this up! I didn't plant those sensors. Blackburn did."

"Wrong again. He couldn't have. Kee Blackburn was with me, *night and day*."

"She's lying!"

His grip tightened on the gun. He advanced on Rheada, pushing her back. She felt the cold circle of metal poke her ribs and nearly faltered.

From the corner of her eye, Rheada could see that Orin's full attention was on her. The gun he had held on Crow was now pointed at the ground. She didn't relish being at Crow's mercy any more than Miguel's, but she could deal with only one threat at a time.

"Look around you, Ortiz. They don't think I'm lying. *Raven* sleeping with undercover? Wouldn't happen. *That's* what everyone knows."

Her thoughts stumbled for a second, caught on the fact that that was exactly what *had* happened: She had slept with an undercover agent. More, she had fallen in love. She had given her heart to a man who was hunting her, with the goal of turning her in—or maybe worse, given the hate she had seen in his eyes.

And as good as she was sure he was, he had failed. He hadn't caught Raven . . . but she was still going to lose everything.

Her heart contracted with such a sharp pain, Rheada barely controlled a gasp. She gritted her teeth and focused on Miguel. And the words she needed to say came straight from the wound in her heart.

"I'll tell you what else they know, Ortiz. They know that Raven has never been caught. That's because I'm careful, Ortiz. I don't trust easily." The wound widened inside, stabbed deeper with each word, but she didn't stop—she *wouldn't* stop: because this was the truth. If she could, she would have turned to Kee and said the words straight to his face.

"I have trusted him with everything." Her quiet voice lifted on the canyon air. "I trust him with my life."

Miguel stared at her as if he were hypnotized.

Rheada took one more step, her gaze never wavering. "He's not undercover, Ortiz. You are."

Before the last words left her mouth, she rocked back and swept her arm up, slamming her wrist against the barrel, knocking the rifle loose from Miguel's hands. She dove for the gun. Her hands fought Miguel's. The rifle went off, several rounds piercing the air.

"No!" Kee yelled. Rheada heard a scuffle behind her.

Miguel overpowered her, pushing her back, as he reached for the rifle. Someone dove over her, tackling Miguel. It was Kee, and his yell—a low, primal roar—as he landed on Miguel, reverberated through Rheada.

Another shot rang out. Two cries of pain came from the heap that was Miguel and Kee. Rheada scrambled to them. The gunfire couldn't have been the rifle! It had sounded more like a handgun. Kee had to be okay.

She pushed at Miguel. His limp body rolled aside, and Rheada saw blood on Kee. Her heart jumped to her throat. It was Miguel's blood, she told herself.

A hand grabbed at her arm, pulling her from the ground. "Leave them." It was Crow.

"Go to hell," she hissed. She yanked her arm free and reached for Kee.

Please, let him be okay.

He groaned. The sound swept through Rheada, flooding her with relief and joy, leaving her light-headed and dizzy. He leaned up on an elbow. His face was lined with pain. Rheada's relief veered sharply to anxiety. Her hand went to his arm, wanting to comfort, to help, to *touch*. The thought spun through her: *He saved my life.*

Her fingers were a mere fraction from him, when his head jerked up as if he had sensed her. His black eyes narrowed on her with a hatred that sliced the air. "Don't."

He pushed himself from the ground, leaving Rheada in a wake of chilling air.

Don't had been Kee's response before, when she had told him she loved him. *You'll be sorry.*

She *was* sorry, but not for loving him. She couldn't change that, she realized, even as she tried to harden her heart. No, she was sorry that *he* had loved *her*. He hated himself for that. She could see that in the torment in his eyes. She would give anything right now to take that torment from him . . . except she was the cause.

She sat there now, weighted to the ground.

A slender hand touched her shoulder. Tilly's face bent to hers. Her sister's eyes shone with worry.

The heartfelt concern on Tilly's face cracked the dam of Rheada's defenses. Her own eyes filled on a swift rush of emotion, and she pulled Tilly to her in a hug. Tilly squeezed back and Rheada's body remembered how much she had missed her sister.

"You shouldn't have come back," Tilly whispered.

"I never left, Tilly." As she said the words, Rheada realized that the truth was that she never *could* have left. The wound at her heart felt mortal.

She pulled Tilly close, hanging on to the one person in the world she had. She knew, though, that they still weren't home free. "It's not over yet."

Tilly paused. "You can't take them to the mask, Rheada. It's not there anymore."

Rheada pulled back slightly and smiled at Tilly. "I know that, but they don't."

Chapter 21

KEE'S right arm hurt like hell. He ignored the pain—and the nausea that rolled from his gut to his throat—his only thought to get his hands on Miguel's rifle. He couldn't see it, but it had to be here.

A boot stepped into Kee's view just to his left. The boot kicked at Miguel, rolling the man's body over—and there was the rifle, just two feet from Kee.

The next instant, a hand reached down and lifted the gun from the ground.

Kee glanced up. Crow stood over him, rifle in one hand and a handgun in his other. His gaze was on Miguel.

"Well, that son of a bitch is finally dead." He chuckled. "Orin, too," he added with a glance over his shoulder.

Kee looked past Crow and saw that Orin was in a dead heap on the ground. He thought of the gunfire he had heard and realized Crow had overwhelmed Orin.

"Good news for you, Blackburn."

"Yeah. Good news."

Crow looked down to Kee's arm. "Looks like the bullet got you, too. I almost got two for the price of one." His face sobered and he leveled the rifle on Kee. "Get the hell up."

Kee took his time, rising first to a crouch. He could leap at Crow, catch him off balance—

Suddenly, a hand grabbed his collar and yanked him off the ground. Kee deliberately stumbled back a step, hoping to catch Crow's man off guard. Instead, his leg found dead air. His foot went out from under him and he hit the ground, bracing himself at the last second with his right arm. Pain shot up his arm to his chest with the force of an internal explosion. Shards of light streaked his vision.

He looked up, struggling to focus. Crow was staring down the barrel of the rifle at him. "Maybe I'll just shoot you."

Kee heard a gasp.

Crow glanced at Raven. She still had her arm around her sister. Crow's other hand lifted and aimed the handgun at

Raven's forehead. "You, too. I could shoot all three of you and be done with it."

Raven didn't blink. "But then you would never get the mask, would you, Crow?"

He smiled. "Oh, you'll tell me where the mask is." He shifted the gun a fraction toward Raven's sister. "Tell me," he ordered.

"She doesn't know."

Kee was surprised at the calmness in Raven's voice.

"But *you* do," Crow pointed out. "Tell me, or you can tell her goodbye."

Crow took a step, bringing the gun within an inch of the sister's forehead, his gaze never wavering from Raven. His lethal intent electrified the air.

"Shoot her or Blackburn and I'll never tell you." She stared him down, her face hard.

Crow's face turned mean. "You *will* tell me," he growled.

He slammed the gun against Raven's head. She hit the ground. Kee felt the blow in his gut. His body lurched toward her before his mind kicked in, jerking him back.

What the hell do I care about Raven?

But he couldn't take his eyes from her. He watched her as, with obvious effort, she pulled herself from the ground and faced Crow.

"I'll take you to the mask on one condition, Crow. Kee and my sister go free."

She stared at Crow. Even Kee couldn't tell if she were bluffing. *No one* could match the absolute fearlessness he saw in her face.

One of Crow's men approached him. "Let's just get out of here, Crow."

Crow shook his head.

"Forget them. Forget the damn mask," the man persisted. "We don't need it. We have enough."

Crow's eyes flared with frustration. "No." He breathed out the word as if it were his last. "We're not forgetting the mask."

He looked at Raven. Slowly, his lips curved into a thin, evil smile. Kee's gut twisted into a sick knot.

Crow grabbed her and pulled her from the ground. "Fine. We'll do it your way, Raven." He yanked her close to him. "You'll be *my* little bird."

"No!"

It was Raven's sister. She lunged for Crow. He swung his rifle against her head and she crumpled to the ground.

Kee was on his feet, taking a step toward Crow, without any thought of what the hell he was doing. Crow leveled the rifle on him. "You heard the lady, Blackburn. Take off." His eyes flashed a threat. "Before I change my mind."

Crow stepped over Miguel's body. "You two," he yelled to his men. "Take my Jeep. You come with me," he said to the third man. Crow started down the canyon, dragging Raven along. She looked over her shoulder to her sister, then to Kee. She had a look of goodbye in her eyes.

The moonlight had made a ring of white on her black hair—hair he had forced his hands through, tangled his fingers in as he pulled her close. Kee watched the circle of white until it disappeared—it was as if a halo were suddenly swallowed in blackness.

The Jeep with Crow's two men hurtled past, throwing rocks and dirt in the air. The headlights careened wildly, flashing on Crow and Raven, then passing on.

Fierce, primal rage erupted in Kee. He had to clamp down his mouth to hold in a scream. He'd never felt so damned helpless. His gaze darted over the ground for a weapon, a gun, a stick, anything. His hand closed around a rock. He saw Crow's evil sneer in his mind.

How the hell did I let him outsmart me?

He stood, rock in hand. He would bash the son of a bitch's head in.

His mind slammed shut on the insanity of his thoughts. He would kill a man over Rheada?

Raven, goddamnit!

No, he wouldn't kill a man over her. He was hunting her, goddamnit. He *hated* her.

He wanted to go after her now, grab her, make her admit she had lied, that everything was a lie. She didn't love him. She was nothing more than a dirty pot thief.

I hate her. He repeated the words, calling upon the hate inside himself, but his mind wouldn't cooperate. He kept remembering lying with her, making love; his body remembered the rush of wanting her, of realizing that she wanted him. The more he tried to obliterate the memories, the stronger they grew. He was losing his mind. It was as if he were split in two, torn apart, beyond repair.

"Are you coming?"

Kee whirled on the voice, then saw the sister. He had forgotten she was even there.

Of course he had forgotten her. He had never even known there was a sister . . . and now he was stuck in the middle of nowhere with Raven's *sister*. Suddenly, the irony struck him funny. He laughed aloud, relishing the echo of his sound in this wild place.

"I take that as a no." She started off in the opposite direction of the canyon entrance.

"Where the hell are you going?"

"After my sister," she answered over her shoulder. She approached the body of the man she had called Orin. He was lying still on the ground. She hesitated for a second, then stepped over him and kept walking. If she continued in that direction, she was going to walk right into the canyon wall.

In five strides, Kee caught her and grabbed her arm. "*Where* are you going?" he asked again.

She jerked her head to him. Her eyes were wide, frightened, *driven*. "I told you. I'm going after my sister."

"This way?" He nodded to the looming cliff face.

"I didn't want Crow to know how I got here, so I parked my Jeep on top and climbed down a path at the front of the canyon. I didn't trust him." She paused, and her gaze lingered at the spot where they had last seen Crow and her sister. "One smart thing, I did, huh?" Her eyes started to fill. She lifted her chin, not allowing one tear to fall. It was a mannerism Kee had witnessed in Rheada.

Raven. His jaw clenched against the incessant slip of his own mind.

"I can drive us within a short hike of the canyon they're going to," she said, walking again.

"Wait a minute!"

"For what?" She faced him. "A bus? If we hurry, we can make it there about the same time they do."

Did he trust her? Or was this another charade, another game of smoke and mirrors like the sisters had worked on him from day one?

He watched her start to climb the talus slope. She was

obviously planning to go up that cliff, with or without him. Kee had to make a decision. All he knew was that he sure as hell wasn't letting Raven slip through his hands. With a last look down the canyon, toward Raven, he turned and followed her sister.

She tackled the rock face with all the subtlety of an angry, driven mountain lion, charging forward, her hands and feet scrambling for holds, meanwhile sending slides of rocks and dirt down on Kee. Her urgency matched, then amplified, his own, but he was hard-pressed to keep up with her. Though he had a longer reach with his legs, his right arm severely handicapped him.

Another shower of rocks tumbled from beneath her feet straight down the wall to Kee. He pressed his face to the cliff, his strong left arm clinging, his right thrown above his head for protection. With every strike of stones on his arm, splinters of pain exploded in his body.

When the deluge ended, he shook the dirt from his head and arm, and looked up to see that she was now walking a narrow ledge, a natural path of stone that wound nearly to the top of the cliff. He had to rock-climb the last ten feet, and was about to hoist himself over the top when her arm stretched to him, grabbed his collar and dragged him up.

All he could hear was his own heavy breathing. All he could feel was the pounding of pain in his arm. Kee folded his arm to his chest, and felt the stickiness of blood trickling from under his shirt cuff to his hand. Blood soaked his shirt down to his wrist. He didn't think the bullet could be lodged in his arm, though he couldn't be sure.

His arm thundered as blood pumped down and pounded against the wound. He bit his teeth down on the blood-soaked cloth, gripped the cuff with his left hand, and ripped the material in one swift, torturous motion. He drew a sharp hiss at the pain. From the corner of his eye, he caught the sharp glance of Raven's sister.

A cursory glance at the wound confirmed his guess: His flesh was pretty torn up by the bullet, but he wouldn't bleed to death. A small miracle, considering his death had seemed inevitable down in that canyon. Yet, here he was alive—he didn't have a bullet in his head and he wasn't choking on dirt from the bottom of a pit. Thanks to Raven.

Why the hell had she saved his life? Twice?

He heard a rip and saw that her sister had torn some cloth from the bottom of her shirt. She wrapped it around the wound, and finished by tucking the ends into a makeshift bandage. Her hands, careful and skilled, reminded him of when Rheada had cleaned and bandaged his hand.

"You need stitches," she said, sitting back on her heels.

Those had been Rheada's words to him at the hospital. Images flashed in his mind—of her concerned eyes, her gentle touch.

"Are you going to be all right?"

Kee realized he had been staring off into space past her shoulder. He focused on her, found dark eyes studying him. Though she was smaller, younger, she looked so much like Rheada.

Raven, goddamnit!

Why did he even have a *second* of trouble remembering who the hell he was thinking about?

"I'll be fine."

"Good," she said, jumping to her feet and heading off again, this time across the plateau. Kee stood and followed, watching her. He couldn't help but notice her gait—straightforward, agile, like her sister's. They were two, sleek, stealthy cats, prowling the night, watching over each other, *covering* each other, fooling the world . . . fooling him . . . seducing him.

Flashes of memory cut through him: the flinch of her muscles as he had thrust within her, finding the barrier; then the passion that had filled her eyes.

Emotions charged through him, forcing a thought onto him that he wouldn't accept. His mind stumbled, tripped, grasping for the anger he had felt.

He hated her, he told himself.

A sudden, stabbing pain drew his gut into a knot, his whole insides into torment. The pain hadn't come from his arm; it hadn't come from the wound; it was tearing him up from *within*—as if the bullet had found his heart.

* * *

A half hour later, they were parked at the edge of another canyon. She had driven pell-mell over slickrock, pushing the Jeep over impossible terrain. Here was one area in which the two sisters definitely differed—with one barely able to keep a vehicle from stalling out and the other one lucky not to fry the engine. When she stopped, it was as if the whole night breathed a sigh of relief.

Kee pressed down on the door handle, but before he reached his foot to the ground, her hand was on his arm, stopping him.

"I understand you're mad," she said. "I don't blame you. I didn't mean for this to involve Rheada."

What? What the hell is she talking about?

"All she ever dreamed of was escaping this life. And all I wanted was for her to be with me. A real bitch, aren't I?" She laughed, but it had the strangled sound of being choked at her throat.

"Truth is, I was selfish and scared. I wanted her with me like she always had been. I even told her she would never make it legit. I'm really sorry."

What the hell was she saying? Kee couldn't get his mind around her words. Raven wanted to go legit, but her sister didn't? It didn't make sense.

Kee flashed on the memory of Rheada putting the shard back. He thought of all the boxes of relics returned by tourists, and her copious notes and records about each one. He had conjectured *then* that she might be trying to go straight. So maybe it was true. So what? That didn't change anything.

He wished her sister would just *shut up*. But that wasn't going to happen.

"I tried to tell her that I was doing this *for* her. It was my chance to set things right. Make Crow pay for what we *both* lost." She paused. "She never wanted to be Raven. She did it for me. This was my turn to do something for her."

Her voice, pleading with him to understand, tugged at something dangerous to him deep inside. It was as if her hand were pulling open a door and releasing a monster he wouldn't be able to control. Every bit of him tensed against the threat to his very sanity.

"I'm glad Rheada found you."

Kee shot a glance to her, ready to tell her to go to hell.

"She has needed someone just like you," she said, before Kee had a chance to say a word. "Someone who would look after *her* for a change. She deserves that. She deserves to have her own life. I was wrong." She was looking at him, the moon reflected within the sheen on her eyes. "I just wanted you to know this, in case—" Her voice broke. She swiped a hand in front of her face as if to banish the pressing emotions. "In case everything goes wrong tonight," she finished.

He stepped out of the Jeep into the night air, and started walking away from her, away from his thoughts, away from whatever it was inside him clamoring to get out. He was at the edge of the canyon, staring down into the abyss, when she caught up to him.

He felt her hand on his arm. "I understand you're mad and you don't want to talk to me. I don't blame you, but you've *got* to listen. You have to stop her."

Stop her. What the hell was going on? Kee jerked his head to her. "What are you talking about?"

"You have to stop her," she said again. "Stop this charade of hers. She knows the mask isn't there. I don't know what she thinks she's going to do when Crow finds the cave empty."

"What do you mean, the mask isn't there?"

"It isn't there. I took it. I tried to tell her, but she said she already knew. She already *knew* the cave was empty when she struck the deal with Crow."

Kee shook his head, trying to understand. "I don't get it. Why—"

"To save our lives," she hissed, as if he were dense. Her grip on his arm tightened. "Don't you see? When Crow realizes that she lied, he'll kill her." She took her first step over the edge of the canyon. She lowered herself over the side, then stopped and looked back at Kee. "He'll kill her, when it should be me." The sheen of emotion was gone from her eyes. She stared back at him, her gaze clear and strong, with the force of everything she held to be true.

She disappeared over the side and Kee was left standing there, staring, frozen to the spot, his mind impaled on the *truth* he had seen in her gaze. Raven had negotiated a deal that could only result in her certain death?

It wasn't true. She wouldn't do that for him. She knew he

was undercover. She knew he had been hunting *her*. She knew
that everything Miguel said had been true.

But even as he argued the logic, Kee thought of her demand
that he and her sister be left behind. His mind filled with the
image of her as Crow dragged her away—the message of
goodbye he had seen in her eyes. She had saved her sister's
life and his own life—twice—in exchange for her own?

How could she do that after learning of his lies? She should
hate him, goddamnit! She should be fleeing from him, using
all her wiles to escape into the night, knowing that every second he would be on her path, chasing her down . . . because
he hated her.

I hate her!

His hands gripped into fists at his sides, desperate to grasp
the hatred that should be there. But he couldn't feel it. He
couldn't find the hatred, or even the anger. It was as if he were
empty, drained, plumbed to his core. He could feel his body
swaying like a thin reed with no anchor.

A sharp caw at his shoulder startled Kee down to his toes.
He jerked his gaze to the side and saw a blur of black. The
raven was hovering only a foot from his face, its pointed beak
open, its keen, beady eyes staring straight at him. Kee stepped
back. The raven moved with him, angling closer. Kee had to
move again, this time to the side as the bird edged closer.

Kee stole a glance to the ground and realized he was near
the spot where Rheada's sister had begun her descent.

Caw!

The screech was an order—and the bird was leaving no
room for Kee to disobey. Its sharp beak and flapping wings
were only inches from his face. Kee crouched and lowered
himself over the side. He glanced up and saw the raven had
landed on the ground and was staring over the side at him,
and as Kee descended, the bird followed on foot, making small
clucking sounds from his throat as if in encouragement. At
one point, the raven hopped to Kee's shoulder, its huge, muscular body pressing down, bobbing and shifting its weight
with Kee's movements. Just as Kee was accommodating the
extra burden, the raven lifted with a single flap of its wings
and floated downward. Kee looked below, and saw Rheada's
sister waiting on a ledge.

"Blackjack! You came." The raven folded its wings and settled beside her.

Kee jumped down the last few feet. "You know this bird."

"It's Rheada's bird."

Of course. Raven. So she really did have a bird.

Irrational frustration built in Kee. "I suppose the rest of the legend is true? That this bird talks to her, whispers secrets to her, protects her—" His voice had an empty meanness, not supported by specific anger.

She glanced up at him, her face confused—and stricken, as if what she had thought to be true about him wasn't. Her hand closed protectively across the back of the bird. "He's a guardian."

"A guardian." He had the insane urge to laugh aloud, or yell that if this bird was so great, maybe *it* should be the one to save Rheada's life!

Jumbled emotions surged violently through Kee. He couldn't control the wave. He couldn't think. Hell, he didn't know *what* to think anymore. Everything he had known to be true was a lie—even what he had known about himself, what he had been *sure* of: that he hated Raven. He couldn't even draw up that hatred from within.

When he got her in his hands, when he could get her answers about his sister, then he would be able to think again.

"Where do we go from here?" he demanded.

She paused, then answered. "I've been watching and listening. I'm sure they're not here yet. They'll come from that direction." She pointed down the canyon. "The cave is up this way, a little higher on the cliff, but not far."

Kee crouched and stared down the canyon. He mentally lowered himself into the familiar role of hunter, predator. Detached from his emotions, his mind clicked over strategies. He noticed that canyon erosion on both sides had created steep slopes of cliff debris. There was no level ground at the bottom, which would make walking tough for anyone down there. Maybe he could use that to his advantage. "If I can come up from behind them, maybe I can pick off one or two of Crow's men, get their guns."

He straightened to leave, then heard voices.

"They're already here." She yanked down on his arm, pulling him to the ground. "Now what?"

He strained to hear, to pinpoint their location. Then he caught the reflection of the moon on metal. He focused hard, and pulled the outlines of the people from out of the darkness. Suddenly, he recognized a shape, a movement. It was Rheada. His pulse jumped with recognition. His gaze froze on her.

She seemed to glide, her steps light and easy, in one smooth, flowing motion. The group headed into the canyon with Rheada leading and Crow right behind her. The rest followed in a loose line. While everyone else was breathing hard, struggling over the rough terrain, she never slipped. She never braced herself, because there wasn't one awkward step. It was almost as if she were walking on different ground than the rest of them—ground that rose to *meet* her while falling away for everyone else.

"This is bullshit!" It was Crow. "There's nothing down here. I know this canyon."

"Obviously not well." Rheada's calm voice drifted up the canyon wall and surrounded Kee. "The cave is right up here."

A light swept up the cliff wall. Kee ducked behind a large boulder, pulling the sister with him.

"I don't see anything." The beam skidded over rocks and crags.

"You can't from here." Her voice came from farther down now. "Not until you're almost to the cave. I'll show you when I get up there."

"Hold it!" Crow yelled. His light jerked from the cliff wall down to the ground.

Kee walked the ledge, trying to keep pace with Crow, who was now walking down the canyon. When he couldn't see Crow—because of trees or the jutting cliff—Kee could still see the beam from Crow's flashlight. Suddenly, the bouncing of the light halted. Crow had stopped.

"Come here," he ordered.

Rheada stepped into the light. She might have obeyed his order, but her expression was defiant, as if *she* were the one in charge.

Crow strode to her and pressed the gun to her temple. "I've heard the legends about Raven," he said, his voice deathly quiet. Kee leaned farther over the edge to hear. "How fast you are, no matter the terrain," Crow continued. "That you can scramble over anything, even straight up cliffs as sure as a mountain lion." He traced her cheekbone with the barrel of the gun.

Kee's body tightened to a coil.

"Maybe you think you can get away," Crow said.

She stared at Crow for a beat. "I could have escaped a hundred times by now, Crow."

Crow's gun raked down her cheek. Kee saw her flinch. He gripped the edge to keep himself from jumping, knowing that if the thirty-foot fall didn't kill him, Crow's gun would.

She laid her hand on her cheek, but never looked away from Crow. Her head tilted, as if considering the dangerous man standing right in front of her. Then she turned and started to walk to the cliff.

"Get back here!"

"I'm climbing to the cave, Crow."

The sister grabbed Kee's arm. "She's coming up alone," she whispered. "We can get to her!"

She started to move along the cliff face. Kee had to reach fast to grab her. "She's not coming alone." He nodded toward Crow, who was now climbing after Rheada. "You stay here," he ordered.

"I'm *not* staying here," she hissed.

"I need you to watch *them*. Throw rocks at them if they start up." Before she could protest, Kee moved away, praying she would stay put and out of his way.

Inching along the cliff, he stole glances below and could see Rheada and Crow, now maybe only twenty feet away at an angle from him.

"Don't you want to know why I didn't run?" she called over her shoulder.

Crow snorted. "Maybe because I would have shot you?"

"I didn't run, Crow, because I want to see your face when you get in that cave."

Why is she baiting him? Kee's heart thundered at his chest. He tried to move faster, gripping anything he could with his hands, the merest jagged outcropping a fingerhold.

"Oh, you'll see my face, little bird. That'll be the *last* thing you see," he grunted.

"I want to see your face when you realize you can't *touch* the mask," she taunted. "You've heard of the Anasazi curse. Every pot thief knows about it."

"What's she talking about, Crow?" one of Crow's men called out from below. Kee recognized the voice as that of the same man who had wanted to forget the mask in the first place.

"She's talking shit—"

"What kind of curse do you think the Anasazi would put on the first living Kachina mask, Crow?"

"Shut up." His words were punctuated with his effort.

"They would put a death curse on it," she continued. She was nearly as high as Kee now, though at least twenty feet away.

"Crow—" whined his man.

"Get up here!" Crow yelled over his shoulder.

"They don't *want* to follow you up here, Crow."

Kee had to marvel at her strategy—effectively scaring Crow's men into staying below. Though he wished she would stop baiting him.

"They're smarter than you, Crow."

Kee winced.

"You little bitch." With a seeming burst of energy, Crow scrambled after her, grabbing her ankle. "You will shut up, *now*."

All Crow had to do was yank and she would free-fall thirty feet to her death.

"There's the cave, Crow." She nodded to a deep shadow.

Crow paused, his hand still gripping her ankle. Kee didn't move. He didn't breathe. Abruptly, Crow released her, and pulled himself up to where Rheada stood. "You're going first." He smiled. "You'll be the one picking up the mask. Any *curse* will be on you."

Kee saw a flicker in her eyes of determination laced with something else—a glint of arrogance. It was the kind of look that inspired awe: that she could stare down her adversary without a hint of trepidation.

Kee's mouth went dry.

"Get moving." Crow nudged her with the gun.

Kee followed them, edging across the rocks as silently as possible. He watched as first Rheada, then Crow, disappeared within a hole in the canyon wall. He crawled in headfirst, and had to pull himself along by his elbows through the narrow tunnel. He gritted his teeth against the pain screaming from his arm through his body. He could hear the muffled noise of them crawling, then it stopped. A moment later, he heard Crow yell, "Where the hell is it?"

She laughed.

"Where the hell *is* it?"

The fury in Crow's voice echoed in the tunnel, building to a palpable force beating at Kee's chest.

"Did you seriously think I would help you?" Her voice, strong, determined, reached into Kee and grabbed him by the throat. He wanted to scream at her to shut up!

"I made a vow when I was twelve years old," she said, "to never betray the Anasazi. Do you think I would break that promise for *you*?"

Her last words came with a flurry of noise, followed by the sound of gunfire.

Chapter 22

KEE clawed his way over the last few feet of the tunnel. Crow was holding Rheada from behind, fending off her blows. Kee spotted the gun on the ground. He dove from the mouth of the tunnel.

Crow ran straight for Kee, with Rheada, then shoved her at Kee, sending them both against the wall. Kee's head whipped back, slamming against the rock. For a second, all he saw were shards of light, but he could feel his arms still around her, wrapped tight, holding her close.

He squinted his eyes open, focused, and found he was on the ground, the gun within his reach. Crow jerked his head to him, and his gaze lit on the gun. The next instant, he disappeared into the tunnel.

Crow's flashlight lay abandoned, its beam splayed on the opposite wall. Crow was gone and Kee didn't care. He wouldn't care if he never saw the bastard again.

For right now, they were alone in the cave and her heart beat against his, both thumping in the same rhythm.

I could stay like this. As soon as the thought registered, his muscles tensed, hardening from the chest out. He pushed away, shifting her aside.

She looked up at him as he moved, her gaze at first slightly dazed, then her dark eyes searched his. "Why did you come here?" she asked.

He saw her real question in her deep gaze: *Did you come to save me or hunt me?*

It was a simple question, and Kee didn't know the answer. Frustration ignited and flamed up his veins. He pushed up from the ground and started for the tunnel, stopping at the entrance to face her. "Why the hell did you bring him to an empty cave?"

She stood with obvious effort, pulling herself up with her hands on the rough cavern wall. She looked tired, at the end of her energy. When she finally met his gaze, however, Kee saw the same strength he had witnessed when she had faced Crow. "That really doesn't matter, does it?"

But it did matter, damnit! He wanted to shake the answer from her, make her admit that it had been all for herself, not for her sister . . . not for him.

"Does anything matter to you . . . *Raven*?"

He said the name that had haunted him, driven him; he said it with all the harshness he could muster. He would find that hatred inside him, goddamnit!

She winced. "Not anymore," she answered quietly. The expression in her eyes raked through him, confusing him.

Did he mean to cause her pain?

He shut his eyes, trying to squeeze her out of his mind, but images of her flooded him. He couldn't control them, couldn't obliterate them. The harder he tried, the clearer they were: her eyes staring at him, trusting him . . . loving him.

But that wasn't true! She wasn't who she said she was! She was Raven! The pot thief! She was the one who had lured his sister into the darkness.

His eyes flew open. Immediately, she stepped back as if pushed by some fierceness she saw in him.

"Tell me about Sarah Yazzie." He didn't recognize his own voice. It came from deep inside him, from someplace black.

She took another step back, her gaze riveted on him. "Who?"

"Sarah Yazzie. A Navajo girl. Only fifteen years old. Just a kid! But that didn't stop you from using her, did it?"

"I don't know who—"

"Round face. Your height. Have there been so many that you can't think of her?" He found the vein of anger and slit it open wide.

"I don't *know* any Sarah Yazzie!" She was backed against the wall. "Who is she?"

"*Was*. She *was* my sister."

She gasped. "Your sister. What is it you think—"

"I don't think. I know. She went looking for *you*. For the infamous *Raven*." The name that had conjured hatred now stuck in his throat.

Rheada couldn't think. She could barely breathe. His anger had sucked all the air from the cave, drawn all the life from her blood. "No—there was no girl—I would never—"

He didn't let her finish. In two strides he was inches from her face. "You would never what? Use someone? But that's a lie, isn't it? You used me. You even used your goddamn sister. Your *own* sister!" He grabbed her shoulders with enough force to crack a board. "Tell me what you know!"

His brow furrowed as if yanked by a desperate need deep inside him. Frantic to help, Rheada tried to concentrate, but she couldn't focus past his eyes—pitch-dark pools of hatred staring back at her, as if he were tapping into a bottomless well.

Suddenly, he let go, stepped back, and jammed his hand into his back pocket. He pulled out a photograph and held it in front of her face. The black-and-white picture was bent and creased—the unintentional damage of loving hands handling it many, many times.

"That was Sarah. Tell me you don't remember." His voice held a plea, as if he could not bear one more moment of uncertainty. Rheada's heart hurt for Kee.

She stared hard, puzzling the picture together in her mind, and a memory emerged. "It might be . . . it was a year ago—"

"What?" He stepped closer to her. Rheada looked up into his dark eyes, where, for now, the hatred had been replaced with his urgent need to know. They were eyes that had once looked at her with passion. She ached at the loss.

"Tilly and I were moving camp to stay ahead—" She stopped, stricken by her own past. They had moved to stay ahead of the law, ahead of men like Kee. She couldn't say the words, but she saw the sharp understanding, the *validation* of his judgment in his eyes. He would damn her with her own words.

She reminded herself it didn't matter anymore. He already hated her. She had already lost him.

As she drew a breath to continue, the staccato sound of rapid gunfire echoed through the tunnel.

"What's happening out there?" She started for the tunnel.

Kee grabbed her arm. "I don't give a damn about that. Finish telling me!"

But Rheada wasn't listening to him. The sound of the angry gunfire filled her senses, terrifying her, as if *she* were under attack. Who was Crow shooting at? Suddenly, she knew. She whirled to Kee. "Tilly brought you here, didn't she?"

His eyes flared with a desperate anger. "I don't give a damn if the whole world is ending. Tell me about Sarah!"

The need in his eyes reached right to her heart. Unbidden, her hand went to his jaw. "I will. But right now I'm going to help *my* sister."

She climbed into the tunnel. She could hear Kee right behind her, both of them scrambling through the earth and rock passage. She could also now hear yelling—Crow and her sister.

Rheada paused at the entrance and peered into the black night. A stream of automatic gunfire cracked the air. It seemed to come from the ground.

"Bitch! Put it down!" It was Crow and he was still up on the cliff. Rheada edged toward the outside, and peered to the left, the direction from where she had heard his voice. She couldn't see him.

"You're going to die anyway, Crow, but I can make it slow and painful." It was Tilly, speaking from the canyon floor, though Rheada barely recognized her sister's voice. She sounded primitive, ready to deliver on her violent threat.

Rheada pulled into a crouch to crawl out of the cave onto the cliff wall. Kee's hand jerked her down. "You want to get shot? Get back here!"

Her heart gave an irrational lurch, as if yanked by a thread of hope that he might *still* care. He didn't care, her mind taunted. He just wanted answers about his sister.

"Don't worry," she said. "I'm the best, remember?" With a swift jerk of her arm, she broke his grip and tumbled forward, out of the cave.

"Admit it, Crow! Now!" Tilly yelled. Gunfire sprayed up the cliff wall, breaking off rocks and rising dust.

Rheada flattened herself against the rock face. What had gotten into Tilly? What was it she wanted Crow to admit?

Crow wasn't talking. Rheada looked to her left—past where Kee now stood at the opening of the cave—to the cliff face beyond. A crevice in the rock wall formed a long, deep shadow, but Rheada thought she could see some movement. She stared closely, and knew she had found Crow. He was cornered in the crevice. All Tilly had to do was level a line of gunfire straight up the crack and she'd split him in two.

"You coward!" Tilly screamed. "You think you can slither away? Face me!"

Her scream bordered on madness. Did Tilly think Crow had killed them in the cave?

"Tilly!" Rheada called out. "Tilly, it's Rheada." From the corner of her eye, she could see Kee edging toward Crow.

"I've got him, Rheada," Tilly said. "He's not getting away." She punctuated her words with another spray of gunfire. A stream of sand and rocks cascaded twenty feet.

Rheada could see Tilly now. Her sister stood alone, the automatic rifle at her shoulder.

"Tilly, I'm okay. Everything's all right."

"No it's not. Nothing is right." Tilly's voice broke. She paused. When she spoke again, every word rang clear in the night. "He took away our father, Rheada. He made you become Raven. He's going to answer for that crime right now."

"Crow killed Daddy?" For a moment, Rheada was a young girl, kneeling with Tilly alongside their father. That day, their lives had changed. She had been someone's child—then suddenly she was the only one to take care of both of them. All those child's fears swept through her now with a renewed vengeance. She turned toward Crow. Kee was in her line of sight. His face was turned to her, and she could feel his gaze on her, but Rheada stared past him, through him, to the murderer in the shadows. "*You* killed him?"

Crow didn't say anything.

"I'll make him talk." Tilly unleashed another barrage. Bullets pelted the cliff, this time just past Kee. Rheada's pulse jammed at her throat. Tilly could accidentally hit Kee. In her rage, she could even think Kee was Crow.

"Tilly! Listen to me!" Rheada edged along the cliff in the opposite direction, away from Crow and Kee. "He's not worth it!"

"How can you say that, Rheada?"

Rheada worked her way along until she found a ledge. It widened to a path that angled down the cliff. Now she could see Crow's men, lying still on the ground. "You're not a murderer, Tilly," she said, hoping it was still true, hoping Crow's men had only been knocked out.

"He ruined our lives."

The path dipped to a step, then another step. Suddenly,

Rheada realized she was on the ancient staircase. She froze in place.

"And he's not getting away with it." Tilly fired the gun. The explosion of gunfire behind her forced Rheada's steps. She had to stop Tilly!

She descended two more steps. A rock wall climbed on each side of the staircase, creating a steep, narrow stairway.

Caw!

Flapping wings appeared right in front of Rheada. Blackjack hovered, blocking her path. She knew she shouldn't ignore him. She also knew this was her only way down to Tilly. "Move, Blackjack!" She swiped her hand through the air.

The huge bird dipped below the swing of her arm and settled on a step, his wings still outspread, effectively barring her descent.

"He ruined your life." Tilly's voice now sounded distant, muffled by the stone wall. "He took away any chance you had of a *real* life."

Rheada's life *was* in ruins. If Crow hadn't killed their father, she would not have had to take care of Tilly, she wouldn't have become Raven . . . and Kee's sister would not have sought the *legendary* Raven, and then disappeared.

The sharp need for justice sliced through Rheada. Hot anger bled into her veins like poison, pumping to every part of her, taking over her body and mind, and whispering that the only cure was in vengeance—a vengeance she could almost taste. Her revenge was all that mattered.

Suddenly, she saw Kee's face, his eyes, filled with the same black need that gripped her. It was eating him up from the inside, consuming him. He blamed *her* for whatever had happened to his sister—blamed her, and hated her, with as much blind vehemence as Tilly blamed Crow. But blaming Crow wouldn't change anything—it wouldn't vanquish Raven from Rheada's life . . . and it wouldn't ease Kee's pain.

She pushed her toe toward Blackjack. "Get out of the way, Blackjack."

He flew up in her face. *Caw!* His screech was earsplitting, heart-stopping. His black eyes looked frantic, as if even her next step might cause catastrophe. Rheada hesitated before the guardian who had always protected her. She softened her gaze. "I *have* to get to Tilly, Blackjack."

Her eyes on Blackjack, Rheada slid her toe forward to the edge of the step and lowered her foot to the next stone. As she put her full weight down, the step tilted, pitching her forward. Solid rock shifted, the ground fell away, as if her mere step had upset the balance of every connecting stone. She grabbed for the stone wall, but it too was swaying. She stumbled down steps as they moved under her feet.

"Rheada!"

She couldn't answer Tilly. The whole cliff seemed to be collapsing beneath her. It was like a stone house of cards, constructed by the Anasazi.

She clawed at sandstone that then disappeared from her fingers. Falling rocks pummeled her. She covered her head with her arms for protection. Her body tumbled with boulders and slabs of sheer cliff. It occurred to her that she might die— killed in this Anasazi trap. The irony should have hurt. Instead, Rheada felt a certain calmness grow: At least now, she would be free of Raven.

Something yanked incessantly at her head. The rumble of cascading stones still echoed in her ears. Her hair must be caught between rocks. Then she felt sharp stings at her hand. What was poking her? She wanted to swipe it away. She tried to raise an arm, but couldn't move.

Squawk!

Was that Blackjack? Her mind tried to focus. She tried to open her eyes, but couldn't. She was encased in rock. Smothered in stone. She couldn't breathe.

"Rheada!" It was Tilly.

Rheada felt a weight being lifted from her.

Caw! Caw! Caw!

"Move, you damn bird!"

Rheada could picture Blackjack strutting across the rocks, commanding Tilly. The image made her chuckle, then cough as her breath drew in unsettled dust.

"Rheada, hold on!"

Rocks lifted from around Rheada's head and there was Tilly, with actual tears on her face. Rheada hadn't seen her sister cry since the night they had found their father. She cupped Tilly's face with her hand, and rubbed the tear off with her thumb. "Hi."

Tilly's eyes shone. "Fine time for you to decide not to listen to Blackjack."

With Tilly's help, Rheada wiggled loose from the rest of the rocks, and pulled herself up to stand. She was shaky, but amazingly, nothing seemed to be broken. She looked up to the cliff, afraid she would see that the whole cliff had disappeared, burying Kee, but the only destruction was the staircase. She scanned the rest of the rock wall, but couldn't see Kee. Her breath caught as she kept looking, searching the dark cliff wall.

"Tilly, do you have a flashlight?" She glanced over to see Tilly climbing down the pile of rubble. Rheada spotted the rifle lying at the bottom a moment before Tilly picked it up. She couldn't intend to still kill Crow!

"Tilly! No! Let Crow go. Killing him won't change anything." Rheada looked at her sister, into matching eyes that stared back at her. The knowledge of all they had been through was there. "Let the past go, Tilly."

"Hold it!"

It was Kee. Rheada's heart jumped. Her gaze jerked in the direction of his voice. It came from the shadows of the crevice. Now she could see that the shadows there were wider than the contour of the crevice. Kee must have made his way to Crow. "You're all right?" she called up to Kee. The shadows moved, mutated to the silhouettes of two men. Rheada couldn't tell which was Kee. "Kee! Are you all right?"

"Drop the gun, Tilly." It was the voice of a lawman, taking charge.

"Rheada? What's going on?"

Rheada faced the question in Tilly's voice, in her eyes. She realized that Tilly had believed her: that Kee *wasn't* undercover.

"I said *drop it!*"

Rheada didn't acknowledge Kee. She was staring at Tilly, watching the understanding dawn in Tilly's gaze.

"Everything Miguel said was true?"

"Yes," Rheada said.

Tilly let out a sound of disbelief. She looked up at the cliff and back to Rheada. "Then why did you save him? Why risk your life for a cop?"

"Because everything *I* said was also true. *All* of it."

"The two of you stay right there!"

Rheada heard the hate, the anger, in Kee's voice. It didn't matter to him that she had saved his life and nearly lost her own: Nothing had changed for him.

As she saw the confusion, the disbelief, grow in Tilly's eyes, Rheada's heart twisted, as if determined hands would wring out any last vestige of hope. The painful truth surged to her eyes. "I still love him," she whispered. "But it doesn't matter."

Tilly walked to her, put her hand on Rheada's shoulder. "We can't stay here."

"I know."

But Rheada couldn't move. She couldn't take a step away . . . and she couldn't look at Kee. She was paralyzed by every wrong choice she had ever made.

"Come on." Tilly's hand pulled her.

Rocks slid down the cliff. Rheada yanked her arm free from Tilly and stared up to Kee. She heard noises of struggle. Stones bounced and cascaded to the canyon floor. Kee was obviously fighting off Crow.

"Hand me the gun!" Rheada reached an arm back to Tilly. When Tilly didn't respond, Rheada whirled on her sister. "Give it to me, Tilly!"

"Who are you planning to shoot?"

Rheada could feel the desperation pounding at her temples. "Just give me the gun!"

Tilly stared back for a beat, her gaze on Rheada. Then her eyes softened, as if Tilly were considering her older sister, the one who had always protected *her*. Suddenly, Tilly's gaze shifted, but not before Rheada saw her make a decision. Tilly stepped out of reach, and in one motion brought her arm up, took sight past Rheada, and fired.

Rheada's heart stopped. God, she hadn't meant for Tilly to kill anyone! She whirled back to face the cliff, afraid of what she would see. A man's form was slumped on the ledge. A tall, lean shadow was clinging to the cliff. It had to be Kee.

"We're leaving here!" Tilly called out. "Take Crow. Take my Jeep. Get the hell out of our canyons."

"Not without Raven," Kee yelled.

Tilly leveled her gaze on Rheada. "There is no Raven," Tilly said, her eyes shining. "It's over."

Rheada's throat constricted around the finality of Tilly's statement.

"No, it's not over! What about my sister?" Kee's anguished scream echoed throughout the canyon. "Goddamn you, Rheada, tell me!"

The split second of near-overwhelming joy Rheada felt to hear her name on his lips was crushed by the full force of condemnation in his voice. He hated her. He didn't care if she lived or died. All he wanted was answers about his sister . . . and then Rheada could just go to hell.

She felt her strength dissolve beneath the intense hate emanating from the man she looked to, the man she loved.

Was he right? Was everything she believed about herself a lie? Fear built in her beyond any she had ever known—it quaked through her, cracking the foundation of her very being. If everything she believed was a lie, what was she left with?

Her thoughts fractured at the answer. She stared ahead, speechless, unfocused.

"Answer me!"

Kee's demand drove through her—in an insane way shored her, giving her a purpose, at least for this moment.

"We were passing through Canyon Blanco," she said, forcing the words past the ache at her throat. "A Navajo girl was camped there." Rheada let the memory fill her. She would remember all she could, for Kee. "She had a fire, but no provisions that we could see. Not even a pack mule. So we stopped and spent the night there. After we made some dinner, she talked and confided that she had left home. She never did tell us her name."

"That's it?"

She didn't want to say the rest. She was about to add to his hatred. She steeled herself against the assault on her heart. "She kept staring at me, as if a question were burning in her mind. Finally, she admitted she was looking for Raven."

Damning silence descended from the canyon wall. Rheada's last hope that he could forgive her, forget that she had been Raven, died. "I said that I had heard that Raven had left the canyons," Rheada said, her voice flat. "I told her that

Raven had quit. That she hated the lies and that she wanted to start an honest life." It was the truth. Would Kee hear? Rheada raised her gaze to him. "I told her to go home."

"She didn't go home."

His pain seared Rheada's heart.

"All I have ever wanted was to leave here, Kee. The last thing I would do is encourage her." Could he hear the plea in her voice to understand?

"You're *exactly* the one who encouraged her! The great Raven!" He laughed—a harsh crack of sound that tore through Rheada.

"I didn't ask your sister to look for me!" she screamed at him. "I didn't *ask* to be Raven!"

The word "Raven" resounded through the canyons, over and over, hurled from canyon wall to canyon wall, the echoes overlapping, the sound of her own voice mutating, changed by each touch of the terrain, until it seemed every rock sang the name. Rheada covered her ears but she couldn't block out the chorus of "Raven." It enveloped her and settled on her shoulders as a heavy mantle.

With a flap of his immense wings, Blackjack settled at her feet and gazed up at Rheada, as if awaiting his next order. To him, she was Raven. To the canyons and cliffs, she was Raven. To Kee, she was Raven . . . and to the world, she was nothing. She could never go back to Aztec, to her home, her business.

Tilly tugged at her arm. Only her sister knew her as Rheada, and she would drag her back into the darkness. Rheada realized it was the only place left for her.

She let Tilly pull her away from the cliff, away from Kee. She gave him a last glance over her shoulder. She couldn't see Kee, but she could see her dreams crash against him and smash to pieces.

In that mortal moment, as she felt her insides dying, everything became clear. It was a crystal instant of insight: Raven the myth was stronger than Rheada Samuels, the woman. It was all she had left.

Chapter 23

RHEADA stared into the night as Tilly drove Crow's Jeep past familiar canyons, and deeper within the labyrinth. The first hint of dawn limned the crest of the cliffs in deep blue, pushing back the blanket of stars. It was a dawn like hundreds of others—just the two sisters, traveling well-known ground . . . except these canyons weren't home anymore. They were the enemy, closing ranks behind Rheada, cutting her off from the life she had been building.

She thought of her home, her business, the tours she had developed, the customers who had become friends. What would happen to her little building, to the place she had made home?

She knew she was thinking crazy. None of it mattered. It was just a building holding things—things that couldn't care about her or what had happened to her.

An ache climbed up to her throat and she swallowed, and stared hard out the window, forcing herself to see the canyons that were again her home. But her mind was continually pulled back to that small adobe in Aztec: the sticky front door she had to push through, but that Kee slid open so easily; the kitchen where he had cooked up coffee in that old, bent pot that had traveled these very canyons; the wide, worn floorboards, solid against her back when she pulled Kee down to her.

Instant heat suffused her veins, and an urgent throb pulsed deep in her core. Her body remembered every sensation: her fingers tangled in his black hair; the rise of her blood beneath his dark, sensuous gaze; the moment of sharp pain; and the full *rightness* of him within her. He had stared down at her with passion in his eyes—a look that said he wanted her, he *needed* her. She tried to shut off her mind, but the memory owned her, just as completely as his look had claimed her. At that moment, he was just Kee, she was Rheada, and they had found each other against all odds.

She had seen into him that night—seen a man with secrets,

with deep pain, who was as desperate as she was to reach out and hold on to something real.

He couldn't have been lying to her! Not then, or when they had lain together in her bed ... or when he had come to her rescue. She could hear his voice calling out to her. She remembered his gentleness, lifting her from the boxes.

How was it possible that had happened only the night before this? In little more than a day, her life was in as many pieces as the broken pottery on her closet floor. Her thoughts fixated on those jagged shards, and she wrapped her arms tightly across her middle, desperate to ease the growing emptiness inside. She had failed at everything, at every promise she had made herself. Now, like some nocturnal creature, unable to bear the glare of daylight, she was retreating into her caves.

And Kee, where would he go?

She knew the answer: He would continue to hunt for answers about his sister. He had a goal. Unlike Rheada, he had not yet been defeated.

The rumble of the Jeep died suddenly. Rheada realized they were sitting at the mouth of Blackjack Canyon, where their childhood had begun ... and ended.

She didn't want to be here. She couldn't bear the weight of these memories, when her dreams had been new, and precious, and *believable*.

"Not here—" she started.

"We have to talk, Rheada."

Tilly's stern voice pulled Rheada's gaze from the window to her sister. Tilly had shifted in her seat and was facing Rheada, a determined furrow to her brow—that particular Tilly expression of stubbornness.

"Not tonight, Tilly—"

"It has to be tonight, Rheada. Because we don't have much time."

"What are you talking about?"

"I have a meeting with Cecilio Diaz."

"Who—"

"He's one of the candidates for the Alliance of Indigenous Peoples," Tilly said. She paused, staring at Rheada. "I plan to give him the mask."

"Why? I don't understand—"

"Give me a chance to explain, Rheada. I know how you feel about the mask. I know you think it should stay hidden—"

"We *agreed* on that, Tilly. That mask is evil. It has the power to destroy, I know it to my core. Look what it almost did to us."

"I agree that it has the power to destroy if it's in the hands of the wrong person," Tilly said.

None of this made any sense. Rheada started to object, but Tilly cut her off.

"Have you followed the campaign at all?" Tilly asked.

"No. And since when have you become so political?"

"Since I read this." Tilly dug in her pocket, pulled out a newspaper article, and handed it to Rheada.

Rheada read from the headline. " 'Candidate gets support of U.S. Pueblo leaders. Zamora claims descendence from both Aztec and Anasazi.' " Rheada looked at Tilly. "He can't prove this."

"I think that's exactly what he plans to do," Tilly said.

"How?"

"With the mask. He's the one who hired Crow."

"What makes you so sure?"

"Orin told me. He said that Crow was connected to the biggest buyer of all time and that this buyer was specifically looking for the Poseyemu mask." She paused, staring out the window, her jaw tense. "Then one night, he let slip something about a *candidate,* and wasn't it ironic that pot thieves were controlling an election. I knew then he was talking about Zamora." She was glaring straight ahead, into the night. "Orin didn't care who got the mask. All he cared about was the huge amount of money he was going to get."

Rheada thought she saw a visible shudder run through her sister. She put her hand to Tilly's shoulder.

Tilly glanced to her. "He was such a sleaze, Rheada. But I pulled it off. He *believed* I was Raven. He *bragged* about being with Raven. And I got an idea for my *own* plan." She gave a weak smile and Rheada's heart clenched for the burden her sister had carried.

Tilly's gaze strengthened. "I couldn't let the mask go to Zamora. Any man who would hire a thug like Crow couldn't be the one destined to have the mask." Tilly paused. "Do you remember what Daddy said about the fall of Chaco? That greed for power had brought it all down? What if Poseyemu wasn't great, Rheada? What if he was the *cause* for the destruction?" Tilly leveled a steady gaze. "I think Zamora is trying to repeat history."

Rheada stared back, not believing what she was hearing. "Tilly, you can't be serious about this."

Tilly handed another newspaper article to Rheada. "Read this."

Rheada unfolded the small piece of newsprint, and read the headline aloud. " 'Zamora arrives in Santa Fe for debate.' " There was a picture of Zamora with an entourage, with the caption "Who are his supporters?"

The beginning of the article restated Zamora's claim of ancestry, but then raised questions about the funding of his campaign. It mentioned the allegations that he trafficked in illegal artifacts and that the attorney general was investigating. Rheada's gaze stuck on the next lines. "If the rumors of pot thievery are true, Zamora may have more to worry about than a federal investigation. According to well-informed sources, the Anasazi protected their possessions with a curse."

Rheada's gaze flew to the headline and the writer's byline. "Carlos," she whispered.

"Who's Carlos?"

Rheada glanced at Tilly. "The reporter. The one Miguel killed." Rheada stared down at the newspaper. Carlos hadn't been writing for some adventure magazine. He was an investigative reporter, digging up dirt on Zamora and she was holding probably the last article he had written.

"I talked to him," Rheada said quietly. "I'm the one who mentioned the curse." She paused. "He also asked about the mask."

For a moment, both sisters were quiet. "Rheada, it's not the trafficking in pots that got my attention. Look at the picture."

It was just a picture of people around Zamora. The caption read, "Who are these young girls?" Rheada looked closer at the grainy black-and-white photo. They were *so* young, so innocent-looking.

Rheada's heart jumped, as if bolting away from something terrible.

"He keeps girls, Rheada."

"Oh, God." Rheada looked at the small faces. They were maybe fifteen years old at the oldest. All of them were looking at Zamora with adoration—all but one. She stood a little apart and was staring straight ahead. Something else about her pulled Rheada's gaze closer—something familiar.

Suddenly, she recognized the face. Rheada's heart fairly leaped to her throat. It was Sarah.

"Zamora's corrupt. He's dangerous. And he could end up being the leader of all the Indians of the Americas."

Rheada barely heard Tilly. She was staring at Kee's sister. The paper rustled in her trembling hands.

Tilly grabbed Rheada's arm. "Rheada, are you listening to me?"

Rheada looked up at her sister. "Tilly, that's Kee's sister."

"What? How do you—"

"He showed me her picture tonight. Jammed it in my face, actually." Rheada looked back at the article.

"Why?"

"Because he was sure that Raven had something to do with her disappearance."

"She's the one you were telling Kee about tonight," Tilly whispered. "The girl in the canyon." Rheada watched the memory of that night grow in Tilly's eyes. Both of them had been stunned by Sarah's request to find Raven . . . and neither of them had spoken of it since.

"This is the same girl, Tilly. Kee's sister, Sarah."

"That's why he was hunting you?"

Rheada nodded.

"But you had nothing to do with that girl!"

"Tilly, she went looking for *Raven*. For me."

Rheada couldn't tear her gaze away from the picture, from the eyes of that young girl. She looked as if she were staring into the distance, to a point beyond the horizon. It was the exact same look Rheada had seen in Kee's eyes, as if he were fixated on something just out of reach. In Kee's case, Rheada realized, the goal had been his sister. But what was his sister's goal? And why was she with Zamora?

"You sent her home, Rheada. It's not your fault she didn't listen."

Rheada stared at Sarah. "Kee thinks she's dead." As soon

as she said the words, Rheada's thoughts took on an urgency. She had to do something. But what?

"That picture proves she's not," Tilly said.

"But Kee doesn't know that." Rheada wondered if there were a way she could contact Kee, tell him about Sarah—except she didn't know where to find him. And something told her he could slip into the night and leave little more of a trace than she did.

You could find him, Raven.

It was a taunting voice at her ear, as if Raven *herself* had come alive.

Yes, Rheada thought, she could find him. But did she want to? Did she want to point him straight to the man who had Sarah? She had seen the warrior in his eyes when he faced Crow and Miguel. Then, he had been strong for her. He had been preparing himself for anything, to defend her. She had known then that Kee was a man capable of killing. What would he do to the man he believed had taken advantage of his sister?

Rheada heard Tilly's door open. "Where are you going?"

"To get the mask. I told you, I'm delivering it to Diaz."

Suddenly, a plan formed in Rheada's mind. "No, not to Diaz, Tilly. We're taking it to Zamora."

"No!"

Tilly's yell echoed off the cliffs and raised a family of ravens from a nearby tree. Screeching caws rent the air. Immense black wings flapped. The calm morning sky erupted into a black, angry cloud. It was as if Tilly's voice had called forth a storm of ravens.

Rheada jerked her gaze to her sister and was at once taken aback. Tilly stared back, her keen eyes shiny black. Her youthful, fiery personality had focused to a sharp, determined flame. A belief, a *conviction*, burned in Tilly—with a brightness Rheada recognized. It came from deep inside, with the same core need, as had Rheada's *own* determination to get out of these canyons . . . the difference being that Tilly's drive wasn't to get away, but to face destiny.

Rheada had always known her sister was strong and brave—more courageous than herself. Why hadn't Rheada also seen Tilly's strength of character? She stared at her now, humbled by her own sister.

"Stashing the mask isn't enough," Tilly said quietly. "We have to do the right thing, Rheada. You taught me that. Somehow, even as a child, you knew the mask needed protection, a guardian. You made me vow never to betray it."

That she could have inspired Tilly was beyond Rheada's comprehension. For a moment, Rheada couldn't speak, unable to believe that she could have inspired anyone. She hadn't done anything right, including leaving her own sister behind in order to pursue a dream—a dream she was never meant to have.

Her sister was right: Not only could they not escape their past, but it was up to them to take advantage of who they were. But as moved as Rheada was by Tilly's convictions, she couldn't forget Kee's sister—she couldn't forget Kee.

"Tilly, if everything you say about Zamora is true, then Sarah is caught at the mercy of a terrible man. And she ended up there because she was looking for Raven, for me. I didn't become Raven to cause that. I have to help her."

"That won't get you Kee."

The sharp truth cut at Rheada's heart. "I know," she managed.

"And you would give up the mask for one girl? You would risk its power with that corrupt man?"

I'm corrupt. The thought sliced through Rheada. If her life was a series of bad choices, now was her chance to turn it around, do something *good* as Raven.

A plan took hold of Rheada, gripping her with the force of a gloved hand at her throat.

Zamora liked girls. Zamora liked power. What if Rheada traded *herself*—the *Raven*—for Sarah? How could he resist?

"Maybe we don't have to give up the mask," Rheada said. "Maybe there's a way we can *both* get what we want."

Kee sat, one hand wrapped securely around the bottle of scotch. He was in his cave. He knew he wasn't really in a cave, he was in the bar. But he could pretend. What was one more goddamn lie to himself?

He ignored the glass and brought the bottle to his lips and swallowed and told himself another lie: The liquor was poison, running down his gullet, to his arteries, and to every vein in his body. Soon, it would kill off the one thought he had left, the one that ran through his mind over and over—that he had failed. He didn't know what had happened to Sarah.

He had been so sure the answer lay with Raven. Hell, he had been sure that Sarah's life had probably *ended* with Raven. But Kee knew now that wasn't possible. Rheada wouldn't have hurt Sarah. She would have sent her home, just as she said. Whatever Rheada was, she wasn't a killer. He'd seen that last night when she talked her sister out of shooting Crow, the man who just might have killed their father.

A groan from the seat next to him drew Kee's gaze. Crow was slumped over, still unconscious. *Good*. The son of a bitch was lucky to be alive.

Eight years ago, Rheada had said. Eight long years they had lived without a father, because of Crow. Rheada couldn't have been more than fourteen—orphaned along with her sister, and left with only their wiles to survive in those canyons. All Rheada could have known to do was what her father had already been doing. She couldn't have brought her dad back to take care of them, any more than Kee could bring Sarah back.

His own pain rose—pain for Rheada and for his own sister. Kee's hand tightened on the bottle. The wound at his arm throbbed mercilessly, but the pain was no match for the immense *hurt* that claimed every inch of him. He ached to his bones, as if he were disease-ridden and rotting from the inside—a walking dead man with no hope.

He lifted the bottle and gulped. He wondered how many bottles it would take before he passed out. Then he wondered whether he should crash a bottle over Crow's head, do the man in right here. Complete Tilly's job.

He stared at Crow's dirty head, but what Kee was seeing was Rheada on the cliff begging with Tilly to put down the gun. Why had she stopped her sister? She had to hate Crow for what he had done.

I didn't ask to be Raven!

He could hear her anguished scream here, a hundred miles away from the canyons, as if her voice would haunt him wherever he went, the rest of his life.

Kee sat there, the bottle poised over Crow's head. Suddenly, there was pressure on his arm, forcing the bottle to the table.

"I don't allow killing in the bar."

Kee dragged his head around and tried to make his blurry eyes focus. He pulled his gaze up to the huge man and found Max staring down at him. "Just saving the taxpayers money, Max."

"I'm talking about you." Max pushed the bottle out of Kee's reach.

Kee's reactions were too slow to stop Max. Every bit of his helplessness and frustration rose within him. "Back off, Max."

The utter despair in Kee's eyes reached right into Max. He was like a wounded wild animal curled in a corner.

"Back off or what, Kee?" Max leaned forward, placing his fists on the table. He kept his gaze on Kee, though it was hard not to dart a glance to the unconscious man—it was like ignoring a skunk two feet away. "What are you going to do?" He finally looked at the man. "You've got about as much fight in you as your friend here." He reached across the table and grabbed a handful of hair, and lifted the man's head.

Max had half expected to see the dark stranger who had haunted his bar. It wasn't that man, but Max recognized the face. "So you got yourself Crow." Max let go of his hair. Crow hit the table with a dull thud. "Good job." Max was actually impressed. The pot thief was as slippery as he was notorious.

Kee's arm reached past Max to the bottle. "He's all yours, lawman."

Max watched Kee throw back another swallow. He closed his eyes and took a long gulp of the scotch, as if to drown out any lingering memories . . . or drown himself in liquor, whichever came first. Max stared, bewildered by Kee's apathy. "If you didn't want Crow, why did you bring him in?"

"He killed a man last night. That good enough for you?"

For the life of Max, he couldn't figure out Kee. If Kee hadn't been after Crow, then who? Max pulled a chair out from the table and sat down. "And where's the man you were looking for? The one you asked me about in the bar?"

"He's the dead one," Kee said matter-of-factly.

But Max saw in Kee's eyes that nothing was simple or matter-of-fact. The man had seen hell . . . worse, he looked as if he were ready to take up residence there.

The bar door opened and Max watched Kee glance up, his

eyes squinting into the daylight, studying the person who was entering. Max swore he saw a flicker of hope reach beyond the boozy blur in Kee's eyes. A regular patron walked in and Kee lowered his gaze to the bottle. It was painfully obvious to Max exactly who Kee had hoped would walk through that door—the same woman who had walked in the door only two weeks before.

"Where's Rheada?" Max asked.

"I don't know."

"You don't know or you don't care?"

He looked away from Max. "I don't know," he said finally.

"What, did you lose her? You can catch a notorious pot thief and you can't keep track of a woman?"

Kee slanted a look to Max. "She's the best." His lips curved to a half smile and he tipped the neck of the bottle in the air in a sad toast. Then his eyes closed slowly, as if he were kissing the bottle, his lips welcoming the liquor like a lover.

"You're killing yourself," Max said.

"I told you before, Max. I don't need saving, so back off." Kee repeated the threat, but his voice didn't hold any power. It was the tired voice of a man who had given up.

Kee was right: He didn't *need* saving. He was almost past saving. Max was staring at a man who had condemned himself and now was carrying out the sentence. The only thing that might bring him to life was to force an attack.

"Maybe you're not *worth* saving," Max said.

Kee's eyes flashed. It was just the signal Max had hoped for. "I don't blame Rheada for walking away."

Pain licked the blackness in Kee's eyes. Max cursed himself, but he couldn't relent. Not if he gave a damn.

"That's what happened, isn't it, Blackburn?" Max leaned even closer. He could smell the wilderness on Kee. "She turned around and walked away, and you're not man enough to go after her."

"Shut up," Kee hissed.

"You drove her off, didn't you?" Max whispered into Kee's face. "You hurt her and drove her off. You son of a bitch."

Kee grabbed Max's collar with a swiftness the old pro almost envied . . . until he looked into eyes that bore a murderous blackness. "I *am* a son of a bitch."

Just as swiftly, his gaze changed focus, and turned inward,

as if redirecting his lethal intent on himself. "You're right," he said in a distant voice, and dropped his grip on Max's shirt. The hardened veneer of Kee's face cracked. Lines of pain spread from his eyes.

"That's it, isn't it?" Max let out a harsh laugh. "You've taken a look at yourself and hate what you see. You figure Rheada has to hate you, too."

Kee didn't answer. He just raised the bottle from the table.

"But what if she doesn't?" Max pressed on.

Kee's hand stopped in midair, the bottle poised for a drink.

"You're not the men you hunted, Kee," Max said. "You're not even the man you *became* when you hunted them. That's just a hard layer you've covered yourself with."

The bottle in Kee's hand trembled slightly as if buffeted by a small shock wave. Max saw Kee's jaw set in some valiant, but vain, attempt for control. Finally, he set down the bottle.

"You've lived the lies *too long*, Kee. You've started to believe them. But you're not those men! You're better than that son of a bitch." Max's fist hit the table close to Crow's head. The thief groaned.

"You've just worn the skin of undercover too long," Max said. "There's a real man who's *worth* Rheada behind that mask you wear."

"Mask." Crow's head rose slowly, like that of a monster coming to life. Dried blood matted hair to his forehead. Bleary eyes peered across the table to Max. "What the hell? You're not Zamora." He started to push himself up from the table and Kee shoved him down.

Crow looked at Kee, his face at first bewildered, then he focused. "Shit," Crow mumbled. He shook his head, groaned, and put a hand to his forehead.

Max's eyes narrowed as he saw that Crow wasn't tied up.

"Shit," he said again. "What the hell did you hit me with?"

Crow sounded pathetic, but Max was watching the man's other hand, which was braced on the side of the table. The next instant, Crow jerked up and pushed forward on the table at the same time, but Max was ready with his weight against the opposite side. He shoved back. Crow lost his balance. Kee was up, out of his chair, and slamming Crow's head into the wall with unbridled rage.

"You don't deserve to live!" Kee yelled.

Max grabbed Kee's arm and tried to pull him off, but anger had hold of Kee's brain—anger fueled by all the liquor. It was as if this were exactly what Kee had wanted—and why he hadn't bound Crow. He was a wildcat, thrashing against both men. He knocked Max to the ground. When Max pulled himself up, he saw that Kee had hauled Crow up by his neck and held a gun to his temple.

"You deserve to *die,* Crow." Kee's voice sent a shudder up Max.

"Kee," he said slowly, taking a few steps toward him. "Don't do this."

"Everything Tilly and Rheada said was true, wasn't it, Crow? You killed their father, didn't you? Didn't you?" he demanded, pressing the gun hard at Crow's temple.

Crow looked damn scared. His eyes darted from Kee to Max. "You gonna let him shoot me?"

"He knows you're worthless, Crow. You *orphaned* those two girls." Now Kee was pressing the gun so hard to Crow's throat, the man's artery stood out, beating in a frantic pulse.

"I didn't even know he *had* kids! He told me he'd sell the mask to me, but then he backed out."

"And you killed him."

Crow was silent, his eyes wide and staring at Kee.

"You killed him for a mask?" Kee's voice was incredulous.

"It's worth a fortune." Then Crow started laughing hysterically. "Those girls had it all along, all these years." He stopped and leveled a crazy-mean stare at Kee. "We all lost tonight, cowboy. I'm out money. Zamora is out the mask. You lost the girl. Why don't you just let me go, and we'll call it even?"

Kee's arm stiffened. Max was sure he was going to pull the trigger. Instead, it was his voice that was lethal. "Why did you tell me that Raven killed a girl?"

Crow's face screwed into a hateful sneer. "Because I hate that bitch. She was stealing my business. She had this goddamn *legend* going for her. I wanted her dead."

"I don't get it—" Kee started.

"You asked if I'd seen a girl, remember? Well, when I told you that about Raven, it sure put a fire in your belly, right? What do I care how Raven gets hers?"

Kee stook a small step back, then caught Crow's jaw in a direct blow with his fist. Crow slumped to the floor. Kee stuffed the gun at his back waistband and rounded the table.

"Where the hell are you going?" Max said.

Kee stopped and faced him. The anger was gone from his eyes, replaced with a keen determination. "I'm giving it one more try." He offered a small smile. "You don't happen to know where Zamora is, do you?"

Max shook his head, trying to catch up with Kee's thinking. "Why Zamora? I don't understand. What did I miss here?"

"The mask. They've got it, Max. Tilly and Rheada. I know it. And my instincts tell me they're going to do something with it. Maybe they plan to give it to Zamora themselves."

"To that bastard? They'd be better off giving it to the other guy, Diaz. Zamora is corrupt."

The smile died on Kee's face. "What do you mean he's corrupt?"

"There's rumors that he keeps girls."

Kee's eyes flared. He ran a frustrated hand through his hair. "They wouldn't—" He paced. "If that's true, they wouldn't sell it to him."

"Unless they don't know," Max said quietly. The fact that Kee had been ready to go after Rheada, even with the lamest of leads, was enough for Max to give him hope. "And they'd have their choice of Zamora or Diaz tonight."

"What do you mean?"

"They're at the Plaza Hotel in Santa Fe for a debate. But it's going to be tough for anyone to get close to either of those men. I've heard the security is really tight. There's already been one assassination attempt on Zamora."

Kee considered Max. "Do you know anything about the security setup?"

Max laughed. "Have you looked at yourself lately, Kee? You look more like the assassin than security."

Kee's eyes sparked and he smiled. "Tell them I've been undercover and I'm coming out." Kee stared back for a beat, his face thoughtful. "I wonder how Rheada is getting to Zamora. She can't very well walk past every cop in the Southwest."

Max shrugged. "If she's any good, that's exactly what she'll do."

Kee chuckled. "Yeah." He turned to leave.

Max glanced at the grungy heap that was Crow. "And what am I supposed to do with him?"

"Stuff him and mount him over the bar," Kee called over his shoulder. "You could use a trophy."

"I don't need a trophy, Blackburn."

Kee stopped at the door and looked at Max. "I don't, either."

Chapter 24

RHEADA walked straight into the lobby of the Plaza Hotel, Blackjack sitting quietly on her bent forearm. Immediately, she sensed danger all around. It seemed that every other man she passed was a cop or a suit with a wire at his ear. Rheada kept walking, though a voice inside begged her to reconsider—and it came from a part of her that was Raven.

Rheada brushed within inches of men who would love to lock up the notorious Raven—and she battled every instinct within to bolt. She kept going, fighting the strong force within her screaming for her to flee, to escape. She kept her eyes staring ahead, ignoring with all her will the inner demands to dart glances left and right, scan the terrain, watch for danger. As her heart beat frantically, she called on the confidence, the *sureness,* of Raven's stealth and cunning.

But Raven had retreated to a hard nugget of fear in Rheada's gut, tying her in a knot, paralyzing her, until she was sure she would freeze up right there in the middle of the lobby. She found a huge stucco pillar, edged around to the back and leaned against it.

What if I can't do this?

But she had to. She had to persuade Zamora to free Sarah, and the only way was to convince him of her own worth as Raven.

She stepped beyond the pillar, and started across the marble floor. Her footsteps echoed on the cold, hard stone—a far cry from the soft sand of Raven's canyons. Fear gripped her thoughts. She stumbled and retreated, pressing her back against the column of stone.

What had happened to her? For eight years she had been Raven, able to sneak into and away from any place she chose without detection. Now that she needed that skill most, now when she could use it for something *good,* she couldn't?

Frustration rolled through her veins. Blackjack's beak rubbed gently up and down her cheek. His quiet chortles tickled on her skin. Rheada ran her hand down his satiny back.

"Tell me what's wrong, Blackjack. Why am I so afraid? Raven wouldn't be afraid."

She tried to conjure up that identity in her mind's eye—Raven, the one who owned the night and the canyons—but what she saw was a flutter in the night, a rise of black hair, the *hint* of a presence, as elusive as a wisp of the imagination.

Run, whispered the voice. *Get away before we're caught!*

Rheada's legs shook with the effort to stand her ground.

I will not run! She had spent her life on the run. All the time she had told herself that Raven was only a means to an end—the way to Rheada's freedom, to a new life. But that had been a lie. Raven had been only the means to Rheada's imprisonment. She was caught in the lies and the subterfuge.

The irony was that up until last night, her greatest fear had been of someone *discovering* her past, uncovering her identity as Raven. Now, for the second time in less than twenty-four hours, she would gladly proclaim that identity . . . in exchange for someone's freedom. Raven would be the means to *someone else's* freedom—even if it meant the cost of her own.

It was the right thing to do.

Her mind filled with images of *herself* in the daylight, leading tours, talking to perfect strangers whose faces were bright with excitement for what she shared.

And she saw herself with Kee, pulling him down to her, pressing her mouth to his, longing to hear her name on his lips . . . Rheada.

It suddenly occurred to her that it was Rheada who had done those things, not Raven. As Rheada, she had found the courage to reach out and grab for something she wanted—her new life, Kee . . . and as Rheada she now made the decision to exchange Raven for Sarah.

Rheada breathed in deep, and stepped out from behind the column, only to nearly collide with a man talking on a two-way radio. The voice inside yelled at her to run, at least to hide, but Rheada wasn't listening anymore. She set her sights on the front desk and slipped into the crowd.

A steady stream of people pushed through the corridor: Indians she recognized as being from Southwest tribes, and other Indians who looked to be from Central or South America. Some turned to look at the woman with the raven on her arm, but most were oblivious to her as they rushed by.

There were reporters with all kinds of equipment. A man with a huge camera on his shoulder cut past Rheada. Blackjack shifted his weight, keeping himself balanced on her arm. Rheada bent her arm close, cuddling Blackjack to her, as she made her way through the sea of strange faces.

Suddenly, a sense of familiarity drew her gaze to one man—to his shoulder-length black hair and his particular gait. Blackjack tensed on her arm, his claws holding tight, and he leaned in the very direction that Rheada was staring, as if he too were drawn to the man.

Rheada's heart gave a jump of recognition. It was Kee! Her steps veered to follow him, but then she lost sight of him as he was swallowed in the crowd. Her heart raced, urging her to follow, to find him, but Rheada told herself it couldn't be him. He had no reason to be here. It had only been her hopes rising to the surface and fooling her.

She turned back, against the constant flow of people. Blackjack gripped hard, and his wings rose once, as if he would pull her down the corridor.

"No, Blackjack. We're going this way," she murmured, placing a firm hand on his back.

He strained against her, and Rheada held him close. She could feel his heart beating as rapidly as her own, echoing the surge of excitement she had felt. It occurred to Rheada how odd it was that Blackjack should have any reaction at all to Kee, but she couldn't ponder the thought. She couldn't let herself be distracted by anything, especially thoughts of Kee.

"Please, Blackjack. Cooperate," she whispered to him. She glanced back to the front desk, and let her mind run over the words she had rehearsed. Then, with a deep breath, she strode to the counter.

Several people stood waiting, but two flutters of Blackjack's wings brought the clerk's attention.

"Get that *crow* out of here."

"This is a raven, sir," Rheada said, with all the cool authority she could muster. "He is the protector of legends, messenger of the Anasazi, the guardian of the Southwest."

As if on cue, Blackjack puffed out his chest, and slowly unfolded his wings, spreading them to their full span of four feet. He stood there, body stretched, wings wide and proud, and absolutely still as if he were an extraordinary sculpture.

"Oh, my," said a woman nearby. "What a beautiful bird."

Others pressed in to see, and a chorus of exclamations rose, all of which only flustered the clerk even more.

"Miss, this is a high-class hotel. You can't have that wild *creature* in here."

Rheada pressed her lips to Blackjack and whispered, "He thinks he is a bear, Blackjack, but he is a mouse."

Rheada lowered her arm and Blackjack stepped down gracefully to the counter, and, with wings still extended, he strutted toward the clerk, his sharp talons clicking on the glossy marble.

The man's eyes flew wide and he stepped back. "Get that bird off my counter!"

"He won't harm you," Rheada reassured him.

A crowd had formed behind her. She decided to take advantage of the audience. "Ravens are birds of royalty. He realizes you are a man of authority," Rheada said, playing off the man's obvious need to stay in charge. "He is simply showing his respect."

Blackjack walked to the end of the counter, stopped, and faced the distressed clerk. Then he slowly folded his wings close to his body and stood quietly, staring at the poor, bewildered clerk.

The crowd behind Rheada was quiet. Even the clerk now looked more curious than upset. They all stared at the great black bird, sitting there so solemn and regal. Rheada felt a flush of pride rise up her cheeks.

"The raven is our relative. From the earliest time, the raven has been at our side, sharing our food, joining man with nature." The lobby was hushed. Without looking, Rheada knew that everyone's eyes were on her and Blackjack. "The oldest Pueblo legend tells of the raven traveling alongside the people on their migrations to their final home. In him is the memory of all time, the knowledge of where we have been, and the wisdom of where we are going."

Rheada gazed on her companion. Blackjack hadn't moved. He looked so still as to not even be breathing. She had meant only to impress the clerk, but her own words plumbed feelings of deep love. Blackjack had always been there for her, guiding her. But would he stay at her side always? Would he even be with her at the end of today?

Her breath caught at her throat, choking on the next words she had to say. Then Blackjack turned his head and pinned her with his keen gaze.

"*Caw-aw-aw*," he called softly.

She stared back and found the strength to continue. "This raven comes from the canyons of the Anasazi. He carries their secrets. He is called Blackjack." Rheada drew a deep breath. "He is a gift to Esteban Zamora."

Blackjack walked back across the counter to Rheada and stepped onto her raised arm, where he settled. He bent his head and pressed his beak to her cheek and rubbed up and down. Rheada had to fight a sudden, frightening swell of emotion—as if she truly *were* about to lose something she loved.

She tilted up her chin to force the tears back from her eyes, and looked at the clerk. He was on the phone. He cupped the mouthpiece and looked at her.

"Your name?" he asked.

Rheada drew a deep breath and said the words she had never thought to say. "Tell him Rheada Samuels is delivering the Raven."

Caw!

Kee heard the raven. At first he thought he must have imagined it: The sound echoed off miles of marble and stone, distorting and growing through the hallways, so that by the time it reached him the sound was more like that of a muted horn, playing one, lone note. But what his ears misinterpreted, the rest of him immediately recognized: It was a raven. More specifically, it was *the* raven—Blackjack.

He didn't ask himself how he knew it was Blackjack. He pushed back through the crowds toward the lobby—one man against a tide of people—his eyes searching beyond the sea of heads for that *one* head he would instantly know. Rheada was here. He would find her.

He didn't know what he would say when he did. He didn't have a thought in his head beyond a *need* to look into those eyes again, to have her eyes look into *him*. That need propelled him forward.

He rounded the corner to the lobby. His gaze darted to every person there, scrutinizing, dismissing, continually seeking.

Caw!

Kee's gaze flew to the far corner of the lobby. He thought the raven's call came from there, though he couldn't see Rheada in the swarm of humanity that had come to see Diaz and Zamora. He pushed forward, elbowing his way through the solid mass of people. He heard gasps and exclamations about his rudeness, but Kee couldn't slow even to apologize.

Caw!

As if on the raven's command, the crowd seemed to part, and Kee glimpsed Rheada. He saw Blackjack sitting on her arm. He saw her jet-black hair, floating at her shoulders. Then, as she turned the corner, just before the crowd closed behind her, he saw the silhouette of her face—the set of her jaw, the pallor of her skin, the sheen in her eyes. She had the fearful, determined look of someone resigned to a terrible fate.

Kee's heart leaped to his throat. "Rheada!"

Caw!

Blackjack's call drifted back to Kee. But Rheada didn't appear. Kee shoved aside people.

Suddenly, a hand grabbed his arm. He wrenched it loose without a backward glance and forged ahead, but another hand caught his other arm and yanked him to a stop.

"You'll stop right there."

Kee whirled, ready to deck the guy, and found himself facing a crew cut, narrowed dark eyes, and a suit. Hotel security, Kee figured.

"This way," the man ordered, pulling on Kee's arm.

Kee jerked his arm back, bringing the man within inches of his face. "I'm on the task force."

The man didn't say anything, just kept tugging Kee across the flow of the crowd . . . and away from Rheada. Frustration pricked up Kee's scalp.

"Let go, asshole, or you'll regret it," Kee hissed.

Suddenly, there was a gun at Kee's ribs. "Shut up and get moving," the man ordered. He pinned Kee's arm behind him, shoved the gun deep into Kee's side, and forced him forward. It was textbook maneuvering and Kee realized the man wasn't hotel security, but probably federal—maybe even on the task force himself, which meant the man wouldn't listen, wouldn't stop, and probably wouldn't hesitate to shoot.

They passed a mirror and Kee saw a long-haired man, his

menacing pitch-black eyes set in dark circles. He looked desperate and dangerous. Kee realized with an inner shudder of horror that he was looking at himself. Max was right: Kee looked like an assassin. In the same split second, Kee knew he didn't have a prayer of convincing this agent of anything.

"This is T4. Lobby." The agent spoke into a radio. "I have a suspect." He listened for a moment. "Understood."

The agent pulled Kee across the lobby to a side door. Kee's mind worked fast. That door led either to the command center or to the agent's first available choice for containment. Kee's gaze darted over the surrounding area. He didn't see any suits stationed outside. If Kee had any luck at all, that door led to an empty room.

As the agent reached for the knob, Kee angled his body ever so slightly for an advantage. The latch clicked open. Kee pushed hard with his shoulder against the door, catching himself but also the agent off balance. They tumbled into a room that Kee instantly recognized was for office supplies.

He pulled his arm free from the agent, slammed shut the door, then whirled on the agent, trying to knock the gun from his hand. The agent was quick, swerving to the side and away. Kee tackled him, throwing them both to the floor. He grappled for the gun, pinned the agent's arm against the floor. Kee drove a fist into the man's side. The agent let out a loud grunt. Kee had a fleeting thought about the noise. He knew he didn't have forever to take care of this guy. Every second he was here, he risked discovery. More important, though, he risked never finding Rheada.

He slammed a fist to the guy's jaw, again and again, until the agent's head lolled to the side. Kee grabbed the gun. He searched the metal shelves for something to tie up the agent. He finally had to settle for two extension cords. From a roll of duct tape, he bit off enough to slap over the man's mouth. Then Kee dragged the man to the back corner and shoved a stack of boxes in front of him.

Kee cracked the door open and peeked out to the slice of hallway that he could see. Two agents were angling across the lobby straight for the room. Kee darted a glance around him, grabbed one of the boxes of paper, hefted it to his shoulder, and walked out of the room.

* * *

Rheada was ushered past the conference room where Zamora and Diaz would hold their debate and out to an enclosed court-yard. A riot of flowers erupted from a myriad of terra-cotta pots.

"Welcome!" A booming voice arose from behind the flow-ers and filled the courtyard.

With Blackjack holding firmly to her arm, Rheada pushed aside blossom-laden branches, and found herself facing a small man with a grand smile. It was Zamora. Though she immediately recognized him from the newspaper picture, Rheada was still caught by surprise. She had expected an evil-looking man, but his face showed no conflict, only merriment, with laugh lines that spread from the corners of twinkling black eyes. He was also smaller than she had imagined, barely her own height. For no reason, it occurred to her that he could walk unhindered through the short Anasazi doorways.

"It is true!"

The comment jerked Rheada from her thoughts back to Zamora. He was laughing, and the robust sound circled through her. Now she couldn't be sure he had said the words or she had only imagined them.

"Come join me!" He gestured behind him.

His enthusiasm, the joy in his voice, was infectious. She felt an irresistible pull toward the man, as if he could draw all the goodness within her into view.

Zamora stepped to the side and, for the first time, Rheada saw they weren't alone. Three girls sat at the wrought-iron table. The one in the middle was Sarah.

Rheada's heart skipped. Her thoughts stumbled, tripping over the wonderful sensations she had been experiencing, only to come face to face with Zamora's true power: his hold over young girls. Rheada had to clench her jaw against the torrent of condemnations that rose swiftly in her throat.

"Please! Sit down!" Zamora offered a chair. "There's noth-ing to fear." His voice, so gentle and coaxing, nearly overcame Rheada.

She drew herself straight. "I'll stand," Rheada said.

Zamora settled in a chair and smiled back at her. "As you wish," he said amiably.

His eyes twinkled with merriment. For a moment, Rheada couldn't pull her gaze away, so strong was his magnetism.

There's nothing to fear. She heard the words as clearly as if he had repeated himself, yet she had been staring at him and his lips hadn't moved. Suddenly, Rheada had the very real sense of having met her match.

Zamora's focus shifted to Blackjack and Rheada saw the man's eyes soften as his gaze lingered. She swore she saw affection grow in his eyes, as if he were gazing upon a long-lost dear friend.

Zamora's eyes grew more intent, almost hypnotic, as he stared, unblinking, at Blackjack. Blackjack leaned toward Zamora. Zamora's smile broadened. Blackjack flexed his wings, his gaze never wavering from the man. The two looked as if they were communicating silently. An eerie unrealness settled over Rheada.

Zamora looked back to Rheada and he stared, still smiling, but with an expectant look on his face that Rheada immediately recognized: He was waiting for her to present him with the bird.

She laid a firm hand across Blackjack's back, in part to hold him closer . . . in part to seek strength for herself within the familiar, comforting feel of his satiny feathers. But Blackjack wouldn't allow himself to be held close. He wiggled free, again flexing his wings. The next instant, he took off, his legs distended, his great wings flapping twice. He landed on Zamora's arm and settled there with the unhesitant ease of familiarity.

Rheada stared, speechless, her emotions jammed at her throat. Blackjack had never flown to *anyone*. Not her father. Not even Tilly. Now he would fly to this total stranger?

"Thank you," Zamora said.

Rheada's heart lurched. A keen ache pierced her clean through.

Zamora looked at Blackjack. "It is good to see you."

Rheada stared, taken aback. She couldn't have heard right. He sounded as if he *knew* Blackjack.

Zamora murmured to Blackjack in a language Rheada couldn't understand, though the words did sound vaguely familiar. One word sounded Keresan, the language spoken by the Pueblo Indians of Santo Domingo; another sounded Hopi; still another, Tewa, the language of the Jemez Pueblo Indians. Interspersed among these languages were words from entirely *different* languages. Through it all, Blackjack's full attention was given to the man, his keen gaze on him, his head bobbing as if comprehending and *agreeing* with whatever Zamora was saying.

Caw-aw-aw.

Without thinking, Rheada took a step forward, answering Blackjack's call—then stopped herself and stared, heartstruck that Blackjack was talking to *Zamora.* His soft call had *always* been for her . . . until now.

His chortles grew louder. His head bobbed excitedly. Suddenly, Blackjack was silent. In the same instant, Zamora's gaze shifted to Rheada. "And now you have something to say?"

His abrupt question startled Rheada and left her uneasy, as if she had slipped into another world where her thoughts were already known. He was a step ahead of her, already knowing what she would say. *Who is this man?*

Rheada shook her head. Her gaze caught that of Sarah's. The girl was staring at her, the brow furrowed on her young face. Whoever this man was, Rheada told herself, whatever his power over people, she had to follow through with her plan to free Sarah.

She took a breath and looked back at him. He stared at her with glistening black eyes, so sparkling that they could be the stars in the night sky. Unbidden, a calmness spread through Rheada. She didn't need a breath for courage or to clarify her thoughts. Suddenly, her thoughts, her *mission,* were clear.

She leveled her gaze on Zamora. "I understand you have a particular interest in Anasazi artifacts, is that right?"

He didn't smile or frown. He only studied her, his face an expression of benign contemplation. "I don't like the term 'artifacts.' It makes them sound dead, don't you think? And the word 'Anasazi.' " He wrinkled his nose into such an expression of displeasure, Rheada nearly apologized.

"Did you know," he continued, "that 'Anasazi' is a Navajo word? This wasn't the name of the people."

And this wasn't the direction of the conversation that Rheada had anticipated. Even more unsettling was Zamora's clear focus, as if he knew personally what he was talking about.

She cleared her throat and tried to regain control of the

situation. "I can tell you've done your research."

His quick, broad grin was disconcerting.

"I too am very knowledgeable about—" She paused, searching for a word that wouldn't set Zamora off again. "Of the ancient ones," she finished. "I've spent my life in their canyons. I know places of theirs that are unknown to anyone else."

Zamora's right brow rose. His eyes twinkled, almost mischievously, as if he were some kindly, wise mentor humoring an upstart. Rheada felt a moment of panic. Had she underestimated this man?

She stole a glance at Sarah and forged ahead. "Over my lifetime, I have collected the best of what the *Anasazi* left behind. And I alone know where to look for anything a *collector* might be interested in—"

"You are very sure of this," Zamora interrupted.

"Yes," Rheada said. She took a step forward, staring confidently at Zamora. "I know," she said quietly, "what a collector such as yourself wants." Rheada slid her gaze over to the girls and lingered for a pointed beat. Fear for them—and for what she was about to say—tightened her throat. She swallowed and looked back at Zamora. "I can give you what you want."

"Really? How would you know what I want?"

Rheada narrowed her eyes on Zamora. "You want what is rare. What is unspoiled." She chose her words carefully. "What no one else has had." Would Zamora understand that she was talking about both his interests in artifacts and girls?

She kept her gaze steady on him and watched his own expression turn curious. He leaned forward in his chair. "What do *you* want?"

The twinkle in Zamora's eyes increased to a million tiny lights, a sparkling effervescence that was more beautiful than anything Rheada had ever seen. She stared—unable to resist the magic in his eyes—and his question echoed in her head—not as words, but as a music of memories, each note a feeling, altogether a harmony that rose inside her and filled her with a deep sense of *life*.

I want my life to matter.

The thought appeared as clear and bright as a full moon, a *digging* moon.

Her mind instantly rebelled. Her life wasn't only about hiding in canyons, skulking through the night, and stealing artifacts . . . except here she was, trading on those very things to Zamora.

Caw-aw-aw.

Blackjack's call pulled her from her thoughts. She almost didn't dare to look at him, for fear she would find him once again *talking* to Zamora. But he was looking at her, his keen eyes shiny. With two flaps, he rose from Zamora's arm and landed on hers. His muscular weight comforted her—like the welcome intimacy of a familiar arm across her shoulder, as Kee's arm had been only yesterday.

"What matters, of course, are the choices we make," Zamora said. His voice was quiet as the whisper of conscience.

Rheada yanked her gaze from Blackjack to Zamora. How had he known she was facing a choice? As she stared at him, at the unfathomable twinkling in his eyes, she realized it didn't matter how he knew. All that mattered was that she *did* have a choice and now was the time to make it.

"You're right. In fact, I have come here to offer you a choice, a trade," Rheada said. "Myself for these girls."

"What?" It was Sarah. Rheada saw her startled reaction from the corner of her eye.

"Why this trade?" Zamora asked calmly.

"Because for whatever reason you chose these girls, I can serve you better."

"Esteban, what is she—"

Zamora reached a hand to Sarah's arm to quiet her. Rheada couldn't understand Sarah—unless she was completely bewitched by the man.

"Why you?" Zamora asked.

Rheada stared back evenly, though inside she quavered with the effort to withstand the *enchantment* of his eyes. "Because I am Raven."

He smiled. "Yes, I have heard of Raven." He tilted his head, considering her. "I thought you wanted to retire."

Rheada controlled a gasp of surprise. "Your information was wrong," she managed. "Why would I retire? I'm the best at what I do."

His expression turned solemn. He leaned forward, staring at her, his eyes steady, relentless, as if he could see deep within her. Her insides stirred, retreating from his laser focus. She scrambled to hide her dreams and her hopes beneath a hard mask. She had to be tough, resolute, she told herself. She had to show Zamora only the criminal in her heart if she was to win. It should be easy. She *was* a criminal. She had made bad choices all her life. Now was her chance to do something right for once.

Except she couldn't hold on beneath his stare. She couldn't keep her heart from cracking. She couldn't stop the wave of emotions from flooding her. Oh God, what if he saw how *sorry* she was?

"I see," he said quietly.

Rheada's heart slammed against her chest.

"You *are* the best," he said.

His pronouncement was a gentle caress that broke the last of her defenses. The emotions welled in her eyes.

"That's why *this one*," he said with a glance to Blackjack, "chose you. He had waited at the woman's burial for the right person."

Rheada blinked. How could he possibly know how she had found Blackjack?

"Do you know who was buried there?"

Rheada couldn't speak. She could barely shake her head in answer. Her thoughts had leaped back to that day when she was just a child, back to when she had still had a father. She remembered the wealth of turquoise surrounding the burial. Her father had never seen such riches buried with an Anasazi woman. He said that she must have been important.

"That was the mother of Poseyemu." His voice was full of sadness. "The first Kachina." He paused. "What do you know about the mask?"

It is evil. The thought struck her like a fist.

"You should be careful of the legends you believe," he said quietly.

A glance at Zamora told Rheada that she had let her emotions rule her expressions. She didn't say a word.

Zamora was quiet for a moment, then asked, "Is the mask safe?"

Rheada's gaze jerked to Zamora. He was a trickster, trying to enchant her! Foreboding skittered up Rheada's spine. He was about to ask for the mask. He would *demand* it. She steeled herself against his incredible power of persuasion.

"You have it, yes?"

In the face of his gaze, Rheada feared her voice would betray her. She shook her head no.

He looked at her and Rheada could see the knowledge in his eyes that she was lying. Then he smiled. "I'm glad to know it is safe," he said. "It belongs to the past."

Movement at the rooftop overlooking the courtyard drew Rheada's attention. She started to glance there, when, from the corner of her eye, she saw the flowering branches move and she glimpsed something black. She jerked her gaze back to the roof. The sun glinted off a shiny object. The next instant, the reflection disappeared.

Something wasn't right. Blackjack knew it, too. He took off, soaring straight to the rooftop. Rheada's instincts screamed run, hide. Instead, she went straight to Sarah.

She rounded the table and grabbed her arm. "Let's go. Now!"

"What are you doing?" Sarah tried to wrench free from Rheada, but Rheada held firm.

"It's okay," Rheada said. "You can trust me."

Gunfire exploded. Rheada recognized it as a rifle.

"No!" It was a man's voice—a voice Rheada knew, one her heart leaped to. But she couldn't take the time to even look over her shoulder to see Kee.

The next instant, she heard shots fired from a gun, not the rifle. She yanked Sarah out of her chair, wrapped herself around her, and started to run.

Another rifle shot split the air. Rheada felt a sharp pinch at her side. She staggered against the table, but held tight to Sarah.

"God, no!"

Kee's yell—deep, primal—reached into Rheada, shored her up. She straightened and hauled Sarah with her to the far corner. She pushed Sarah to the ground and covered her with her own body. The sounds of gunfire and rifle shots reverberated against the cement walls of the courtyard.

Sarah cried out. Rheada thought she'd been hit. She raised her head to look, her heart pumping wildly. What she saw was Sarah staring toward the table, her eyes wide, tears streaming down her cheeks.

Rheada glanced over to see Zamora slumped in his chair, red oozing from his chest. She had to hold tight against Sarah's struggles to get to him.

Caw! Caw! Blackjack flew down from the roof, his piercing calls ripping the air. He sounded more like he was screaming. He landed beside Zamora, and pushed at the silent man's arm with his beak.

Rheada craned her neck to try to see Kee. She saw a flash of sunlight on black just beyond one of the huge pots. She tried to stretch farther, to see Kee. Her side erupted in searing pain that took her breath away. Rheada put a hand to her side and felt the unmistakable stickiness of blood. She'd been shot.

The pain traveled swiftly, taking over her senses, blurring her vision, muting all noise. As darkness blanketed her, all Rheada could think was she had saved Sarah.

It wasn't a sacrifice.

Chapter 25

KEE scrambled across the courtyard. He gave a cursory glance to Zamora, who was slumped across the table. Whether the man was dead or alive, Kee didn't care. He was looking for Rheada.

But then he thought he heard something, a whimpering coming from under the table. Kee knelt and found two girls huddled there, protecting each other. "It's over," he murmured. He reached a hand to one of them. "You can come out."

She shrank back from him with fear on her face. It flashed on Kee that he didn't exactly have the clean-cut look of a cop. "It's okay. I'm not going to hurt you." He offered a smile, and kept his palm extended to her.

Finally, she put her hand in his and let him pull her from under the table. The other girl followed. They were both so young, barely teenagers, no older than Sarah.

At the thought of his sister, Kee's heart ached—a pain he couldn't reach, he couldn't soothe.

"Are you all right?" It was the girl.

Kee couldn't answer. The hurt owned him, clenching his muscles, stunning him with its power. He turned away, unable to speak, and straightened from the ground.

He pushed a branch of blossoms aside. He saw a young girl, alone, bracing herself on the pot in order to stand. He recognized the familiar round face. But he could only stare, at first not believing. He had to be hallucinating. Or he had lost his mind. It couldn't be Sarah.

"Kee?"

Her voice jolted him, brought him to life. His legs walked to her. His hand reached for her tentatively, a part of him still afraid that she wasn't real, that he hadn't found her, alive.

Now he noticed that her expression was dazed, her eyes slightly unfocused, and there was a cut on her forehead. "Are you hurt?" His own voice came out choked.

She swiped at her forehead. "No."

He wanted to pull her into a hug, but she drew back. Kee's

arm fell limp to his side. Every night, he had imagined what he would do if he had another chance—he had never thought she would pull away. Her eyes opened wide. "What—" she stammered. "What are you doing here?"

"I've—" He had almost said, *I've been looking for you.* But he hadn't been. He had believed she was dead. He had been on a quest for vengeance, when all along she had been alive. "I thought you were dead," he whispered.

"I know."

"What?" He couldn't be hearing this.

Her gaze pulled away, as if she couldn't look at him. "I thought it best if you *did* believe that."

"Why?" But the word barely carried past his lips. He couldn't find the breath in him.

She looked to the side, past Kee. Suddenly, her eyes flew wide. "Esteban!" She ran toward him.

Kee grabbed her. "It's okay, Sarah. He can't hurt you."

Her gaze flew to his. "He saved me!" She wrenched free of Kee and ran to the table.

"No—" Kee couldn't make any sense of it. He couldn't think past what Sarah had said—that she had wanted him to believe she was dead. "I don't understand—"

She was standing beside Zamora. "He found me," she said. Her hand brushed the hair back from Zamora's forehead. "He protected me."

Kee's mind stumbled over her words, as he watched his sister's tenderness for this man, this *stranger,* while she wouldn't even allow him to hug her.

He protected me.

Not Kee, she was saying. Kee hadn't been there for her. "How could you let me think you were dead?" He took a step toward her. "Why, Sarah?"

"He told me to."

"What?"

Sarah's gaze rose. She had been looking at Zamora. Her eyes shone with the pain of loss . . . and love. "He told me you needed to go on a journey."

Kee thought of all the cold nights where his only warmth had been the red-hot coals of anger in his gut. His harsh reality then had been the realization he was capable of doing anything, even watching someone die, just to get answers about

Sarah. The only journey he'd been on was to hell, without hope for anything more.

"I knew he had to be right," Sarah said. "After I left home, I got lost. I saw a campfire and was walking to it. But a raven appeared, flying in my face, forcing me in the other direction. He was very determined." She smiled down at Zamora. "The raven led me to Zamora."

"A raven . . ." Kee couldn't even finish a coherent sentence.

"Yes," she said. She tilted her head as she looked at Kee.

Kee shook his head. "You followed a raven."

"I don't care what you think," Sarah said. "It's true. And when Esteban told me you needed something to believe in, I knew that had to be true. Because we all need that." She looked back to Zamora. "I needed that."

But Kee wasn't thinking she was lying. He was thinking that he had done the same thing. He had also followed a raven—*the* Raven. He had followed her right out of the caves, into the sunlight, and finally to here, to his sister . . . and what he had found himself believing was that he never wanted to be without Rheada again.

He had thought he could do anything, everything, on his own. He had been damn *determined* to do it on his own. Now that he thought about it, Rheada had had that same determination to make a life on her own. He wondered, right then, whether she would let him make that life along with her . . . that was, if he could find her.

Kee stood there, staring at the miracle of Sarah alive. He walked to her and wrapped his arms around her, savoring the *feel* of her safe in his arms.

"I also followed a raven," he confided. His gaze went to Blackjack. The raven sat on Zamora's arm. He was staring at Zamora, his head cocked to one side, as if waiting for something to happen, for the man to move.

"You followed that bird?" She was looking at Blackjack.

"In a sense," Kee said. He slanted his eyes toward Blackjack. Kee had the absurd notion to ask the bird where she was.

"Raven brought that bird to Esteban." A measure of distrust laced her voice. "I don't understand," she continued. "She offered to *trade* herself for me and the others."

"She what?" Kee arched back to look into Sarah's face.

"She told him that she could give him whatever he wanted, if he let us go. Why would she do that?"

Because Rheada saves people. She had saved his own life twice. But more, she had given him reason to hope.

"Because she thought you were in trouble," Kee said.

"But she barely knew me."

Kee looked at his sister and the truth filled his heart. "She did it for me." He leaned back, gripping her shoulders. "Where did she go, Sarah?"

Her eyes grew solemn. "Kee, she's—" She stopped. "I think she's—"

Kee's heart jumped to his throat. "Show me where she is, Sarah!" He pulled Sarah with him behind the huge flowering bushes. She led him around a cluster of pots, and pushed through a tangle of branches that closed behind them.

There, on the ground, was Rheada.

Kee knelt and gently rolled her toward him, into his lap. His hand felt a sticky wetness at her side. Then he saw the blood.

Time stopped. The world teetered on its axis and would fall. With no anchor, *he* would fall.

She can't be dead!

He touched fingers to her neck and thought he felt a pulse. He couldn't be sure. His own pulse was racing, as if he had stepped off a cliff.

"Sarah, call an ambulance!"

All hell broke loose behind him. The doors slammed open. He heard men shouting orders.

"Get someone. Anyone!" he yelled to Sarah over his shoulder.

Kee glanced down at Rheada. He brushed hair back from her face with a trembling hand. "You can't die, Rheada." He pulled her close. "You can't." He cradled her. "We haven't had our chance yet. *You* haven't had a chance yet. Goddamnit, you have to live!"

Rheada stirred in his arms.

Kee gasped for air—as if he had been yanked back from a free fall. "Rheada?"

Her eyes fluttered open. "Your sister?" The words were broken on her jagged breathing.

"You saved her life."

Her face grew calm. Too calm. Fear spiked through Kee. He roused her. "You're going to be fine. Rheada, stay with me!"

Her eyes peeked open. "Say that again . . . my name."

"Rheada." Kee's heartbeat pounded at his throat. "You saved my life." He heard footsteps running across the stones to them. "They're coming to take care of you."

"You're the one I need," she said. She smiled.

Every bad choice he had made, every wrong act, disappeared as if by magic, from just the love in her eyes.

"Don't move!" It was a man's voice. A strong yank on Kee's hair jerked him backward.

"I'm Special Agent Kee Blackburn!" he yelled, trying to hold on to Rheada without hurting her.

"Let go of her and back off!"

Rheada smiled up at Kee. "Tell him you're one of the good guys."

The sunlight of her smile poured over Kee, warming him to his soul. "They won't believe it," he joked.

She squinted up at him. "Yeah, you do look terrible. Maybe you should quit."

"Now!" yelled the man.

From the corner of his eye, Kee saw a gun leveled at his temple, but he couldn't help a chuckle. "It's okay," Kee said, his gaze locked on Rheada. "We're all on the same side."

They ended the tour on the ridge overlooking Chaco Canyon. The ancient Anasazi city lay below them, curving out into the valley like a great man with arms spread. Rheada turned into the wind to face her group of tourists.

"One thousand years ago, the daughter of a Chaco priest married the son of an Aztec chief. It was the marriage of two powerful nations, meant to create one empire. Instead it tore apart the peoples of the Southwest."

Kee stood at her side, his fingers close enough for hers to grasp, but she didn't need to. She had waited a lifetime to tell this story. "The child of this union, half Anasazi and half Aztec, was tormented. According to a legend, he was killed. Warlords of Chaco avenged the child's murder with the assassination of the Aztec prince. The cycle of revenge and murder ripped apart the fabric of this great civilization. The clans scattered to the cliffs. That is one version of the legend."

Rheada paused. The wind lifted from the canyon below. And on the wind rose the sound of ancient drumbeats. "But now I will tell you the true story.

"That boy did not die. The mother—just a young girl herself—took her baby son and disappeared into the night. She left behind all the people she knew and the only home she had ever known."

Rheada paused again. Voices of the ancient ones joined the drumbeats.

"She made this choice to save his life. They lived secret lives, all the time in hiding, until the day she died and her son was left alone. He was still a young boy and his life was in danger. And now he faced his own decision. He could stay in hiding. Or he could run far away, save himself, survive. But that was not to be his destiny."

Kee's hand slipped within hers and Rheada's heart surged at the touch. She thought of the dreams she had held to her heart when she was in the canyons. When she had made the choice to leave the canyons, plunging forward with only hope, never once had she dreamed that her destiny would be to find a man like Kee.

She took a breath and continued. "He chose neither. Instead he traveled to the scattered clans. He created rituals. He taught the people dances. He brought together the masks from the Aztecs and the ceremonies of the Anasazi. Finally, he led them down from the caves and cliffs to their proper places."

Kee's hand pressed closer to hers. She smiled up at him. "They had feared him," she said, looking into his eyes. "They had driven him into the night. And in the end, *he* was the one to lead them to somewhere safe."

The chanting voices and rhythmic drumbeats echoed off the cliff walls and surrounded Rheada. The sounds filled her so that at first she thought the man's voice came on the song.

But it was Kee. His deep voice rumbled through her. "He was called Poseyemu. They called him this because he was born to a woman who was stronger than the sun."

His hand gripped hers tighter. His warmth spread into her. She could feel his life beat at her palm.

"Why did I tell you this story?" Rheada turned and looked

into the eyes of the man she loved. "Because what we fear most may be exactly what saves us."

Kee led her away from the group. "You might also have told them to be careful of the legends they believe."

Rheada looked up at Kee in surprise. "Zamora said the same thing to me."

He smiled. "He was right."

"Yes, he was." Rheada could still feel the intensity of Zamora's gaze, as if he could see right through to her core, to what was important. "He was right about a lot of things. You know, he wasn't surprised when I showed up with Blackjack. I even had the sense that he had been expecting me. As if I had passed some sort of test."

She thought of the mischievous twinkle in his eyes and chuckled.

"What's funny?"

"I just wish he hadn't dropped out of the election. He would have made a good president."

"He said he had other legends to bring to life," Kee said. Then he looked down at Rheada as they walked. "I have another plan, though." His eyes twinkled and Rheada wondered what in the world Kee could have in store.

He stopped at a curve of the cliff wall. Stretched before them was the valley of Chaco. "It's so beautiful here," he said.

The deep quietness of his voice, the simple sincerity of his words, filled Rheada with more awe than the grand vista before them. She had never felt so at peace, so *safe*.

"Beautiful," he said again.

And now, from the sound of his voice, Rheada could tell he was looking at her. A warm surge of awareness poured through her. She turned to him, but at that moment Kee let go of her hand. He pulled a trowel from his back pocket, crouched, and started to dig.

"What are you doing?"

He didn't answer, just continued digging until he had a hole a foot deep. Then he stood and took Rheada's hands in his. She could feel something within his palm.

"This is for you, Rheada."

He released her hands and Rheada looked down at a shard

in her hand, one she immediately recognized. It was the shard of the raven she had buried.

Rheada gasped. Her gaze flew to Kee.

He looked back, his eyes warm, though a wry grin pulled at his mouth. "Tilly thought it would make a good souvenir," he said.

"That's Tilly for you," Rheada managed to say, though emotions choked her throat. She could barely think past the wonder of Kee smiling on her as he held the shard of the raven.

"I pointed out to her," Kee continued, "that no relic, no *legend*—" He fell quiet and just gazed at her. The emotion that filled his eyes echoed the same within her. "None of that could compare with the real thing."

Rheada's eyes filled, but this time she let the tears slide over the edge and down her cheek. She had nothing to hide from anyone, not anymore.

She looked down at the relic in her hand. She ran her thumb over the ancient picture, then dropped the shard into the hole, and covered it with dirt. The miracle of a *future* settled over her. Tilly and Sarah were back at the office planning great journeys. But here, standing on the edge of the cliff with Kee, Rheada realized that the most extraordinary journey of all was that of finding the courage to believe.

"It really *was* a test," she murmured.

"What?"

She rose and slipped her arms around Kee's waist and smiled up at him. "Nothing."

"Some things belong *only* to the past," he said quietly. Intense passion filled his eyes. "*You* belong in the world, Rheada. In the sunlight. With me." He pulled her close and lowered his mouth to hers.

Rheada's gaze filled with his eyes, with the destiny she saw there.

Dear Reader,

Georgia O'Keefe is said to have described the Anasazi cliff dwellings in Mesa Verde as a "little city of stone . . . looking down with the calmness of eternity." The ancient dwellings of the Southwest evoke this sort of inspiration, as if the songs and poetry and deep spiritual connection of these long-dead inhabitants can reach across time to us. More than a peaceful existence, however, is tangled within the sage and held close by the canyon shadows. Of equal endurance is the mystery surrounding the Anasazi.

The Anasazi built great cities in canyon valleys. The cities of Chaco Canyon included thirteen towns with 2,500 buildings, some five stories tall—the tallest "apartment" buildings on the continent until New York City. Chacoan influence reached far beyond the canyon, encompassing 40,000 square miles with 400 miles of graded roads, some 40 feet wide. Chaco was obviously the hub of a great civilization. Yet, suddenly, inexplicably, Chaco was abandoned.

Though archaeologists a century ago discovered disturbing evidence of violence at Chaco, the Chaco Phenomenon was continually cast in the benevolent light of an egalitarian society. The question of why the cities were abandoned was answered environmentally: overbuilding, erosion, and drought. But then why did the inhabitants flee to cliffs, and build their homes in dark, dank caves? Why not just move to another valley and build along a river?

Instead, the Anasazi moved into caves high up on cliff walls. These cliff dwellings made for an arduous life for these farmers. And their engineering skills, so brilliantly and beautifully executed in Chaco, were now focused on fortresses in caves. There were obviously enemies in their midst. I believe the answer lies within the carefully memorized oral histories of the Anasazi's descendants: today's Pueblo Indians.

Power on the scale of Chaco would resonate across the

centuries. Pueblo people speak of "White House," a legendary city of wonder, but also a place profoundly out of harmony. Several recent scholarly books have looked more closely at this dark side of Chaco and revealed evidence of systematic terror—institutionalized violence used to enforce political power. Some claim proof of ritualized human sacrifice and cannibalism employed by a warrior elite to exact absolute control. Even Navajo legend includes a story about the dark power at Chaco. In the legend, a corrupt ruler used black magic to draw people to him and they became his slaves.

We don't know who these warrior elite were. Perhaps they were fanatical priests. Perhaps they were refugees of the Toltec empire. Connections to Mexico and South America are numerous and undebatable, including a vast trade network. Interestingly, there is also proof of an Aztec land far north of not only Mexico, but Anasazi settlements. The 1847 Desturnall map, the official map of the Treaty of Guadalupe-Hidalgo (the treaty that ended the United States' war against Mexico), cites an area along the Colorado River in Utah called "Antigua Residencia de los Aztecas": ancient homeland of the Aztecs.

Did a warrior cult infiltrate Chaco? Did a warrior cult *create* the Chaco Phenomenon? Is this why the Anasazi fled their great cities and retreated into impossibly difficult cliff dwellings? What, then, drew them back out—out of the dark caves to settle the Puebloan villages which are still inhabited today?

Despite hundreds of books and undoubtedly hundreds of thousands of field notes, documents, and research papers about the Anasazi, these mysteries remain unsolved . . . or perhaps deliberately obscured. We have, after all, the direct descendants of the Anasazi to talk to: today's Pueblo Indians of New Mexico and Arizona. But forces exist barring our reach into the past—invisible but strong walls as endurable as the sandstone walls of the ancient cities. For one, Puebloan history is oral, passed down through ritual storytelling. Early written accounts are by and large from the conquerors, and consequently biased. The second force emanates from the Puebloans themselves, who protect their rituals and beliefs beneath a cloak of secrecy.

One belief in particular intrigued me and seemed to hold a clue to the mysteries: the Kachinas. These are the masked supernaturals who visit the pueblos and bridge the worlds of men and gods. They carry the prayers of the living to the deities. They intercede with the forces of nature to sustain life. They are at the core of Puebloan religion, yet their origin is shrouded in the past, as if the Kachinas emerged full-blown from the caves along with the Pueblo Indians.

In a very real way, the Kachinas lead the Puebloans along their spiritual path. I had to wonder if they had led the Puebloans out of the caves. The Kachinas also offered another connection to the Mesoamericans: the ritual of masked gods. This connection, however, also posed a problem: If the Mesoamericans had been a source of the terror, then why would the Anasazi accept and thoroughly integrate these masked gods?

In my research, I uncovered one more bit of tantalizing information: a mythological hero shared by nearly every pueblo village. His name was Poseyemu. His importance is legendary, yet full of contradictions. He was a war leader and a creator; a hunter and a farmer, connected to both blood and mist; a teacher of rituals, yet also a trickster. All agreed, however, that he was a leader and guided the people from the underworld.

During the time I was researching, Albuquerque hosted spiritual leaders from across the Americas. Native peoples from many countries have been enmeshed for decades, even centuries, in struggles over land, language, and civil and political rights. The spiritual leaders were beginning a dialogue among people who have shared traditions and for whom those traditions have been severed. There have also been several conferences for the alliance of indigenous people, the idea being to work together for common goals.

The efforts of these leaders inspired me. Suddenly, I had an insight into the Anasazi mystery. That it was perhaps not a question of them versus enemies, but of powerful indigenous cultures struggling with identity, unity . . . and emergence. Perhaps the Kachinas were born in the terrible elitist society of Chaco, but their true spiritual power evolved in the fearful days in the caves. In the dark past, Kachinas led people past the terrible secret to life, to the place they were supposed to be. I want to be clear, however, that Poseyemu as the first Kachina is purely my own conjecture, including the legend I weave regarding his birth and life.

Some additional notes about specifics in the book. There

are fictional as well as real locations used throughout the book. In the case of the real locations, I have still taken some license in descriptions, as in the town of Aztec and some of the surrounding canyons. While specific pictographs and petroglyphs I mention don't exist in those canyons, they do exist in the Southwest. Badger Canyon is a composite of slot canyons winding off Lake Powell.

The Anasazi "curse" of artifacts is an enduring legend in the Southwest. Witnesses include National Park and Forest Service rangers. A ranger at Mesa Verde was quoted as hearing "disembodied voices" in the ruins that yelled at him in unknown languages. The rangers continually receive packages of shards from tourists, with notes begging the rangers to return the "unlucky" artifact. In one story, a man's life nearly disintegrated into illness and loss of business after he stole an Anasazi axe. In a fitful sleep one night, he stumbled over the axe and nearly severed his foot. He swore that when he went to bed that night the axe was on his dresser wrapped in plastic. He also swore that a raven had led him to the axe.

Ravens occupy a special place in the Southwest. Part of Indian mythology, they are also ever-present at prehistoric ruins. Ceremonial ravens have been found in Anasazi ruins, carefully wrapped and preserved in corn husks. Present-day ravens are ever-watchful curators over the Southwest's open-air "museums." At the end of every one of my hikes over slickrock, I can be assured that at least one raven will greet me as the sentry to the ruin. The largest of the songbirds, with a distinct vocabulary among themselves, ravens are also known as one of the most intelligent birds. They're reputed to be able to remember hundreds, if not thousands, of "treasures" they might hide over a season. Visionary, wise and loyal, the raven was the only choice for Rheada's companion.

I hope you enjoyed the story and the journey to the Southwest. I hope too that I conveyed at least some of the tantalizing mysteries of the Anasazi. I love to hear from my readers. You can write to me at PO Box 23203, Albuquerque, NM 87192, or by e-mail: lbaker10@aol.com.

Sincerely,
Laura Baker